WIZARD

. . . returns us to the awesome interior of Gaea, the world-sized alien first encountered in Varley's monumental bestseller, TITAN.

Gaea's discoverer, Cirocco "Rocky" Jones, is now herself an inhabitant, plotting wizardry in the remote highlands between two of Gaea's brains. Gaea is old, perhaps dying. Wearily, she assures her usefulness to Earth by performing tawdry miracles.

Enter two pilgrims: Chris'fer, late of San Francisco. And from the Coven on the dark side of the moon, Robin, small, nine-fingered, female with snake . . .

Berkley Books by John Varley

MILLENNIUM
THE OPHIUCHI HOTLINE
PICNIC ON NEARSIDE
(formerly titled THE BARBIE MURDERS)

The Gaean Trilogy by John Varley

TITAN
WIZARD
DEMON

·THE·WIZARD·

JOHN VARLEY

Wizard

BERKLEY BOOKS, NEW YORK

This Berkley Book contains the complete
text of the original hardcover edition.
It has been completely reset in a typeface
designed for easy reading, and was printed
from new film.

WIZARD

A Berkley Book / published by arrangement with
the author

PRINTING HISTORY
Berkley/Putnam edition / August 1980
Berkley edition / January 1981
Sixth printing / December 1983
Seventh printing / August 1984
Eighth printing / January 1985

ISBN: 0-425-08166-4

A BERKLEY BOOK ® TM 757,375
The name "BERKLEY" and the stylized "B" with design
are trademarks belonging to Berkley Publishing Corporation.
PRINTED IN THE UNITED STATES OF AMERICA

For
K.L. King,
Kenneth J. Alford,
and
John Philip Sousa

Contents

GAEA

PROLOGUE:

Fairest of the Fair

For three million years Gaea turned in solitary splendor.

Some of those who lived within her knew of a broader space outside the great wheel. Long before the creation of the angels avian beings flew the towering vaults of her spokes, looked out the clerestory windows, and knew the shape of God. Nowhere in the darkness did they see another like Gaea.

This was the natural order of things:

God was the world, the world was a wheel, and the wheel was Gaea.

Gaea was not a jealous God.

No one had to worship her, and it never occurred to anyone to do so. She demanded no sacrifices, no temples, no choirs singing her praises.

Gaea basked in the heady energies to be found near Saturn. She had sisters scattered through the galaxy. They too were Gods, but the distance between them enforced Gaea's theology. Her conversations with them spread over centuries at the speed of light. She had children orbiting Uranus. They were Gods to those living inside them, but they hardly mattered. Gaea was the Supreme Titan, the Fairest of the Fair.

Gaea was not a distant concept to her inhabitants. She could be seen. One could talk to her. To reach her, all one had to do was climb 600 kilometers. It was a formidable trip, but an imaginable distance. It put heaven within reach of those daring enough to make the climb. She averaged one visitor in a thousand years.

Praying to Gaea was useless. She did not have the time to listen to all those within her, and would not have done so if she could. She would speak only to heroes. She was a God of

1

blood and sinew whose bones were the land, a God with massive hearts and cavernous arteries who nourished her people with her own milk. The milk was not sweet, but there was always enough of it.

When the pyramids were being built on Earth, Gaea became aware of changes going on within her. Her center of consciousness was located in her hub. And yet, in the manner of earthly dinosaurs, her brain was decentralized to provide local autonomy for the more prosaic of her functions. The arrangement kept Gaea from being swamped with detail. It worked very well for a very long time. Around her mighty rim were spaced twelve satellite brains, each responsible for its own region. All acknowledged Gaea's suzerainty; indeed, at first it was hardly proper to speak of her vassal brains as separate from herself.

Time was her enemy. She was intimately acquainted with death, knew its every process and stratagem. She did not fear it. There had been a time when she did not exist, and she knew another such time would arrive. It divided eternity, neatly, into three equal parts.

She knew Titans were subject to senility—she had listened as three of her sisters degenerated into ravings and fantasy, then fell silent forever. But she could not know how her own aging body would play her false. No human suddenly throttled by her own hands could have been more surprised than Gaea when her provincial brains began to resist her will.

Three million years of supremacy had ill-prepared Gaea for the arts of compromise. Perhaps she could have lived in peace with her satellite brains had she been willing to listen to their grievances. On the other hand, two of her regions were insane, and another so darkly malevolent that he might as well have been. For a hundred years the great wheel of Gaea vibrated with the stresses of war. Those epic battles came close to destroying her and resulted in huge loss of life among her peoples, who were as helpless as any Hindu before the Gods of Vedic myth.

No titanic figures strode the curve of Gaea's wheel, throwing thunderbolts and mountains. The Gods in this struggle were the lands themselves. Reason vanished as the ground opened and fires fell from the spokes. Civilizations a hundred thousand years old were swept away without trace, and others fell into savagery.

Gaea's twelve regions were too headstrong, too unreliable to unite against her. Her most faithful ally was the land of Hyperion; her implacable enemy, Oceanus. They were adjacent territories. Both were devastated before the war became an armed truce.

But revolt and war were not to be enough disgrace for an elderly God; elsewhere worse disaster approached. In the wink of an eye the airwaves were flooded with the most astonishing noises. At first she thought it was a new symptom of encroaching dotage. Surely she had invented these impossible voices from space with names like Lowell Thomas, Fred Allen, and the Cisco Kid. But she eventually caught on to the trick. She became an avid listener. Had there been mail service to Earth she would have sent in Ovaltine labels for magic decoder rings. She loved Fibber McGee and was a faithful fan of Amos and Andy.

Television hit her as hard as talkies had stunned audiences in the late 1920s. As in the early days of radio, for many years most television was of American origin, and it was these programs she liked best. She followed the exploits of Lucy and Ricky and had all the answers to *The $64,000 Question*, which she was scandalized to discover was rigged. She watched everything, something she suspected not even the producers of many of the shows did.

There were movies and there was news. In the electronic explosion of the eighties and nineties there was much more as entire libraries were transmitted. But by that time her studies of human culture were more than academic. Watching Neil Armstrong's performance confirmed something she had long suspected. Humans would come calling by and by.

She began preparing to meet them. The outlook was not good. They were a warlike breed, possessed of weapons that could vaporize her. They could not be expected to take lightly the presence of a 1,300-kilometer living wheel-God in "their" solar system. She recalled Orson Welles's Halloween broadcast of 1938. She remembered *This Island Earth* and *I Married a Monster from Outer Space*.

All her planning came to naught when Oceanus, ever eager

for a chance to sabotage Gaea in any way he could, destroyed *DSV Ringmaster,* the first ship to reach her. But the humans failed to fulfill her worst expectations. The second ship, though armed and ready to destroy her, stayed its hand long enough for explanations to be made. In this Gaea was aided by the surviving members of the first expedition. An embassy was established, and everyone politely ignored the ship which took station at a safe distance, never to leave her neighborhood again. She did not worry about it. She had no intention of ever provoking it to loose its deadly cargo, and Oceanus's range of mischief was limited.

Scientists came to study. Later, tourists came to do what tourists do. She admitted anyone as long as he signed a statement absolving her from responsibility.

In due time she was recognized by the Swiss government and allowed to establish a consulate in Geneva. Other nations quickly followed, and by 2050 she had become a voting member of the United Nations.

She looked forward to spending her declining years studying the endless complications of the human species. But she knew that for real security the human race must need her. She must become indispensable, at the same time making it clear that it would be impossible for any one nation to claim her as its prize.

She soon found a way to accomplish that.

She would perform miracles.

1.

Flag of Caprice

The Titanide galloped from the fog like a fugitive from a demented carousel. Take a traditional centaur—half horse, half human—and paint it in Mondrian white lines and squares of red, blue, and yellow: that was the Titanide. She was a nightmare quilt from hooves to eyebrows, and she was running for her life.

She thundered down the seawall road, arms held out behind her like the silver lady on a Rolls-Royce, steam snorting from her wide nostrils. Close behind her was the mob, riding tiny citipeds and brandishing fists and clubs. Above them a police Maria slid into position, bellowing orders that could not be heard over the hoot of its klaxons.

Chris'fer Minor backed farther into the arched tunnel where he had hidden when he heard the sound of the riot horns. He pulled his jacket tight around his neck, wishing he had chosen another refuge. The Titanide was sure to head for the fort as the only cover in sight. There was nowhere else to go except the bridge, protected behind a high fence, and the Bay.

But the Bay was where she headed. She flew over the cracked asphalt of the parking lot and leaped the suspended chain barrier at the edge of the seawall. The jump was of Olympic caliber. She was beautiful in the air, sailing far enough to clear the rocks and most of the shallow, foamy water. The splash was awesome. Her head and shoulders emerged, then more of her until she looked like a human standing in waist-deep water.

The people were not satisfied. They began to tear out chunks of asphalt and shy them toward the alien. Chris'fer wondered what the Titanide had done. This mob had none of the feral festivity of pure alien-baiters. They were angry about something specific.

The rioteer in the hovering Maria turned on the sunburn

gun, a device normally reserved for use against armed disturbances. Clothes began to smolder, hair to crackle and curl. In no time the parking lot was empty, and the former mob sizzled and cursed in the cold Bay waters.

Chris'fer heard the drone of approaching paddycopters. It was hardly the first riot he had witnessed. While he was curious about the cause, he knew that hanging around was a sure way to spend the week in jail. He turned and passed through the short corridor into the oddly shaped brick building.

Inside was a trapezoidal concrete courtyard. It was surrounded by a three-tiered gallery. The outer wall was pierced regularly by half-meter square holes. There was not much else to say about the building; it was an abandoned hulk, but a well-swept one. Here and there wooden easels supported signs with old-fashioned gold lettering on them, pointing the way to various parts of the building, giving history and details in small print.

Near the center of the courtyard was a brass flagpole. At the top a flag whipped in the stiff breeze coming through the Golden Gate: centered in a field of black, a six-spoked golden wheel. It was impossible to look up at that flag without having one's eye drawn farther, to the imposing sight of the bridge span hanging unsupported in space.

This was Fort Point, constructed in the nineteenth century to protect the entrance to the Bay. All its cannons were gone now. It would have been a redoubtable defense against an enemy from the sea, but none had ever come. Fort Point had never fired a shot in anger.

He wondered if the builders had thought their creation would last two hundred and fifty years, structurally unchanged from the day the last brick was laid. He suspected they had, but would have been dumbfounded to stand where he now stood, to look up at the orange metal of the bridge arching so insolently over the brick behemoth.

Actually, the bridge had not fared nearly so well. After it had been brought down in the quake of '45, it had been fifteen years before a new roadway was slung between the undamaged towers.

Chris'fer took a deep breath and shoved his hands into his pockets. He had been trying to put off what he had come here for, terrified of being turned down. But it had to be done. There was a sign indicating his direction. It said:

THIS WAY TO THE GAEAN EMBASSY

THE AMBASSADOR IS⬚IN⬚

The word "in" was on a dirty piece of cardboard hanging from a nail.

He followed the pointing hand through a door and into a hallway. Interior doors opened right and left into bare brick rooms. The Gaean Embassy held nothing but a metal desk and some hay bales stacked against a wall. Chris'fer entered, then saw there was a Titanide sprawled behind the desk.

She wore a comic-opera uniform on her human torso, festooned with brass and braid. Her horse body was palomino, and so were the hands and forearms that protruded from her jacket sleeves. She was apparently asleep, snoring like a chain saw. She embraced a gold military shako with a long white plume, her head thrown back to expose a tawny palomino throat. There was an empty liquor bottle sitting tilted in the hat, and another beside her left hind leg.

"Is somebody out there?" The voice from behind an interior door marked *Her Excellency, Dulcimer (Hypomixolydian Trio) Cantata.* "Tirarsi, show them in, will you?" There was a tremendous sneeze, followed by a snort.

Chris'fer went to the door, opened it hesitantly, and stuck his head in. He saw another Titanide sitting behind a desk.

"Your . . . ah . . . she appears to be passed out."

The Titanide snorted again. "She's a he," Ambassador Cantata said. "And it ain't unusual. She's spun so far off the wheel she doesn't even remember how it turned." "Spinning off the wheel" was rapidly replacing "falling off the wagon" and other euphemisms for a drinking problem. Titanides brought to Earth were notorious drunks. It was not just the alcohol—which they had known before they left Gaea—but the maguey plant. Its fermented, distilled nectar was so adored by Titanides that Mexico was one of the few Earth nations with a Gaean export trade.

"Come in, then," the ambassador said. "Take a seat over there. I'll be with you in a minute, but first I have to see where Tzigane got to." She started to rise.

"If you mean a sort of quilted Titanide, she jumped into the Bay."

The ambassador froze with her hindquarters nearly up and her hands flat on the desk. Slowly her rump settled again.

"There's only one 'quilted Titanide' in West America, and he's a male, and his name is Tzigane." She narrowed her eyes at Chris'fer. "Was this a recreational plunge, or did he have a more pressing reason?"

"I'd say he discovered a sudden need to be in Marin County. There were about fifty people chasing him."

She grimaced. "Hanging around bars again. He got one taste of human ass, and now he can't seem to get enough. Well, sit down, I'll have to try to square this with the police." She picked up an old-fashioned blind phone and told it to connect her with City Hall. Chris'fer pulled the only chair in the room closer to the desk and sat on it. While she talked, he looked around her office.

It was large, as it had to be to accommodate a Titanide. It contained many nineteenth- and twentieth-century antiques and art objects, but very little furniture. A long-handled water pump was bolted to the floor in one corner, and the bare bulb that hung from the center of the room was hooded by a leaded Tiffany shade. A freestanding wood stove was near the room's only window. There were paintings and posters on the walls: a Picasso, a Warhol, a J&G Minton, and a little black sign with orange letters reading "Some Day I'm Going to Have to Get ORGANIZED!" Behind the desk were two photos and a portrait. They depicted Johann Sebastian Bach, John Philip Sousa, and Gaea as seen from space. On the desk was a silver bucket of limes.

Half the floor was covered in a thin layer of hay. There were bales of it stacked in a corner. Ambassador Cantata hung up the phone and reached for an open bottle of tequila and the bucket, popped a lime into her mouth, crunched it, and drank half the bottle. She made a face at him.

"You wouldn't have any salt, would you?"

He shook his head.

"Too bad. Want a drink? How about a lime? I think I have a knife. . . ." She started to rummage through drawers, stopped when he politely refused.

"He looked like a female to me," Chris'fer said.

"Huh? Oh, you mean Tzigane. No, I'm familiar with the mistake—it was the breasts that fooled you; we all have them—but he's a male. It's the frontal organs that determine it. Between the front legs. Tzigane's are kind of hard to see from a distance, with that pattern of squares. I, for your information, am female, you may call me Dulcimer, and what is your name and what can I do for you?" He sat up a little straighter. "My name is Chris'fer Minor, and I want a visa. I'd like to see Gaea."

She had written his name on a form from a stack on her desk. Now she looked up and moved the form away.

"We sell visas in all the major airports," she said. "No need to see me. Just come up with the cash and put it in the vending machine."

"No," he said, voice a little unsteady. "I want to see Gaea herself. I have to see her. She's my last chance."

2.

The Mad Major

"So it's miracles you're wantin', then," the Titanide said in a flawless Irish accent. "You want to stand in the high place and ask Gaea to grant you a great wish. You want her to spend her precious time on a problem that seems important to you."

"Something like that." He paused, stuck out his lower lip. "Exactly like that, I guess."

"Let *me* guess. A medical problem. Further, a *fatal* medical problem."

"Medical. Not fatal. See, it's—"

"Hold on, wait a minute." She raised her hands, palms facing him. This was going to be a brush-off, Chris realized.

"Let me fill in some more of this form before we go on. Is there an apostrophe in Chris'fer?" She licked the tip of her pencil and filled in the date at the top of the page.

The next ten minutes were taken up with the information asked for in every government office in the world: unident number, spouse's name, age, sex... ("WA3874-456-11093, none, twenty-nine, hetero male..."). By the age of six any human could recite it asleep.

"'Reason for wishing to see Gaea,'" the Titanide read.

Chris'fer fitted his fingertips together, partially hiding his face behind them.

"I have this condition. It's... rather hard to describe. It's a glandular or neurological thing; they're not really sure. There's only a hundred cases of it so far, and the only name for it is Syndrome 2096 dash 15. What happens is I lose contact with reality. Sometimes it's extreme fear. Other times I go off into delusional worlds and am likely to do just about anything. Sometimes I don't remember it. I hallucinate, I speak in tongues, and my Rhine potential alters sharply. I get very lucky, believe it or not. One doctor suggested it was this extra

10

psi that's kept me out of trouble so far. I haven't killed anyone or tried to fly by stepping off a building."

The Titanide snorted. "You sure you want to be cured? Most of us could do with a little extra luck."

"This isn't funny, not to me. No drug stops it; all I can do is be tranquilized when it happens. For years I've been put through every psychological diagnosis there is, and all it did was prove that the problem is medical. There is no trauma in my past causing it, and no current problem, either. I only wish there was. They can *adjust* anything psychological. Gaea is my last hope. If she turns me down, I'll have to go into a hospital for life." Without realizing it, he had made his hands into a hard knot at his chin. He relaxed them.

The ambassador regarded him with huge, fathomless eyes, then looked back to her form. Chris'fer watched her write. In the space marked "Reason for visa:" she wrote "ill." She frowned at it, scratched it out, and wrote "crazy."

He felt his ears burning. He was going to protest, but she asked another question.

"What's your favorite color?"

"Blue. No, green . . . is that really on there?"

She turned the form slightly, let him see that, yes, that really was on there.

"Are you sticking to green?"

Baffled, he nodded slowly.

"How old were you when you lost your virginity?"

"Fourteen."

"What was his or her name, and what color were his or her eyes?"

"Lyshia. Blue-green."

"Did you ever have sex with him or her again?"

"No."

"Who, in your opinion, is the greatest musician of the past or present?"

Chris'fer was getting angry. Privately he thought Rea Pash-korian must be the best; he had all her tapes.

"John Philip Sousa."

She grinned without looking up, and he could not understand it. He had expected an admonition to be serious or to stop trying to curry favor, but she seemed to be sharing the joke. With a sigh, he settled in for the rest of the questions.

They got less and less relevant to his proposed trip. Just

when he thought he had a pattern, the emphasis would change. Some questions involved moral situations; others seemed random madness. He tried to be serious, not knowing how much this questioning would affect his chances of getting in. He began to perspire, though the room was cold. There was just no telling what the right answers were, so all he could do was be honest. He had been told that Titanides were good at detecting falsehoods from humans.

But at last he had had enough.

"'Two children are tied down in the path of an approaching gravity train. You have time to release only one of them. They are both strangers to you, both the same age. One is a boy, and one is a girl. Which do you rescue?'"

"The girl. No, the boy. No, I'd rescue one and go back and . . . *damn* it! I'm not going to answer any more of these questions until you—" He stopped abruptly. The ambassador had thrown her pencil across the room and now sat with her head in her hands. He was seized with a fear so sudden and so intense that he thought it was the beginning of an attack.

She stood and walked toward the wood stove, opened the door in front, and selected several logs. Her back was to him. Her skin was the same color and texture as a Caucasian human's, from head to hooves. Her only hair was on her head and her magnificent tail. While she was sitting behind the desk, it was easy to forget she was not human. When she stood, her alienness was pronounced, precisely because half of her was so unremarkable.

"You don't have to answer any more questions," she said. "Thank Gaea, this time they don't matter." When she spoke Gaea's name, it sounded bitter.

As she fed wood into the stove, her tail flicked over her back and remained arched out of the way. She did what every horse does in every parade—usually in front of the reviewing stand—and with the same lack of shame. It was apparently done without conscious thought. Chris'fer looked away, disturbed by it. Titanides were such an odd mixture of the commonplace and the bizarre.

When she turned, she took a shovel which had been leaning against the wall, scooped up the pile and the straw it had landed on, and tossed it into a bin against the wall. She glanced at him as she sat down and looked wryly amused.

"Now you know why I don't get invited to parties. If I don't think about it all the time, every damn second...." She let him imagine the consequences.

"What did you mean, 'this time it doesn't matter'?"

Her smile vanished.

"It's out of my hands is what I mean. It's hard to believe, the number of things that kill you humans, and more new ways every year. Do you know how many people ask me to see Gaea? Over two thousand every year, that's how many. Ninety percent of them are dying. I get letters, I get phone calls, I get visits. I get pleas from their children, husbands, and wives. Do you know how many people I can send to Gaea in a year? Ten."

She reached for the tequila bottle and took a long pull. Absently she picked up two limes and ate them in one bite. She was facing the wooden stove, but her eyes were focused at infinity.

"Just ten?"

She turned her head and looked at him with scorn.

"Boy. You're something. You are really something. You had no idea."

"I—"

"Spare me. I think you feel pretty sorry for yourself. You think you've got it rough. Fella, I could tell you stories...never mind. People study for *years* to learn how to psych me out, me and the three other ambassadors. To be one of the forty." She hit the stack of forms with her fist. "There are books an inch thick analyzing this form, telling people how to answer. Computer studies of how past winners answered." She picked up the stack and hurled it, and it came apart into a short-lived snowstorm that settled all over the room.

"How would you pick? I've approached it every possible way, and there's no good answer. I've tried to think like a human would think, make a decision like a human would, and the first thing they always seem to start out with is nine or a dozen forms, so I wrote up a form and hoped the answers would be in there, but they weren't, any more than they were in the crystal ball or the damn dice. Yeah, I actually own a crystal ball. And I've shot craps for people's lives. And nineteen hundred and ninety of my decisions every year are *still* wrong. I've done my best, I swear I have, I've tried to do the job right. All I want to do is go back to the wheel."

She sighed so deeply that her nostrils quivered. "There's

something about the wheel, I think. Every hour you go through a cycle. You can't feel it, not really, but if it's gone, you know it. You can no longer sense the center of things. The clock of your soul is no longer advancing. Everything has flown apart; everything gets more distant."

When she had been silent for a full minute, Chris'fer cleared his throat.

"I didn't know any of this."

She snorted again.

"I'm surprised you came here and took this job, feeling the way you do. And . . . I'm surprised that you sound like you resent Gaea. I thought she was, well, like a God to Titanides."

She regarded him levelly, spoke with no emphasis.

"She is, Herr Minor. I came here because she is God and because she told me to come. If you meet her, it would be best to remember that. Do what she tells you. As for the resentment, of course I resent it. Gaea doesn't require that you love her. She just wants obedience, and she damn well gets it. Nasty things happen to those who don't listen to her. I'm not talking about going to hell; I'm talking about a demon eating you alive. I don't love her, but I have a tremendous respect for her.

"And you'd better watch it, I'd say. There's a streak of fatalism in you. You came here unprepared, ignorant of things you could have learned if you'd even read the *Britannica* article. That won't work in Gaea."

Chris'fer slowly realized what she was saying but still could not quite believe it.

"Yes, you're going. Maybe it's your luck working for you. I wouldn't know about luck. But I got a directive from Gaea. She wants some people who are crazy. You're the first one this week who qualifies. I can even feel good about sending you. I was bracing myself for turning down a great humanitarian in favor of some slobbering killer. Compared to that, you'll do fine. Come with me."

The outer office now held a swaying but revived Titanide and three humans. One, a young woman with reddened eyes, came toward the ambassador. She tried to say something involving a child. Dulcimer (Hypomixolydian Trio) Cantata danced nimbly by her and hurried out into the corridor. Chris'fer saw the woman seek comfort in the arms of a hard-faced man. He looked away hurriedly. He could not have seen accusation in her eyes; there was no way she could know he had been chosen.

He caught up with the Titanide in the tunnel and had to jog to equal her walking pace. They went around the fort on the north side, by the Bay.

"Get rid of that apostrophe," she said.

"Huh?"

"In your name. Change it to Chris. I hate the apostrophe."

"I—"

"Don't make me mention that I wouldn't send someone with a silly name like Chris'fer to Gaea."

"All right, I won't. I mean, I will. Change my name."

She was unlocking a gate in the fence that kept the public away from the bridge. She opened it, and they went through.

"Change your last name to Major. Maybe it'll jar you out of that fatalism."

"I will."

"Have it done in court, and send me the papers."

They reached the bottom of a huge concrete bridge support. A metal ladder had recently been bolted to it. It dwindled in the distance but appeared to reach all the way to the roadway with no safety cage.

"Your passport is on top of the south tower. It's a little Gaean flag, like the one outside the embassy. Climb this ladder, go up the cable, get it, and come back. I'll wait here."

Chris'fer looked at the ladder, then at the ground. He wiped his sweating palms on his pants.

"Can I ask why? I mean, I'll do it if I have to, but what does it mean? It's like a game."

"It is a game, Chris. It is random; it makes no sense. If you can't climb this measly ladder, then you aren't worth sending to Gaea. Come on, get going, kid." She was smiling, and he thought that, despite her professed sympathy for humans, it might amuse her to see him fall. He put his foot on the first rung, reached up, and felt her hand on his shoulder.

"When you get to Gaea," she said, "don't expect too much. From now on you are in the grip of a vast and capricious power."

3.

The Screamer

The Coven was established late in the twentieth century, though not under that name. It was more political than religious. Most accounts of the group's early days state that the original members were not at first serious about many of the things they did. Few of them believed in the Great Mother or in magic. Witchcraft was, at first, merely a social glue that held the community together.

As time went on and the dilettantes grew bored, as the moderate and the fainthearted moved away, the remaining core began to take its rituals seriously indeed. Rumors of human sacrifice began to be heard. It was said the women on the hill were drowning newborn male babies. The resulting attention served to draw the group tighter against a hostile outside world. They moved several times, ending in a remote corner of Australia. There the Coven surely would have perished, since all had sworn not to reproduce until parthenogenesis was a reality. But the Screamer arrived and changed all that.

The Screamer was an asteroid—millions of tonnes of metallic iron, nickel, and ice, with impurities running through it like the veins in a cat's-eye marble—that became, one fine May morning, a sizzling line of light through the southern sky. The ice burned away, but the iron, nickel, and impurities smashed into the desert on the edge of property owned by the Coven. One of the impurities was gold. Another was uranium.

It was well that the Screamer hit near the edge since even at that distance the blast killed sixty percent of the faithful. News of the asteroid's composition quickly spread. Overnight the Coven changed from just another forgotten deathlehem into a religion rich enough to stand beside the Catholics, the Mormons, and the Scientologists.

It also brought the group unwanted attention. The Australian Outback would seem an unlikely place to begin a search for a refuge remote from society, but the desert had proved far too reachable. The Coven wanted to find a new meaning for the word "remote."

This was the 2030s, and it so happened there was an ideal place to go.

When two bodies orbit around a common center of gravity, as the Earth-Moon system does, five points of gravitational stability are created. Two are on the orbit of the smaller body, but sixty degrees removed. One is between the two bodies; another, on the far side of the smaller one. They are called LaGrangian points and designated L1 through L5.

L4 and L5 already held colonies and more were building. L2 seemed the best choice. From there the Earth would be completely hidden by the Moon.

They built the Coven there. It was a cylinder seven kilometers long with a radius of two kilometers. Artificial gravity was provided by spin; night, by closing the windows.

But the days of isolation were over almost before they began. The Coven was one of the first nongovernmental groups to move into space in a big way, but they were not the last. Soon the techniques of space colonization were refined, cheapened, standardized. Construction companies began to turn them out the way Henry Ford had turned out Model T's. They ranged in size from the merely gigantic to the Brobdingnagian.

The neighborhood began to look like Levittown, and the neighbors were *odd*. Just about any sizable lunatic fringe, band of separatists, or shouting society could now afford to homestead in the LaGrangians. L2 became known as Sargasso Point to the pilots who carefully avoided it; those who had to travel through it called it the Pinball Machine, and they didn't smile.

Some of the groups couldn't be bothered with the care and feeding of complex machinery. They expected to exist in pure pastoral squalor inside what was really just a big hollow coffee can. The developers were often happy to accommodate them, reasoning that all that expensive hardware, if installed, would only be abused. Every few years one of these colonies would come apart and fling itself and its inhabitants across the sky. More often, something would go wrong with the ecology and people would starve or suffocate. There was always someone willing to take one of the resulting hulks, sterilize it with free vacuum, and move in at a bargain price. The Earth never ran short of the alienated and the dissatisfied. The United Nations was happy to get rid of them and did not ask too many questions. It was a time of speculation—of instant fortunes and shoddy practices. Deals were made that would have shocked a Florida real estate developer.

The Sargasso Point incubated cultures more like carcinomas than communities. The most repressive regimes humanity had ever known took shape and died in the LaGrangians.

The Coven was not one of them. Though they had been around only fifty years at L2, it qualified them as founders. Like the first settlers everywhere, they were appalled at the quality of people moving in around them. Their own early days were forgotten now. Age, wealth, and the unforgiving environment had mellowed then hardened them into a viable group with a surprising amount of personal freedom. Liberalism had reared its head. Reform groups had replaced the original hardliners. Ritual was once more put in the background, and the women turned to what most of them had no way of knowing was actually the group's original ethic: lesbian separatism. The term "lesbian" was no longer strictly accurate. On Earth, for many of the women, lesbianism had been a response to injustices suffered from the male sex. In space, in isolation, it became the natural order, the unquestioned basis of all reality. Males were dimly recalled abstractions, ogres to frighten children, and not very interesting ogres at that.

Parthenogenesis was still a dream. To conceive, the women had to import sperm. Eugenics was easy in one sense: male fetuses could be detected early and stilled in the womb. But with sperm, as with everything else, the watchwords were still *caveat emptor*.

4.

Little Giant

Robin toed herself lightly down the curved corridor. The gravity at the hub masked her weariness, but she felt it in her back and shoulders. Even downheavy she would not have shown it or the weight of depression she always carried from watchstanding.

She wore a white, water-cooled vacuum suit of ancient vintage, her gloves and boots stuffed into the helmet carried under her arm. The suit was cracked and patched, its metalwork tarnished. Hanging from the utility belt were a Colt .45 automatic in a handmade holster and a carved wooden fetish festooned with feathers and a bird's claw. Barefoot, with long finger- and toenails painted dark red, hair blond and unkempt, lips stained purple, bells hanging from pierced earlobes and nostril, she might have been a barbarian sacking technology's greatest achievement. But looks can be deceiving.

Her right arm began to tremble. She stopped and looked at her hand with no change of expression, but the emerald Eye tattooed in the center of her forehead began to weep sweat. Hatred boiled up like an old friend. The hand was not her, could *not* be her hand, because that would mean the weakness was hers, and not something visited on her from the outside. Her eyes narrowed.

"Stop that," she whispered, "or I will cut you off." She meant every word and dug her thumbnail into the patch of scar tissue where her little finger had been to prove to herself that she meant it. The hardest part, surprisingly, had been getting the knife to the right spot with a hand that jerked at random. It had hurt, but the attack had vanished in the amazing agony.

The shaking stopped. Sometimes the threat was enough.

There was a story that she had bitten off her finger. She had never uttered a word to deny it. There was a quality called labra that the witches valued. It had much to do with honor,

19

with toughness and stoicism, with Eastern concepts of obligation. It might entail dying to a purpose, and with style, or paying any price to cancel debts, to individuals or society. Insisting on standing watches when one was subject to fits of palsy held much labra. Cutting off one's finger to stop the attacks had even more. The witches said Robin had enough labra to fill the wombs of ten ordinary women.

But standing watches when she knew it could endanger the community held no labra at all. Robin knew it, and so did the more thoughtful members of the Coven, those who were not dazzled by her young legend. She stood watches because no one on the council could look into the intensity of her eyes and deny her. The third Eye, impassive and omniscient, only added weight to her assertion that she could prevent the attacks by sheer effort of will. A dozen witches had earned the right to wear the third Eye. All were twice Robin's age. No one would stand in the way of Robin the Nine-fingered.

The Eye was supposed to be a badge of infallibility. There were limits, and everyone tacitly understood this, but it was useful. Some of the wearers used the Eye to back up absurd assertions, to take anything they wanted merely by saying it belonged to them. They earned only resentment. Robin always told the absolute truth about the small things, reserving the Eye for the Big Lie. It earned her respect, which was something she needed more than most. She was only nineteen years old, and might at any moment froth at the mouth and fall helpless to the ground. One needed respect at those vulnerable moments.

Robin never lost consciousness during her attacks, never had difficulty recalling what had happened. She simply lost all control over her voluntary muscles for a period of from twenty minutes to three days. The attacks could not be predicted except in one respect: the higher the local gravity, the more frequently they came. As a result, she spent most of her time near the hub, no longer going to the full gravity on the Coven floor.

It limited her activities, made her an exile with home always in sight. The ends of the cylinder called the Coven were a series of terraced concentric circles. Homes were in the down-heavy rings where people felt more comfortable. The Coven floor was reserved for farming, livestock, and parkland. Up-light was machinery. Robin never went below the gee/3 level.

What she had was not a curable epilepsy. The Coven's

doctors were as good as any on Earth, but Robin's neurological profile was new to them. It was to be found only in recent medical journals. The Terrans were calling it High-gee Complex. It was genetic disorder, a recent mutation, that resulted in cyclic abnormalities of nerve sheaths, aggravated by the composition of blood when the body was in gravity. In weightlessness the altered blood chemistry acted to inhibit the attacks. The mechanism of the disease was unclear, and the drugs to treat it were unsatisfactory. Robin's children would have it or carry it.

The reason for her predicament was known. She was the practical joke of some faceless lab technician. For many years, unknown to them, their orders for human sperm had been handled by a man who knew of them and who did not like lesbians. Though the shipments were carefully checked for disease and many common genetic disorders, it was impossible to screen out a syndrome the existence of which was not known to the Coven doctors. Robin and a few others were the result. All but Robin were dead.

There was one side effect of the meddling no one knew about yet. The women had been getting sperm from short men born of short parents. With no standard but their own, they did not realize they tended to be small.

Robin pushed through the swinging door to the shower room, stripping off her suit as she went. One woman was sitting on the wooden bench between the two walls of lockers, drying her hair. At the far end of the room another stood motionless with water spraying into her hands, cupped beneath her chin. Robin put her suit in her locker and got Nasu out of the drawer in the bottom. Nasu was her demon, her familiar: a 110-centimeter anaconda. The snake coiled around Robin's arm and darted her tongue; she approved of the damp heat of the shower room.

"Me, too," Robin said. She went to the shower, ignoring the woman who looked sidelong at her tattoos. The two painted snakes were common enough in the Coven, where tattooing was universal. The design on her belly, however, was uniquely her own.

As soon as she got the taps turned on and had endured a chilling blast of water, there was a great clanging of pipes and the showers stopped. The woman next to her groaned. Robin bounced up to the nozzle and put a death grip on it, wringing it like a chicken neck. Then she dropped down and began to scream. Her companion joined in, and eventually the third woman did, too. Robin put her guts into it, trying, as she did in all things, to scream louder than anyone else. Soon they were coughing and chuckling, and Robin realized someone had been calling her name.

"Yeah, what is it?" A woman she knew slightly—perhaps her name was Zynda—was leaning around the edge of the door. "The shuttle just brought a letter for you."

Robin's jaw dropped, and for a moment she looked blank. Mail was a rare thing in the Coven, whose members, put together, knew no more than a hundred outsiders. Most of it was packages ordered through catalog sales, and the bulk of that came from Luna. It could be only one thing.

She sprinted for the door.

It was nervousness, not her affliction, that caused her hands to shake as she handled the flimsy white envelope. The postmark over the kangaroo stamp read "Sydney," and it was addressed to "Robin Nine-fingers, The Coven, LaGrange Two." The return address was engraved and read "The Gaean Embassy, Old Opera House, Sydney, New South Wales, Australia, AS109-348, Indo-Pacific." It had been more than a year since she had written.

She managed to get it open and unfolded, and read:

Dear Robin,

Sorry to be so long in answering.

Your plight has touched me, though perhaps I shouldn't say it as you made it clear in your letter that you aren't looking for sympathy. This is well, as Gaea never grants cures for nothing.

She has informed me that she wishes to see representatives of Earthly religions. She mentioned a group of witches in orbit. It sounded unlikely, and then your letter arrived, almost as if some divine providence had intervened. Perhaps your deity had a hand in it; come to think of it, I know mine did.

You should take the first available transportation. Please write and tell me how it all came out.

> *Sincerely,*
> *Didjeridu (Hypoaeolian Duet) Fugue*
> *Ambassador*

"Billea tells me Nasu ate her demon."

"It wasn't her demon yet, Ma. It was just a kitten. And she didn't eat it. She squeezed it. It was too big to eat."

Robin was in a hurry. Her duffel bag stood half full on her bunk, and she was tearing through her dresser drawers, tossing unwanted items left and right, throwing the things she would take in a pile beside her mother.

"Whatever the story is, the kitten is dead. Billea wants compensation."

"I'll say it was my kitten."

"Child." Robin recognized that tone. Constance was the only one who could still use it with her.

"I didn't mean it," Robin conceded. "Take care of it, will you? Give her anything of mine."

"Here, let me see that. What are you taking with you?"

"This?" Robin turned and held the blouse over herself.

"It's only a half-blouse, child. Put it back."

"Well, of *course* it's a half. Practically everything I *own* is, Ma. Are you forgetting your bloodrite gift?" She held out her left arm with the snake tattoo coiling around it from little finger to shoulder. "You don't think I'm going to Gaea and not show it off, do you?"

"It leaves your breast bare, child. Come here. There are some things I need to talk to you about."

"But, Ma, I'm in a—"

"Sit." She patted the bed. Robin dragged her feet, but she sat. Constance waited until she was sure she had Robin's attention. She put her arm around her daughter. Constance was a big dark woman. Robin was small, even for the Coven. She stood 145 centimeters in her bare feet and massed 35 kilos. There was little of her mother in her. She had the face and hair of her anonymous father.

"Robin," Constance began, "there never seemed a need to speak to you of these things, but now I must. You're going into a world very different from ours. There are creatures out there known as men. They're . . . not like us at all. Between their legs they have—"

"Ma, I already know that." Robin squirmed and tried to shake off her mother's arm. Absently, Constance squeezed her shoulder. She looked at her daughter curiously.

"Are you sure?"

"I saw a picture. I don't see how they could ever get it *in* if you didn't want them to."

Constance nodded. "I often wondered myself." She looked away for a moment, coughing nervously. "Never mind. The truth of it is, life on the outside is based on the desires of these men. They think of nothing else but inserting their penis into you. The thing swells up to be as long as your forearm, and twice as thick. They hit you over the head and drag you into an alley . . . or, I guess, into an empty room or something like that." She frowned and hurried on.

"You must never turn your back on one of them, or they will rape you. They can do you *permanent damage*. Just remember, you're not at home, but out in the peckish world. Everyone out there is peckish, men and women alike."

"I'll remember, Ma."

"Promise me you'll always cover your breasts and wear pants in public."

"Well, I probably would wear pants anyhow, among strangers." Robin frowned. The concept of strangers was not a familiar one. While she did not know all the Coven by name, they all were by definition her sisters. She had anticipated meeting men in Gaea, but not peckish women. What an odd thought.

"Promise me."

"I promise, Ma." Robin was startled by the strength of her mother's embrace. They kissed, and Constance hurried from the room.

Robin looked at the empty doorway for a moment. Then she turned and finished her packing.

5.

Prince Charming

Chris had taken the Titanide ambassador's advice and done
some reading on Gaea before boarding the ship that would take
him there. He was not a stupid man, but planning was not his
long suit. He had seen so many of his plans ruined by attacks
of insanity that he had fallen out of the habit.

He discovered that Gaea was not high on the list of places
to visit in the solar system. There were many reasons for this,
ranging from dehumanizing customs procedures to the lack of
first-class tourist accommodations. He found an interesting
statistic: on the average, 150 people arrived at Gaea daily.
Something fewer than that number left. Some of the missing
were people who decided to stay. Emigrating was informal,
and Gaea had a resident human population of several thousand.
But some were fatalities.

Gaea tended to attract the young and adventurous. Men and
women came who were bored with the sameness of Earth.
Often they arrived after a tour of human habitats around the
solar system, where they found more of the same but in pres-
surized domes. Gaea offered an Earthlike climate. That meant
freedom from the regimentation found on more hostile planets
and elbow room that Earth no longer could provide.

He learned a lot about Titans in general, about Gaea's chil-
dren at Uranus—who admitted only accredited scientific observers and spoke condescendingly of Gaea, the Mad Titan.
He studied Gaea's physical structure and maps of her interior.
She was a spinning hollow wheel with six hollow spokes. Even
to humans who had grown up with space colonies at the
LaGrange points, her dimensions beggared the imagination.
She had a radius of 650 kilometers, a circumference of 4,000.
The living space on the rim was shaped like an inner tube 25
kilometers across and 200 kilometers high. Between each of
the six spokes was a flat, angled mirror that deflected sunlight

through transparent windows in the rim roof, so that parts of the rim were always in daylight while the areas beneath the spokes were perpetually dark. Gaea was habitable throughout; even the spokes supported life, clinging to the sides of cylinders 400 kilometers high. Maps of Gaea were unwieldly, being sixteen times longer from east to west than from north to south. To study the maps properly, it was necessary to fasten the ends together to make a loop, set the map on edge, and sit in the middle.

He was glad he had spent the time on it. Gaea was nearly invisible from space. Though he crowded around the ports with the others as the ship was snared by Gaea's docking tendrils, he could see little. With the exception of the reflecting mirrors, her outer surface was flat black, the better to absorb all the sunlight available to her.

He had done his homework and did not expect any surprises. It turned out there was only one, but it was a disaster.

As expected, his group was taken to join the other tourists arriving that day for the beginning of forty-eight hours of quarantine and decontamination. These procedures were one of the reasons Gaea did not attract the rich or the trendy. The routine was a cross between a hospital, Ellis Island, and Auschwitz. Uniformed human quarantine officers told everyone to disrobe and surrender all personal possessions. This included Chris's medication. His arguments were met with firm refusals. There were no exceptions to be made under any circumstances, and if he did not wish to surrender the pills, he was free to return to Earth at once.

The decontamination was in earnest and carried out with dehumanizing efficiency. Naked bodies, male and female together, were put on moving belts to be taken from one station to the next. They were washed and irradiated. There were emetics and diuretics to be taken, enemas to be endured. After a waiting period the whole process was repeated. The attendants made no concessions to privacy. Examinations were done in huge white rooms with dozens of tables, crowded by naked, shuffling people. Everyone slept in a common bunkroom and ate tasteless food dished out on steel trays.

Chris had never felt comfortable in the nude, even with other men. He had something to hide. While it was certainly not visible on his body, he suffered from the irrational fear that by removing his armor of clothing, he was exposing his differentness. He stayed away from situations where social nudity was the custom. As a result, he *was* conspicuous; in a sea of black and brown and tanned skin, he was pale as milk.

The attack came early on the first day. The chemicals in the pills had nothing to do with it, for they were certainly still in his bloodstream. It was the placebo effect which had been removed. Though his condition was not a psychological one, it was by now more complex than that. He was subject to anxiety from worrying about the psychochemical problem, and the punch line was that the anxiety attacks could trigger the serious ones. When his palms and the back of his neck began to perspire, he knew it was coming.

Soon he began to experience visual distortion and an acute sensitivity to sound. He had to assure himself each minute that everything was still real, that he was not on the verge of a heart attack, that people were not laughing at him, that he was not dying of a brain tumor. His feet were distant, pale, cold things. It was all a charade, and he had to act his part in it, pretend he was normal when everyone knew he was not. It was funny, really. He pretended to laugh. Then he pretended to cry, laughing secretly, knowing he could stop crying any time he wanted to, right up to the moment a man touched him on the shoulder and Chris punched him in the nose.

After that he felt better. He laughed at the man struggling to his feet. They were in the shower room—they spent most of their time there, he thought, feeling cross for a moment. But the annoyance passed. The man on the floor was shouting, but Chris couldn't have cared less. He was more interested in the erection he was getting. He thought it was a fine thing and knew all the naked women would agree with him. There was a wet splat behind him, and he turned and saw the man he had hit had fallen again. The dumb idiot had taken a swing at Chris from behind and slipped in a puddle.

He felt like fucking something. It didn't really matter what. The urge hardly amounted to an obsession. He could have been diverted from the project quite easily, but it sounded like fun.

"Who wants to fuck?" he yelled. Many of the people in the shower turned to look at him. He spread his arms, sharing his delight in the fine thing. A few people laughed. Most looked away. He was unperturbed.

A big blond woman caught his eye. He loved her instantly,

from the long, wet hair against her back to the fine swell of
muscle in her calves. He went to her and pressed his love
offering against her hip. She looked down, then quickly up to
the grin on his face, and slapped him with a soapy hand.

He put his palm against her face and shoved her back and
down. She hit with a thud of buttocks and a sharp clack of
teeth and was too startled by it all to attempt to dodge the kick
he aimed at her, but the kick didn't connect anyway because
a man grabbed Chris by the arm and spun him around, and
they both slipped and went down in huge confusion. By this
time men were coming from all directions to defend the blond
woman. It got very involved.

Chris didn't mind. Practically from the outset of the brawl
he found himself at the edges of it, so he joined the majority
of people hurrying to be as far from the fight as possible. It
turned into a crush against one wall with the showerheads
spraying warm water down on acres of skin, a great deal of
which was female skin. Chris embraced them at random, and
it wasn't long before he got a smile in response. The woman
was small and dark-haired, which was great because he had
had it with big blonds, and she giggled when he threw her over
his shoulder and carried her off to the big, deserted barracks
and tossed her into an upper bunk. Soon he was happily for-
nicating.

And it was really unfair, just a terrible injustice, because
he felt he could have kept at it all day long except this fascist
attendant happened by and told them they had to be in the exam
room for some damn colonic irrigation or other similar idiocy,
and she just wouldn't listen when Chris explained that he'd
had it with tubes up his ass. It was really annoying him, so
he stood up and planted his feet—the woman made a funny
gurgle when Chris stepped on her chest—and took a swing at
the uniform, who had already stepped back and who had her
weapon out and took careful aim and *shot* him.

He woke in a pool of vomit streaked with blood. And what
else is new? he wondered, but didn't really want to know.
There was a three-day growth of beard on his chin, caked with
dried blood. He didn't remember much, knew that was the one
thing he had to be grateful for.

They wanted to know if he was going to be a good boy
now, and he assured them he would.

The woman who had shot him helped him clean up. She

seemed anxious to give him the full details of his stay in jail and the events that had led up to it, but he closed his mind. He was given his personal effects and taken to some sort of elevator. When the doors shut behind him, he saw that the capsule was free-floating in a yellow fluid that moved through a gargantuan pipe. Once those facts were noted, however, he ceased to think about it.

The trip took nearly an hour, and for that time he thought of nothing. He emerged beneath the mind-numbing curved sky of Gaea, stood on her terrifying curved ground, glanced around, failed to be terrified or numbed. He was at the limits of numb. Overhead, a thousand-meter blimp was passing by. He looked at it blankly and thought of pigeons. He waited.

6.

Tent City

Nasu was in a terrible mood. Robin bore two fresh stigmata on her forearm to attest to her demon's temper. Anacondas do not react well to washing and prodding; the snake was terrified and bewildered by the events of the last two days, and her way of expressing it was to lash out at the nearest target, which was Robin. In all the time they had been together, Nasu had bitten Robin only three times before.

Robin was not doing much better herself. Some of the things she had been warned about had turned out to be chimeras. But the heat was terrible.

The temperature was thirty-five degrees. She had verified that astonishing fact—announced by the guide who met her group at the surface—by finding a thermometer and staring at it in disbelief. It was preposterous to run an environment that way, but the people shrugged it off. They complained but expressed no determination to *do* something about it.

Her urge was to tear off her clothes. She fought it as long as she could, but her mother had been wrong about so many other things she decided it was safe to disobey her in this. Many of the people in the dusty streets of Titantown were nude; why shouldn't she be? She compromised, keeping her loins covered as a signal she would fight any rape attempt. Not that she really feared rape anymore.

The first penis she saw, in the mass showers of quarantine, had made her laugh and earned her a sour look from the proud owner. All the rest had been just as comical. She couldn't imagine its swelling enough to harm her but reserved judgment until she could observe a man raping with one.

But there wasn't any raping the first night, though she stayed awake a long time to watch for it and fight off attackers. The second night there were two men raping in one corner of the barracks. The bunks all around the couples were empty, so

Robin sat on one and watched. The hilarious dangling things had swollen more than she thought they would, but not really very much. The women did not seem to be in pain. Neither had been knocked unconscious, nor were they face down. One, in fact, was on top of the man.

One woman told Robin to go away, but she had seen enough. If someone managed to knock her out, the experience would be distasteful but not very dangerous. She regularly dilated herself more than that for cervical exams.

She watched the women after the raping was over, looking for signs of shame. There did not seem to be any. So at least that much was true; peckish women had been taught to take degradation in stride. Slaves usually did, she remembered, at least outwardly. She wondered what rebellions smoldered inside.

No one made love for as long as she observed. Robin supposed they had to hide it from the men.

Titantown had begun under a huge tree but, with the end of the Titanide-Angel War many years before, it had spread to the east. Most Titanides still lived under the tree or in its branches. Some had moved out into tents of multicolored silk bordering the crazy thoroughfare that was the nearest thing in Gaea to a tourist attraction. It was chockablock with salons and saloons, hippodromes and nickel pitches, emporia, divertissements, hijinks, kickshaws, bagatelles, burlesque, and buffoonery. Sawdust and Titanide droppings were trampled underfoot, and the dusty air was thick with the smells of cotton candy, perfume, greasepaint, marijuana, and sweat. The place was laid out with the customary Titanide disdain for formal streets and zoning regulations. A casino faced the Intergalactic Primitive Baptist Church, which stood next to an interspecies bordello—all three structures as flimsy as a promise. The sweet voices of Titanides at choir practice mixed with the clatter of roulette wheels and the sounds of passion coming through thin tent walls. In a high wind, the whole bewildering hurly-burly could be swept away in moments, to reappear a few hours later in a new configuration.

The elevator to the hub ran once in a hectorev—which she learned was five Coven days or four point two Earth days— so Robin found herself with thirty-six hours to kill. Titantown looked educational, though she was not sure what it was for.

Coven concepts of amusement had not prepared her to regard this kind of carnival as a place to have fun. The witches' idea of a good time tended toward athletic contests, feasts, and festivals, though they loved practical jokes and tellers of lies.

Her mother had given her several hundred UN marks. Robin stood on the plank balcony of her tree house-hotel room, looked out over the noise and dust and bright colors below, and felt rising excitement in her breast. If she couldn't find a way to raise hell down there, she'd turn in her third Eye.

Gambling was a bust. She won a little, lost a little, lost a little more, and could not bring herself to care. Money was a crazy peckish game, and she did not pretend to understand it. Her mother had said it was a means of keeping score in the great dominance display of the penile culture. That was all Robin needed to know.

She decided to keep an open mind, though many things seemed quite unpromising as amusements. At first, she followed the people who seemed to be having the best times, then did what they did. For half a mark she purchased the use of three knives to throw at a man who capered and taunted in front of a wooden target. He was very good. She couldn't hit him, and neither could anyone else while she watched.

She followed a drunken couple into *Professor Potter's Wonder Zoo!*, where Gaean animal oddities were displayed in cages. Robin thought it fascinating and couldn't understand why the couple left after only a perfunctory glance, looking for some "action," as the man put it. Well, then, she would find action.

In one tent she witnessed a man raping a woman on a stage and found it very boring. She had already seen this, and even the contortions could not make it of further interest. Then two Titanides repeated the performance, and it was well worth seeing, though semantically troubling. She thought one Titanide was raping the other, but then the rapist pulled out and was penetrated by the rapee. How could that be, logically? If both sexes could rape, was it still rape? Of course, the problem applied only to Titanides. Each had a male and a female organ in the rear, and a male or a female in front. The announcer presented the show as "educational" and explained that Titanides thought nothing of engaging in public anterior sex, but reserved frontal lovemaking for private moments. He also taught Robin a new verb: to fuck.

The Titanide anterior penis alarmed Robin. Normally sheathed and partially concealed by the hind legs, it was a formidable instrument when revealed. It looked exactly like the human model, but was as long as Robin's arm and twice as thick. She wondered if her mother had been confused, attributing this fearsome thing to human men.

There were other educational and scientific sideshows. Many of them featured violence. This did not surprise Robin, who had expected nothing more of peckish society and who was no stranger to violence herself. In one small tent a woman demonstrated the powers of some form of yoga by sticking pins in her eyes, driving a long saber through her midriff until it emerged from her back, then deftly amputating her own left arm with scalpel and saw. Robin was sure the woman was a robot or a hologram, but the illusion was too good to penetrate. At the next show she was as good as new.

She bought a ticket to an all-Titanide production of *Romeo and Juliet,* then found herself giggling so much she had to leave. A more apt title might have been *The Montagues and the Capulets Join the Cavalry.* It was also apparent that the script had been tampered with. Robin doubted the bard would have minded having Titanides play the roles but thought she would have resented having Romeo turned into a man by peckish revisionists.

Drawn by the sound of music, she wandered into a medium-sized tent and gratefully sat down on one of many long benches. In the front, a line of Titanides sang under the direction of a man in a black coat. It seemed to be yet another show, but for the lack of a ticket-taker. Whatever it was, it felt good to get off her feet.

Someone tapped her shoulder. She turned and saw another man in black. Behind him stood a Titanide wearing steel-rimmed glasses.

"Excuse me, would you please put this on?" He was offering her a white shirt. He had a friendly smile, and so did the Titanide.

"What for?" Robin asked.

"It's customary in here," the man said apologetically. "We believe it improper to uncover ourselves." Robin saw the Ti-

tanide was wearing a shirt: the first time she had seen one
cover his or her breasts.

She shrugged into it, willing to humor screwy beliefs if she
could sit and listen to the lovely music. "What kind of place
is this anyway?"

The man sat beside her and grinned wryly.

"Well you may ask," he sighed. "Sometimes it tests the
faith of the most devout. We're here to bring the Word to the
outer planets. Titanides have souls just as humans do. We've
been here twelve years now. Services are well-attended; we've
performed a few marriages, a few baptisms." He grimaced and
looked toward the group in front. "But I think when all is said
and done, our flock comes here for the choir practices."

"Not true, Brother Daniel," the Titanide said, in English.
"'I-believe-in-godthefather-maker-of-heav'n'earth-and-in-je-
suscrise-hisonly-sonourlord—'"

"Christians!" Robin yelped. She leaped to her feet, making
the two-fingered protective sign with one hand, holding Nasu
out with the other, and began to back away, her heart pounding.
She did not stop running until the church was lost in the dust.

She had been in a church! It was her one big fear, the one
bogey from her childhood about which she had no doubts.
Christians were the very root and branch of the peckish power
structure. Once in their hands, a merry pagan would be injected
with drugs and subjected to hideous physical and mental tor-
tures. There could be no escape, no hope. Their terrible rites
would soon warp one's mind beyond all hope of redemption;
then the convert would be infected with a nameless disease
that rotted the womb. She would be forced to bear children in
pain to the end of her days.

Gaean cuisine was interesting. Robin found a place that
smelled good and ordered something called a Bigmac. It
seemed to be mostly carbohydrates wrapped around grease. It
was delicious. She ate every bite, feeling reckless.

While she was mopping up mustard with her fingers, she
became aware that a woman at the next table was watching
her. She watched back for a while, then smiled.

"I was admiring your paint job," the woman said, getting
up to slide in next to Robin. She had scented her body and
wore a carefully artless collection of thin scarves that just
happened to cover most of her breasts and all of her groin. Her

face looked fortyish until Robin realized the lines and shadows were cosmetics intended to make her look older.

"It's not paint," Robin said.

"It's. . . ." Real wrinkles appeared on her brow. "What is it then? Some new process? I'm *fas*cinated."

"An old process, actually. Tattooing. You use a needle to drive ink into the skin."

"That sounds painful."

Robin shrugged. It *was* painful, but there was no labra in talking about it. You cried and screamed when it was happening, and never mentioned it again.

"My name's Trini, by the way. How do you take it off?"

"I'm Robin, may the holy flow unite us. You don't take it off. Tattooing is forever. Oh, you can edit a little, but the pattern is there to stay."

"How . . . what I mean is, isn't that rather inflexible? I like to get a three- or four-day skin job as much as the next person, but I get tired of it."

Robin shrugged again, getting bored. She had thought this woman wanted to make love, but it appeared she didn't.

"You don't rush into it, of course." She craned her neck to see the wall menu, wondering if she had room for something called sauerkraut.

"It doesn't seem to hurt the complexion," Trini said as she lightly ran her fingertips over the coil of snake that looped Robin's breast. Her hand dropped and came to rest on Robin's thigh.

Robin looked at the hand, annoyed that she could not read this peckish woman's signals. The face was no help, either, when she looked there. Trini seemed to have made a study of being casual. Well, she thought, it never hurts to try. She had to reach up to put her arm over the bigger woman's shoulder. She kissed her on the lips. When she pulled away, Trini was smiling.

"So what is it you do?" Robin leaned forward to take the reefer from Trini, then settled back on her elbows again. They were reclining side by side, facing each other. Trini's disheveled mop of hair was backlighted by the open window of her room.

"I'm a prostitute."

"What's that?"

Trini rolled onto her side, doubled up with laughter. Robin giggled with her for a while but subsided long before Trini did.

"Where the hell have you *been?* Don't answer that, I know, cooped up in that big tin can in the sky. You really don't know?"

"I wouldn't have asked if I did." Robin was annoyed again, not liking to feel ignorant. Her gaze, looking for a place to light, settled on Trini's calf. She stroked it absently. Trini shaved her legs, for no reason that Robin could see, and left the hair on her arms alone. Robin shaved anywhere she had a tattoo, which was her left arm and right leg, part of her pubic area, and a wide circle around her left ear.

"I'm sorry. It's called the oldest profession. I provide sexual pleasure for money."

"You sell your body?"

Trini laughed. "Why do you say that? I sell a service. I'm a skilled worker with a college degree."

Robin sat up straight. "*Now* I remember. You're a whore."

"Not anymore. I free-lance."

Robin confessed she did not get it. She had heard of the concept of sex for money but was having difficulty integrating it with her still-hazy concepts of economics. There was supposed to be a slavemaster in the picture somewhere, selling the bodies of the women he owned to men less rich than he.

"I think we have a semantic problem. You say 'whore' and 'prostitute' like they're the same thing. They used to be, I guess. You can work through an agency or out of a house, and that's being a whore. Or you can be on your own, and that's a courtesan. On Earth, of course. Here, there's no laws, so it's every woman for herself."

Robin tried to make sense of it but had no luck. It did not fit with what she knew of peckish society that Trini should keep the money she made. That would imply her body was her own property, and of course, it wasn't, in men's eyes. She was sure there was a logical contradiction in what Trini had said but was too tired to worry about it just then. One thing seemed clear, though.

"How much do I owe you, then?"

Trini's eyes widened. "You think...oh, no, Robin. This I do for myself. Making love to men is my job, what I do for a living. I make love to women because I like them. I'm a lesbian." Trini looked slightly defensive for the first time. "I think I know what you're thinking. Why would a woman who doesn't like men make a living having sex with them? It gets a little—"

"No, I wasn't thinking that at all. That first thing you said is about the *only* thing you've said that makes sense. I understand that perfectly and see that you're ashamed of your peckish enslavement. But what's a lesbian?"

7.

Harmony Heaven

Chris hired a Titanide to take him to something called the Place of Winds, where he was told he could get an elevator ride to the hub. The Titanide was a blue-and-white long-haired pinto female named Castanet (Sharped Lydian Duet) Blues, but it was Chris who had the blues. The Titanide spoke some English and attempted to engage him in conversation, to which Chris replied in grunts, so she passed the trip playing her brass horn while at a full gallop.

He began to take more interest in the trip as they left Titantown behind. The ride was as smooth as a Hovercraft. They passed through brown hills and rode for a time beside a swift-flowing tributary of the river Ophion. Then the land began to rise toward the imposing presence of the Place of Winds.

Gaea was a circular suspension bridge. Her hub served as the anchor against centripetal force. Radiating down her spokes were ninety-six cables that tied the hub to the subterranean bone plates of the rim. Each cable was five kilometers in diameter, composed of hundreds of wound strands. They contained conduits for heating and cooling fluxes, and arteries for the transport of nutrients. Some of the cables met the ground at right angles, but the majority emerged from the vast spoke mouths overhead to slant through a twilight zone for a time before fastening in a daylight area.

The Place of Winds was the Hyperion terminus of a slanting cable. It looked like a long arm reaching out of darkness, its fingers gripping the land in a fist of rubble. Somewhere in the maze of ridges and tumbled boulders high winds sang as air was pumped upward to spill in the hub and fall through the spokes. It was Gaea's millennial air conditioner, the means by which she prevented the formation of a pressure gradient and maintained a breathable oxygen pressure in a column of air 600 kilometers high. It was also the angels' stairway to heaven.

But Castanet and Chris were not headed there; the elevator was on the other side.

It took Castanet nearly an hour—or one rev, Chris reminded himself—to go around the cable. The far side was daunting. Incalculable tonnes of cable rested on the air above them, as if a skyscraper had been erected parallel to the ground.

The land beneath the cable was uncharacteristically barren. It could not have been merely lack of sunlight; Gaea was known for her prolificacy, supporting life forms adapted to any environmental extreme, including perpetual darkness. But only in the vicinity of the elevator terminus itself was there any plant life.

It was a dark, soft capsule, four meters long and three high, with a dilated opening in one end. The other was pressed against a sphincter of a kind common in Gaea. These openings led to the circulatory system, which, if one dared, could be used as transport. The capsules were corpuscles that included— in the dual-function organization that was a Gaean trademark— a life-support system. An oxygen-breathing animal placed inside could survive until it died of starvation.

Chris climbed in and seated himself on the free-form couch-shape inside. There were filaments growing from the inner walls, useful in strapping oneself securely. Chris used them. It was his third ride in what native Gaeans called the bumper cars. He knew the ride could be rough as the thing bumbled through eddied currents around switch points.

The interior was luminescent. With the opening sealed behind him, Chris wished he had brought a book. He faced a three-hour ride with no company but his churning stomach and the knowledge that at the end of the line he would be interviewed by a God.

There was a sucking sound as the capsule was drawn into the protective maze of valves within the cable. It blundered from auricle to ventricle until, with an unexpected surge of power, it headed for heaven.

The dancer was under a suspended spotlight, floating in and out of a yellow cone spilling through the still air. He was a tap-dancing fool in top hat and tails, spats and boiled shirt. Like all the best dancers, he made it look easy. The soles of his black shoes and the metal foot of his cane hammered a complex tattoo that echoed in the unseen cavern of the hub.

He was performing fifty meters from the door of the common, ordinary elevator which had brought Chris on the last leg of the trip. A bell rang, and Chris turned to see the door closing.

The dancer disturbed him. It was as if he had walked into a theater showing an obscure film that was half over. The man must refer to something; the artist must have had something in mind. But there he danced, divorced from all meaning, sufficient unto himself. His face was concealed in the shadow cast by the brim of his hat; only his pale pointed chin was visible. He should remove his hat, Chris thought, to reveal an empty skull: the face of death. Or else stop dancing and indicate with his elegantly gloved hand where Chris's path lay. He gave no such signal, refused to turn himself into a symbol of anything. He just kept dancing.

He finally made his move when Chris approached him. The spotlight winked out, and another came on twenty meters distant. The man's silhouette clattered through darkness until it was again fleshed out in light. A third light came on, a fourth, a diminishing series. He leaped from one to the other, pausing for an improvised rhythmic statement before hoofing it to the next one. Then the lights died. The sound of taps on marble was gone.

The darkness of the hub was not absolute. High above was a single, dimensionless red line of light, sharp as a laser. Chris stood between high shadows: Gaea's cathedral collection. Spires and towers, flying buttresses and stone gargoyles were cool gray against fathomless black. Did they have interiors? His books had not said. He knew only that Gaea collected architecture and specialized in places of worship.

The regular tapping of heels in the distance soon resolved itself into a human woman in a white jumpsuit, like the ones the quarantine personnel had worn. She came around the corner of a squat stone temple, paused to sweep the area with a flashlight. The glare blinded him, moved past, returned to pin him like an escaping felon, then lowered.

"This way, please," she asked.

Chris joined her, feeling awkward in the low gravity. She led him on an irregular path through the monuments. Her boots were white leather, with stilted heels that clacked authoritatively. She made it look easy, while Chris tended to bounce like a rubber ball. The spin of the hub imparted only one-fortieth gee; he weighed just a few kilograms.

He wondered what she was. It had not occurred to him, in quarantine, to doubt the humanity of the employees. Up here, it was somehow different. He knew Gaea could, and often did, make living creatures to order. She could create new species, such as the Titanides, who were only two centuries old as a race, and give them free will and the benefit of her neglect. Or she could make one-shot individuals just as free and uncontrolled.

But she also made things called tools of Gaea. These creatures were nothing more than extensions of herself. She used them to build full-scale replicas of cathedrals, to communicate with small life forms—to do anything she could not accomplish through her normal ecology of existence. He would soon meet one of these tools, who would call herself Gaea. Gaea was actually all around him, yet it would do him little good to speak to the walls.

Chris looked again at the tall woman with the flowing black hair. Was she a tool or a real human?

"Where are you from?" he asked.

"Tennessee."

The buildings were built to no plan. Some shouldered close in what Chris thought of as celestial slum districts; others were widely separated. The haphazard arrangement was as likely to form a plaza as an alley. They squeezed between a replica of Chartres and a nameless pagoda, crossed a huge square paved in marble on the way to Karnak.

The writer of the book Chris had read confessed bafflement as to why Gaea built these things. And why, having done so, did she leave them in the dark, all but invisible? It made one feel like a flea lost in the musty bottom of a child's toy box. The structures might have been counters in a trillionaire's Monopoly set.

"That's my favorite," the woman said unexpectedly.

"Which?"

"That one," she said, pointing her flashlight. "National."

It seemed familiar, but after so many in such a short time one pile of stone was beginning to look like any other.

"What's the point of this? You can barely see them."

"Oh, Gaea doesn't need visible light," she assured him. "One of my great-grandparents worked on that one. I saw it, in Washington."

"It doesn't look like that."

"No, it's a mess. They're going to demolish it."

"Is that why you came here? To study great architecture as it was?"

She smiled. "No, to build it. Where can you do this kind of work on Earth? They worked on these things for hundreds of years. Even here, it takes twenty or thirty, and that's with no labor unions or building codes and no worries about cost. On Earth, I was building things a lot bigger, but if they weren't done in six months, they'd hire somebody else. And when you were finished, what you had looked like a turd had fallen out of the sky. Here, I'm working on the Zimbabwe Mormon Tabernacle."

"Yes, but what is it good for? What does it mean?"

Her look was full of pity. "If you have to ask that question, you wouldn't understand the answer."

They were in an area of subdued lighting. It was impossible to find the source of light, but for the first time there was enough to see the hub roof, more sharply curved than that of the rim but still more than 20 kilometers away. It was an intricate basket weave, each reed being a thousand-meter cable strand. To the near wall was fastened a white cloth the size of a cyberschooner's mainsail. A movie was being projected on it. Not only was it two-dimensional, but it lacked color and sound as well. A pianola near the projection booth provided musical accompaniment.

Between the booth and the screen was an acre of Persian carpet. On divans and pillows lounged two- or threescore men and women in loose, colorful garments. Some of them watched the movie; others talked, laughed, and drank. One of them was Gaea.

She did not do justice to her photographs.

Few pictures had been taken of the particular tool Gaea was pleased to present as "herself." In them, scale was indeterminate. It was one thing to read that Gaea was a small woman, quite another to stand facing her. No one would have noticed her warming a park bench. Chris had seen thousands like her roaming the urban wastelands: little, lumpy ragpickers.

Her jowly face had the texture of a potato. She had soft dark eyes squeezed between a heavy brow and folds of fat. Her frizzy hair, shot with gray, had been trimmed off evenly at shoulder level. Chris had found a picture of Charles Laughton to see if an oft-expressed comparison was true. It was.

She grinned sardonically.

"I know the reaction, son. Not as impressive as a goddamn burning bush, am I? On the other hand, what do you think Jehovah had in mind when He did that? Scare the pants off some superstitious Jew goatherder, that's what. At ease, boy. Pull up a pillow and tell me about it."

It was surprisingly easy to talk to her. There was this to be said about her unorthodox choice of Godly aspect: it suited, in a way impossible to pinpoint, the image of Gaea as Earth Mother. One could relax in her presence. Things long held inside could be brought out, bared, in a trust that grew as one spoke. She had a knack all good therapists or parents should have. She listened and, beyond that, made him feel that she understood. It was not necessarily a sympathetic ear, nor was it uncritical love. He did not feel that he was her special favorite, or even any great concern. But she was interested in him and the problem he presented.

He wondered if it was all subjective, if he was projecting all his hopes onto the dumpy woman. Nevertheless, he wept unself-consciously as he spoke and felt no need to justify it.

He seldom looked at her. Instead, his eyes roamed, lighting on a face, a goblet, a rug, without really seeing anything.

He finished what he had come to say. There were no reliable reports about what might happen next. People who had returned with cures were curiously vague about their interviews with Gaea and about the average of six months they spent inside her after the audience. They would not speak of it, no matter what the inducement.

Gaea watched the screen for a time, took a sip from a long-stemmed glass.

"Fine," she said. "That's pretty much what I got from Dulcimer. I've examined you thoroughly, I understand your condition, and I can guarantee a cure is possible. Not only for you, of course, but for—"

"Excuse me, but how did you examine—"

"Don't interrupt. Back to the deal. It *is* a deal, and you probably won't like it. Dulcimer asked you a question, back at the embassy, and you didn't answer it. I'm wondering if you have thought about it since and if you have an answer now."

Chris thought back, suddenly recalled the problem of the two children tied down before an approaching train.

"It doesn't mean much," Gaea conceded. "But it's interesting. There are two answers I can see. One for Gods, and another for humans. Have you thought about it?"

"I did, once."

"What did you come up with?"

Chris sighed, decided to be honest. "It seems that it's likely that . . . if I attempted to rescue either of them, I would probably die while trying to set the second one free. I don't know which I would free first. But if I tried to free one, I would have to try to free the other."

"And die." Gaea nodded. "That's the human answer. You people do it all the time—go out on a limb to pull back one of your kind and have the limb break under you. Ten rescuers die while looking for one lost hiker. Terrible arithmetic. It's not universal, of course. Many humans would stand by and watch the train kill both children." She looked at him narrowly. "Which would you do?"

"I don't know. I couldn't honestly say I'd sacrifice myself."

"The answer for a God is easy. A God would let them both die. Individual lives are not important, in other words. While I'm aware of every sparrow that falls, I do nothing to prevent the fall. It's in the nature of life that things should die. I don't expect you to like that, to understand it, or to agree with it. I'm just explaining where I stand. Do you see?"

"I think so. I'm not sure."

Gaea waved it away. "It's not important that you approve, just that you understand that is how my universe works."

"That I understand."

"Fine. I'm not *quite* as impersonal as that. Few Gods are. If there were an afterlife—which, by the way, there isn't, not in my theogony or in yours—I'd probably be inclined to reward the fellow who jumped onto the tracks and died trying to save those children. I'd take the poor bastard into heaven, if there were one. Unfortunately"—she gestured expansively, with a sour look—"this is the closest anyone will ever come to heaven, right here. I make no great claims for it; it's a place, like any other. The food's okay.

"But if I admire someone for something he or she has done, I reward them in *this* life. Do you follow me?"

"Well, I'm still listening."

She laughed, reached over, and slapped his knee.

"I like that. Now, I don't give anything for free. At the same time I don't sell anything. Cures are awarded on the basis of merit. Dulcimer said you couldn't think of anything you'd done to deserve a cure. Think again."

"I'm not sure I know what you want."

"Well, for things done on Earth it would have to be independently documented. The invention of a life-saving device, the origination of a worthwhile new philosophy. Sacrificing yourself for others. Have you seen *It's a Wonderful Life* by Frank Capra? No? It's a shame how you people neglect the classics for the whims of fad and popular taste. The protagonist in that story did things that would have qualified him, but they weren't documented in the papers, and he could hardly bring up a busload of character witnesses to testify to me, so he'd be out of luck. It's too bad, but it's the only way I can operate Have you thought of anything?"

Chris shook his head.

"Anything you did since you talked to Dulcimer?"

"No. Nothing. I suppose my energies have been directed mostly toward my own problem. Perhaps I should apologize for that."

"No need, no need. Now to the deal. The thing is, I deal only with heroes. You may assume that I'm a snob with ephemerals and that I must draw the line somewhere. I could have used wealth as a criterion, and you'd be facing a more difficult task than you are now. It's harder to get rich than it is to become a hero.

"In times past, I wouldn't even be talking to you. You would have first needed to prove that you are heroic. In those days the test was simple. The elevator was closed to free beings. If they wanted to see me, they had to climb up through a spoke, 600 kilometers. Anyone who made it was by definition a hero. A lot didn't, and were dead heroes.

"But since I became a healer to the human race, I revised the plan. Some of the people who need cures are physically too weak to get out of bed. They can't slay dragons, obviously, but there are other ways of proving worth, and now they have a chance. Think of it as a crumb thrown in the direction of human concepts of fair play. Understand, I don't guarantee the fairness of any of this. You take your chances."

"That I also understand."

"Then there you are. Unless you have a question, you may be on your way. Come back when you're worthy of my notice." But she did not yet turn away.

"But what do you want me to do?"

She sat up straighter, began ticking off points on her fingers. They were stubby little sausages crusted with jewelry, the ring bands buried in fat.

"One. Nothing. Go home and forget about it. Two. The simplest. Go to the rim, and climb back up here. You have about one chance in thirty of making it. Three." She forgot about counting, swept her arm to include the people on the couches around her. "Join the party. Stay amusing, and I'll keep you healthy forever. All these people arrived as you did. They decided to play it safe. There's plenty of films, and as I said, the food is good. But the suicide rate is high."

Chris looked around, looked closely for the first time. He could imagine that it would be. Several of the people did not really look alive at all. They sat staring at the huge screen, dull presences that seeped depression like a gray Kirlian miasma.

"Four. Go down there, and *do* something. Return to me a hero, and I will not only cure you but give Terran doctors the answers that will enable them to cure the seventy-three people who have the same thing you have.

"That's the bottom line. Now it's up to you. Do you jump onto the tracks, or do you stand and wait for someone else to do it? These people are hoping someone braver will come along, someone suffering from what they have. There is one man in fact, who *has* what you have. There he is, the one with the hungry eyes. If you go down, live or die, you can be his salvation. Or you can join him and wait for a *real* chump to arrive."

Chris looked at the man and was shocked. Hungry-eyed was precisely the way to describe him. For one frightening moment, Chris saw himself standing beside the man.

"But what do you want me to *do?*" Chris moaned. "Can't you just give me a hint?"

He felt that Gaea was rapidly losing interest in him. Her eyes kept straying to the flickering images on the screen. But she turned to him one last time.

"There are one million square kilometers of terrain down there. It is a geography such as you have never imagined.

There is a diamond the size of the Ritz sitting on top of a glass mountain. Bring me that diamond. There are tribes living in ruthless oppression, the slaves of fell creatures with eyes red and hot as coals. Free them. There are one hundred and fifty dragons, no two alike, scattered through my circumference. Slay one of them. There are a thousand wrongs to be righted, obstacles to be overcome, helpless ones to be saved. I recommend that you set out to walk around my interior. By the time you return to your starting point I guarantee your mettle will have been tested many times.

"You have to decide now. This man here and seventy-two others on Earth await you. They are damn well tied to the railroad tracks. It's up to you to save them, and you'll begin knowing that you may not be able to save yourself. But if you die, your death will count for something.

"So what will it be? Order a drink, or get out of my sight."

8.

The Aviator

Robin knew better than to stomp. She had not spent the last twelve years banished to the uplight regions of the Coven for nothing. But emotionally she was stomping.

Someone was supposed to be guiding her back to the elevator, but she quickly outdistanced her. Like an ant among elephants, she threaded her way through monuments.

Ridiculous things. Was she supposed to be impressed? If waste was impressive, she was overwhelmed.

Cathedrals. Tap dancers. A bloated, obscene thing passing herself off as the Great Mother, surrounded by listless sycophants. And to top it off?

Heroes.

She spit in the general direction of Notre Dame.

Why should she want to be the salvation of twenty-six strangers? One of them was undoubtedly her father. Gaea had pointed that out, to get a blank look in return. Fatherhood was as alien to Robin as stock options.

Nothing came for free, Gaea had said. What about those twenty-six who were counting on Robin to search out a nasty, dangerous death? Her whole being rebelled against the idea. Had even one of the sufferers been of the Coven she would have moved heaven and Earth to help her. But outsiders?

She had been on a fool's errand from the start. There was no need to compound the mistake. Staying among that pitiful pack of ass kissers was absolutely out of the question, and so was playing Gaea's game. She would go back to where she belonged, live her life as the Great Mother intended.

She found the elevator and pressed the summons beside it. A bell rang, and she got in. Bad design, she realized, looking around for grips to hold. There were two buttons to push—one marked "Heaven," the other "DOWN!" She hit the second one and raised her hands to catch the ceiling if it descended too fast. In that position, with that expectation, it was not alarming to feel her feet leave the floor. There was a blank moment before she realized the ceiling was not getting any closer. In fact, it was slowly receding. She looked down.

She saw her boots. Six hundred kilometers below them she saw Nox, the Midnight Sea.

Time slowed to a crawl. She felt adrenalin sweep to her extremities in a burning surge. Images swirled: brief, yet crisp with detail. The air tasted good. There was a raw power in her limbs as she reached out with hands and feet grown curiously distant. Then there was dissociation as fear and despair threatened to obliterate her.

When she began to scream, her waist was just passing the level of the elevator floor. She continued to sink, cursing and screaming lustily. The walls stayed just out of reach until they were far above her. The elevator was a diminishing box of light.

Robin's calculations were not begun in the hope the answer would put her back among the living. She could see her death many kilometers below. What she wanted to know was how many seconds. Minutes? Could she possibly have hours to live?

Growing up in the Coven was a help. She knew about centripetal movement, could work that type of problem more readily than she could have dealt with gravitation. Robin had never been in a gravitational field of any consequence.

She began with a known factor, which was the one-fortieth gee that prevailed at the hub. When the elevator floor opened under her, she had begun to fall at a velocity of one-quarter meter per second. But she would not accelerate at that rate. A moving body in a spinning object does not fall along a radial line but appears to move against the direction of spin. In effect, she would be moving in a straight line if viewed from the outside, while the wheel turned under her. Her downward acceleration would at first be slight. Only when she had built up a considerable sidewise velocity would the rate of her fall really begin to increase, and she would experience this as wind coming from the direction opposite the spin.

She looked around quickly. The wind was already strong. She could make out the tops of trees growing from one vertical wall. This was the storied horizontal forest of Gaea. Had Gaea been turning the other way, Robin would have been smashed

in seconds or minutes. Since the fall had started at the near
wall, she still had time.

There were a few simplified calculations she could make.
She was handicapped by not knowing the precise air density
in Gaea. She had read it was high, something like two at-
mospheres at the rim. But at what rate did it fall off as one
approached the hub? It never got too thin to breathe, so she
could get an estimate by assuming one atmosphere at the hub.

It was oddly comforting to lose herself in the math. She
didn't mind having to start over, though she was struck with
the futility of the project. She kept at it from a desire to know
when death would overtake her. It was important to die right.
She gripped the strap of the bag containing Nasu and started
again.

She came up with an answer she didn't like, tried again,
and a third time when the answers didn't match. Averaging,
she got a figure of fifty-nine minutes to impact. As an added
bonus there was the impact speed. Three hundred kilometers
per hour.

She was falling with her back to the wind. Since she was
moving toward both the rim and the approaching wall, it meant
her body was at a slight angle. The hub was not quite under
her feet. The receding wall was not quite vertical to her. She
looked around.

It was breathtaking. Too bad she could not appreciate it.

The Coven, if dropped from her point of departure, would
have been a tin can falling down a smokestack. The Rhea
Spoke was a hollow tube, flared at the lower end, completely
encrusted with trees to dwarf the biggest sequoia. The trees
rooted in the walls and grew outward. She could no longer
make out even the largest as individual plants; the inner walls
were a featureless sea of dark green, all around her. The interior
was lit by twin vertical rows of portholes, if one could use that
name for openings at least a kilometer in diameter.

She craned her neck, looking into the blast of wind. Nox
looked closer. There was something else, something that hovered at the top of her view.

It was the vertical Rhea spokes. They fastened to islands
in the Midnight Sea and leaped straight up, converging until
they met near the bottom of the spoke and entwined themselves
in a monumental pigtail.

She had to see. Twisting in the air, she managed to stabilize herself with her teeth to the gale and opened her eyes. The spokes were in front of her, getting closer by the second.

"Oh Great Mother, hear me now." She mumbled her way through the first death incantation, unable to look away from what had become a rushing dark wall before her. The cable seemed to rotate like a barber pole, the result of her rapid progress past the wound strands.

It took a full minute to sweep past the cables. At the closest approach she held her right arm close to her side. The conviction was strong that if she reached out, she could touch it, though she knew she must be more distant than that. When she was past, she twisted in the air once more and watched the thing recede from her.

One hour didn't sound like that much time. Surely one could remain in absolute terror that long. She began to wonder if something was wrong with her because she no longer felt terror. Before the approach of the cables had rekindled her fright, she had attained a kind of peace. She felt it stealing over her once more and welcomed it. There is a sweet calm that can come with the realization that one's death has arrived, that it will be swift and painless, that there is no good to be gained by sweating and clawing air and cursing fate.

It couldn't last forever. Why couldn't it last just twenty more minutes?

She was skipping back and forth now between fatalism and fear. Knowing there was nothing she could do was not enough. She wanted to live, she was not going to, and there were no words to express the sorrow of that.

Her religion was not one that believed in answered prayers. The Coven did not pray at all, in that sense. They asked nothing. There were things they could demand, positions to be earned in the afterlife, but in a tough spot you were on your own. The Great Mother was not going to interfere in anyone's fate, and it never occurred to Robin to ask Her to. But she did wish there was *something* she could turn to for help, some power in all this vastness.

And then she wondered if that was what Gaea wanted. Could she listen, all the way down here, minutes from destruction? After the first tremendous shock of it, Robin had not been greatly surprised that Gaea had done this terrible thing.

It seemed to mesh well with the insanity she had been talking. But now she wondered why, and the only reason she could think of was to terrorize Robin into acknowledging Gaea as her Lord.

If true, there might be something Gaea could do. Robin opened her mouth, and nothing came out. She tried again and screamed. Through some welcome spiritual alchemy, her fear was transmuted into anger so consuming it shook her more powerfully than the winds.

"Never!" she shouted. "Never, never, never! You stinking cancer! You abomination! You loathsome, repulsive perversion! I'll meet you in your grave, and I will disembowel you and choke you with your reeking guts! I'll stuff you with coals; I'll bite out your tongue; I'll spit you on cold iron and fry you for eternity! I curse you! Hear me now, oh Great Mother, hear me and mark me well! I pledge my shade to the eternal torment of the one called Gaea!"

"Good for you."

"I'm not even *started* yet! I'll—"

She looked toward her feet. One meter beyond them was a grinning face. There was not much more she could see, considering his angle; just his shoulders, amazing bulge of chest, and the wings folded on his back.

"You're taking this very calmly."

"Why shouldn't I?" Robin asked. "I thought I had it figured out, and I'm still not sure I was wrong. You swear, by whatever powers you hold holy, that Gaea didn't send you?"

"I swear by the Squadron. Gaea knew she was not tossing you to certain death, but she had no hand in this. I do it freely, on my own."

"I figure I'll hit the wall in about five more minutes."

"Wrong. The bottom of the spoke flares, like a bell, remember? It's enough that you'll come out and fall at a sixty-degree angle over East Hyperion."

"If you're trying to cheer me up. . . ." But it did have some effect. Her first estimate of sixty-eight minutes was right, it turned out. But her figure for terminal velocity was low; she would be falling longer. She wondered what the angel could do to help her with that.

"It's true I can't carry you," he said. "Really, you amaze

me. I get all sorts of reactions from people. Mostly they tell me what I have to do, when they're rational at all."

"I'm rational. Now can we get on with it? Time must be a factor here."

"But it's not, you know. I mean, not yet. I can help you only when we get closer to the ground, and what I'll do is slow you down. Until then you might as well relax. But I guess I don't have to tell you that."

Robin didn't know what to say to him. She was on the edge of hysteria, and her defenses against it were weakening. The only way to deal with that, she had found, was to pretend you are calm. If you can pretend well enough to fool someone else, you might even fool yourself.

He was falling in front of her now. As she looked at him, two things occurred to her: he was one of perhaps five people she had ever met smaller than herself, and she had no reason to assume he was a male. She wondered why she had done so. He had no external genitalia; there was nothing but a patch of iridescent green feathers between his legs. It must have been his wiriness. In her short time in Gaea she had come to associate angularity with males. He seemed to be made of bones and cables, covered with equal amounts of bare brown skin and multicolored feathers.

"Are you a child?" she asked.

"No. Are you?" He grinned. "At least you've started to live up to my expectations. Your next question is: am I male or female? I am extremely male and proud of the affliction. I say affliction because male angels live about half as long as females, and are smaller and have less range. But there are compensations. Have you ever made love in the air?"

"I have never made love at all in the sense you probably mean."

"You want to try? We have about fifteen minutes, and I can guarantee you an experience you won't forget. How about it?"

"No. I can't imagine why you would want to."

"I'm a deviant," he said cheerfully. "I have this thing for fat. Can't seem to get enough of it. I hang around waiting for fat human women to drop by. I do them a favor, and they do me a favor. Everybody's happy."

"Is that your fee then?"

"No. Not a fee. I'll save you anyway. I don't like to see

people squashed to death. But what do you say? It's not so much to ask. Just about everybody's been eager to return the favor."

"I'm not."

"You're odd, you know? I've never seen a human with markings like you. Were you born with those? Are you a different species of human? I can't understand why you won't make love with me. It's over so quickly. All it takes is a minute. Is that so much to ask?"

"You ask a lot of questions."

"I just want to . . . oops! It's about time to start turning, or you're going to hit . . . watch out!"

Robin had turned in panic, imagining the ground almost upon her. Her shoulder caught the rushing winds the wrong way, and she began to tumble.

"Just go limp again," the angel advised. "You'll straighten out. That's better. Now see if you can twist around. Keep your arms out to your sides, and angle them back."

Robin did as he said, ending in a swan dive. They were passing through the twilight zone now, close enough that the land below her was moving visibly. The angel moved in behind her and encircled her with his arms. They were hard and strong as ropes, one crossing her breasts, the other over her loins. She felt the cool pressure of his cheek feathers against her neck, then the warmth of his lips on her earlobe.

"You're so soft, so much lovely padding. . . ."

"By the Great Mother, if you are going to rape me, do it now, and a curse be on you for a lying peacock! We haven't got all day." Robin was shivering, fear of falling and the threat of nausea combining to batter at her self-control.

"What's in the bag?" he said tersely.

"My demon."

"All right, *don't* answer! But hold onto it. Here we go."

His arms were like clamps now as he carefully began to open his great wings. Weight tugged at her, changing her free fall to the feeling of hanging upside down. It became impossible to keep her legs straight out behind her. When she let them drop, the unstable pair rocked briefly around the balance point of the angel's wings, below his shoulder blades.

The ground tilted as the angel banked cautiously. His goal was to head her toward Ophion, where it flowed beneath the cable joining the Place of Winds to the hub. The river was deep, wide, and slow in that country, running in a southeasterly direction. To that end, he had to go first south for a time, then north, to align their glide with the river. Then he must extend Robin's fall by flattening the angle of his descent. Otherwise, she would have hit far short of the water.

They passed over a group of craters. Robin didn't ask what they were. It *couldn't* have been people; ninety meters per second would not give them that much kinetic energy. But other, heavier objects released at her point of departure could have done it.

The angel extended his wings to the fullest now. The ground below was hilly and forested, but ahead, the straight stretch of river could be seen. It did not look as if they would reach it, and there could be no pulling up and going around. The angel could lift little more than his own body weight.

"I think I'll have you down to seventy or eighty kilometers per hour when you hit," he said, shouting in her ear. "I will try to brake us in short bursts when I'm sure you'll reach the river. You'll be coming in at an angle."

"I can't swim."

"Neither can I. You're on your own there."

It was a confusing experience. The tug of his arms increased sharply, and she took a deep breath, her heart hammering. Then they were gliding again, seemingly still high above the brown waters. Another tug; she put her hands out reflexively, but they were still airborne. The third tug was the hardest of all. For long seconds Robin could not draw a breath.

And now the shoreline was getting closer, streaking by on her right. Ahead, the river curved westward.

She thought she hit on her back but was too stunned to be sure. The next thing she remembered clearly was clawing through muddy water toward the light.

Swimming turned out to be strenuous. It was amazing the things one could do when the water rose over one's upper lip.

The angel stood on the shore as she clambered out. It was not something he did well; his feet were not built for it. They were clawlike, with long, skeletal toes, made for grasping tree limbs. Robin crawled a meter or two on dry land, then went over on her side.

"Here, give me that," the angel said, yanking the bag from

her hand. "I deserve something for my work; you can't argue with that." He opened it, gasped, closed it quickly, and let it fall, backing away.

"I told you," Robin wheezed.

The angel was angry and impatient. "Well, what have you got?"

"There's a little money. You can have it all."

"I have no use for it. The only place to spend it is at the Titanides' madhouse."

Robin sat up and used her fingers to comb wet hair from her face.

"You speak English well," she said.

"What do you know? It can say nice things if it wants to."

"I'm sorry. If I hurt your feelings, I didn't really mean to. I just had a lot to worry about."

"Not anymore."

"I appreciate that. You saved my life, and I'm grateful."

"All right, all right. I learned to speak English from my grandmother, incidentally. She also taught me that nothing comes for free. What do you have besides money?"

There was a ring, a gift from her mother. She offered it to the angel. He held out his hand and examined it sourly.

"I'll take it. What else?"

"That's all I've got. Just the clothes I have on."

"I'll take them, too."

"But all my other things—"

"Are in the hotel. It's over that way. The day is warm. Enjoy the walk."

Robin removed her boots and poured water from them. The shirt came off easily, but the pants clung to her clammy skin.

He took them, then stood looking at her.

"If you only knew how much I love fat human women."

"You're not having this one. And what do you mean, fat? I'm not fat." She was made uneasy by his eyes, a distinctly new sensation. Robin had no more body modesty than a cat.

"You're twenty percent fat, maybe more. You're coated with it. You bulge all over with it." He sighed. "And those are the *damnedest* markings I ever saw." He paused, then grinned slowly. "At least I got to see you. Happy landings." He tossed the clothes to her and leaped into the air.

The force of his wings rocked Robin back on her heels, stirred a choking cloud of dust and leaves. For a moment his majestic wingspread blotted out the sky; then he was rising, vanishing, a silhouette stick-man in a riot of feathers.

Robin sat again and surrendered to a bad case of the shakes. She glanced at her carrier bag, writhing angrily as a thoroughly upset anaconda tried to gain her freedom. Nasu would have to wait. She would not starve, even if the attack lasted for days.

Robin managed to turn over, fearing she would blind herself by staring at the sun, and soon had lost all control of her body. The timeless Hyperion day marched on while she twitched in the amber sunlight, helpless, waiting for the angel to come back and rape her.

9.

The Free-Lance

Gaby Plauget stood on the rocky shelf and waited for the noise of the massive diastole to abate. A normal Aglaian intake cycle produced a sound like Niagara Falls. Today the sound was more like air bubbles rising from the neck of a bottle held underwater. The intake valve with the Titan tree jammed in it was almost completely submerged.

The place was called the Three Graces. It had been named by Gaby herself, many years before. In those days the few Terrans living in Gaea were still naming things in human speech, usually adhering to the early convention of using Greek mythology as a source. Knowing full well the other meaning of the word, Gaby had read that the Graces assisted Aphrodite at her toilet. She thought of Ophion, the circular river, as the toilet of Gaea and of herself as the plumber. Everything eventually ran into the river. When it clogged, she was the one who flushed it.

"Give me a plumber's friend the size of the Pittsburgh Dome and a place to stand," she had once told an interested observer, "and I will drain the world." Not having such a tool, she found it necessary to come up with methods less direct but equally huge.

Her vantage point was halfway up the northern cliff of the West Rhea Canyon. Formerly, the canyon had possessed a distinctly odd feature: the river Ophion did not flow out of it into the flatlands to the west, but in the other direction. It was Aglaia which had made that possible. Now, with the mighty river pump's intake valve impaired, common sense had caught up with Gaeagraphical whim. The water, with no place to go, had turned Ophion into a clear blue lake that filled the canyon and backed up onto the plains of Hyperion. For many kilometers, far up the curving horizon of Gaea, a placid sheet of water covered everything but the tallest trees.

Aglaia sat like a purple grape three kilometers long, lodged in the narrowing canyon neck, her lower end in the lake, her far end extending to the plateau 700 meters above. She and her sisters, Thalia and Euphrosyne, were one-celled organisms with brains the size of a child's fist. For three million years they had mindlessly straddled Ophion, lifting its waters over the West Rhea Summit. They took nourishment from the flotsam that continually floated into their vast maws, and were large enough to ingest anything in Gaea except the Titan trees, which, being part of the living flesh of Gaea, were not supposed to become detached.

But these were the twilight ages. Anything could happen, and usually did. And that, Gaby reflected, was why a being the size of Gaea had need of a troubleshooter the size of Gaby.

The intake phase was completed now. Aglaia was swollen to maximum size. There would be a few minutes before the valve began to shut, as if Aglaia held her breath in anticipation of her hourly eruption. Silence settled through the golden twilight, and many eyes turned to Gaby, waiting.

She went down on one knee and looked over the edge. There did not seem to be anything left undone. Deciding when to make the move had been a hard choice. On the one hand, the contracting valve would hold the tree wedged more firmly than ever during the systolic phase. On the other, the water which Aglaia had swallowed would now come rushing out, exerting great force to dislodge the obstruction. The operation did not depend on a delicate touch; Gaby planned to give the tree the biggest jolt she could manage and hope for the best.

Her crew was awaiting the signal. She stood, held a red flag over her head, and brought it down sharply.

Titanide horns sounded from the north and south canyon walls. Gaby turned and scrambled nimbly up the ten-meter rock face behind her. She bounded onto the back of Psaltery, her Titanide crew chief. Psaltery thrust his brass horn into his pouch and began galloping down the winding trail toward the radio station. Gaby rode him standing up, her bare feet on his withers, her hands holding his shoulders. She was protected by the Titanide trait of running with the human torso leaning forward and the arms swept back like a child imitating a fighter plane. She could grab the arms if she slipped, but it had been many years since she had needed to.

They arrived at the station as the systolic backwash was

beginning to be felt. The water was ten meters below them and the blocked intake valve half a kilometer up the canyon; nevertheless, as the torrent began to make a boiling bulge in the new lake and the water level began to rise, the Titanides stirred nervously.

The noise was building again, this time overdubbed with something new. At the top of the Aglaian plateau, at the Lower Mists, where the outflow valve would normally be spraying a stream of water hundreds of meters into the air, nothing was coming out but gas. The dry valve produced a sound Gaby thought of as contrabass flatulence.

"Gaea," she muttered. "The God that farts."

"What did you say?" Psaltery sang.

"Nothing. Are you in contact with the bomb, Mondoro?"

The Titanide in charge of etheric persuasion looked up and nodded.

"Shall I tell her to snuff it, my leader?" Mondoro sang.

"Not yet. And stop calling me that. Boss is sufficient." Gaby looked out over the water, where three cables emerged. She followed them with her eyes, searching for the raveling that would precede a break, and then regarded her impromptu fleet hovering overhead. After so many years the sight could still awe her.

They were the three largest blimps she could round up on a few days' notice. Their names were Dreadnaught, Bombasto, and Pathfinder. All were over a thousand meters long, each of them an old friend of Gaby's. It was friendship that had brought them here to help her. The larger blimps seldom flew together, preferring to be accompanied on their dirigible journeys by a squadron of seven or eight comparatively tiny zeps.

But now they were in harness, a troika the likes of which had seldom been seen in Gaea. Their translucent, gossamer tail surfaces—each large enough for the playing of a soccer match—beat the air with elephantine grandeur. Their ellipsoid bodies of blue nacre jostled and slithered and squeaked against each other like a cluster of carnival balloons.

Mondoro held up a thumb.

"Blow it," Gaby said.

Mondoro leaned over a seedpod the size of a cantaloupe which nestled in a tangle of vines and branches arranged between her front knees. She spoke to it in a low voice, and Gaby turned toward Aglaia, expectantly.

After a few moments Mondoro coughed apologetically, and Gaby frowned at her.

"She is angry at us for leaving her so long in the dark," Mondoro sang.

Gaby whistled tunelessly and tapped her foot, while wishing for a standard transmitter.

"Sing to her then of light," Gaby sang. "You're the persuader; you're supposed to know how to handle these creatures."

"Perhaps a hymn to fire . . ." the Titanide mused.

"I don't care what you sing," Gaby shouted, in English. "Just get the damn stupid thing to blow." She turned away, fuming.

The bomb was lashed to the trunk of the Titan tree. It had been placed there, at considerable risk, by angels who flew into the pump during the diastolic cycle, when there was air above the inrushing waters. Gaby wished she had an army surplus satchel charge to give the angels. What she had sent instead was a contraption made of Gaean fruits and vegetables. The explosive was a bundle of touchy nitroroots. The detonator was a plant that produced sparks, and another with a magnesium core, wedded to a brain obtained by laboriously scraping plant matter from an IC leaf to expose the silicon chip with its microscopic circuitry. The chip was programmed to listen to a radio seed, the most fickle plant in Gaea. They were radio transceivers that sent messages only if they were phrased beautifully, that functioned only if the things they heard were worth repeating.

Titanides were masters of song. Their whole language was song; music was as important to them as food. They saw nothing odd about the system. Gaby, who sang poorly and had never interested a seed in anything she sang, hated the things. She wished for a match and a couple of kilometers of waterproof, high-velocity primacord. Above her, the blimps kept the lines taut, but they would not last much longer. They did not have stamina. Kilo for kilo, they were among the weakest creatures in Gaea.

Four Titanides had gathered around the transmitter, singing complicated counterpoint. Every few bars they slipped in the five-note sequence the detonator brain was listening for. At some point the seed was mollified and began to sing. There was a muffled explosion that made Aglaia shiver, then a gout of black smoke from the top of her intake valve. The straining lines slackened.

Gaby stood on her toes, afraid to discover that the blast had merely broken the cables. Splinters that were themselves as large as pine trees began to spew from the opening. Then there was a cheer from the Titanides behind her as the bole of the Titan tree appeared, wallowing like a harpooned whale.

"Make sure it's five or ten kilometers from the intake when you stake it down," Gaby sang to Clavier, the Titanide delegated to handle the mop-up. "It will take awhile for all that water to be pumped out, but if you take the trunk to the water-line now, it will be high and dry in a few revs."

"Sure thing, Chief," Clavier sang.

Gaby stood watching her crew take care of the equipment borrowed from Titantown while Psaltery went to get Gaby's personal luggage. She had worked with most of these Titanides before, on other jobs. They knew what they were doing. It was possible they did not need her at all, but she doubted any of them would have tackled it except under divine orders. For one thing, they did not have Gaby's contacts with the blimps.

But Gaby had not been ordered to do anything. All her work was performed under contract and paid in advance. In a world where every being had a prescribed place she defined her own.

She turned at the sound of hoofbeats. Psaltery was returning with her belongings. There was not much; the things Gaby needed or valued enough to carry at all times could be stuffed into a small hiker's backpack. The things she most valued were her freedom and her friends. Psaltery (Sharped Lydian Trio) Fanfare was one of the best of the latter. He and Gaby had traveled together for ten years.

"Chief, your phone was ringing."

The ears of the other Titanides perked up, and even Psaltery, who was used to it, seemed subdued. He handed Gaby a radio seed identical to all the others. The difference was that this one connected to Gaea.

Gaby took the seed and withdrew from the group. Standing alone in a small grove of trees, she spoke softly for a time. The Titanides were not eager to hear what Gaea had to say—news of the doings of Gods is seldom good news—but they could not help noticing that Gaby stood quietly for a time when the conversation was obviously over.

"Are you up to a trip to the Melody Shop?" she asked Psaltery.

"Sure. We in a hurry?"

"Not really. Nobody's seen Rocky for almost a kilorev. Her Nibs wants us to check in and let her know it's almost Carnival time."

Psaltery frowned.

"Did Gaea say what the problem might be?"

Gaby sighed. "Yeah. We're supposed to try to sober her up."

10.

The Melody Shop

Titanides were terribly overpowered. Of all the beings in Gaea, they alone seemed improperly designed for their habitat. Blimps were precisely as they must be to live where and how they did. Everything about them was as functional as their fear of flame. Angels were so close to impossible they had left Gaea no room for her customary playfulness. It had been necessary for her to design them to tolerances of grams and subordinate everything to their eight-meter wingspans and the muscles needed to power them.

The Titanide was obviously a plains animal. Why then was it necessary to make it able to climb trees? Their lower bodies were equine—though cloven-hoofed—and in the light gravity of Gaea they could have done quite well with legs slimmer than any thoroughbred's. Instead, Gaea had given them the quarters of a Percheron, the fetlocks of a Clydesdale. Their backs, withers, and hips were broad with muscle.

It turned out, however, that Titanides, alone of Gaea's creatures, could withstand the gravity of Earth. They became Gaea's ambassadors to humanity. Considering that the race of Titanides was less than two centuries old, it became obvious that their strength was no accident. Gaea had been planning ahead.

There was an unexpected dividend for the humans living in Gaea. A Titanide's walking gait had none of the jouncing associated with Terran horses. They could move like clouds in the low gravity, their bodies maintained at a constant height by light touches of their hooves. The ride was so smooth, in fact, that Gaby had no trouble sleeping. She reclined on Psaltery's back with one leg hanging over each side.

While she slept, Psaltery climbed the winding trail into the Asteria Mountains.

He was a handsome creature of the naked-skin type, colored like milk chocolate. He had a thick mane of orange hair that grew not only from his scalp but down his neck and over a lot of his human back, worn in a series of long braids, like the hair of his tail. As with all his species, his human face and torso appeared to be those of a female. He was beardless and had large, wide-set eyes with sweeping lashes. His breasts were large and conical. But between his front legs was a penis that looked all too human for many Terrans. He had another, much larger one between his hind legs, and under his lovely orange tail was a vagina, but to a Titanide it was the frontal organs that made the difference. Psaltery was male.

The trail he followed through the woods was tangled with vines and new growth, but occasionally it was possible to see that once it had been wide enough for a wagon to pass. In some of the clearings broken patches of asphalt could be seen. It was part of the Circum-Gaea Highway, built more than sixty years ago. Gaby had had a hand in its construction. To Psaltery, it had always been there: useless, seldom-traveled, slowly crumbling.

He reached the top of the Aglaian plateau, the Lower Mists. Soon he was out of them and trotting beside the Aglaian Lake with Thalia in the distance, thirstily sucking the waters. He climbed to the Middle Mists, to Euphrosyne and the Upper Mists. Ophion became a river once more, briefly, before entering the double-pump system that lifted it to the Midnight Sea.

Psaltery turned north before reaching the last pumps and followed a small mountain stream. He forded it in white water and began to climb. He was in Rhea now and had been for quite some time, but the boundaries in Gaea were not well-defined. The journey had started in the middle of the twilight zone between Hyperion and Rhea, that hazy area between the perpetual weak daylight of the one and the eternal moonlit night of the other. He had been proceeding into night. Somewhere on the middle slopes of the Asterias he reached it. The Rhean night presented no visibility problems; Titanide night vision was good, and this close to the boundary there was still much light reflected from the plains of Hyperion curving up behind them.

He ascended the steep mountainside along a narrow but

well-defined path. In a series of alpine switchbacks he made his way through two passes and into the deep valleys on the other side. The Rhean mountains were sheer and rocky, with slopes averaging seventy degrees. There were no more tall trees, but the land was upholstered in lichens thick and smooth as the felt on a pool table. Dotted over that were broad-leafed shrubs the roots of which scrabbled into the living rock, sending out taproots that could be as long as half a kilometer before they reached the nourishing body of Gaea—the mountains' real bones.

Soon he could see the Melody Shop's beacon rising between two peaks. Rounding a bend, he came upon a sight that was unique, even in Gaea, who had made a hobby of creating the unusual.

Between two peaks—each as sharply pointed as the Matterhorn—was slung a narrow saddle of land. It was flat on top with a perpendicular drop on each side. The plateau was called Machu Picchu, after a similar place in the Andes where the Incas had built a stone city in the clouds. A single ray of sunlight had inexplicably wandered from the flood that poured through the distant Hyperion roof. It angled sharply into the night, where it drenched the plateau in buttery gold. It was as if the sun had found a pinhole through the blackest clouds imaginable, late on a stormy afternoon.

There was only one structure on Machu Picchu. The Melody Shop was a two-story wooden house, whitewashed, topped by a roof of green shingles. At this distance it looked like a toy.

"We are here, Chief," the Titanide sang. Gaby sat up, rubbing her eyes, turned, and gazed out over Cirocco's valley.

"'Look on my works, ye Mighty, and despair,'" she muttered. "Salty, that gal ought to have her head examined. Somebody ought to tell her that."

"You did, the last time you were here," Psaltery pointed out.

"Yeah, I did, didn't I?" Gaby winced. The memory was still painful. "Just drive on, would you?"

The two descended the path to the narrow neck of land leading to Machu Picchu. There was a rope-and-wood suspension bridge spanning a deep chasm just before the plateau. The bridge could be brought down with a few chops of an ax, isolating Cirocco's stronghold to all but an aerial approach.

A young man was seated on the far side of the bridge, wearing climbing shoes and a khaki outfit. From his gloomy expression Gaby figured him for one of the endless procession of suitors who made their way, year after year, to conquer the mysterious and lonely Wizard of Gaea. When they arrived, they found she was far from lonely—with three or four lovers already in attendance—and deceptively easy to conquer. Getting into her bed was not hard if a man did not mind the crowd. Getting out intact was something else. Cirocco tended to drain men's souls, and if their souls were shallow enough to be drained, she no longer needed them. She had seventy years on all of them. This alone made her fascinating, but ninety-five years of sexual activity made her preternaturally skillful, far beyond their experience. They fell in love with her by the score, and she gently turned them out when they became obnoxious about it. Gaby called them the Lost Boys.

She eyed this one suspiciously as she crossed the bridge. They had been known to jump. She decided he would probably make it when he managed to grin at her emphatic gesture toward the trail leading back to Titantown and the pieces of his old life.

She jumped from Psaltery's back as he neared the wide front porch. Though the tall doorways of the house had been built with Titanides in mind, none of them would enter unless personally invited by the Wizard. Gaby took the four steps of the front stoop in one easy leap and had her hand on the brass doorknob before she noticed an arm hanging off the side of the porch glider. Between the side slats of the seat she could see a bare foot. All else was covered by a dirty Titanide horse blanket that looked very like a serape.

When she pulled the blanket back, she looked down at the open-mouthed face of Cirocco Jones, formerly Captain of the Deep Space Vessel *Ringmaster*, now the Wizard of Gaea, Hindmother of the Titanides, Wing Commander of the Angels, Admiral of the Dirigible Fleet: the fabled Siren of the Titan. She was out cold. Cirocco was sleeping off a three-day binge.

Gaby's face could not hide her disgust. She teetered on the edge of walking away from it; then her expression gradually softened. The ghost of affection sometimes came back to her when Cirocco was like this. She smoothed unkempt dark hair from the sleeping woman's brow and was rewarded by a loud snort. Hands fluttered vaguely, searching for the blanket, and the Wizard rolled over.

Gaby got behind the glider and grasped its bottom. She lifted, and the chains creaked overhead as her onetime superior officer rolled out and hit the porch with a thud.

11.

The Purple Carnival

Hyperion was thought by many to be the loveliest of Gaea's twelve regions. In point of fact, few had traveled enough to make an informed comparison.

But Hyperion was a fair country: gentle, fertile, and washed in an eternal pastoral afternoon. He contained no rugged mountains but a plenitude of rivers. (Hyperion was always referred to with the male pronoun, though none of Gaea's regions was either male or female. They were named for the Titans, first children of Uranus and Gaea.) There was Ophion, wide and slow and muddy for most of its length. Flowing into it were nine major tributaries. They were named for the Muses. To the north and south the land rose gradually, as it did in all of Gaea's regions, until it ended in cliffs three kilometers tall. At the top of the cliffs were relatively narrow shelves known as the highlands. Here could be found plants and animals unchanged from the days of Gaea's youth. From there the land continued to rise until it could no longer support a rocky carapace. The naked body of Gaea became visible, still rising, becoming vertical and then arching over the land below, completely enclosing it with a translucent window to admit sunlight. The air at that altitude was not cold, but the walls were. Water vapor collected there and froze into a thick band of ice. It continually broke off to smash into the slopes of highland mountains, melt, rush down in narrow cascades, leap from the towering cliffs, and continue more placidly in the Rivers of the Muses. Eventually, as all things did, it joined the uniting flow of Ophion.

The west and central lands of Hyperion were clothed in thick forest. For part of its length Ophion became more lake than river, extending a finger of swamp from the central vertical cable terminus into the northeast. But throughout most of his area, Hyperion was prairie: a region of gently rolling hills with spacious skies and what looked like amber waves of grain. It was known as the Titanide Plains.

The grain grew wild, and so did the Titanides. They dominated the land without overpowering it, building little, content to herd a variety of animals that burrowed to suck Gaea's milk. They had no serious competitors for the land, no natural predators. There had never been a census, but 100,000 would have been a good estimate of their number. Had there been 200,000 the land would have been seriously crowded. Half a million would have meant starvation.

Gaea had patterned Titanides on human beings. They loved their children, who did not have to be taught to walk and talk and thus, child for child, required much less rearing than human infants. A Titanide child was independent in two Earth years, sexually mature in three. When the child left the nest, the parent was usually eager to have another one.

All Titanides could have children.

All Titanides *wanted* to have children, usually as many as possible. Infant mortality was low: disease, unknown. Life spans were long.

It could have been an equation of disaster. In fact, Titanide population had been stable for seventy years, and the reason was the Purple Carnival.

The rivers of Hyperion—Ophion and the Muses—divided the land into eight regions known as Keys: loose administrative areas analogous to human counties. The Keys did not mean a great deal. Anyone was free to move from one to another. But Titanides were not great travelers, tending to live in the region of their birth. The most important divisions within the species of Titanides were the chords, which resembled the human races. Like humans, Titanide chords could be crossed with no ill effect. Unlike humans, there was no racial tension. There were ninety-four established chords. All lived side by side, spread through each of the eight Keys of Hyperion.

The largest Hyperion Key was bounded by the rivers Thalia, Melpomene, and a southward curve of Ophion. This was the Key of E, and it contained Titantown and the Place of Winds. To the south was the Key of D Minor; to the west, C Sharp and F Sharp Minor.

Twenty kilometers north of Titantown in the Key of E a lone rock stood between the swamp and a wide, flat plain ringed by low hills. The rock was called Amparito Roca. It was 700 meters high and about as wide, sheer-sided but scalable, and had been thrown there from an unknown distance during the Oceanic Rebellion, many megarevs before. The craterlike area it dominated had been created when Amparito Roca bounced before coming to rest and was known as Grandioso.

Once in every ten kilorevs—420 Earth days, a period often called the Gaean Year—Titanides from the Hyperion Keys trekked to Amparito Roca in noisy, colorful caravans, taking enough provisions for a festival lasting two hectorevs. In Titantown the midway shut down, and the Titanides folded their tents, leaving the human tourists to fend for themselves. Every Titanide made the journey, but of the humans, only natives and pilgrims could attend the great festival.

It was the biggest event in the Titanides' lives, combining Christmas and Mardi Gras and Cinco de Mayo and Tet into one monster celebration, as if all the people of Earth had gathered together for a week of drinking and singing.

It was a time of great happiness and bitter disappointment. Dreams begun and nurtured ten kilorevs ago could bear fruit at the Purple Carnival. More often they came to naught. The crowds filling Grandioso on the first day of Carnival would soon be winnowed to a few, and the crowds leaving on the last day were more subdued than those which had arrived in song and laughter. Yet there would be no despair. You won or you lost; it was all in how Gaea turned.

The prize to be won in the bowl of Grandioso was the right to bear children.

The Purple Carnival commenced with the rendition of a march by the Key of E Quality-Plus Marching Band, 300 strong. This time it was "On Parade," by John Philip Sousa. Robin, perched on a ledge fifty meters up the red-brown side of Amparito Roca, had no way of knowing what she was about to experience. She listened to the opening bars, a solo trumpet call of remarkable crispness, then gripped the rock when the ensemble joined in, fortissimo, with three descending notes that were gone almost before they were uttered, yet which had possessed a volume and clarity little short of miraculous. The air was still trembling, astonished to have contained such a sound, while the trumpet repeated its earlier brash statement, only to be swallowed once again by the arrival of the massed winds, this time in earnest.

The Quality-Plus Band had never heard of uniforms. They had never heard of directors either. They would have hated the first, had no need of the second. With ensemble music, music that was written down to be performed rigidly, all any Titanide needed was someone to provide a downbeat. Everything else was implicit on the paper and would be performed exactly as written, perfect the first time and every time thereafter. Titanides never needed rehearsal. They designed and built their own instruments, could play any horn, fiddle, drum, or keyboard they encountered with a few minutes' familiarization, and built few instruments alike.

The music moved Robin. It was a formidable accomplishment for the band, though they were never aware of it; Robin had never liked march music, associating it with peckish militaristic displays, with soldiery and aggression. The Titanides forced her to hear it as exuberance, as sheer, brassy vitality. She rubbed the goose bumps on her arms and leaned forward, hanging on every note.

This was the kind of celebration she could understand. The air held a promise, a vibrant excitement that tasted delicious. She had felt it even before she caught up with the cloud of dust that had marked the Titanide column on its way to Carnival, felt it in spite of being still shaken by her fall, her encounter with the angel, and her long helplessness on the banks of Ophion. Upon reaching the parade of partygoers she had been welcomed without reservation. Somehow they all knew she was a pilgrim, though Robin was herself far from sure she qualified for the status. Nevertheless, the Titanides overwhelmed her with gifts of food, drink, song, and flowers. They had carried her on their backs, where she had to share space with saddlebags and sacks of food, and on their wagons, which creaked and swayed beneath staggering loads. She had wondered what in the name of the Great Mother they were carrying that so burdened wagons with as many as twelve wheels, pulled by hitches of from two to twenty Titanides.

Now she overlooked the bowl of Grandioso and thought she knew. A good part of the cargo must have been costume jewelry. Stark naked, Titanides were often flashy as a neon kaleidoscope, but to a Titanide it was never enough. Even in town, for no special occasion, they averaged a kilo of bangles, beads, bracelets, and bells. If they had bare skin, they painted it; if covered with hair, they stained it, braided it, bleached it. They pierced their long ears, their nostrils, their nipples, labia, and foreskins and wore in them anything that flashed or jangled. They drilled holes in their adamantine hooves—clear and red as rubies—and bolted on gems of contrasting colors. One seldom saw a Titanide without a fresh flower braided into the hair or tucked behind an ear.

That was all apparently just a warm-up. For the Purple Carnival the Titanides threw restraint to the winds and got decked out.

The music reached a pounding climax and then was gone, though it reverberated in the rock. It seemed to Robin that something so alive as that sound should not be allowed to die, and indeed, it wasn't. The band tore into the "National Emblem," by E.E. Bagley. From that moment there was never to be a pause in the music.

But during the brief hiatus Robin saw that someone was going to join her. She felt annoyed at the imminent interruption—she would have to speak to this woman in the worn leather boots and green pants and shirt just when she had settled down to some serious listening. She considered leaving. The woman chose that moment to look up and smile. Her gesture seemed to say, "May I join you?" Robin nodded.

She was certainly agile enough. She bounded up the rock face it had taken Robin ten minutes to climb, hardly using her hands.

"Hi," she said, sitting beside Robin with her legs dangling off the ledge. "I hope I'm not disturbing you."

"It's okay." Robin was still watching the band.

"They don't really march, of course," the woman said. "The music excites them too much to stay in step. If Sousa saw them, he'd scream."

"Who?"

The woman laughed. "Don't let a Titanide hear you say that. John Philip Sousa is right up there with sex and good wine in their top ten. And damn if they don't make *me* like him, the way they play it."

Robin would not have known proper marching if she had seen it and could not have cared less. The Titanides' leaping and dancing were fine with her. Sousa must have been the man who wrote the march, but that was unimportant, too. The woman had said the music moved her in spite of herself, and it had done the same thing to Robin. She turned her head to study the new arrival.

The woman was not much taller than Robin, and that was refreshing. There had been entirely too many giants since she came to Gaea. Her face in profile was relaxed, with an oddly innocent quality belied by the way she carried her body. She might have been only a few years older than Robin, but somehow she didn't think so. The light brown color of her unlined skin had the look of a tan. Sitting, she did not move anything but her eyes, which missed nothing. She seemed bonelessly relaxed; it was an illusion.

She let Robin look her over for a reasonable time; then, with a slight movement of her head, her attention was completely shifted. Her eyes smiled before her mouth did, but when the lips caught up, they revealed even white teeth. She put out a hand, and Robin took it.

"I'm Gaby Plauget," she said.

"May the holy flow unite...." Robin's eyes widened.

"Don't tell me they still remember me in the Coven. Really?" Her grin grew even bigger, and she squeezed Robin's hand. "You must be Robin the Nine-fingered. I've been looking for you all day."

12.

The Bride-Elect

Chris came out of it in the middle of a dance. Operating on some automatic level, his body continued to move as it had been moving for some seconds before he could make it stop, at which point he was bumped from behind by a large blue Titanide. Chris had a grin on his face. He got rid of it.

Someone grabbed his elbow and pulled him from the line of dancers, turned him, and he was face to breast with another Titanide.

"I *said*, we have to get going *now*, or I'll be late for my own *review*," she said, and held one large hand in an odd position. When he did nothing, she raked her other hand through her long pink hair and sighed. "Well, step *up*, Chris! Come on!"

Something made him lift his bare foot and put it in the Titanide's palm. Call it a ghost reflex, his body remembering a learned operation his mind had forgotten. It was the right thing. She lifted; he grabbed for her shoulder and found himself astride her back. Her skin was hairless, predominately yellow but mottled with small brown spots like a ripe banana. Against his bare legs she had just the right temperature and texture: human skin stretched over a different frame.

She twisted at the waist, leaning to one side far enough to get one arm around his shoulders. Her big, almond eyes were glittering with excitement. To his amazement, she kissed him hard on the lips. She was so big she made him feel six years old.

"For luck, precious. We've got the mates and the mode. All we need now is luck, and you're my charm." She let out a howl and dug the ground with her back legs, springing forward at a full gallop as Chris hugged her waist and hung on.

He was not entirely unused to this sort of occurrence. There had been other times when he recovered from amnesia in midstride, so he thought he was prepared for almost anything.

He was not prepared for this.

The whole world was filled with bright sunlight, dust, Titanides, tents, and music. Especially music. They passed through waves of it, encountering what certainly must have been all the forms invented by humans and the vastly greater number known to Titanides. It should have been acoustical insanity, but it was not. Each group was aware of the things being done by adjacent groups. With improvisational prestidigitation they played off each other, re-worked themes, and threw them back for elaboration: re-metered, sweetened. Chris and the Titanide passed through families of music—ragtime next door to cakewalks, shouldering close to swing and nineteen varieties of progressive jazz, with small pockets of inhuman strangeness hushed or clarioned.

Some of it was inaccessible to Chris. The best he could do was think, yes, it might be interesting if music were like that. To Titanides all sound was music. The kinds humans loved were just a corner of the theater, nothing but a subset of the family music. One thing Chris heard was just sustained notes in clusters of three or four, each a few cycles away from the tonic. The Titanides managed to turn the resultant beats, the difference and summation tones, into music in and of itself.

Moving in the crush of Purple Carnival was a voyage through the innards of a 50,000-channel sound mixer with living electronics. Somewhere a Master Titanide thumbed the huge switch panel, augmenting here, muting there, bringing up one melodic line only to fade it out in a few seconds.

Things were sung in the direction of his companion. (Was it proper to call her his mount? His steed?) She usually waved and returned a short song. Then a Titanide called out, in English.

"What have you got there, Valiha?"

"A four-leaf clover, I hope," Valiha called back. "My ticket to maternity."

It was nice to have a name for her. She seemed to know him, embarrassingly well, as a matter of fact, and she would expect him to know her. Not for the first time, he wondered what he had been up to.

Their destination was a crater with eroded walls, half a kilometer in diameter. He groped for a name, just out of reach, and came up with Grandioso. Meaningless, but it felt right, as things sometimes did after an episode. The rock that sat on the edge of the crater had a name, but it wouldn't come.

From the sides of Grandioso he could look back and see the Titanide encampment, a mad brawl like the tuning of a thousand orchestras, a turmoil of color that trailed a dust plume far downwind.

The interior of the bowl was another world. It held many Titanides, but they had none of the anarchic revelry of those outside. Grandioso was covered in a carpet of short green grass and had been marked off in a grid of white lines. The Titanides had arranged themselves in small groups, never more than four in a square, like counters in a game. Some of the squares held gaudy but temporary-looking structures like floral floats. Others were nearly bare. Valiha entered the maze, went in three squares and over seven. She joined two other Titanides in a square that held a few objects like holly wreaths and a selection of polished stones, all laid out in a pattern that meant nothing to Chris.

She introduced him to the others, and he heard himself named as Long-Odds Major. What had he been telling her? The two Titanides were a female named Cymbal (Lydian Trio) Prelude and a male with the unlikely name of Hichiriki (Phrygian Quartet) Madrigal. Valiha, he learned, was also a member of the Madrigal chord. They were distinguished by their yellow skin and cotton-candy hair. Her middle, parenthetical name was Aeolian Solo. He gathered that the middle names of Titanides designated breeding. Little was clear beyond that.

"And all this . . . ?" Chris hoped that not completing the sentence would protect the secret of his ignorance of things she thought he knew. He gestured at the white lines, at the rocks and flowers. "What mode did you say this was going to be?"

"A Double-flatted Mixolydian Trio," she said, apparently nervous enough to chatter about anything, regardless of having discussed it before. "It's on the sign there in front. You realize that's not really what it is—a Double-flatted Mixolydian Trio is musically meaningless; it's just a string of English words we use for the real words that you can't sing. Oh, I guess I didn't say, but that mode means that Cymbal was the foremother and Hichiriki was the forefather. If we get tapped, Cymbal will be the hindfather."

"And you the hindmother," Chris said, feeling safe.

"Right. They produced the egg, and Cymbal will quicken it in me."

"The egg."

"Right here." She reached into her pouch—how handy to have a built-in pocket, Chris thought—and tossed him something the size of a golf ball. He almost dropped it, and Valiha laughed.

"It doesn't have a shell," she said. "But haven't you seen one before?" A slight frown creased her forehead.

Chris had no idea. This one was quite hard, apparently solid. It was a perfect sphere, pale gold with brown whorls like fingerprint smudges. It had milky areas in its translucent depths. Someone had printed a series of Titanide characters on it.

He gave it back to her, then looked at the sign she had mentioned earlier. It rested on the ground, a ten-centimeter metal plate engraved with symbols and lines:

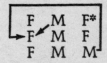

"The *F* stands for female," someone said, behind him. He turned and saw two human women talking to each other. They both were short and rather pretty. The smaller one had a green, staring Eye painted on her forehead. There were more drawings partially visible on her legs and arms. She looked young. The other, darker one was the voice he had heard. He could not guess her age, though she did not look older than her middle thirties.

"The *M*, of course, is male. The star at the right is the semi-fertilized egg produced by the foremother, and the arrow pointing up from the bottom line shows the first fertilization. This is a Double-flatted Mixolydian Trio, which means the foremother is also the hindfather. Mixolydian ensembles are those with two females participating, except for Aeolian Duets, where the whole ensemble is female. All Aeolian modes are all-female. Lydian modes have one female and one, two, or three males, and the Phrygian mode, of which there is only the quartet, has three females and one male, the forefather."

Chris stepped out of the way as the smaller woman knelt

to peer at the legend on the sign. He wanted to find out how he fitted into the picture and hoped he could learn by eavesdropping. It was a tactic he had used well in the past after memory lapses, a common one among people with mental problems, whose almost universal urge was not to reveal the extent of their condition.

The woman sighed as she straightened up.

"I guess I'm still missing something," she said with a faint accent Chris could not place. She pointed to Chris as if he were a statue. "How does *he* fit in?"

The older one laughed. "Not at all, into a Mixolydian Trio. There are two modes that include humans—the Dorian and Ionian—but there are none of those here today. You'll seldom see them. No, if anything, he's part of the decorations. He's a fertility fetish. A good-luck charm. Titanides are very superstitious at Carnival."

She had been looking at him while she spoke; now her eyes met his for the first time, searched for something, and did not seem to find it, and she broke into a smile. She extended her hand.

"I don't think you really are, though, anymore," she said. "I'm Gaby Plauget. I hope I didn't offend you."

Chris was surprised at the strength of her grasp.

"I'm—"

"Chris Major," She laughed again. It was innocent laughter, impossible to take the wrong way. "I shouldn't do that. You've probably gathered I know a little about you. We haven't met, though."

"I get the feeling that . . . never mind." Chris thought he knew the name from somewhere, but she had said they had not met, so he dropped it. If he spent too much time trying to recall shadow experiences buried in his head, he would never get anything done.

She nodded. "I'll tell you more later. I'll see you around." She fluttered the fingers of one hand, still grinning, and returned to the other woman. "Look at the top row of symbols as one Titanide," she explained. "Hind legs to the left, head to the right. The top row represents a female: vagina in back, penis in the middle, another vagina between the forelegs. The second row is also a female, and the third row is a male. Now does it make sense? Top row is foremother and hindfather, middle row is hindmother, bottom row. . . ."

"What was that she was saying to you?"

Chris turned, saw Valiha looking nervous.

"Well, just what did I say to *you?*"

"That you were very lucky, and you . . . you mean it's not true?" Her eyes grew wide, and she put her hand to her mouth.

"I seem to have times of being lucky," he said. "It's not reliable, though. And I don't recall how we met, or what we've talked about, or what we've done together. I'm blank from . . . well, the last thing I remember is talking to Gaea in a big room at the hub. I'm sorry. Did I make some kind of promise?"

But Valiha had returned to her two partners. They put their heads together and sang a sweet moaning melody. He gathered they were talking it over. He sighed and looked around for Gaby and her companion, but they had moved far down the row, walking toward a large white tent that stood on the edge of the judging field.

Valiha asked him to be near for the review when it came. She wanted to know if he brought bad luck when he was not crazy, and he said he didn't think so. It was clear the three Titanides were upset and did not know what to do. He thought it might be best to melt into the crowd, not burden them with what seemed to him the black cloud of doom he carried with him. With that intention he started off down the field, not hurrying, studying the groupings of Titanides.

It made more sense now. Each square contained an ensemble the purpose of which was to be certified for reproduction. To that end they had created proposals according to arcane rules of their own. They grouped themselves in twos, threes, and fours, each specifying one of the twenty-nine possible modes of procreation, each having already produced a semifertilized egg: the first stage of the Titanide sexual minuet.

Chris wondered, as he ambled slowly between the groups, just how many of these proposals would ever be put into effect and who made the decisions. It didn't take a lot of insight to realize that Gaea was a finite world. He supposed that with industrialization Gaea could be made to support many more sentient beings than she now did, but a limit would soon be reached. It followed that only a small number of the groups around him would be chosen to procreate. He made a guess at how few that would be, thought he was being conservative, and later learned he had overshot the mark by a factor of five.

Such competition produces stress, and stress leads to irrationality. Had Titanides been humans, there would have been much fighting at Carnival, but Titanides did not fight among themselves. Losers retired to weep in private. They emerged after a period of sorrow to wild drinking and dancing and much talk about next time. But before that they grasped at anything, decorating their assigned squares with talismans, amulets, and charms, becoming for a time intensely superstitious, like bettors at racetracks or primitives aware of their status as small beings doing their best to attract God's attention.

The displays they created to enhance their proposals ranged from the baroque to the minimalist. Chris saw one group of two who had built a shaky pagoda festooned with broken glass, flowers, empty cans, and beautiful ceramic pots. Another square was carpeted in white feathers, sprinkled with blood. Some practiced tableaux or short skits; others juggled knives while standing on their hind legs. There was a starkly simple display that Chris found irresistible, consisting of a worn gray stone with an egg sitting on it, set off by a twig and two tiny flowers.

There was one square with a single occupant. Chris at first thought the rest of the ensemble had not yet arrived, but when he studied the sign in front of the proposal, he was even more puzzled:

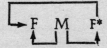

According to Gaby's explanation, each row on the sign represented a Titanide. Further, the sign seemed to indicate that this female intended to be forefather, foremother, hindfather, and hindmother to her child. He looked at her. She was a lovely creature, covered in snowy fur, sitting down with a single clear green egg resting on the grass between her knobby front knees. He couldn't resist.

"Pardon me. I don't think I understand just how...."

She was smiling at him, but her look showed incomprehension. She sang a few notes to him, lifted her shoulders eloquently, and shook her head.

He left her, still curious as to just what it was she intended to do.

He had meant to steal away, but somehow he was still around when the Wizard emerged from her tent and began making her review. Chris happened to be close by. He decided to watch for a while.

She was a big woman and made no attempt to hide the fact, carrying herself erectly, shoulders back, chin out. Her skin was light brown, her hair a fine mahogany, blowing carelessly to each side of a part down the center. Her brow was a bit too prominent, her nose too long and her jaw too wide to play glamour roles in the movies, but she had a power in her movements, something about her that transcended more conventional beauty. She walked on the balls of her bare feet, a quarter-gee gait Chris had seen before that involved the knees' bending very little with each stride, with her hips doing most of the work. It was feline and very sexy, though not meant to be; it was simply the most efficient way to walk in Gaea.

He followed her for a while as she moved up and down the rows of applicants. She was accompanied by a brace of Titanide bucks of the Cantata clan: light-skinned and hairless but for their heads, tails, forearms, and lower legs, and large even among Titanides. One carried a clipboard; the other, a gold box. They were apparently identical twins. They wore only gold bracelets and bands around arms and legs. The Wizard looked less regal. Her sole garment was a faded brick-red blanket with a hole she could put her head through, covering her to the knees. Her arms were often lost in its folds, but when they came out, Chris could see she wore nothing under it.

The Wizard ignored the white lines on the ground, moving from one square to another as it suited her. Her Titanide retinue and the small number of other observers stuck to the lanes between squares, however, and Chris did, too. One of the Cantatas was making sure she looked at every group, checking off squares on his board, once calling the Wizard back when she turned at the wrong place.

She knew many of the Titanides. Often she would stop to sing with them, kissing some, embracing others. She walked slowly through the groups after first reading the sign in front and looking the Titanides up and down with no expression on her face. Sometimes she stopped and appeared lost in thought, then would confer with an aide, mutter something to him, and move on. At some squares she asked questions of one or more candidates.

She went through the entire group that way, then started through again. Chris began to be bored with it. He decided to say good-bye and good luck to Valiha and her ensemble.

"Where *were* you?" Valiha hissed.

"I'm really not going to do you any good," Chris said. He noticed that the lovely Titanide egg had been balanced on the neck of an empty tequila bottle at Valiha's feet. He gestured to it. "I'll have no more effect than that trash."

"Please, Chris, humor me in this. You promised you would." Her eyes were pleading, and he thought uncomfortably that, yes, he had promised something like that. He looked away from her eyes, looked back, and nodded.

"All you have to do is stand just on the edge of the line. You can't come into the square during the review...shhh! Quiet, everybody, she's coming!"

Chris turned, and there she was, moving up the line behind him. She was judging the row opposite Valiha's, going fairly quickly, and passed just a few meters from Chris. After she had taken a few more steps, she paused, tilted her head slightly, then turned and looked at him with her brow lowered. He felt awkward but could not look away. Eventually one corner of her mouth turned up.

"So you're back with us," she said. "We met, briefly, about a dekarev ago. I'm Cirocco. You can call me Rocky." She did not offer her hand but continued to look him over. He felt underdressed in the shorts he had awakened in. The Wizard glanced at Valiha, did a double take, and fixed her with the gaze that had so unsettled Chris. Then she moved into the potential Double-flatted Mixolydian Trio.

"You're Valiha," Cirocco said. The Titanide made an odd curtsy in reply. "I knew your hindmother well." She was walking around Valiha, rubbing her hand along the smooth mottled flanks. She nodded to Hichriki and Cymbal, bent to squeeze Valiha's right-hind fetlock, then resumed her smoothing motions. She came around front again, reached up and stroked

Valiha's cheek. She knelt and rubbed the Titanide's foreleg
with both hands, then turned her head and spoke to Chris.

"You've fallen into good company," she said. "Valiha's an
Aeolian Solo. I believe it's the only one I've ever granted for
this particular Madrigal-Samba mix. In another two or three
hundred kilorevs her descendants might form a chord of their
own. What she's proposing here is well thought out, though.
It's a consolidation instead of the rather daring Locrilydian
Duet she proposed last Carnival. But she's only . . . oh, make
it five Earth years old, and the young want to do it all themselves, don't they, Valiha?"

A tinge of pink colored the Titanide's yellow cheeks as the
Wizard stood up. She looked away and blushed deeper when
Cirocco laughed and patted her hip.

"I expected you to be singing an Aeolian Solo this time,"
Cirocco teased. She glanced at Chris, who felt uncomfortable
with the exchange. It all had too much of the aspect of a horse
show for his taste. He expected her to peel back the Titanide's
lips and look at her teeth.

"'Singing an Aeolian Solo' is a Titanide euphemism for
conceit," Cirocco explained. "A Titanide female can effec-
tively clone herself, being all four parents to her offspring by
using frontal and hind self-insemination. But I don't let 'em
do it too damn often." She put her hands on her hips, then
reached up again and brushed the back of her hand down the
Titanide's chest. "Are these breasts ready for this great responsibility, my child?"

"They are, Captain."

"You've chosen well in the foreparents, Valiha. Your hindmother would have been proud." She turned and picked up the
egg from its glass pedestal. It grew very quiet as the Wizard
held the sphere up to the light, then brought it to her lips. She
kissed it, opened her mouth, and carefully put it in. When she
took it out, it was already changing color, to become as clear
as glass in a few seconds. Now Valiha was the only one moving, and what she did was to set her hind legs apart, lift her
tail, and lean her torso forward. Her pink hair fell over her
face, and she waited. Chris had a momentary return of memory:
being present while two Titanides engaged in anterior intercourse—something they did often and with great relish during
Carnival. This was the female position, ready to be mounted

by the Titanide taking the male role. The Wizard walked around
behind Valiha, who quivered in anticipation.

Chris looked away, wincing. Her arm had gone in past the
elbow. When it came out, the egg was no longer in her hand.

"Queasy?" The Wizard had a towel, which she used to dry
her arm and then tossed to a waiting aide. "Ranchers do that
sort of thing all the time."

"Yes, but these are . . . well, they're people. It just struck
me as undignified. Maybe I shouldn't say that."

Cirocco shrugged. "Say what you please. This is what they
know. They think our marriage customs are pretty dull, and
maybe they've got a point." She narrowed her eyes at him.
"Say, are you and Valiha shooting marbles?"

"I don't know what you mean." As he said it, he had the
uncomfortable feeling that maybe he did know what she meant.

"Never mind. She seems to be a friend anyway."

"She seems to be. I don't really remember." He looked over
her shoulder, where he could just see the three Titanides crest-
ing the lip of the crater as they raced away to consummate the
ensemble.

"Must be tough. I can see why you came here. Well, you
ought to be there at the celebration anyway. If she'd been less
excited, she'd have given you a ride." She sang to one of the
Titanides, who held out his hand in a familiar way.

"This is Harp of the Cantata Chord. He doesn't speak any
English, but he'll take you to the party and bring you back in
a few revs. Sober, I hope. Meet me in the tent over there. We
have some things to talk about."

13.

Hospitality

It was cool and dim inside the Wizard's Carnival tent. Its top was heavy and opaque while the sides were of white silk, slitted to admit the breeze. Overhead, a cloth panel moved slowly back and forth, fanning the hanging veils and scarves festooning the ridgepole. Gaby, Robin, Psaltery, and Chris sat on huge pillows, waiting for the Wizard.

The Titanides liked to make the Wizard's quarters sumptuous at Carnival time. Layer upon layer of hand-loomed carpets had been spread on the ground, dominated by one featuring the great six-spoked wheel. Two walls were heaped with pillows. A third showcased the Snow Throne. It was made of twenty-kilo transparent viny-leaf bags of Highland Mind Powder, the finest cocaine in the universe and Gaea's chief export. The Titanides built the throne fresh each Carnival, stacking the crystalline containers like sandbaggers on a levee.

There were two low tables heaped with the finest Titanide cuisine, steaming hot or sitting in sweating silver bowls of shaved ice. Titanides came and went steadily, removing things that had cooled, replacing them with fresh delicacies.

"You should try some of that stuff," Gaby suggested. She saw Chris jerk his head up and smiled. Hyperion did that to newcomers. The light never changed, and people stayed awake forty or fifty hours without knowing it. She wondered how much sleep the poor child had managed since the beginning of Carnival. She remembered her own early days in Gaea, when she and Cirocco had marched until they literally dropped. It had been a long time ago. She remembered feeling very old. Now she wondered if she had ever been that young.

She had been, once, on the banks of the Mississippi River near New Orleans. There had been an old house with a dusty attic where she would hide every night, trying to escape the sound of her mother's screams. There was a dormer window she could raise to let in the air. With the window open the tugboat whistles almost drowned out the sounds from below, and she could see the stars.

Later, with her mother dead and her father in prison, her aunt and uncle took her to California. In the Rockies she first saw the Milky Way. Astronomy became her obsession. She read every book she could find, hitchhiked to Mount Wilson, learned mathematics in spite of the California school system.

She did not let herself care about people. When her aunt left, she took her four children but not Gaby. Her uncle didn't want her, so she went with the social services women without a backward glance. By the time she was fourteen she found it easy to go to bed with a boy because he had a telescope. When he sold it, she never saw him again. Sex bored her.

She grew into a quiet, beautiful young woman. The beauty was a nuisance, like smog and poverty. There were ways to deal with all three things. She discovered a certain scowl that would keep boys from bothering her. There was no smog in the mountains, so she learned to hike with a telescope on her back. Cal Tech would accept a penniless student, even a female one, if she was the very best there was. So would the Sorbonne, Mount Palomar, Zelenchukskaya, and Copernicus.

Gaby did not like traveling. Nevertheless, she went to the Moon because the seeing was good. When she saw the plans for the telescopes to be taken to Saturn, she knew she had to be the one to use them. But at Saturn was Gaea, and disaster. For six months the crew of *Ringmaster* alternated between sleep and total sensory deprivation in the black belly of Oceanus, Gaea's upstart Godling. To Gaby, it was twenty years. She lived every second of it. It was plenty of time to examine a life and find it wanting. There was time to realize she had not a single friend, that there was no one she loved and no one to love her. And that it mattered.

That was seventy-five years ago. Since then she had not seen one star and had never felt the lack. Who needs them when you have friends?

"What was that?" Robin asked.

"Sorry. Just bouncing over the chuckholes of my mind. Us old folks do that."

Robin gave her an exasperated look, and Gaby grinned. She liked Robin. Seldom had she met anyone with so much stubborn pride and so many sharp edges. She was more alien than a Titanide, knowing little of what everyone called "human" culture, aware of her ignorance, and mixing blind chauvinism with an eagerness to learn more about it. It was a touchy business, talking to Robin. She would make a dubious companion until one had earned her trust.

Gaby liked Chris, too, but where her urge was to protect Robin from herself, she wanted to protect Chris from the crazy outside world. It couldn't make much sense to him, and yet he struggled gamely on, his world view quite warped from a lifetime of domination by a series of malevolent spirits who spoke with his voice, saw with his eyes, and sometimes lashed out with his hands. He could no longer afford emotional involvement, for one of his alter egos would betray it soon enough. Who would trust him after he had once revealed the large or small confidences of love?

Chris caught Gaby looking at him and smiled uncertainly. His straight brown hair tended to fall over his left eye, causing him to toss his head. He was a tall man, a meter eighty-five or ninety, of medium build, with an angular face that might have looked cruel but for the evidence of pain around his eyes. The first impression of hardness was given by his slightly flattened nose and heavy brow.

His body, too, might have looked powerful, yet he seemed so lugubrious, sitting there in his scanty shorts and pale, pale skin, that it was impossible to see him as menacing. His arms and legs were strong, and he had good shoulders, but there was too much fat around the waist. He was not too hairy, which was to Gaby's liking.

All in all, Gaby could see why Valiha found him attractive. She wondered if Chris knew yet that she did.

Cirocco swept in, followed by her matched pair of Titanides. She glanced around, mopping her face with a wet towel, and headed for a corner of the tent.

"Where's Valiha?" she asked. "And wasn't there supposed to be a Titanide for Robin?" She slipped out of her serape and stepped behind a shoulder-high cloth partition. Water began to spray from a nozzle suspended above her. She turned her face into it and shook her head. "If you'll just pardon me for a moment, folks. It's so damn hot out there."

"Valiha is still with her group," Chris volunteered. "You didn't tell me I should bring her with me."

"You're getting started too fast here, Rocky," Gaby protested. "Why don't you begin at the beginning?"

"Sorry," she said. "You're right. Robin, I haven't met you yet. Chris, I met you, but you don't recall it. The thing is, Gaea told Gaby that you two were on your way down here—"

"On our way down?" Robin squeaked. "She *dropped* me."

"I know, I know," Cirocco said soothingly. "Believe me, I detest that. I've protested it every way I can, but it hasn't done any good. Don't forget, I work for her, not the other way around." She looked at Gaby, expressionless, held her gaze for a moment, then resumed her soaping.

"Anyway, we knew you were on your way, and we knew you'd probably both make it. Oddly enough, most of the pilgrims do. About the only way to die in the Big Drop is to panic. Some people—"

"You could drown," Robin put in, darkly.

"What can I say?" Cirocco asked. "Obviously it's dangerous, and it's a disgusting thing to do. Do I need to apologize any more for something I have no part of?" She looked at Robin, who said nothing but finally shook her head.

"As I was saying, some people fight the angels who are trying to help them, and the angels can do only so much. So her purpose—as she has expressed it to me, understand, don't think I'm defending this—is to teach you to respond safely in a crisis. If you panic, you'll never be a hero. Or so her thinking goes."

Chris had been looking increasingly puzzled.

"If all this is supposed to mean something to me, I'm afraid I missed the important part."

"The Big Drop," Gaby explained. "It's probably just as well you don't recall. Gaea drops pilgrims out of a false elevator after her interview. They fall all the way to the rim."

"You still don't remember any of it?" Cirocco asked. The flow of water stopped, and one of the Titanides handed her a towel.

"Nothing. From the time I left her until not long ago, it's blank."

"That would be understandable, even without your condition," Cirocco said. "But I've talked to one of the angels." She glanced at Robin. "It was old Fat Fred."

Gaby laughed. "Is *he* still around?" She saw Robin's glare and tried to get rid of the smile on her face, with no success.

"He's still around, still chasing human tail. He told me about meeting two wildcats. One eventually cooperated, and he eased her down in Ophion. Another was just plain crazy. He couldn't approach him at all, but he followed him in, thinking that when the ground got close, the man would come to his senses. Imagine his surprise when the guy hit dead center on the back of a blimp."

"Who was it?" Gaby asked. "The blimp, I mean."

"Fred said it was Dreadnaught."

Gaby looked surprised. "That must have been just after I had him and two others help me unclog Aglaia."

"No doubt." Cirocco paused in her toweling to look intently at Chris, who quickly looked away. She stepped out of the shower and into a white robe held by one of the Titanides. She wrapped it around herself and sat cross-legged on the floor in front of the three humans and the Titanide. Her servant knelt behind her and began brushing her wet hair.

"I'm wondering about luck," she said. "Gaea told me about your condition, of course, and mentioned luck. Frankly, I don't want to believe that anyone could be that lucky. It goes counter to everything I've learned. Of course, most of that is seventy years out of date."

"It's regarded as pretty well-proven," Chris said. "From what I've heard, most people think none of the psi powers will ever amount to much. They've got equations that describe what's happening, but I don't pretend to understand them. Free-will particle theory, reality strata . . . I read an article about it."

"We don't get many newspapers out here." Cirocco frowned at her hands. "I don't like it. Never did."

"Einstein didn't like quantum mechanics," Gaby pointed out.

"You're right," Cirocco sighed. "But I'm always surprised at how things turn out. In my day they were sure they'd have the genetic code cracked in a few more years. We were going to wipe out all physical diseases and genetic conditions. And nobody thought we'd be solving psychological problems any time soon. So just the opposite happened. A couple things were a hell of a lot harder to do than anybody imagined, and there were breakthroughs in areas where nobody expected them. Who can figure it? Anyway, we were talking about luck."

"I don't know what it is," Chris put in. "But I do seem to get luckier at times."

"I don't like to think of what it implies if it's true that luck guided you to a landing on Dreadnaught's back," Cirocco said. "It depends on how far you take your reasoning, but you might say a Titan tree came loose and jammed in the Aglaian pump so Gaby would call Dreadnaught into that area for you to land on his back. And I refuse to believe the universe is that deterministic!"

Gaby snorted. "So do I, but I believe in luck. Come on, Rocky. Why should you object to a puppet master pulling a few of your strings? Don't you know what it feels like by now?"

Cirocco shot Gaby a deadly glare, but for a moment her eyes had looked haunted.

"Okay," Gaby soothed, holding out her hands. "I'm sorry. We won't get off on that, all right?"

Cirocco relaxed quickly enough and nodded almost imperceptibly. She brooded for a moment, then looked up.

"I'm forgetting my manners," she said. "Hornpipe, ask these folks what they'd like to drink, and bring a couple of those trays over here where we can all reach them."

Gaby welcomed the pause. The last thing she wanted was to get into a fight with Cirocco. She stood and helped Hornpipe with the food, introduced Psaltery to Robin and Chris, and Cirocco to Robin. There were polite comments about the food and drink, small jokes and pleasantries exchanged. She had them all laughing at one point with a tale of her first encounter with a Titanide soup the main ingredient of which was live worms marinated in brine. In fifteen minutes everyone seemed more relaxed with a little something alcoholic inside.

"As I was saying," Cirocco resumed at last, "we heard you would be coming down here. I don't know what your plans are, but I figure if you were going to leave, you would have done so by now. How about it? Chris?"

"I don't know. I really haven't had any time to make plans. It seems like just a few hours ago that Gaea told me what I had to do."

"And confused you completely, I imagine."

He smiled. "That's a fair description. I guess I'm planning to stay, but I don't know what I'm going to do while I'm here."

"That's the nature of the test," Cirocco said. "You'll never know until you're facing it. All you can do is go out seeking. That's why we call you a pilgrim. What about you, Robin?"

Robin looked down at her hands and said nothing for a while, then looked steadily at Cirocco.

"I don't know if I should tell you what my plans are. I don't know if I can trust you."

"That's direct anyway," Cirocco said, half smiling.

"She has this grudge to settle with Gaea," Gaby explained. "She didn't trust me for a while either. Maybe she still doesn't."

"I'm going to kill her," Robin said with quiet deadliness. "She tried to kill me, and I swore I would get her. You can't stop me."

Cirocco laughed. "Stop you? I don't think I'm needed for that. Did you bring a couple of nuclear weapons with you?" She glanced at the .45 on Robin's hip. "Is that thing loaded?"

"What good is an unloaded gun?" Robin asked, honestly baffled by the question.

"You've got a point. Anyway, you can set your mind at ease about one thing. I'm not Gaea's bodyguard. She has eyes and ears enough for that, without needing me. I wouldn't even tell her you're after her. It's none of my concern."

Robin considered it. "All right. I plan to stay. Pretty soon I'll start out climbing a spoke, and when I get there, I'll kill her."

Cirocco looked at Gaby, and her eyes seemed to say, *where did you get her?* Gaby shrugged and smiled.

"Well . . . ah . . . okay. I don't guess there's much I can add to that."

"Why don't you go on, Rocky? She still might be interested."

"I don't think so," Robin said, standing. "I don't know what you're going to propose, but if it has anything to do with going out and being 'heroic'—" she looked as if she wanted to spit, but couldn't find a place not covered with rug— "you can count me out. I won't get involved in that kind of game. I have a score to settle, and I mean to take care of it and then get out of here, if I'm still alive."

"So you're going to climb the spoke."

"That's right."

Cirocco turned to Gaby again, and Gaby understood the

look. This was your idea, she was saying. You take it from here if you want her along.

"Listen, Robin," Gaby said. "Your object is to get back to the hub, of course, but since you already had your one free ride, the elevator won't work for you. There's about one chance in thirty of your making it to the top alive. Less, really, since you'll be doing it alone. Cirocco and I did it, but we were damn lucky."

"I know all that," Robin began, and Gaby hurried on.

"What I'm saying is, what we're proposing just might get you to the top safer and faster. I'm not asking you to play Gaea's game: I'm dead set against that, myself. I think it's . . . well, never mind what I think. But consider this. She's not asking you to hurt anyone or do anything dishonorable. She suggested that you start out to travel around the rim. That's what we propose to do."

"There are some things I have to attend to," Cirocco said.

"Right. We happen to be going in the same direction, and Gaea told us you and Chris were on your way here. Rocky and I have done this before, with other pilgrims, together and separately. We try to keep them out of trouble until they learn their way around.

"What I'm saying is, you could go with us. You'd learn some things that might help you if you're still determined to climb it. I'm not saying it won't be dangerous. Get out of Hyperion, and everything in Gaea can be dangerous. Hell, even a lot of Hyperion can kill you. But here's the beauty of it. It might happen that along the way you'll do something that Gaea would see as heroic. It wouldn't be anything you'd be ashamed of, I can promise you that. I'll give Gaea that much—she knows how to pick her heroes. This is only if the opportunity arises, you understand. You wouldn't have to think of it as playing her game, or seeking anything in particular. Just go with us. And when you get back, you'll get a free ride to the top. What you do with it is your own business." She sat back. She liked Robin, but damn if she could do anymore than that to protect her. In a way, Gaby felt like Fat Fred, the angel; there were people who would give an arm or a leg for the help she and Rocky were offering, and here she was trying to sell this stiff-necked little pup on the idea.

Robin sat down. She had the grace to look slightly abashed.

"I'm sorry," she said. "I'm grateful for the offer, and I'll gladly go with you. What you say makes sense." Gaby wondered if Robin had seen the same picture she had imagined: two or three hundred kilometers up the vertical spoke interior, Robin is suddenly seized with paralysis. No one who had taken the Big Drop was anxious to repeat it.

"Chris?"

"Me? Sure. I'd be a fool to turn you down."

"That's what I like," Cirocco said. "A realistic appraisal." She stood, removed her robe, and donned her faded serape. "Make yourselves at home. Food and drink are on the house. Carnival is over in about eighty revs, so enjoy yourselves. I'll meet you all at the Enchanted Cat in one hundred revs."

14.

Gingeroso

"Hey, lover, if you don't come out of there soon, I'm coming in with you."

Chris was looking down at the water running off his body, splashing on his naked feet. There was a bar of soap in his hand. He looked up and got a faceful of spray.

Unusual to blank twice in a row.

"Leave me some water, will you?" It was a female voice, the voice of a stranger. Now where had he been, what was the last clear memory . . . ? He turned off the water and stepped from the tiny shower stall. The walls and floor were bare wood planks. Through an open window he could see the ground thirty meters below. He was in a tree, probably in the Titantown Hotel. He peered cautiously around the doorjamb. The small connecting room held some lightweight furniture and a substantial bed, and on the bed was a nude woman, also substantial. She sprawled on her back in a pose that would have looked enticing had she not been so bonelessly relaxed. Was this before or after? he asked himself, but his body knew the answer. It was after.

"Ah, finally," she said, lifting her head as he came out. "I don't know how much more of this heat I can take." She rose and stood before the bedroom window, lifted her mass of black hair from her shoulders, and fastened it with a pin. Chris thought she was lovely and was sorry he had missed having her. Most things he missed were just as well forgotten, but she looked like the exception. She had long legs and a perfect complexion. Her breasts were perhaps a trifle too large, but he would have liked the chance to prove that experimentally.

She glanced at him. "Oh, no, you don't. Not again, not now, brother. Haven't you had enough?" She hurried into the shower.

He couldn't find his shorts. Poking around, he saw a few unusual implements and many jars of creams and oils. He frowned, looked around some more, and there it was, tacked to the wall. It was yellowing and torn, but it was a prostitution license, issued five years before in Jefferson County, Texas.

"What's wrong now?" she asked when she came out, drying her neck and shoulders. "You sure are changeable, you know?"

"Yeah, I do know. What do I owe you?"

"We talked about that, remember?"

"No, I don't because I might as well tell you I can't remember anything for the last . . . I don't know how long. From before I met you. And that's just how it is, and I don't want to talk about it, but I can't even remember your name, I can't find my clothes, and would you just tell me how goddamn much I owe you so I can get out of here and not bother you anymore?"

She sat beside him on the bed, not touching him, then reached out and took his hand.

"Like that, huh?" she said, quietly. "You told me about that, but you said a lot of things, and I didn't know what to believe."

"That part was true. Everything else was probably lies. If I told you I had a lot of money somewhere, that was a lie. I had some when I arrived, but after my last blackout all I had left was a pair of shorts."

She knotted the towel around her waist, went to a wooden bureau, and took something from the top. "You threw the shorts away just after you picked me up," she said. "You were going back to nature." She smiled, not teasingly, and tossed something to him.

It was a small gold coin. Stamped into one side were the words "BLANK CHECK" and some Titanide symbols. On the other side was a signature: "C. Jones." Something was coming back to him, and he closed his eyes to squeeze it into recall.

"You said that entitled you to anything in Titantown. 'Just as good as money.' I'd never seen one, but you were on a spending spree, and everyone seemed to honor it."

"I cheated you," he said, knowing it was true. "Only Titanides have to honor it. I was supposed to use it to . . . use it to . . . to outfit myself for a trip I'm supposed to make." He stood up, suddenly panicked. "I bought a lot of things, I remember that now. I was supposed to . . . I mean, where are—"

"Easy, easy. That's all taken care of. I had them take it over to La Gata, like you said to. It's safe."

He sat down slowly. "La Gata. . . ."

"That's where you're supposed to meet your friends," she prompted. She glanced at a gyroscopic Gaean clock on the bureau. "In about fifteen minutes."

"That's right! I have to . . ." He started for the door, then stopped with the feeling he was forgetting something.

"Do you have a towel I could borrow?"

Wordlessly she handed him the one she was wearing.

"I . . . uh, I'm sorry that I don't have anything to give you. I don't know what sort of line I gave you, but I guess I'm surprised you didn't ask for—"

"Money in front? I wasn't born yesterday. I knew what I was getting into." She went to the window and put her hands on the sill, looking down at the town below. "I've been here for quite a while. The Earth was never too good to me. I like the people here. At least, I think of them as people. I guess I'm starting to go native." She looked at him as though she expected him to laugh. When he didn't, one corner of her mouth turned up. "Hell, I own a third interest in a Titanide myself. You stay here long enough, you start shooting marbles."

She went to him and kissed him on the cheek. "I can't believe we did all that and you can't remember any of it. Sort of hurts my professional pride." For a moment he thought she was going to cry and could not imagine what was wrong.

"There's a girl going with you on your trip," she said.

"Robin?"

"That's the one. You tell her I said 'hi,' and to be careful. And good luck. Wish her good luck for me. Will you do that?"

"If you'll tell me your name again."

"Trini. Tell her to watch out for the Plauget woman. She's dangerous. When she gets back, she's always welcome here."

"I'll tell her."

15.

The Enchanted Cat

Titantown was sheltered by a massive tree that had formed when many smaller trees united into one colony organism. Though Titanides never indulged in town planning, their own preferences imposed a certain structure on the settlement. They liked to live within 500 meters of the light, so their dwellings tended to form a ring under the tree's outer periphery. Some of the homes were set sensibly on the ground. Others perched on the gigantic limbs that spread horizontally and were supported by subsidiary trunks themselves as large as sequoias.

Scattered through the residential ring but predominately inward were the workshops, forges, and refineries. Farther out, toward the sunlight and sometimes in the open air, were bazaars, shops, and markets. Throughout the city were public buildings and facilities: the fire brigades, libraries, storehouses, and cisterns. The public water supply was from wells and collected rainfall, but the well water was milky and bitter.

Robin had recently spent a lot of time in the outer ring, using the medallion Cirocco had given her to purchase supplies for the trip. She had found the Titanide artisans polite and helpful. They invariably steered her to the highest-quality merchandise when something less elaborate would have done as well. Thus, she now owned a copper canteen with elaborate filigree chasings which would have made it seem right at home on the Czar's banquet table. The hilt of her knife was shaped to fit her hand. It sported a ruby like a great glass eye. They had tailored her sleeping bag from material so lushly embroidered that she hated to let it touch the ground.

Hornpipe, the Titanide she had met in Cirocco's tent, had been her guide, singing translations to merchants who did not speak English.

"Don't worry about it," he had said. "You'll notice no one else is paying money either. We don't use it."

"What's your system, then?"

"Gaby calls it noncoercive communism. She says it wouldn't work with humans. They're too greedy and self-centered. Pardon me, but that's what she says."

"That's okay. She's probably right."

"I wouldn't know. It's true we don't have the problems associated with dominance that humans seem to have. We don't have leaders, and we don't fight one another. Our economy works through chords and earned entitlements. Everyone works, both at a trade and on community projects. One accumulates standing—or maybe you would call it wealth or credit—by accomplishment, and by aging, or by need. No one lacks the necessities; most have at least some luxuries."

"I wouldn't call it wealth," Robin pointed out. "We don't use money, either, in the Coven."

"Oh? What is your system, then?"

Robin thought it over as dispassionately as she could, recalling the assigned community work backed up by a schedule of punishments, up to and including death.

"Call it coercive communism. With a lot of barter on the side."

La Gata Encantada was near the trunk of the great tree. Robin had been there once, but the darkness was perpetual in Titantown, and there were no road maps. There were no roads. One needed a lantern and a lot of luck to find anything.

Robin thought of the core of the city as the entertainment district. The description would serve, though as everywhere else in Titantown there were shops and even homes scattered among the dance halls, theaters, and pubs. There was an area between the outer ring and the trunk which held few structures. It was the gloomiest part of Titantown, given over to small garden plots that thrived in the warm, damp darkness. Most of the town was lit with big paper lamps; here there were few of them.

It was the closest thing she had seen to what she thought of as a park. Her mother had warned her about parks. Men hid in them to spring out and rape women. Of course, few humans came this far into Titantown, but there was nothing to prevent them from coming. She had thought she was over her worries about rape, but she couldn't help it. There were places where the only useful light was that cast by her own lantern.

There was a hissing sound that made her jump. She stopped to discover the cause and found lines of low, fleshy plants emitting a fine spray. No one reared in the Coven, with its chugging lines of sprinklers crossing the curved agricultural floor, could have failed to see the purpose of the mist. She smiled and inhaled deeply. The smell of damp earth took her back to her childhood, to simpler days spent playing in fields of ripe strawberries.

The pub was a low wooden building with the customary wide door. A sign hung outside: two circles, the top one smaller and with two points on top, slanted eyes, and a toothy grin.

Why a cat? she wondered. And why Spanish? If Titanides learned a human tongue, it was invariably English, but there it was, painted above the doorway, "La Gata Encantada," without even the customary Titanide runes. They were a strange race, Robin decided. They were so like humans in so many ways. Most of their skills were the same as human skills. The things they made were, for the most part, things humans made, too. Their arts were similar to human arts, with the exception of their transcendant music. Their odd system of reproduction was the only thing distinctly their own.

But not quite, she realized, as she walked into La Gata, past the water trough that was a fixture in every Titanide public building. The floor was sand with a layer of straw. All in all, the Titanides dealt with the problem of combining urbanization and incontinence better than, for instance, New York City in the horse-and-buggy era. The city swarmed with small armadillolike creatures whose sole food was the ubiquitous piles of orange balls. In private homes the problem was dealt with as it occurred, with shovels and waste bins. But where many Titanides gathered it was impossible. They threw fastidiousness to the winds and simply did not worry about it. Hence the water troughs, to wash one's feet before going home.

Other than that, La Gata Encantada looked very like a human tavern, but with more space between the tables. There was even a long wooden bar complete with brass rail. The place was full of Titanides who towered over her, but she had ceased to worry about crushed toes. She would have fared worse in a crowd of humans.

"Hey, human girl!" She looked up to see the bartender waving at her. He tossed her a pillow. "Your friends are in back. You want a root beer?"

"Yes, please. Thank you." She knew from her first visit that root beer was a dark, foamy alcoholic brew made from roots. It tasted like the beer she was used to, but stouter. She liked it.

The group had gathered at a big round table in a far corner: Cirocco, Gaby, Chris, Psaltery, Valiha, Hornpipe, and a fourth Titanide she didn't know. Robin's drink arrived before she did, in a monster five-liter mug. She sat on her pillow, putting the table at the level of her breasts.

"Are there cats in Gaea?" she asked.

Gaby looked at Cirocco, and they both shrugged.

"I never saw one," Gaby said. "This place is named after a march. Titanides are march-happy. They think John Philip Sousa is the greatest composer who ever lived."

"Not quite accurate," Psaltery objected. "He is neck and neck with Johann Sebastian Bach." He took a drink, then saw Robin and Chris were looking at him. He went on, by way of clarification.

"Without being condescending, both are basic and primitive. Bach with his geometry of repeated sound shapes, his calculus of inspired monotony; Sousa with his innocent flash and bravura. They approach music as one would lay the bricks of a ziggurat: Sousa in brass and Bach in wood. All humans do that to some extent. Your written music even looks like brick walls."

"We had never thought of that," Valiha contributed. "Celebrating a song and then preserving it to be performed exactly the same the next time was a new idea. The music of Bach and Sousa is very pretty, with no needless complications, when written on paper. Their music is hyperhuman."

Cirocco looked owlishly back and forth between the two Titanides, then shifted her gaze to Robin and Chris. She had trouble finding them.

"And now you know as much as you did before," she said. "Never did like Sousa, myself. Bach I can take or leave." She blinked, looking from one to the other as if waiting for them to dispute her. When they didn't, she took a long drink from her glass of beer. A lot of it spilled over her chin.

Gaby put a hand on her shoulder. "They're going to cut you off at the bar pretty soon, Captain," she said lightly.

"Who says I'm drunk?" Cirocco roared. A brown-gold sudsy wave washed over the table as her glass toppled. The

room was quiet for a moment, then noisy again as all the Titanides took care not to notice the incident. Someone appeared with a towel to mop up the beer, and another glass was set in front of her.

"No one said that, Rocky," Gaby said quietly.

Cirocco seemed to have forgotten it.

"Robin, you haven't met Hautbois, I believe. Hautbois (Sharped Mixolydian Trio) Bolero, meet Robin the Nine-fingered, of the Coven. Robin, this is Hautbois. She comes from a good chord and will keep you warm when the cold winds blow."

The Titanide rose and executed a deep bow with her front legs.

"May the holy flow unite us," Robin mumbled, bowing from the waist, while studying what she assumed was meant to be her companion on the trip. Hautbois had a plush carpet of hair seven or eight centimeters deep. Only the palms of her hands, small areas around her nipples, and parts of her face revealed bare skin, which was a rich olive green. Her pelt was also olive, but marbled with whorls of brown like fingerprint patterns. Her head and tail hair was white as snow. She looked like a huge, fluffy stuffed animal with big brown button eyes.

"You met Hornpipe, didn't you?" Cirocco went on. "Ol' Horny here is the . . . well, call it the grandson of the first goddamn Titanide we ever met. His hindmother was the first Hornpipe's Mix-oeey. . . ." She paused, having trouble with the word. "Mix-oh-eye-*oh*-nee-an. Mixoionian. She was the first Hornpipe's Mixoionian get. Then she bred with her forefather. That doesn't sound so hot from the human standpoint, but I assure you it's great eugenics with Titanides. Hornpipe's a Lydian Duet." She belched and looked solemn. "As are we all."

"What do you mean?" Chris asked.

"All humans are Lydian Duets," Cirocco said. She produced a pen and began drawing on the table.

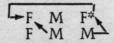

"Lookee here," she said. "This is a Lydian Duet. Top line is female, bottom line male. The star is the semi-fertilized egg.

The top arrow shows where the egg goes, and the bottom arrows show who fucks who, primary and secondary. The Lydian Duet: foremother and hindmother are female; forefather and hindfather are male. Just like humans. Only difference is Titanides have to do it twice." She leered at Chris. "Double the pleasure, huh?"

"Rocky, hadn't we better—"

"It's the *only* mode where Titanides get together the same way humans do," Cirocco said, hitting the table with her fist. "Out of twenty-nine possibilities this is the only one. There's duets that are all female, three of 'em. Aeolian Duets. Lydian Duets all have a male, but often as not he's the hindmother." She frowned and counted on her fingers. "More often than not. Four out of seven. In the Hypolydian the female fertilizes herself frontally, and in the Locrilydian she does it to herself anterally. An-*teer*-e-or-ly."

"Rocky. . . ."

"Does she really have intercourse with herself?" Chris asked. Gaby gave him a disgusted look, but it hardly mattered since Cirocco did not seem to have heard him. She was nodding over the table, peering at the diagram she had drawn.

"Not as you are thinking," Hautbois volunteered. "That's physically impossible. It's done manually. Semen is collected and then implanted. Semen from a rear penis can fertilize a front vagina, but only on the same individual, not between—"

"Folks, folks, give me a break, please. How about it?" Gaby looked from one to the other, finally settling on Cirocco. She grimaced and stood up. "Ladies and gentlemen and Titanides, I had hoped to get this trip under way with a little more organization. I think Rocky had some things she wanted to say, but what the hell. That can wait."

"C'n wait," Cirocco muttered.

"Right. Anyway, the first part of the trip is dead easy. We'll just float down the river without a care in the world. About all there really is to do is load everything onto the boats and shove off. So what do you say we get up and get going?"

"Get going!" Cirocco echoed. "A toast! To the road! May it lead to adventure and carry us safely back home." She stood and raised her glass. Robin had to use both hands to lift her own, which she shoved out into the middle with the others in a great clinking and sloshing of beer. She drank deeply and heard a crash. The Wizard had fallen off her stool.

She had not, however, passed out. Robin could not decide if that was to be desired or not.

"Hold on a minute," she said, patting the air with her hands. "You know how it is with beer. Gotta powder my nose. Be right back, 'kay?" She lurched off toward the front of the room.

There was a scream. While Robin was still wondering who it had been, Gaby was up and over the table, somehow managing to shoulder her way through the press of Titanides.

"He's here, he's here! It's him!"

She now recognized the voice as Cirocco's and became curious as to what could have frightened her so badly. Robin was having her doubts about the Wizard's character, but she had not judged her for a coward.

A crowd had formed at one end of the bar, near the door. There was no hope of someone her size seeing over the high horsey hindquarters, so she leaped onto the bar itself and was able to walk almost to the center of the disturbance.

She saw Cirocco being comforted by a Titanide Robin did not know. Gaby stood a little distance away. She held a knife in one hand while with the other she made motions to the man cowering on the floor in front of her. Her teeth showed in the flickering lamplight, bright and feral.

"Get up, get up," she hissed. "You're just like those other turds on the floor, you abomination. It's time someone cleaned you up, and I'm the one to do it."

"I didn't do anything," the man moaned. "I swear, just ask Rocky. I wouldn't do anything, I've been real good. You know me, Gaby."

"I know you too well, Gene. I've had two chances to kill you, and I was a fool to pass up either of them. Get up and face it; at least you can do that. Get up, or I'll slaughter you like the pig you are."

"No, no, you'll *hurt* me." He doubled over, hands in his crotch, and began to sob. He would have been a pathetic sight even standing erect. His face and arms—in fact, all his visible skin—were crisscrossed with old scar tissue. His feet were bare and filthy, and his clothes were tatters. There was a black, piratical patch over his left eye, and most of one ear was missing.

"Get *up*!" Gaby ordered.

Robin was surprised to hear Cirocco speak, in a voice that sounded almost sober.

"He's right, Gaby," she said quietly. "He didn't do anything. Hell, he tried to run as soon as he saw me. It was just such a surprise, seeing him again."

Gaby stood a little straighter. Her eyes lost some of their fire.

"Are you saying you don't want me to kill him?" she asked tonelessly.

"Chri'sake, Gaby," Cirocco mumbled. She seemed calm now, but listless. "You can't just slice him up like a side o' beef."

"Yeah. I know. I've heard that before." She went down on one knee beside him, used the flat of her knife blade to turn his head.

"What are you doing here, Gene? What are you up to?"

He simpered and stuttered meaninglessly for a while. "Just getting a drink, is all. A man's throat gets dry, what with the heat wave."

"Your friends aren't here. There must be a reason for you to come to Titantown. You wouldn't take a chance on meeting *me*, for one thing, unless you had a reason to risk it."

"That's right, that's right, Gaby, I'm scared of you, all right. Yes, sir, old Gene knows better than to get in your way." He thought about that for a moment and didn't appear to like the implications, so he promptly changed course. "I forgot, is all. Hell, Gaby, I didn't know you'd be here, that's all."

Robin could see he was a man so habituated to lying that he himself might not know the truth. It was also obvious that he was truly terrified of Gaby. He must have been twice her size, yet he never thought of fighting.

Gaby stood and gestured with her knife.

"Get up. Gene? Don't make me tell you again."

"You won't hurt me?"

"If I ever see you again, I will hurt you bad. Do we understand each other? I'm saying I won't kill you. But if I ever see you again, anywhere, *ever*, I will hurt you bad. From now on it's your business to be sure our paths never cross."

"I will, I will. I promise."

"When we meet again, Gene," she said, and gestured with her knife, "I'll cut out the other one."

The gesture had not been toward his one good eye, but considerably lower.

16.

The Circumnavigators' Club

Even with Hornpipe's strong arm supporting her Cirocco fell down twice while the Titanides were being loaded. She kept declaring she would make it on her own steam.

The gear Chris had bought was waiting, as promised, in a shed behind La Gata, along with the possessions of the others. The Titanides had saddlebags which strapped around their backs and cinched underneath. Valiha twisted around and fastened hers, ending with a capacious leather and canvas bag on each side of her equine lower half. The arrangement left room for Chris to ride. He jumped aboard and opened the bags, which already contained the things Valiha was bringing. She handed him his baggage, item by item, telling him to balance the contents. When he was done, each bag was less than half full. She said this was as it should be because when they left the river and took to the road, the extra space would be filled with provisions that were already on the boats.

While he was packing, Chris watched Gaby and Hornpipe trying to get Cirocco calmed down and aboard the Titanide. It was rather pathetic and more than a little worrisome. He noticed that Robin, kneeling atop Hautbois a few meters away, was also watching the spectacle. It was nearly pitch-black, the only light coming from the oil lamps the Titanides held, but he could see her frown.

"Having second thoughts about the trip?" he asked her.

She looked up in surprise. They had not spoken before—or at least not when he remembered it—and he wondered what she thought of him. He found her decidedly odd. He had learned that what he thought were paintings were in fact tattoos. Snakes with multicolored scales had wrapped their tails around her right big toe and her left little finger, and their bodies coiled up her leg and arm to slither beneath her clothes. He wondered what the heads looked like and if she sported any other art.

She turned back to her packing. "When I sign on, I stay

on," she said. Her hair was falling into her eyes; with a toss of her head, she revealed her other physical oddity. Most of the left side of her head was shaved to reveal a complicated pentagonal design centering on her left ear. It made her look as if her wig were slipping.

She glanced again at Cirocco, then looked at Chris with what might have been a friendly smile. The tattoos made it hard to tell.

"I know what you mean, though," she conceded. "They can call her a Wizard if they want to, but I know a drunk when I see one."

Chris and Valiha were the last of the eight to emerge from the darkness beneath the Titantown tree. He blinked in the light for a moment, then smiled. It felt good to be moving. It hardly mattered what he was moving toward.

The other three teams made a pretty picture as they crested the first hill and started down the sun-baked dirt road between fields of tall yellow grain. Gaby was in the lead, wearing her Robin Hood greens and grays, mounted on the chocolate brown Psaltery with his orange flame of hair. Behind them was Hornpipe, with Cirocco prone on his back. Only her legs were visible, protruding from the dull red serape. Hornpipe's hair seemed black when seen in dim light; now it sparkled like a nest of fine prisms, flying out behind him. Even Hautbois's brown and olive swirls looked grand in the sunlight, and her dandelion of white head hair was glorious. Robin rode with her back straight and her feet on the saddlebags, dressed in loose pants and a light knitted shirt.

He made himself comfortable on Valiha's broad back. Taking a deep breath, he thought he could taste that elusive quality of the air that often precedes a summer rainstorm. To the west he could see weather rolling in from Oceanus. There were clouds: fat, wet rolls of cotton. They were elongated toward the north and south. Sometimes they came in strings, like sausages, and the higher, thinner ones often appeared to be unrolling, laying a thin sheet of white as they moved. It had something to do with the Coriolis effect, whatever that was.

It was a great day to be going somewhere.

Chris had not believed he could sleep on the back of a Titanide, but it turned out that he could. He was awakened by Valiha.

Psaltery was walking on a long dock reaching into Ophion. Valiha followed, and soon her hooves clomped on wooden planks. Moored to the dock were four large canoes. They were wooden frameworks with a silvery material stretched over the ribs. It made them look like the aluminum craft which had been a standard on Terran lakes and streams for almost two centuries. Their bottoms were reinforced with planks. In the center of each was a mound of supplies covered with red canvas and secured with ropes.

They rode high in the water, but when Psaltery stepped into the stern of one, it sank noticeably. Chris watched in fascination as the Titanide nimbly moved about on the narrow deck, removing his saddlebags and stowing them in the bow. He had never thought of Titanides as a seafaring race, but Psaltery looked as if he knew his way around a boat.

"You'll have to get down now," Valiha said. Her head was turned around, something that always gave Chris a psychosomatic pain in the neck when he saw it. He tried to give her a hand with the straps but soon saw he was in her way. The heavy bags might have been pillowcases stuffed with feathers from the way she threw them around.

"The boats will hold two Titanides and some baggage, or all four humans," Gaby was saying. "Or we can keep the human-Titanide teams together, one per boat. Which way would you like to work it?"

Robin was standing on the edge of the dock and frowning down at the boats. She turned at the waist, still frowning, and shrugged. Then she jammed her hands into her pockets and scowled down at the water, mightily displeased about something.

"I don't know," Chris said. "I guess I'd prefer...." He noticed Valiha watching him. She turned away quickly. "I'll stick with Valiha, I guess."

"Makes no difference to me," Gaby said, "so long as at least one person in every boat knows something about canoeing. Do you?"

"I've done some. I'm no expert."

"Doesn't matter. Valiha can show you the ropes. Robin?"

"I know nothing about it. I'd like to bring up—"

"You go with Hautbois then. We can switch around later, get to know each other better. Chris, will you give me a hand with Rocky?"

"I'd like to make a suggestion," Robin said. "She's out cold. Why don't we leave her here? Half her baggage is liquor, I saw it myself. She's a drunk, and she's going to be a—"

She got no further because Gaby had pinned her to the dock before Chris quite knew what was going on. Gaby's hands were at Robin's neck, forcing her head back.

Slowly, trembling slightly, Gaby released the pressure and sat back. Robin coughed once but did not move.

"You must never speak of her that way," Gaby whispered. "You don't know what you are saying."

No one had moved. Chris shifted his feet and heard a decking plank creak loudly.

Gaby got to her feet. As she turned away her shoulders were slumped, and she looked old and tired. Robin stood, dusted herself off with icy dignity, and cleared her throat. She rested one hand on the butt of her automatic.

"Stop," she said. "Stop right there." Gaby did stop. She turned around, not looking as if the situation held any interest for her.

"I will not kill you," Robin said quietly. "What you did demands an accounting, but you are peckish and probably know no better. But hear me and know that you are warned. Your ignorance will not save you. If you touch me again, one of us will die."

Gaby glanced at the weapon on Robin's hip, nodded glumly, and turned away again.

Chris helped her load Cirocco into the front of one of the canoes. He was mystified by the whole situation but knew when to keep his mouth shut. He watched Gaby step into the boat and pull a blanket over the Wizard's limp body. She arranged the Wizard's head on a pillow, managing to make her sleep look almost peaceful until she stirred and snorted and kicked the blanket away. Gaby climbed out of the boat.

"You'd better get in the front," Valiha said as he joined her at the canoe which was to be theirs. He stepped in and sat down, found a paddle, and dipped it in the water experimentally. It suited him well. Like all things Titanides made, it was beautifully crafted, with the images of small animals etched into the polished wood. He felt the boat lurch as Valiha boarded.

"How do you people find the time to make everything so beautiful?" he asked her, gesturing with the paddle.

"If it's not worth making beautiful," Valiha said, "it's not worth making. We don't make so many things as humans do either. We make nothing to throw away. We make things one at a time and don't begin a second until we are through with the first. Titanides never invented the assembly line."

He turned around. "Is that really all there is to it? A different outlook?"

She grinned. "Not the whole story. Not sleeping has something to do with it. You humans waste a third of your lives unconscious. We don't sleep."

"That must be very strange." He had known they didn't sleep but had not really thought of what it implied.

"Not to me. But I do suspect that we experience time in a different way from you. Our time is not broken up. We measure it, of course, but as a continuous flow rather than a succession of days."

"Yeah . . . but what does that have to do with craftmanship?"

"We have more time. We don't sleep, but about a quarter of our time is spent resting. We sit and sing and work with our hands. It adds up."

Travelers on Ophion often remarked on the feeling of timelessness the river gave them. Ophion was both the source and the end of all things in Gaea, the circle of waters that tied all things together. As such, it felt like an old river because Gaea herself felt old.

Ophion was old, but it was a relative thing. As ancient as Gaea herself, Ophion was an infant beside the great rivers of Earth. It was also to be remembered that most humans saw the river only in Hyperion, where it spread out and took things easy. Elsewhere on its 4,000-kilometer circumference, Ophion was as frisky as the Colorado.

Chris had been set for a fast trip. It was just what one did in a canoe: put it on a fast stream and ride the white water.

"You might as well relax," came the voice from behind him. "You'll tire yourself out too soon and then go to sleep. Humans are extremely boring when they sleep. I know this part of the river well. There is nothing to watch out for between here and Aglaia. Here Ophion is forgiving."

He put his paddle on the floor of the canoe and turned around. Valiha sat placidly just aft of the tarp-covered pallet of supplies. The paddle in her hands was twice as large as his own. Valiha looked completely relaxed with all four legs folded under her, and Chris thought that odd because he had not expected a being so like a horse to enjoy sitting like that.

"You people amaze me," he said. "I thought I was hallucinating the first time I saw a Titanide climbing a tree. Now you turn out to be sailors, too."

"You people amaze *me*," Valiha countered. "How you balance is a mystery. When you run, you begin by falling forward, and then your legs try to catch up with the rest of you. You live constantly on the edge of disaster."

Chris laughed. "You're right, you know. I do, at least." He watched her paddling, and for a time there was no sound but the quiet gurgle made by her oar.

"I feel I ought to be helping you. Should we take turns rowing?"

"Sure. I'll row three-quarters of a rev, and you can row the other quarter."

"That's hardly equitable."

"I know what I'm doing. This isn't work."

"You're moving us pretty fast."

Valiha winked at him, then began to paddle in earnest. The canoe almost became airborne, skipping like a tossed stone. She kept it up for a few dozen strokes, then fell back into her relaxed rhythm.

"I could do that for a whole rev," she said. "You might as well face the fact that I'm a lot stronger than you, even at your best. And right now you aren't in condition. Get used to it gradually, okay?"

"I guess so. I still feel I ought to be doing something."

"I agree. Lean back, and let me do the donkeywork."

He did, but wished she had used another euphemism. It hit at the heart of something that had been bothering him.

"I've been feeling uncomfortable," he said. "What it boils down to is, we are—that is, we humans are using you Titanides like . . . well, like draft animals."

"We can carry a lot more than you can."

"All right, I know that. But I don't even have a pack. And . . . well, it somehow makes me feel I'm using you badly when—"

"Nervous about riding me, is that it?" She grinned at him

and rolled her eyes. "Next you'll be suggesting that you walk sometimes, to give me a rest, right?"

"Something like that."

"Chris, there's nothing more boring than taking a walk with a human."

"Not even watching one sleep?"

"You got me. That's more boring."

"You seem to find us tedious."

"Not at all, you are endlessly fascinating. One never knows what a human will do next, or from what motive. If we had universities, the best-attended classes would be in the Department of Human Studies. But I'm young and impatient, as the Wizard pointed out. If you wish, you may walk, and I will endeavor to slow down. I don't know how the others will like it."

"Forget it," Chris said. "I just don't want to be a burden. Literally."

"You aren't," she assured him. "When you ride me, my heart lifts and my feet fly like the wind." She was looking into his eyes with an odd expression on her face. He could not read it, but it made him want to change the subject.

"Why are you here, Valiha? Why are you in this boat, making this trip?"

"You mean just me or the other Titanides?" She went on without waiting for an answer. "Psaltery is here because he goes where Gaby goes. The same for Hornpipe. As for Hautbois, I presume it is because the Wizard often grants a child to those who circumnavigate the great river."

"Really?" He laughed. "I wonder if she'll grant me a child when I get back?" He expected her to laugh, but there was that look again. "But you didn't say why you were coming. You're . . . well, you're pregnant, aren't you?"

"Yes. Chris, I'm really sorry about running off and leaving you. I could—"

"Never mind that. You already apologized, and it makes me nervous to watch it anyway. But shouldn't you be taking it easy?"

"That's far in the future. It doesn't inconvenience us much anyway. And I'm here because it's a great honor to go with the Wizard. And because you are my friend."

Once again there was that look.

* * *

"Can I join you?"

Chris looked up, startled. He had not been asleep, but neither had he been precisely awake. His knees were stiff from maintaining the same position for hours.

"Sure. Come aboard." Gaby's canoe had pulled alongside Chris and Valiha. Gaby stepped from one to the other and sat in front of Chris. She cocked her head to one side and looked dubious.

"Are you all right?"

"If you mean, am I crazy right now, you'd be the best judge of that."

"I'm sorry, I didn't mean to—"

"No, I'm serious." And a little hurt, he admitted to himself. One had to stop feeling apologetic about it sometime or lose all self-respect. "I never know when I'm having what the doctors call an episode. It always seems perfectly reasonable behavior to me at the time."

She looked sympathetic. "It must be terrible. I mean, to. . . ." She looked at the sky and whistled thinly for a moment. "Gaby, shut your big mouth," she said. She looked back at him. "I didn't come to embarrass you, no matter what it might look like. Can we start over?"

"Hi! So good of you to drop in."

"We should get together more often!" Gaby beamed back at him. "There were a few things I wanted to say, and then I'll have to run." She still seemed to feel awkward because having proclaimed that, she said nothing more for several minutes. She studied her hands, her feet, the interior of the boat. She looked at everything but Chris.

"I wanted to apologize for what happened on the dock," she said at last.

"Apologize? To me? I don't think I'm the one who needs it."

"You're not the one who needs it the *most,* obviously. But I can't talk to her until she's cooled off. Then I'll crawl to her on my belly or do whatever she wants me to do to wipe it out. Because she's right, you know. She did nothing to deserve that."

"That was my estimation, too."

Gaby grimaced, but managed to look him in the eye.

"Right. And in a larger sense, none of you deserved it. We're all in this together, and you all have a right to expect better behavior of me. I want you to know that you can in the future."

"I'll accept that. Consider it forgotten." He reached out and shook her hand. When she made no move to leave, he thought it might be time to go a little deeper into the problem. But it wasn't an easy thing to bring up.

"I was wondering. . . ." She raised her eyebrows and seemed relieved. "Well, to be blunt, what can we expect of Cirocco? Robin isn't the only one who isn't impressed so far."

She nodded and ran both hands through her short hair.

"That's what I wanted to talk about, really. I want you to realize that you've seen only one side of her. There's more. Quite a lot more, actually."

He said nothing.

"Right. What can you expect? Frankly, not a lot for the next few days. Robin was telling the truth when she said Rocky's luggage is mostly alcohol. I dropped most of it in the drink a few minutes ago. It took me three days to get her presentable for Carnival, and as soon as it was over, she spun off the wheel again. She'll want to drink more when she wakes up, and I'll let her, a little, because tapering her off is easier than cold turkey. After that I'll keep just a little bit, for emergencies, in Psaltery's saddlebag."

She leaned forward and looked at him earnestly.

"I know this is going to be hard to believe, but in a few days, when she gets over the withdrawal and away from the memories of Carnival, she'll be okay. You're seeing her at her worst. At her best, she's got more guts than all of us put together. And more decency, and compassion, and . . . there's no use my telling you that. You'll either see it for yourself or always think she's a sot."

"I'm willing to keep an open mind about it," Chris offered.

She studied his face in that intense way of hers. He felt every gram of her considerable energy boring in, as if her whole being were intent on knowing what was inside him, and he didn't like it. It felt as if she could see things even he was not aware of.

"I think you will," she said at last.

Another silence descended. Chris felt sure she had more to say, so he prompted her again.

"I don't understand about Carnival," he said. "You said,

'get away from the memories of Carnival.' Why is that necessary?"

She put her elbows on her knees and laced her fingers together.

"What did you see at Carnival?" She didn't wait for an answer. "A lot of singing and dancing and feasting, lots of pretty colors, flowers, good food. The tourists would love Carnival, but the Titanides don't let them go see it. The reason is it's a very serious business."

"I know that. I understand what it's for."

"You think you do. You understand the primary purpose, I'll grant you. It's an effective method of population control, which is something nobody's ever liked, human or Titanide, when it's aimed at them. It's fine for those other trashy folks." She raised her eyebrows, and he nodded.

"What did you think of the Wizard's part in the Carnival?" she asked.

He considered it. "She seemed to take it seriously. I don't know what standards she was using, but she seemed to be making a thorough study of all the proposals."

Gaby nodded. "She does. She knows more about Titanide breeding than Titanides do. She's older than any of them. She's been going to Carnivals for seventy-five years now.

"At first she liked them." Gaby shrugged. "Who wouldn't? She's a very big cheese here in Gaea, which you and Robin don't really seem to grasp yet. At Carnival, she gets her ego built up. Everybody needs that. Maybe she's been a little too eager to get it, but that's not for me to judge." She looked away from him again, and he thought, correctly as it turned out, that she did have a few judgments to make on that subject. He realized Gaby was one of those people who cannot look someone in the face while lying to them. He liked her for it; he was the same way.

"After a while, though, it began to wear on her. There's a lot of despair at Carnival. You don't see it because Titanides grieve in private. And I'm not saying they go out and kill themselves if they don't get picked. I've never heard of a Titanide suicide. Still, she was the cause of a lot of sorrow. She kept at it for a long time after the fun had gone out of it, you understand, out of a sense of duty, but about twenty years ago she decided she had done all that could be expected of anybody. It was time to hand the job over to someone else. She went to Gaea and asked to be relieved of the job. And Gaea refused."

She looked at him intently, waiting for him to understand. He did not yet, not completely. Gaby leaned back in the bow of the boat, her hands laced behind her head. She stared at the clouds.

"Rocky took her job with some reservations," Gaby said. "I was with her, so I know. She went into it with what she thought were open eyes. She did not trust Gaea to be completely true to her word; she was ready for some jokers in the deck. The funny thing, though, was that Gaea *did* live up to her end of the bargain. There were some good years. Some close calls, some really bad troubles, but all in all they were the best years of her life. Mine, too. You'd never hear either of us complaining, even when things got dangerous, because we knew what we were getting into when we decided not to go back to Earth. Gaea did *not* promise an easy ride. She said that we could live to a *very* ripe old age, so long as we kept on our toes. That's all been precisely as promised.

"We didn't think much about getting older because we *didn't*." She laughed, with a hint of self-deprecation. "We were sort of like the heroes of a serial or a comic strip. 'Join us again next week . . .' and there we'd be, unchanged, off on a new adventure. I built a road around Gaea. Cirocco got carried off by King Kong and had to get loose. We . . . hell, shut me up, please. You walk into an old folks' home, you get stories."

"It's all right," Chris said, amused. He had already thought of the comic-strip analogy. The lives of these two women had been so divorced from the reality he knew as to make them seem less than real. Yet here she was, a century old and real as a kick in the pants.

"So Rocky finally came up against it. The joker, and it was a hell of a trick. We should have expected it, though. Gaea does not conceal the fact that she never gives something for nothing. We had thought we were satisfying our end of that deal, but she wanted more. Here's how the swindle worked.

"You saw her put the Titanide egg in her mouth at Carnival?" Chris nodded, and she went on. "It changed color. It turned clear as glass. The thing is, no Titanide egg can be completely fertilized until that change occurs."

"You mean until it's put in someone's mouth?"

"You've *almost* got it. A Titanide mouth won't do the job. It has to be a human mouth. In fact, it has to be a particular human."

Chris started to say something, stopped, and sat back. "Just her?"

"The one and only wonderful Wizard of Gaea."

He didn't want her to go on talking. He saw it now, but she insisted on being sure he saw all the implications.

"Until and unless Gaea ever changes her mind," she went on relentlessly, "Rocky is solely and completely responsible for the survival of the race of Titanides. When she realized that, she skipped a Carnival. She could not face another one, she said. It was too much to put on any one person. What if she were to die? Gaea wouldn't give her an answer. Gaea is perfectly capable of letting the race vanish if Rocky leaves here, if she stops going to Carnival, or even if she dies.

"So she started going to Carnivals again. What else could she do?"

Chris thought of the Titanide ambassador back in San Francisco. Dulcimer, her name had been. He had felt sick when she explained her position to him. He felt worse now.

"I don't understand how. . . ."

"It was very slickly done. When Rocky took the job, she had just convinced Gaea to stop a war between the Titanides and the angels. The animosity between the two races was built into their brains, into their genes, I guess. She had to recall all of them physically and make changes. At the same time Rocky and I submitted to the direct transfer of a great deal of knowledge from Gaea's mind. When it was done, we could both sing the Titanide language and a lot of others, and we knew a hell of a lot about the inside of Gaea. And Rocky's salivary glands had been changed to secrete a chemical which the Titanides had been changed to need for reproduction.

"She didn't start drinking at once. She used to sniff cocaine when she was younger but hadn't for years. She went back to that for a while. Liquor worked better, and that's what she ended up doing. When Carnival time approaches, she tries her best to get away. But she can't."

Gaby stood up and signaled to Psaltery, whose boat was paralleling Chris's ten meters away. He angled toward them.

"All that's beside the point, of course," she said briskly.

"The important thing about a drunk on a trip like this is not why she drinks, but whether she'll be any use to anybody, herself included, if things get tough. I tell you she will, or I wouldn't have suggested you come with us."

"I'm glad you told me," Chris said. "And I'm sorry."

She smiled lopsidedly. "Don't be sorry. You've got problems; we've got problems. We got what we asked for, me and Rocky. It's our own fault if we didn't realize what we were asking."

17.

Recognition

The rain Gaby had been expecting finally arrived when they had been on the river for five hours. She broke out the oilskins and handed one to Psaltery. The others were doing the same, except for Cirocco, who still slept in the front of Hornpipe's canoe. Gaby started to tell Psaltery to bring the boat over so she could get the Wizard out of the rain, then changed her mind. Her impulse was always to pamper Rocky when she was like this. She had to remember what she had told Chris. Cirocco must take care of herself.

Presently the Wizard raised her head and peered at the rain, as though she had never seen anything as inexplicable as water falling from the sky. She started to sit up, then leaned over the side of the canoe and vomited into the brown water. It was a lot of effort for not much return.

When she was through, she crawled to the middle of the canoe, threw back the red tarpaulin, and began rooting around in the supplies. Her search grew more and more frantic. In the back, Hornpipe said nothing but kept paddling steadily. At last the Wizard sat back on her heels and rubbed her forehead with the heel of her hand.

Suddenly, she looked up.

"GaaaaBEEEE!" she yelled. She spotted Gaby, twenty meters away, then stepped onto the edge of the boat and out onto the water.

For a moment it looked as if she could actually pull it off. It turned out to be just the low gravity, however, for with her second step she went in over her knees, and before she could take a third, the water closed over her slightly puzzled face.

"She may be a Wizard," Chris chuckled—"but she's not Jesus."

"Who's Jesus?"

Robin listened to the explanation for a moment, long enough to know it wasn't something that interested her. Jesus was a Christian myth figure, apparently the one who founded the whole sect. He had been dead more than two thousand years, which struck Robin as the best thing about him. She remained cautious until she was able to ask Chris if he believed any of that, and when he said no, she considered the subject closed.

The two of them were sitting on a log a good distance from the rest of the group, all of whom circled the figure of Cirocco, shivering in a blanket next to a roaring fire. A big pot of coffee hung from a metal trivet, slowly blackening in the flames.

Robin was feeling sour. She was wondering what in the name of the Great Mother she was doing on this fool's errand led by a Wizard she wouldn't trust to tie her own shoelaces competently. And Gaby. The less said about her, the better. Four Titanides . . . actually, she rather liked them. Hautbois had shown herself to be quite a teller of tales. Robin had spent the first part of the trip listening to her, from time to time throwing in a yarn of her own, feeling her out to see how gullible she might be. Hautbois would get along well in the Coven; she was not easily taken in.

Then there was Chris.

She had put off getting to know him, feeling uneasy about actually having to meet socially with a male. Yet she already knew a lot of what she had been taught about men was untrue. She could see the tales of men had grown in the telling. She could not imagine ever learning to be comfortable with him, but if they were to make this trip together, she should try to understand him better.

That was turning out to be hard to do, and she berated herself for it. It was not his fault. He seemed open enough. She just could not bring herself to talk to him. It was a lot easier talking to the Titanides. They did not seem as *alien* as he.

So instead of talking, she looked at the water dripping from the edge of the tent fly they had suspended between two trees. There was not a breath of wind. The rain fell straight down, hard and steady, but the rude shelter was enough to keep them dry. The fire was for the coffee and the Wizard; it was quite warm, though not unpleasantly so.

"Hyperion gets a lot darker on a cloudy day then California does," Chris said.

"Does it? I hadn't realized."

He smiled at her, but it was not patronizing. He seemed to want to talk, too.

"The light here's deceptive," he said. "It seems bright, but that's because your eyes open to accommodate it. Saturn only gets about a hundredth as much light as the Earth does. When something blocks most of that, you notice the difference."

"I wouldn't know about that. We handle things differently in the Coven. We keep the windows open for weeks at a time to make the crops grow better."

"No kidding? I'd like to know more about it."

So she told him about life in the Coven and found one more example of a quality that was the same for men and women: it was easy to talk to anyone if he or she was a good listener. Robin knew she was not and was not ashamed of the fact, but she respected someone who, like Chris, could make her feel as if his whole attention were on her, as if he really were absorbing what she had to say. At first this respect, grudging as it was, made her nervous in itself. This was a *male*, damn it. She no longer expected him to assault her twice a day, but it was disorienting to realize that without that stubble of beard and breadth of shoulder, he did not look or act like anything but a sister.

She could tell that he thought many things about the Coven were strange, though he avoided expressing it. That bothered her at first—how could someone from peckish society think *her* world was weird?—but trying to be fair, she had to admit that *all* customs must look strange to one who was unused to them.

"Then those . . . tattoos? Everyone has them in the Coven?"

"That's right. Some have more than I; some, less. Everyone has the Pentasm." She tossed her head to show him the design around her ear. "Usually it is centered on the mother's mark, but my womb is defiled and. . . ." He was frowning his incomprehension. "The—what was it Gaby called it?—the belly button." She laughed, remembering. "What a silly name! We call it the first window of the soul because it marks the holiest bond, that between mother and daughter. The windows of the head are the mind's windows. I have been accused of heterodoxy for putting my Pentasm in guard over my mind rather than my soul, but I successfully defended myself before the tribunal because of my defilement. The windows of the soul lead to the womb, here and here." She put her hands to her belly and her crotch, then hastily took them away when she recalled the difference between herself and the man.

"I'm afraid I don't understand the defilement."

"I can't have children. They would have what I have, or so the doctors say."

"I'm sorry."

Robin frowned. "I don't understand this custom of apologizing for things one didn't do. You never worked at the Semenico Sperm Bank in Atlanta, Gah, did you?"

"That's Georgia," he said, smiling. "Gee Ay stands for Georgia. No, I didn't work there."

"Someday I might meet the man who did. His death would be unusual."

"I wasn't really apologizing," he said. "Not that way. We often say, 'I'm sorry,' just to offer sympathy."

"We don't wish sympathy."

"Then I withdraw the offer." His grin was infectious. Soon she had to smile with him. "God knows I get too much of it myself. I usually just let it pass, unless I'm feeling nasty."

Robin wondered how he could say it so carelessly. Peckish people varied a lot. Some hardly understood what honor meant. Others could be very touchy. She had submitted to indignities upon arrival that she would never have accepted from one of her own people, and the reason was she presumed these folk didn't know any better. At first she assumed they all had no self-respect, but she thought Chris had some—though not a lot—and if he were willing to accept sympathy without protest, he must not see it as always encroaching on his own sense of self-reliance.

"I have been accused of being too nasty," she admitted. "By my sisters, that is. There are times when we can accept sympathy with no loss of honor, so long as it implies no patronization."

"Then you have my sympathy," he said. "As one sufferer to another."

"Accepted."

"What does 'peckish' mean?"

"It comes from our word for your . . . we'd better not talk about that."

"Okay. Then why do you want to kill that man in Georgia?"

She found herself launched on an explanation of what had

been done to her, why it had been done, and that led into an explanation of the peckish power structure and how it operated. It dawned on her that she was speaking to a supposed member of that very power structure. Oddly, she was embarrassed. She had been saying some pretty terrible things, and after all, he had done nothing to her personally. Did that matter? She was no longer sure.

"At least I think I know what 'peckish' means now," he said.

"I didn't mean to accuse you of anything," she said. "I'm sure you see it differently because of the way you were brought up, so—"

"Don't be so sure," he said. "I don't admit to any big conspiracy, you understand. If there is one, nobody's invited me to the meetings. And I do think you . . . your Coven is operating from an obsolete world picture. If I read you right, you'd agree to that at least partially yourself."

She shrugged, noncommittally. He was right, partially.

"When your group cut itself off from the rest of the human race, things might have been as bad as you say. I wasn't around, and I guess if I had been, I would have been part of the oppressor class and think it was the way things should be. But I have been told that things are a lot better now. I won't say they're perfect. Things don't *get* perfect. But most of the women I know are happy. They don't think there's many battles left to fight."

"You'd better stop there," Robin cautioned. "Most women have *always* been happy with the way things were, or at least they said so. That goes back to before peckish society allowed women to vote. Just because we of the Coven believe some things that I now know are overstated or incorrect, don't draw the conclusion that we are foolish about everything. We know that the majority is *always* willing to let things remain as they are until they are led to something better. A slave may not be happy with her lot, but most do nothing to improve it. Most do not believe it *can* be improved."

He spread his hands and shrugged. "You've got me there. And I wouldn't see oppression because I'd be the benefactor of it. What do you think? How bad does it look to you, as a sort of visitor from another planet?"

"Frankly, it is much better than I had hoped. On the surface anyway. I've had to discard a lot of preconceptions."

"Good for you!" he said. "Most people would rather die than discard a preconception. When Gaby told me about where you came from, the last thing I expected you to have was an open mind. But what do . . . uh, peckish women think?"

Robin was feeling an odd mixture of emotions. Most unnerving of all was the fact that she felt pleased that he felt she had an open mind. This in spite of the way he had phrased it, which could be interpreted as an insult to the Coven. The closed, isolated group Gaby had probably described to him would be expected to cling to its own notions fanatically. The Coven was not like that, but it would be hard to explain to him. Robin had been trained to accept the universe as it existed, as she observed it, not to introduce a Finagle factor to make it conform to the equation or even to the doctrine.

It had been easy to discard the notions that males had meterlong penises and that they spent all their time raping women or buying and selling them. (That last was not yet disproved, but if it was happening, it was a subtle bit of social business she had not yet been able to observe.) She faced a disquieting notion: male-as-person. A human being not totally at the mercy of his testosterone, more than just an aggressor penis, but a person one could talk to, who could even understand one's point of view. Following that thought to its logical end took her to an almost unthinkable possibility: male-as-sister.

She realized she had been quiet too long.

"Peckish women? Uh, I really don't know yet. I met a woman who sells her body, though she says that's not the right way to look at it. I don't understand money, so I really can't say if she's right. Gaby and Cirocco are worse than useless in that respect. They have less to do with human society—as you know it—than I do. I have to say I don't know enough of your culture to understand woman's role in it."

He was nodding again.

"What's in your bag?" he asked.

"My demon."

"Can I see it?"

"That probably isn't—" But he had already opened the bag. Well, let it be on his own head, she thought. Nasu's bite was painful but not serious.

"A snake!" he cried. He seemed delighted and reached into the bag. "A py—no, an anaconda. One of the nicest ones I've seen, too. What's his . . . what's her name?"

"Nasu." She was regretting not saying anything now and wished Nasu would go ahead and bite and get it over with. Robin would then apologize because it was a dirty trick. How was he to know Nasu allowed no one but Robin to handle her?

But he was doing it correctly, showing the proper respect, and damn it if Nasu wasn't coiling around his arm.

"You know something about snakes."

"I've had a few. I worked in a zoo for a year, back when I could still hold a job. Me and snakes get along."

When five minutes went by and Chris still wasn't bitten, Robin had to admit the truth of what he said. And it made her more nervous than ever to see him sitting there with her demon wound around his shoulders. What was she to do? The main function of a demon was to warn one of enemies. Part of her knew that made no more sense than the infallibility granted by her third Eye. It was tradition, no more. She wasn't living in the Stone Age.

But a part of her much deeper than that looked at Chris and the snake and did not know what to do.

18.

Wide Awake

Gaby had hoped to get all the way to Aglaia before camping but now saw that was unrealistic. Cirocco was in no shape to continue.

Actually they had not done badly. The Titanides' steady rowing had brought them to the last northward bend before Ophion resumed its generally eastward trend. A driftwood-strewn shelf elbowed into the river's flow and provided a gentle beach for the landing of the canoes. Atop a low bluff was a stand of trees, and it was there the Titanides made camp, with Chris and Robin trying to help but mostly getting in the way.

Gaby judged the rain would continue for several dekarevs. She could have called Gaea and found out for sure—even requested an end to it for good reason. But weather was fairly standardized in Gaea. She had seen a thirty-hour rain follow a two-hectorev heat wave many times, and this looked like one of those. The clouds were low and continuous.

To the northwest she could just make out the Place of Winds, the Hyperion terminus of the slanted support cable known as Cirocco's Stairs. The cable vanished into the cloud layer, a vague, deeper darkness, before rising above it somewhere to Gaby's north. She thought she could detect brightness behind the clouds where it hung over them and reflected light into its own massive shadow.

Cirocco's Stairs. She smiled wryly, but without any bitterness. Almost everyone seemed to have forgotten that *two* people had made that first climb. It did not bother her. She knew that, aside from the highway, she had not left nearly as many marks on this crazy world as Cirocco had.

She walked to the top of the bluff and watched with amusement as Chris and Robin tried to make themselves useful. The Titanides were too polite to refuse most of their offers of help, so things that might have been done in five minutes were taking fifteen. And of course, it was the right thing to do. Chris had not spoken of his background, but he was a city kid aside from a few excursions into Earth's tamed wildernesses. Robin came from a hypercity, no matter that the Coven floor was picturesque crops and cattle. She might never have seen a wild, unplanned thing in her life.

When it came time to cook, however, the Titanides put all four feet down and shooed the young humans away. Titanides cooked almost as well as they sang. For this first day of travel they were digging into the packs and getting items most likely to spoil, the choice morsels brought along to be eaten quickly. They fed the fire and rimmed it with smooth stones, broke out the copper cookware, and did the magical things Titanides could do to turn fresh meat and fish into wonders of improvisation.

Before long the fruits of their labors could be smelled. Gaby sat back and savored the wait, feeling happier than she had in a long time. It took her back to a much simpler meal shared many years ago, when somehow, torn and bruised and with no assurance they would live another day, she and Cirocco had been as close as they would ever be. Now those memories were bittersweet, but she had lived long enough to know one must hold onto the good things to survive. She might have brooded about all the things that had gone wrong between that day and this or worried about Cirocco, who was even now throwing up in her tent and plotting to get her liquor back from Psaltery's saddlebags. Instead, she chose to smell the good food and listen to the soothing sounds of rain mix with the songs of the Titanides and to feel the long-awaited cooling breeze begin to blow from the east.

She was one hundred and three years old, setting off on a trip that, like all her other trips, she might never finish. There were no life-insurance policies in Gaea, not even for the Wizard. Certainly not for the free-lance pest that Gaea tolerated only because she was more reliable than Cirocco.

The thought did not disturb her. She would survive and prosper. There had been a time when her present age would have been impossible to contemplate, but now she knew that centenarians are always young under the skin; she just happened to be fortunate enough to look and feel young as well. In her own case, she was sixteen, in the San Bernardino Mountains, with her telescope and the fire—both built with her own hands—waiting for the sky to darken and the stars to come out. What more could one ask of life?

She knew she was not growing anymore. She no longer expected to. Increasing age, she had found, brings increased experience, knowledge, perspective; it brings many things that one could apparently accumulate forever, but a plateau of wisdom is reached. If she completed her second century, she did not expect to be significantly changed. That had caused her some concern around the time of her eightieth birthday, but she no longer worried about it. The worries of the day were sufficient.

This day held only one worry for her as it drew to a close.

She watched Robin moving around the fire and sighed deeply.

The meal was up to the Titanides' usual high standards but for one literally sour note. Titanide cookery occasionally employed a powerful spice obtained from the crushed and prepared seeds of a watermelon-sized blue fruit. It had an elegant name in Titanide song, but humans generally called it hyperlemon. It was white and granular. A few grains were enough for any recipe.

When the meal was almost ready for dishing out, Psaltery suddenly turned and spit a mouthful of vegetables onto the ground. For a moment his lips were too puckered for speech as the other Titanides looked at him questioningly. He held out a spoon, and Valiha put her tongue to it. She made a face.

It did not take long to discover that a leather bag marked salt actually contained hyperlemon concentrate. The bag had been bought by Hautbois. The conclusion reached after much scandalized discussion among all four Titanides was that the vendor—a reformed tequilaholic named Kithara—had for some reason decided to play a joke on the Wizard's party.

None of the Titanides was amused. Gaby thought it was no big thing, even though a pot of vegetables had to be thrown out. They still had plenty of good salt. A check of other provisions revealed no substitutions. But to a Titanide, ruining good food was a sin. None of them could understand why Kithara had done it.

"I'll be sure to ask him upon our return," Psaltery vowed darkly.

"I would like to be there with you," Valiha said.

"Why make such a fuss?" Gaby wanted to know. "It was a harmless joke. Sometimes you folks get to looking a little somber to me. I'm glad you can make jokes."

"It's not the joke we object to," Hautbois said. "I like them as well as anyone else. But this one was in . . . bad taste."

Though the aging process had passed her by, there was one thing about Gaby that had changed as she grew older. She required less sleep than she used to. Two hours out of twenty were generally enough. Often she stayed awake for sixty or even seventy revs with no ill effects.

The Titanides said she was getting more like them every day and soon would entirely lose the disgusting habit.

Whatever the reason for it, she had decided she could get by without sleeping at this camp. She went off by herself, walked by the river for a time, and when she returned, the camp was quiet but for the low, humming songs of the Titanides in rest phase. They sprawled around the fire, four improbably limber comic nightmares, their hands occupied with unimportant tasks, their minds wandering. Valiha was on her side, propped up on one elbow. Hautbois was on her back, her human torso now in line with the rest of her body, her legs curled in the air like a puppy waiting for her belly to be scratched. Of all the things Titanides could do, Gaby thought that was the funniest.

There were four tents pitched among the trees a good distance from the fire. She passed by her own unoccupied shelter. In the second, Cirocco slept uneasily. She had two stiff drinks in her, and an ocean of coffee. Gaby knew it wasn't the coffee that made her toss and turn.

She paused outside Chris's tent and knew it would just be snooping to look inside it. She had no business with Chris. So it was on to the next one in line. She waited outside for several minutes until she heard someone stirring.

"Can I talk to you for a minute?"

"Who is that? Gaby?"

"Yeah."

"I guess so. Come on in."

Robin was sitting up on her sleeping bag, which rested on a deep pad of moss put there by Hautbois. Gaby lit the lamp

hanging from the ridgepole and saw Robin's eyes glittering
alertly but with no particular malice. She was dressed in the
clothes she had worn all day.

"Did I disturb you?"

Robin shook her head. "Can't sleep," she admitted. "This
is the first time in my life that I've not had a bed to sleep in."

"Hautbois would be happy to get more moss."

"That's not it. I'll get used to it, I suppose."

"It might help if you wore something looser."

Robin held up the elaborately patterned nightgown Hautbois
had laid out for her. "It's not my style," she said. "How could
anyone sleep in something like that? It ought to be in a display
case."

Gaby chuckled, then squatted with one knee on the ground
and picked at a cuticle. Robin was looking at her when she
glanced up. Might as well get on with it, she thought. She
knows you didn't come in to see if she needed fresh towels.

"I guess the first thing is to apologize," she said. "So here
it is. I regret what I did, it was not justified, and I'm sorry."

"I accept your apology," Robin said. "But the warning still
stands."

"That's fine. I understand that." Gaby was picking her
words as carefully as she knew how. Something more than an
apology was called for, but she had to be sure she did not
appear patronizing.

"What I did was wrong in my culture as well as yours,"
she said. "The apology was for the violation of my own moral
code. But you were telling me about something you witches
have, some system of obligations, and the word has slipped
my mind."

"Labra," Robin said.

"That's it. I don't pretend to understand it all. I think I can
be sure I violated it, though, even if I'm not sure just how.
What I'm asking for now is your help. Is there a way to set
things right between us? Is there anything I can do to make
it like it never happened?"

Robin was frowning. "I don't think you want to get into—"

"But I do. I'm willing to do quite a bit. Is there anything?"

"Y-e-e-s. But—"

"What?"

Robin threw up her hands. "Much like any primitive culture,
I suppose. A duel. Just the two of us."

"How serious a duel?" Gaby asked. "To the death?"

"We're not less *that* primitive. The purpose is reconciliation, not murder. If I thought you needed killing, I'd just do it and hope my sisters would back me up when the tribunal came around. We would fight bare-handed."

Gaby considered it. "What if I won?"

Robin gave an exasperated sigh.

"You don't understand. The winner isn't important, not in that sense. We wouldn't be trying to prove which is the better woman. The fight would only prove who is the stronger and quicker, and that has nothing to do with honor. But by agreeing to fight with a provision not to kill each other, we each acknowledge the other as a worthy, and thus honorable opponent." She paused and for a moment looked quite wicked. "Don't worry about it," she said. "You wouldn't win."

Gaby matched her grin and once again found herself liking this strange child. More than ever she wanted her solidly on her side when trouble started.

"How about it then? Am I worth fighting?"

Robin took a long time answering. Many things had occurred to Gaby since the fight was proposed. She wondered how many of them Robin was considering now. Should she let Robin win? That might be hazardous if Robin suspected she was not fighting wholeheartedly. If Robin *did* lose, would she really bury the hatchet? Gaby had to take her word for that. She thought she understood the little witch well enough to know her concept of honor would not have allowed her to suggest it if she could not behave as advertised. So the fight would be serious and probably painful.

"If that's the way you want it," Robin said.

Robin was taking off her clothes, so Gaby did the same. They were half a kilometer from the river, far enough to make the campfire just a dim light seen through pouring rain. The field of combat was a shallow depression in the rolling land. There was little grass, but the dirt was firm enough: heat-baked ground only beginning to soak up moisture after six hours of steady rain. Still, the footing would not be good. In places there were puddles and mud.

They faced each other, and Gaby sized up her opponent. They were a close match. Gaby had a few centimeters in height and a few kilos in mass.

"Are there any forms we should observe? Any rituals?"

"Yes, but they're complex, and they wouldn't mean anything to you, so why don't we just dispense with them? Mumbo jumbo and alagazam, you bow to me and I bow to you, and we'll consider the rituals satisfied, okay?"

"Rules?"

"What? Oh, I guess there should be, shouldn't there? But I really don't know how much you know about fighting."

"I know how to kill someone with my hands," Gaby said.

"Let's just say we do nothing that would permanently injure the other. The loser should be able to walk tomorrow. Other than that, anything goes."

"Right. But before we start, I was curious about that tattoo on your stomach. What is that for?" She pointed to Robin's midsection.

It might have been better—Robin could have looked at herself rather than at Gaby's pointing hand—but she was still caught off guard when Gaby kicked with the foot she had been carefully working down into the mud. Robin ducked the kick, but a glob of mud hit her on the side of the face, blinding one eye.

Gaby expected the leap backward and was prepared to exploit it, but Robin's reflexes were a little quicker, and Gaby took a kick in the side. It slowed her just enough for Robin to execute her own surprise move.

She turned and ran.

Gaby ran after her, but it was not a tactic she was used to. She kept expecting a trick and so did not run as fast as she might have. As a result, Robin soon had a comfortable lead. She stopped when the distance between them had lengthened to ten meters, and when she turned, her eye was open again. Gaby thought she would not be seeing as well as before, but the rain had removed most of her disadvantage. Gaby was impressed. When she began to move in on the younger woman, she did so with extreme caution.

It was like a restart. Gaby felt handicapped because she had seldom fought this way before. Her own training had been very long ago, and while she was not rusty, it was hard to remember what one did in those practice sessions. For the last eighty years any fight she found herself in was completely serious, meaning that death could always result. That kind of fight was not at all like practicing. Robin, on the other hand, must do this sort of thing all the time. Her personality would practically guarantee it.

There was no real reason why the fight should last more than a few minutes, even pulling punches. Somehow Gaby didn't think it would turn out that way. When she moved in, she gambled by not throwing any punches or kicks, leaving Robin an opening Gaby felt she could handle if the younger woman chose to exploit it. But she did not, and the two of them grappled for wrestling holds. An agreement had been made without words. Gaby would honor it. By formalizing the contest even further than the rules they had agreed on, Robin was saying she had no desire for either of them to be hurt. That meant Gaby was an honorable opponent who did not deserve to be hurt.

It took quite a while. Gaby realized she had surrendered what advantages she might have had by fighting this way. She didn't mind. She expected to lose, but that didn't prevent her from giving it all she had. Robin would know she had been in a fight.

"Peace!" Gaby yelled. "Uncle, aunt, and a lot of little cousins!"

Robin released her arm, and the knife of pain slowly withdrew from Gaby's shoulder. She lifted her face from the mud and cautiously rolled over. She began to think she might one day regain the use of the arm.

She lifted her head and saw Robin sitting with her head between her knees, panting like a steam engine.

"Two out of three?" Gaby suggested.

Robin began to laugh. She did it loudly and with no self-consciousness.

"If I thought for one minute you meant that," she finally managed to say, "I'd tie you up and keep you in a cage. But you'd probably gnaw through the chains."

"Almost had you a couple of times there, didn't I?"

"You'll never know how close."

Gaby wondered how she could feel so good, considering the fact that she hurt all over. She supposed it must be marathon euphoria, that boneless relaxation which can come when one completes an all-out effort. And after all, she was not injured.

There would be bruises, and the shoulder would be weak for a while, but she was suffering mostly from the effects of exertion, not pummeling.

Robin got slowly to her feet. She held out a hand.

"Let's get down to the river. You need to wash up."

Gaby took her hand and managed to rise. Robin was walking with a limp, and Gaby didn't feel too steady herself, so they supported each other through the first painful hundred meters.

"I really did want to ask you about that tattoo," Gaby said as they approached the river.

Robin wiped her hands over her abdomen, but it was no use. "Can't see it now. Too much mud. What did you think of it?"

Gaby was about to say something polite and noncommittal but thought better of it.

"I think it's one of the most hideous things I ever saw."

"Precisely. It is a source of much labra."

"You want to explain that? Do all witches disfigure themselves like that?"

"I'm the only one. Therein lies the labra."

They walked carefully out into the river and sat down. The rain had relented, becoming a fine mist, while to the north there was a break in the clouds that let some light through.

Gaby could no longer see the tattoo but could not stop thinking about it. It was grotesque, almost frightening. Rendered like an anatomical drawing, it depicted incised layers of tissue laid back with surgical precision to bare the organs beneath. The ovaries were like rotten fruit, crawling with maggots. The fallopian tubes were knotted many times. But the womb itself was the worst. It was swollen, bulging out of the "incision," and dripping blood from a ragged wound. It was clear the injury had been caused from the inside, as though something were tearing its way out. Nothing could be seen of the creature the womb sheltered but a pair of red, feral eyes.

As they went to retrieve their clothes, it began to rain hard again. Gaby was not alarmed when Robin stumbled and fell; the footing was terrible, and she was still favoring a turned ankle. By the time of Robin's fourth fall it was obvious something was wrong. She staggered, trembling, her jaw muscles knotted with determination.

"Let me help you," Gaby said when she could no longer bear it.

"No, thank you. I can make it on my own."

A minute later she fell down and did not get up. Her limbs shook in a slow rhythm, not violently. Her eyes did not track. Gaby knelt and put one arm under Robin's knees, the other under her back.

"Nnnn . . . uunnnnuh. Nnnnuh."

"What? Be reasonable, friend. I can't leave you out here in the rain."

"Yyyuuu . . . ssss. Yu . . . yesssss. Llluuh . . . eeeeve. Leeeeeve muh-muh-muh-meee."

It was a hell of a problem. Gaby put her down and stood over her, scratching her head. She looked toward the campfire, not far away, and back again to Robin. They were atop a low hill; rising water would be no problem. Nor would she drown from the rainfall. This part of Hyperion held no predators that would give her trouble, though some small animals might try a nibble.

This would have to be straightened out later. Some sort of accommodation had to be reached, for Gaby would not do this again. But for now she turned away and headed back toward camp.

Hautbois stood up, alarmed, when Gaby returned alone. Gaby knew the Titanide had seen them leave together; it was likely she even knew what they intended to do, out there in the rain. Gaby reassured her before she could jump to conclusions.

"She's all right. At least, I guess she is. She's having a seizure and doesn't want my help. We can get her when it's time to go. Where are you going?"

"To bring her back to the tent, of course."

"I don't think she'll appreciate it."

Hautbois looked as angry as Gaby had ever seen a Titanide be.

"You humans and your silly games," she snorted. "I don't have to play by her rules or yours either."

Robin saw Hautbois looming through the wall of rain. Damn it, Gaby had sent back the cavalry; that much was obvious.

"I came on my own," the Titanide said as she picked Robin out of the mud. "Whatever human concept you are trying to defend by this insane act can remain unviolated because no human agency is taking you from here."

Put me down, you overgrown hobbyhorse, Robin tried to say, and heard the despised croaks and gurgles drool over her slack jaw.

"I'll take care of you," Hautbois said tenderly.

Robin was calm as Hautbois put her atop the sleeping bag. Stop fighting, submit to it, wait it out, and win eventually. You're helpless now, but you can get back at them.

Hautbois returned with a bucket of warm water. She bathed Robin, dried her, held her up like a defective robot rag doll, and put her into the embroidered finery of her nightgown. Robin might have weighed no more than a sheet of paper as Hautbois lifted her with one hand and slid her into the sleeping bag. She tucked it up around her neck.

She began to sing.

Robin felt heat in the back of her throat. It horrified her. To be tucked in, bathed, dressed . . . it was a terrible affront to her dignity. She should be able to summon more anger than she was feeling. She should be composing the blistering verbal assault she would deliver to this creature as soon as she regained her body. Instead, she felt only the choking lump of an emotion she had long forgotten.

Weeping was unthinkable. Once it was surrendered to, one might never be free of the self-pity. It was her biggest fear, so terrifying that she seldom could so much as name it. There had been times, all alone, when she had wept. She could never do it while with someone.

And yet in a sense she was alone. Hautbois had said it herself. Human rules, Coven concepts, need not apply here. It went beyond that; the Coven did not demand that she never cry. It was her own self-enforced discipline.

She heard moaning and knew it was coming from her mouth. Tears were leaking from the corners of her eyes. The lump in her throat could not be swallowed, so it would have to come out.

Robin surrendered and cried herself to sleep in Hautbois's arms.

Chris reclined on his sleeping bag in the damned half-light and trembled. For hours it had felt as if an attack might be imminent, but it refused to start. Or had it? As he had told Gaby, he was not the one to judge if he was in an episode. But that was not strictly true. If he were having an attack, he would not know it, it would seem perfectly reasonable for his mind to be operating like a machine with worn pulleys and bent gears, but he would not be here *sweating*.

He told himself it was the light and the rain beating on the tent roof. The light was all wrong. As it came through the tent walls, it had to be either early morning and time to get up, or late evening and much too early to sleep. It would not turn into decent night.

What with the rain, it was amazing the things he had been able to hear. There were the quiet songs of the Titanides and the crackle and pop of the fire. Someone had approached his tent, stood outside it, casting her shadow on the walls, and walked away. Later he had heard voices in conversation and people walking away. Much later someone had returned.

And now someone else was approaching. Not even the Wizard would cast a shadow as large as that.

"Knock, knock."

"Come in, Valiha."

She had a towel with her, and while she stuck her head and torso in to hold the tent flaps open, she used it to wipe the mud from her front hooves before stepping onto the canvas floor. She did the same with her back legs, twisting and leaning back while lifting each leg, managing to suggest a dog scratching behind an ear without looking at all awkward. She was wearing a violet rain slicker which was almost a tent in itself. By the time she had removed it and hung it on a peg near the door Chris had worked up considerable curiosity as to the purpose of her visit.

"Do you mind if I light the lantern?"

"Go right ahead."

The tent was Titanide-sized, meaning she could stand erect in the center and had just enough room to turn around. The lamp cast fantastic shadows of her until she hung it from the ridgepole and sat down with her legs folded.

"I can't stay long," she said. "In fact, it might have been a mistake to come here at all. However, here I am."

If she had intended to mystify him, she couldn't have done a better job. Her hands were nervously fiddling with the edge of her pouch, something that was hard for Chris to watch. Her thumbs hooked in the edge of it, and she stretched it out like the elastic band on a pair of bathing trunks.

"I've been upset since I realized that you . . . you really don't remember the hundred revs we spent together after I found you wandering beneath Cirocco's Stairs, after your Big Drop."

"How long is a hundred revs?"

"A little over four days, in your reckoning. One rev is sixty-one minutes."

"That's quite a while. Did we have a good time?"

She glanced up at him, then resumed her fumbling.

"I did. You said you did, too. What has bothered me is that you might have the impression that I was using you solely for a good-luck charm, as I said when you first returned to your senses."

Chris shrugged. "It wouldn't bother me if you had. And if I brought you good luck, I'm glad I did."

"That isn't it." She bit her lower lip, and Chris was surprised to see a tear, quickly wiped away. "Gaea curse me," she moaned, "I can't say it right. I don't even know what I'm trying to say, except thank you. Even though you don't remember." She dug into her pouch and came out with something which she pressed into his hand. "This is for you," she said, and stood and was gone practically before he knew what had happened.

He opened his hand and looked at the Titanide egg. Its dominant color was yellow, like Valiha herself, but there were swirls of black. There was an inscription on its hard surface, in tiny, spidery English characters:

Valiha (Aeolian Solo) Madrigal: Long-Odds Major
26th Gigarev; 97,618,685th Rev (Anno Domini 2100)
"Gaea Says Not Why She Spins."

19.

Eternal Youth

"If you're worried about a paternity suit," Cirocco said, "you can forget it. Titanides don't work that way."

"I didn't mean . . . maybe I'm expressing myself badly."

Chris was in Cirocco's canoe. He sat toward the middle while the Wizard lolled in the bow. Her head was on a pillow. There were puffy blue bags under her eyes, and her complexion was unhealthy. Even so, it was a great improvement on a few hours ago. Chris had elected to travel with Cirocco with the intent of quizzing her about human-Titanide sex but had put it off when he saw her face.

He was not the only one to switch boats. Gaby was now riding with Hautbois and Robin, while Valiha and Psaltery led the flotilla in canoes that rode high in front.

They had passed beneath Cirocco's Stairs, an experience Chris could have done without. The massive cable hanging above him had taken him back to the Golden Gate on that windy day when Dulcimer set his feet on the path which led to Gaea. Cirocco's Stairs looked like a bridge cable. In place of the tower, however, there was just the gaping conical mouth of the Rhea Spoke, dwindling into infinity and taking the unseen cable with it. The cable was an exponential curve, a geometric abstraction made real. A dozen Golden Gates set end to end could not have spanned its terrible immensity.

Now they were a few minutes from the confluence of Ophion with the river Melpomene. Already the waters moved a little faster, eager to challenge the Asteria Mountains, darkly visible in the east.

Chris looked away from the river and tried again.

"For one thing, I know she's already pregnant. I'm presuming a child is not at issue. Am I right in that?"

"You're still thinking in terms of mommies and daddies," Cirocco said. "What you are here is a potential forefather, and

Valiha a potential foremother. The egg could be implanted in . . . oh, say Hornpipe, for instance, and he'd be the hindmother; then any of the other three could fertilize it, including Valiha."

"Not until I knew you a lot better," Hornpipe said from the rear of the boat.

"This isn't funny to me," Chris said.

"I'm sorry. A child is definitely not at issue. One, I wouldn't approve it. Two, no Titanide would even start a proposal for a child without much more thought. And three, you've got the egg."

"Then what *is* at issue here? Is there a great significance to the gift? What is she telling me?"

Cirocco did not look as though she really wanted to answer questions, but she sighed and relented.

"It does not necessarily mean anything. Oh, it means she likes you, that's certain. For one thing, she wouldn't have made love to you unless she did, but she wouldn't have given you the egg unless she *still* did. Titanides are sentimental, see? Walk into any Titanide home, and you'll find a rack of these on the wall. Not one in a thousand ever gets used or is even intended for use. They're common as . . . as condoms on lover's lane."

Hornpipe made a loud raspberry.

"It was a rather low image, wasn't it?" Cirocco managed to grin.

"What's a condom?"

"Before your time, huh? A one-time prophylactic. Anyway, the analogy is apt. Every time a female has frontal intercourse one of these pops out two hectorevs later. That's two hundred revs, in case they aren't still teaching the metric system where you come from. You know, it's a hell of a note when a Titanide knows what a condom is—he's never seen one!—and a human doesn't. What do they *teach* you? That history started in 2096?"

"Actually, I think they include 2095 now."

Cirocco massaged her forehead and smiled weakly.

"Sorry. I digress. Your education or lack of it is none of my business. Back to Titanides . . . most of the eggs get thrown away. If not immediately, then during the next spring cleaning. Some are kept for the sentimental value, long after they've expired. They last about five years, by the way.

"What you have to bear in mind is the dual nature of Titanide sex. Hind sex is for two purposes, one much more common than the other. One is sheer recreation: hedonism. They do it publicly. The other purpose is procreation, when they're allowed to, which is not nearly as often as they'd like. Frontal sex is different. Very seldom is it done just to make an egg. Almost always it's an expression of close friendship or love. Not precisely the love you and I know because Titanides don't pair-bond. But they do love. That's one of the things I know for sure, and my list of those things is short. A Titanide will hind-sex with someone he or she would not dream of front-sexing with. Frontal sex is sacred.

"Now this has been relaxed some when dealing with humans, who *can't* hind-sex. The more liberal elements of Titanide thought hold that it is moral to have frontal sex with a human for fun. It should still be done in private, but one doesn't need to love the human or be close friends. Hornpipe?"

"This is true," the Titanide said.

"Why don't you take over?" Cirocco suggested. "I've got a headache."

When Chris turned around, Hornpipe stopped paddling for a moment and spread his hands.

"There isn't much more to say. Cirocco covered it well."

"Then you're saying the egg is just a keepsake. The reason Valiha seemed upset was that I had forgotten what happened. She isn't in love with me."

"Oh, no, I'm saying nothing of the sort. Valiha is an old-fashioned girl who has never had sex with a human. She loves you desperately."

In Gaea, stormy weather caused the nights to steal more land than they normally occupied. As the party passed the mouth of the Melpomene, they entered an area normally classed as a twilight zone. Now it was night.

But night in Gaea could never become total. In clear weather, even the center of Rhea was as bright as an Earthly night with a full moon. Under clouds the gloom thickened but never became impenetrable. The land in the foothills of the Asteria Mountains was lit by a soft glow from above the cloud layer. Lanterns were set in niches to the rear of the canoes. The group traveled on.

Tall trees began to appear on the shore. They were scattered at first but soon became a thick forest. The trees were a lot like pines, with straight trunks and thin leaves. There was little underbrush. Chris saw herds of six-legged creatures that traveled in prodigious hops, like kangaroos. Cirocco told him the area was a remnant of the protoforest Gaea had brought forth as a young Titan, that simple plants and animals like the ones they now saw still thrived in the highlands.

As they began to move into a narrow canyon, Chris experienced an optical illusion. He thought he was canoeing uphill. The surrounding hills slanted toward the east. The trees grew just a few degrees from the vertical, their tops ten or twenty meters east of their roots. After looking at it for a time, the eye concluded everything was really vertical and the river was defying gravity. It was one of Gaea's jokes.

It began to rain as the Titanides were beaching the boats just below the beginnings of a steep ravine. There was a lot of noise in the air. Chris thought of a huge waterfall or continuous waves crashing on a beach.

"Aglaia," Gaby said as she joined Chris and Valiha in pulling a canoe onto the land. "You probably won't see her unless the clouds break up."

"What's Aglaia?"

Gaby described the workings of the trio of river pumps while the Titanides broke down the canoes. The work went quickly. The silvery skin was loosened from the wooden framework, folded into small bundles, and stowed in the saddlebags. He wondered what they were going to do with the ribs, keels, and floorboards. The answer, apparently, was to leave them behind.

"We can make new canoes when we need them," Valiha explained. "That won't be until we're across the Midnight Sea and into Crius."

"How will we cross the sea then? Hold the Wizard's hand and walk?"

Valiha did not deign to reply.

The humans mounted up, and they were off into gathering darkness.

"I built this road, a long time ago," Gaby said.

"Really? What for? And why isn't it kept up?"

They were on the section of the Circum-Gaea Highway Gaby had traveled on her way to the Melody Shop. The Titanides were taking turns clearing a way through entangling vines.

"Hautbois up there with her machete is one reason. Things grow pretty fast, so the road would require a lot of upkeep and no one was willing to do it. Not very many people ever made the round trip. It was a crazy project in the first place. Nobody wanted it but Gaea, but her wants are pretty important here, so I built it."

"With what?"

"Titanides, mostly. To build the bridges, I'd blimp in a couple hundred of them. For leveling and grading and laying asphalt, I—"

"Asphalt? You're kidding."

"No, you can still see some of it when the light's better. Gaea specified one lane of blacktop, wide enough for a two-meter axle, no grades steeper than ten percent. We put in fifty-seven rope suspension bridges and a hundred twenty-two on pilings. A lot are still standing, but I'd think twice before using them. We'll have to take each one as it comes."

Gaby had mentioned the highway before. Chris decided she wanted to talk about it, for whatever reason, but would need some prompting. He was willing.

"You're not going to tell me you...blimped in? Carried asphalt in on blimps. You said they wouldn't go near a fire, and besides, that sounds like a lot of asphalt."

"It was. No, Gaea whomped up something—several things, actually—that made the job a lot easier. Not too pleasant, though. There was one critter the size of a *Tyrannosaurus rex*, who ate trees. I used fifty of them. They'd clear a path through forests and leave big piles of wood pulp. I think they could digest about a thousandth of what they ate, so they ate a *hell* of a lot of trees. Then there was something else—and I swear this is the truth—a thing about the size of a subway car that ate wood pulp and shit asphalt. You wouldn't *believe* the smell. This wasn't good clean asphalt—which, come to think of it, doesn't smell all that great by itself—this...this *crap* was loaded with esters and ketones and I don't know what. Think of a whale that's been dead for three weeks. That'll give you a start.

"Luckily nobody had to stay close to the things. The saw-mills—that's what we called the tree eaters—they weren't too

bright, but they were docile and could be trained to eat only
trees that were sprayed with a certain scent. We'd go on ahead,
blazing trail, and the sawmills would follow. Then we'd get
behind them and shovel all that wood pulp where we wanted
the road to be. Well, then we'd put the 'stilleries—the asphalt
creatures, you understand. We called them distilleries. We'd
put them on the trail of pulp, and they'd start doing their thing.
We'd stay ten kilometers upwind. There wasn't much chance
they'd go astray because wood pulp was all they could eat.
And not just any wood pulp, but stuff that had gone through
the stomach of a sawmill. They had the brains of a slug.

"Two or three weeks later, when the stuff had detoxified,
I'd move in a crew of forty or fifty Titanides to pull big rollers
and pack the stuff down. Presto. A highway. Of course, dumb
as they were, sometimes the 'stilleries did get a little confused,
like if we'd not swept up the traces of pulp from some spot.
Then they'd get stalled and start to whine like a two-hundred-
tonne puppy. We'd draw lots to see who had to go in and
straighten the damn thing out. That happened several times,
and it was almost worth your life to go in there, let me tell
you. Until I solved it."

"How did you do that?"

"Found a Titanide who'd taken a sword across the face in
the Angel War," Gaby said smugly. "The nerves were cut, and
she couldn't smell. She'd go in and lead the thing on the end
of a rope. When it was all over, I had Rocky give her a
hindmothership at the next Carnival, I was so grateful.

"Of course, it isn't paved all the way. That would be sillier
than usual, even for Gaea. There's no point in spreading blacktop over desert sands or on ice. One-third of Gaea is desert or
frozen over. There we blasted paths when we could and left
a series of way stations. If you ever get in trouble and come
across a hut with the words 'Plauget Construction Company'
on the door, you'll know who put it there."

"How do you get wagons across the ice then?" Chris asked.

"Huh? Oh, the same way you do with any ice. Not that
many people ever took wagons on the Circum-Gaea. You
switch to a sleigh. You follow the frozen Ophion in Thea; it's
about the only way through the mountains anyway. Oceanus
is one big frozen sea, nice and flat, so that's no problem, if
anything in Oceanus can be said to be no problem. In the

deserts, you just find your way across as best you can. We made some oases."

Chris saw an odd expression on Gaby's face. It was a little wistful but mostly happy. He knew she was looking back fondly to the old days, and he hated to ask his next question. But he thought it was why she had been talking in the first place.

"Why did you build it?"

"Huh?"

"What's it for? You said yourself there was no demand for a road. There's been no maintenance and no traffic. Why build it?"

Gaby sat up from her usual position, facing the rear, leaning against Psaltery's back. Chris couldn't get used to the position; he liked to see where he was going. The problem, as Gaby had discovered long ago, was that a Titanide was too high and wide in the torso to see around.

"I did it because Gaea told me to. Hired me to, rather. I told you that."

"Yeah. You also said it was an unpleasant job."

"Not all of it," she pointed out. "The bridges were a challenge. I liked that. I wasn't a road builder—I wasn't even an engineer, though it wasn't hard to pick up the math—so I used a couple people from the embassy at first. For the first five-hundred kilometers I learned from them. After that I worked out my own solutions." She was silent awhile, then looked at him.

"But you're right. I didn't do it because I wanted to. I was paid, like I'm paid for all the work I do for Gaea. I'd have passed this one up, but the wages turned out to be too good."

"What was it?"

"Eternal youth." She grinned. "Or near enough to it. Rocky gets it free, for being the Wizard. I found out not too long after I got here that the offer didn't extend to me. So I worked out this arrangement with Gaea. I'm getting immortality on the installment plan. The thing about being a free-lance, you don't get the medical benefits of a salaried employee. If Gaea ever runs out of things for me to do, I'm washed up. I'll probably shrivel up in a day."

"You're not serious."

"No. I expect I'll just start to age. It might be more rapidly. But I've got this—hey, where's Rocky?"

Chris looked behind him, then realized Hornpipe had gone to the front to blaze trail. A fog had descended, further worsening the visibility. He could barely see Robin and Hautbois, and Hornpipe was completely swallowed in the mist.

Psaltery surged ahead, and Valiha quickened her pace to draw even with Hautbois. The two teams quickly caught Gaby, who was engaged in heated conversation with Hornpipe.

"She said she was going back to speak to you, and—"

"Are you *sure*, Hornpipe?"

"What are you . . . oh. I didn't, honest. She said she was going to ride with you for a while. She might be hurt. Perhaps she fell, and—"

"Not bloody likely." Gaby scowled and rubbed her forehead. "You can stay here, backtrack a little, see if you can find her. The rest of us will go on. I'm pretty sure I know where she is."

Macchu Pichu perched high above the layer of cottony clouds. It was possible to stand on the front porch of the Melody Shop, lit by the incredible celestial spotlight, and look out over a vast sea of mist that stretched between the highland cliff ramparts, north to south. It spilled from the invisible spoke mouth over Oceanus and came tumbling over Hyperion. In places updrafts had rolled themselves into fluffy, hollow tubes as they passed into higher and thus slower-moving regions of the atmosphere. The tubes were cyclonic disturbances set on edge and attentuated until they looked like toppled tornadoes. They were called mistrollers. Occasionally violent storms came out of Oceanus, and those were called steamrollers.

Chris stood watching the clouds while the others went in searching for Cirocco. Presently he heard the sound of glass breaking and a heavy object hitting the floor. Someone shouted. He heard feet pounding up a staircase, pursued by the odd sound of Titanide hooves on carpet. After a while a door slammed, and the sounds ceased. He continued to watch the mist.

Gaby came out, holding a wet towel to her face.

"Well, it looks like we'll be here another day, getting her on her feet." She stood beside Chris, catching her breath. "Is anything wrong?"

"I'm fine," Chris lied.

"It was pretty slick, what she did," Gaby said. "She called

Titantown with a radio seed she'd hidden. Nobody's sure what she said, but it sounded like she was in trouble because she told a friend to blimp in and wait for her beside the road. The fog was her doing. She told Gaea she needed some cover. She slipped away and joined up with the Titanide, who brought her here. She's been here three revs, which is time for a lot of drinking. So we'll have to . . . hey, are you sure you're okay?"

He didn't have time for her questions. The fog was rearing up like a monstrous wave. There were foul beasts hiding in the basement. He could hear them. When he reached out blindly, he grabbed the blackened arm of a pale corpse who yammered, worms crawling from her mouth, reaching out for him. . . .

He began to scream.

20.

Resumption

Robin looked up as Gaby joined her on the porch. She had been sitting on the steps, reading a yellowing manuscript she had found in Cirocco's study. It was a fascinating work, a description of the interactions of flora and fauna and...the only word for them was undecided organisms, all living within a kilometer of the Melody Shop. It was not a scholarly book but was written in an economical style that Robin found wonderfully readable. The manuscript had been sitting atop a roll-top desk beside a shelf of books containing a dozen volumes authored by C. Jones.

"How are the patients?" Robin asked. Gaby looked haggard. She doubted the woman had slept since the encampment by the river... how long ago? Two dekarevs? Three? Possibly she had not even slept then.

"Wrong verb," Gaby said, sitting beside her. "How *is* the patience? Yours."

Robin shrugged. "I'm not in a hurry. I'm broadening my mind. I had no idea the Wizard could write so well."

Gaby batted an imaginary fly in front of her face, looking sour.

"I wish you'd stop calling her the Wizard. It gives her too much to live up to. She's just a human being, like you."

"I know that...maybe you're right. I'll stop."

"Well, I didn't mean to snap at you." She looked out over the lawn. "The patients are doing as well as can be expected. Chris has stopped screaming, but he's still curled up in the corner. Valiha can't get him to eat. Rocky's locked in her bedroom. All the booze went over the bridge, so far as I know. Of course, with an alcoholic, you are never sure. She could have it hidden anywhere." She put her face in her hands as if to rest for a moment. Robin saw her mouth twist and heard a pitiful sound. Gaby was crying.

148

"I have her locked up in her room," she managed to say between the hoarse sobs. "I can't believe it. I can't believe it's come to this. When she sees me, she curses. She pukes her guts out and sweats and shivers, and I can't do a thing about it. I can't help her."

Robin was mortified. She had no idea what to do. Sitting beside a woman one respected and watching her consumed with tears was an unthinkable situation. She did not know what to do with her hands. She fingered the pages of the manuscript in her lap, stopped when she realized she was shredding it.

With a shock, she remembered crying in front of Hautbois. That had been different, of course. Hautbois had said so, and she had soon realized it was all right. But the Titanide had not just sat there.

Hesitantly, Robin put her arm over Gaby's shoulders. Gaby responded, apparently without shame, turning and burying her face in Robin's shoulder.

"It's all right," Robin said.

"I loved her so much," Gaby moaned. "I still love her. What a joke. After seventy-five years, I still love her."

Gaby lifted Cirocco's head from the pillow and held a glass to her lips.

"Drink this. It's good for you."

"What is it?"

"Pure, fresh water. The best thing in the world."

Cirocco's lips were pale in a moist gray face. Gaby could feel the dampness in the tangled hair as she held Cirocco's head steady with one hand in back. There was a lump there, picked up when she cracked it against the brass bar at the head of the bed.

She sipped, then began to drink noisily.

"Hey, hey, not too much at once. You haven't kept much down lately."

"But I'm thirsty, Gaby," Cirocco whined. "Listen, babe, I won't yell at you anymore. I'm sorry I did." Her voice took on a wheedling tone. "But listen, honey, I'd do just about anything for a drink. Just for old times' sake—"

Gaby clapped her hands to Cirocco's cheeks and pressed them together, making her lips pout in a way that would have been comical in other circumstances. Cirocco cringed back, her eyes red and frightened. She far outweighed Gaby but seemed to have no thought of struggling. All the fight had gone out of her.

"No," Gaby said. "No today, and no tomorrow. I didn't know if I could keep on saying no, so I destroyed all the liquor in the house, so don't even bother to ask me anymore, okay?"

Tears were leaking from the corners of Cirocco's eyes, but Gaby, looking closely, was sickened to see a hint of craftiness there. So there was a cache, something put by for an emergency. At least it wasn't in this room. The door must be kept locked.

"Okay. I am feeling better. I'll be up and around soon, and I'm through with drinking. You'll see."

"Yeah." Gaby looked away, then forced herself back. "I didn't come up here for promises. Not that kind. I wanted to know if you're still with us. With me."

"With . . . oh, you mean . . . what we talked about." She looked quickly around the room, as if to surprise concealed listeners. She shivered and seemed to want to sit up. Gaby helped her. Cirocco pulled the blankets tightly around herself. The fireplace roared and crackled and kept the room heated to around thirty-five sweltering degrees, but Cirocco could not get warm.

"I've . . . I've been thinking about it," Cirocco said, and Gaby was sure she was lying. She had been thinking of getting a drink. It didn't matter. Her fears would now speak directly, uncensored by any scheme.

"I was thinking maybe we . . . maybe we should, should think about it some more. I mean, let's don't rush into it. It's a big step to take. I'll . . . sure, I'll still go with you, but we shouldn't . . . really shouldn't go all the way through with it, you know? Shouldn't really talk to, to Rhea and Crius and—"

"Twenty years isn't exactly rushing it," Gaby pointed out.

"Well, yeah, sure, but what I'm saying. . . ." She trailed off, obviously unsure of what she was saying. "If I could just have . . . uh-oh, no, I won't say it. I won't ask. I'll be a good girl, okay?" She smiled weakly, ingratiatingly.

"So you're going to back out?"

Cirocco frowned. "I didn't say that. Did I? Come on, Gaby, you know it's dangerous. You said so yourself. What we ought to do is back off, don't rush into it, and in a little while . . . well, it'll be obvious what . . ." Once more she lost the train of thought.

"Okay," Gaby said, getting up. "I don't know if we have the time, but I thought you'd say something like this. I'm not sure Gene's going to give us the time. I think he was up to something. I don't know what. But this has to be started now, not later. It's just a feasibility study, Rocky. Think of it that way."

"I don't know if I can . . . well, do it without arousing suspicion."

"Sure you can."

"No. No, this is too rash. I've thought it over. Wait; then I'll help you."

"No." She waited for Cirocco to understand her, saw the feeble smile slowly fade. "It may be too late already. If you won't do it, I will. And I think I'd better tell those two pilgrims they might be better off without us."

Cirocco started to say something, but Gaby didn't want to hear it. She left the room as quickly as she could.

The Melody Shop had been designed and built with Titanides in mind. The ceilings were high, and the doors were wide. The few carpets were placed only where there were human-sized chairs, a reminder to Titanides to stay off them. Much of the hardwood floor was covered in sawdust or straw. The big table in the library had a human side and a Titanide side, half with chairs and half with straw floors. It had high windows that faced east, toward the Midnight Sea, and a stone fireplace, now cold. Gaby had gathered everyone there because of the view. While she said what she had to say, they could look out over the land they had yet to cover and thus perhaps make a more informed decision.

"I guess there's no easy way to say this. It's doubly hard because of some of the things I've already said to some of you. But from this point I'm rescinding all promises about Cirocco. She is much worse off than I thought. I don't know yet if she'll be going with me, but whether she does or not, it's time to reevaluate decisions you all made based on wrong information. I told you that Rocky would pull out of it and be useful and . . . and that she'd be an asset rather than a burden. I can no longer stand behind that."

She scanned the six faces. With the exception of Hautbois, she knew what each of the Titanides would say. About Chris and Robin she was not so sure. Chris had problems of his own,

possibly of a temporary nature, and she would never dare guess
what Robin might do.

"It boils down to this. I will be going on around the rim.
Rocky may join me. You all are welcome if you wish to come.
If Rocky goes, she may let one or more of us down in some
important ways. By that I mean a little more than just the fact
we'd have to take care of her if she managed to get drunk
again. That's not the problem. Whether this makes you angry
or not, Chris, and you, too, Robin, either of you could put us
in the same position and probably will. In a way Rocky has
no more control of it than you two do. That I'm willing to
accept. I can't tell you why, I guess, but I do, for all three of
you. I'll take care of you when you're incapacitated, and so
will all the Titanides."

"We actually view your disabilities as no more serious than
the human trait of falling asleep," Hornpipe put in hesitantly.
"It is the same thing for us. When you sleep, we have to look
out for you."

"He's got a point," Gaby said. "Anyway, my fears about
Rocky are that she will let us down through a failure of nerve.
I never thought I'd have to say that, but there it is. I'm no
longer sure she'd put the welfare of the group over her own
personal needs. I feel I hardly know her. But I have to view
her as unreliable.

"As I said, I'm going anyway. What I need to know is what
your plans are. Hornpipe?"

"I'll stay with Cirocco. If she goes, fine."

Gaby nodded. She raised her eyebrows to Psaltery, who
barely bothered to nod. She knew he would go with her.

"Valiha?"

"I would like to continue on," she said. "But only if Chris
goes."

"Right. Hautbois?"

"I must complete the circuit," she said. "I have never been
a hindmother, and this is my best chance."

"Okay. Glad to have you. What about you, Chris?"

It looked like an effort for Chris to so much as lift his gaze
from the table. He had recovered from his latest attack hours
ago, but as usual with attacks in which there had been no
memory loss, he was emotionally exhausted and had no more
self-esteem than a whipped dog.

"I think you're minimizing the problem," he muttered. "The

problem with me, I mean. Why should I expect more of Cirocco than I can of myself?" Valiha reached for his hand, but he jerked it away. "I'll go if you'll have me."

"We knew what we were getting into," Gaby said. "You're welcome here. Robin?"

There was a long pause. Gaby worried while Robin made up her mind. The witch's alternative, so far as Gaby could see, was a climb up the spoke. Robin was capable of setting out on that trip, knowing she would die on the way.

"I'll go," she said finally.

"Sure? Couldn't you back out with honor?"

"Since you offered, yes, I could. But I'll go."

Gaby had no intention of questioning her beyond that.

"That leaves only Rocky and Hornpipe as maybes. All right. Gather up your things. Meet me on the front porch in one rev."

It was a somber departure.

The clouds which had for two hectorevs broken on the precipice of Machu Picchu were now sending outriders rolling over the Melody Shop. The celestial spotlight was blotted out. The great white house stood silent in the gloom, its life drained away. Inside, Gaby was latching the storm shutters.

The saddlebags of the Titanides had been reprovisioned. There was little left to do, but still, Gaby bustled about like a vacationer fearful she would forget something. Chris and Robin both knew she was hoping for Cirocco to make an appearance, and neither of them expected the Wizard to do so.

A bolt of lightning flashed between the twin peaks of Cirocco's mountain retreat. The Titanides did not react, but Chris and Robin milled nervously. Chris stepped into Valiha's hand and settled himself on her back. Robin mounted Hautbois. They all waited.

Gaby came out and jumped onto Psaltery. She looked back at the house, in time to see the doorknob turn. Cirocco came out, tall in her red blanket and bare feet. She looked ashen and weak. She came down the steps carefully and walked over to Psaltery and Gaby. She held her hands over her head.

"I don't have anything. See for yourself."

"I'm not going to search you, Rocky."

"Oh." It didn't seem to matter to her. She dropped her arms, then leaned on Psaltery's flank. "You're right, you know. I'd better go with you."

"All right." There was a note of relief in Gaby's voice, but little enthusiasm.

It began to rain once more as they crossed the rope bridge. On the other side, Robin heard a droning noise. It was hard to find the source with the mountains all around. She heard it get louder and then fade away. Both Gaby and Psaltery were anxiously scanning the clouds.

"What was that?"

Gaby shivered. "Don't ask."

21.

Hands Across the Sea

"It's a good thing these depressions are transitory," Chris said.

"I should say so." Valiha turned her head to look at Chris. "I have never seen anyone as withdrawn as you were. It must take a lot out of you."

Chris silently agreed with that. He was not completely over it but was making the effort to put on a bright face. One more night's sleep, and he might feel life still had some point.

They had not returned to Ophion after their side trip to the Melody Shop. Though the Circum-Gaea Highway followed the river's bank through the Upper Muse Valley, slides had made it impassable in several places. Instead, they took a path through the Asterias. To call it a goat trail would have been like saying a tightrope was the Seaboard Highway. There were places where the humans had to dismount and cling to ropes strung by a Titanide who went ahead, using toeholds so scanty they might have been drawn on the rock. In this, as in so many other things, Titanides were a lot better than Chris. He was beginning to find that annoying. His consolation was that Cirocco and Robin were no better, though Gaby seemed to be part goat and part fly.

There were crevasses to span. The big ones were bridged by lassoing a rock on the other side and crossing hand over hand beneath the rope. Finally, Chris was able to do something better than anyone else. The Titanides could do it, but just barely. He could hardly bear to look as they dangled by their hands.

Any gap less than ten meters wide, however, did not rate a rope bridge. The Titanides simply hurdled it. The first such jump took ten years off his life. After that he closed his eyes.

But at last they descended the final slope. Below them was

a narrow band of forest, a narrower beach of black sand, and Nox, the Midnight Sea. It shimmered in the silvery light. Embedded in the water were nebular drifts of luminescence, cold blue beneath the brighter surface reflections. There were harder, more compact light sources, some a warm yellow and others deep and green.

"The light clouds are colonies of fish about this long."

Chris looked up and found that Hornpipe was walking beside Valiha. Cirocco was holding thumb and forefinger a few centimeters apart.

"They're more like insects, actually, but water-breathing. They're true colonies, with a hive brain like ants or bees. But they don't have a queen. They apparently hold free elections, from what I've been able to learn. Complete with primaries and campaigns and propaganda in the form of pheromones released into the water at election time. The winner is allowed to grow to be a meter long and holds office for seven kilorevs. His function is mainly morale. He releases chemicals that keep the hive happy. If the leader is killed, the hive stops eating and dissolves. At the end of the term the hive eats him. Sanest political system I ever saw."

Chris looked at her hard but could see no hint that she was pulling his leg. He wasn't about to ask her. It was a big surprise that she was talking at all, and he was willing to listen to whatever she felt moved to say. Since leaving the Melody Shop, she had been quiet, exhausted all the time. Though he had seen ample evidence of her human failings, he was more than a little in awe of her.

"Nox is one of the most sterile places in Gaea," she went on. "Not many creatures can live here. The water's too clean. There are abysses in there ten kilometers deep. Water gets pumped out and taken to the heat-exchanger fins, boiled, and distilled. When it comes back, it's crystal-clear. If there was light in here, it would be beautiful; you could see down for hundreds of meters."

"It's rather beautiful as it is," Chris ventured.

"Maybe you're right. Yes, I guess it is beautiful to look at. I don't much care for crossing it. Bad memories." She sighed, then pointed out over the water. "That cable in the middle attaches to an island called Minerva. I guess we have to call it an island; the cable is practically the whole thing. There's no real shoreline. We'll be stopping off there for a short time."

"What are the other lights? The points."
"Submarines."

Upon arriving on the beach, the Titanides disencumbered themselves of their saddlebags and removed gleaming wedges of steel that proved to be the heads of axes. Moving into the forest with their knives, they soon fashioned handles and began felling trees by the dozen. Chris watched from a safe distance after offering to help and, as usual, getting a polite refusal.

The trees were remarkable. Each was fifteen meters high, straight, and fifty centimeters in diameter. They had no branches but at the tops were giant, gossamer fronds. Chris was reminded of darts sticking out of a board.

"Do the trees seem unusual?" Gaby had joined him while he watched.

"What are they called?"

"You've got me there. I've heard several names. None has stuck officially. I used to call them telephone poles, but that dated me too much. In the woods they're called cabin trees by people who're building cabins. By the sea they're raft trees. It's the same plant, either way. It's probably best to call 'em log trees."

Chris laughed. "Every tree is a log tree when it's cut down."

"But there's no tree that's so *good* at it as this one. It's an example of Gaea's cooperative side. She sometimes makes things almost too easy. Watch this."

She walked to the top frond of a fallen tree, took out her knife, and deftly severed it. Chris saw the thin tube was hollow. She put her knife into it and slashed upward. The smooth bark ripped and began to tear. It tore the entire length of the trunk, folded back, and bared a moist bole of yellow wood that might have been machined on a lathe.

"I'm impressed."

"That's not all. Valiha, can I borrow that a minute?" The Titanide gave Gaby her ax. Chris knelt while she examined the perfectly flat end revealed when the bark peeled away. There was a grid of lines on it. Gaby swung the ax against one of the lines. It made a solid *thunk*.

"I'm not as good at this as they are," Gaby muttered. She pulled the blade free and swung again. With a dry clatter the log partitioned itself into a dozen smooth planks. She set one foot on the stack, slung the ax on her shoulder, and grinned as she flexed the muscles of one arm like a scale-model lumberjack.

"I'm im*pressed*."

"It weren't nothin'. Anyway, that's not the end of the amazing wonders. The bark can be turned into strips that are as strong as a steel band. You can use them to lace the logs into a raft. For the next couple revs the stumps will ooze epoxy glue. Only about one in twenty of the trees will fracture into planks. We'll use the regular boles for the bottom of the raft and the planks for decking. That way a stray jolt won't turn the whole thing into a big bundle of lumber. In about four or five revs the raft ought to be ready to launch. End of lecture."

"Not quite," Chris said. "You mentioned this being part of Gaea's cooperative side. Are these trees new things? I mean—"

"Like the Titanides are new? No, I don't think so. More likely they're very old. Older than Gaea. They're one of the species designed by the same folks who built Gaea's forebears, billions of years ago. They seemed to like things handy. So there's the plants that grow transistors and such on one end of the scale, and the basics like these trees and the smilers— which are hypercattle that you can harvest meat from without killing them. Either the designers planned for periods when civilization would fall, or they didn't like noisy factories."

Chris walked down the beach by himself, vaguely troubled. He knew he should be feeling grateful to be along with Cirocco and Gaby, learning all these things that should prove useful if he had to strike out on his own. Instead, he was struck by his own uselessness in the scheme of things. Everything seemed well under control. He couldn't cook, couldn't build a raft, row a canoe—he could not even keep up if called upon to walk. He was supposed to be seeking out adventure, finding a way to become a hero. Instead, he was along for the ride. He no longer truly believed they would encounter anything Gaby and the Titanides could not handle.

The beach sand was very fine. It sparkled, even in the darkness of Rhea. Walking near the trees was tiring, so he moved near the water's edge, where dampness had turned the sand into a firm surface. Nox was still for such a large body of water. Low waves undulated and crested in slow motion. The sound they made was more of a hiss than a roar. Foam lapped at his feet, then melted into the sand.

He had gone out with the intention of washing up. Two days of climbing rocks and riding muddy trails had left him gritty. When he could barely hear the sound of the Titanides' labors, he judged he had come far enough. He stumbled over something nearly invisible against the black sand. It was a pile of clothing.

"Did you bring any soap?"

He squinted toward the sound of the voice and saw a dark circle against the water. Robin raised herself from her squatting position, stood in water up to her waist. Concentric silver rings spread away from her.

"It just so happens that I did," Chris said, digging the soft round ball from his pocket. "The Wi . . . Cirocco said the water was cold."

"It's not too bad. Bring it out here, would you?" She sat again, until only her head showed.

Chris got out of his clothes and cautiously stepped into the water. It was chilly, but he had been in worse. The shore sloped gradually. There were no slimy creatures underfoot, or even any shells. It was smooth, uniform sand, suitable for the filling of hourglasses.

He swam the last few meters, then stood beside her and handed her the ball of soap. She began rubbing it over her upper body.

"Don't drop it," he cautioned. "We'd never find it again."

"I'll be careful. Where did you learn to do that?"

"What? You mean swim? I was so young I don't remember. Just about everyone I know can swim. Can't you?"

"Nobody I know can. Would you teach me?"

"Sure, if we have time."

"Thanks. Would you soap my back?" She handed him the ball.

The request surprised him, but he agreed readily enough. He used his hands perhaps a little more than he had to, and when she did not object, he kneaded her shoulders. There was firm muscle beneath the cold skin. She did the same for him, having to reach high to get his shoulders. He knew he had not even begun to understand her and wished that were not the case. With any other woman he would have felt at ease. He would have kissed her and let her decide what to do from there. He would have accepted her answer, yes or no. With Robin, he didn't feel he dared pose the question.

But why not? he wondered. Did everything have to be done on her terms? Where he came from, it was perfectly all right to make the offer, so long as one was prepared to be turned down. He had no idea how they did such things in the Coven, except to know that the situation could never arise between a man and a woman. Perhaps she was as confused as he, socially.

So when she stopped rubbing his back, he turned, put one hand gently to her cheek, and kissed her on the lips. When he drew away, she looked puzzled.

"What was that for?"

"Because I like you. Don't you kiss in the Coven?"

"Of course we do." She shrugged. "How strange. I hadn't realized it, but you smell different. Not actually unpleasant, but different." She turned from him and dived awkwardly toward the shore. She windmilled her arms and thrashed her legs without really getting anywhere and soon had to stand up and spit water.

Chris sank until the water lapped at his chin. He had never been rebuffed in quite that way before. He knew she had not been aware she was turning him down, but it was still deflating.

"I fell into the river when I got here," she said as they slogged through the shallow water toward the beach. "I did something to get to shore because I knew I had to. But I can't put it all together now."

"You probably didn't have far to go, or the current was helping you."

"Can you show me now?"

"Maybe later."

At the beach he tossed her the soap again. She stood with her feet in the water and washed her lower body. He watched her, wishing there were more light so he could finally get a better look at the tattoos. Abruptly, he decided he had better sit down.

"What's the matter?"

"Nothing."

"I saw what was happening." She frowned at him. "Don't tell me you thought you could—"

"It's called the gallant reflex, okay?" Chris was embarrassed and annoyed. "Reflex. I didn't plan to assault you or anything. You just look very, very good standing there, and . . . who could help it?"

"You mean that just by looking at me...." She covered herself with a hand and a forearm. To Chris, it made her look prettier than ever. "I didn't realize that's what my mother meant, or maybe I thought it was another mistake."

"Why didn't you realize? You seem to think we're so different. I'm just like you. Can't you get aroused by looking at someone sexually desirable?"

"Well, sure, but it didn't occur to me that a man—"

"Don't make it into such a tremendous distinction. We have a lot of things in common, whether you like it or not. We both erect, both have orgasms—"

"I'll bear it in mind," she said, tossed him the soap, scooped up her clothes, and hurried off down the beach.

Chris worried that he might have killed a budding friendship. He *did* like her, almost in spite of himself. Or in spite of her. He wanted to be her friend.

A little later he wondered if she had left because of anger. Going back over the conversation, he realized that the point she had chosen to leave could be given another interpretation.

He did not think Robin would be too comfortable with the idea that he was like her. Or, conversely, that she was like him.

The completed raft would not have won any prizes in a boat show, but it was a marvel from the standpoint of size alone, considering the time it had taken to build it. It slid down the ramp which had been its construction site and hit the water with a mighty splash. Chris joined the Titanides in cheering. Robin was yelling, too. They had both had a hand in the finishing stages. The Titanides had shown them how to handle the glue and let them set deck planks in place while the railings were being installed.

It had ample room for the eight of them. There was a small cabin near the bow, large enough to bunk all the humans at once, and a canopy that could be hung to keep the rain off the Titanides. A mast amidships supported a silver Mylar sail with a minimum of rigging. Steering was done with a long tiller. Just aft of the mast was a circle of stones to support the cooking fire.

Gaby, Chris, and Robin gathered by the gangplank while the Titanides carried aboard saddlebags, provisions they had gathered near the beach, and heaps of firewood. Cirocco had already gone aboard and installed herself at the bow, gazing at nothing.

"They want me to name it," Gaby said to Robin. "Somehow I've gotten the reputation around here as the namer of names. I pointed out that we'll be using this raft for only eight days at the most, but they think every ship has to have a name."

"It seems appropriate," Robin said.

"Oh, you think so? Then you name it."

Robin thought for a moment, then said, "*Constance*. Is that all right, to name a ship after—"

"That's fine. A lot better than the first boat I sailed in here."

For several kilometers it was possible to propel *Constance* with long poles. This was fortunate because the wind had departed along with the rain. Everyone but Cirocco lent a hand. Chris enjoyed the hard work. He knew he was not moving the boat nearly so much as the Titanides, but it felt good to be contributing. He put his back into it until the poles would no longer touch bottom.

At that point four oars were rigged, and they took shifts as galley slaves. It was even harder than the poling. After two hours at the oars Robin suffered a violent seizure and had to be taken into the cabin.

During one of his rest periods Chris went around the cabin and found that Cirocco had abandoned her post, presumably to sleep. He stretched out on his back and felt the muscles protest.

The night sky of Rhea was like nothing he had ever dreamed.

In Hyperion, on a clear day, the sky was a uniform yellow blur, unguessably high. Only by following the sweep of the central vertical cable to where—as a mere thread—it penetrated the Hyperion Window could one really define where the solid sky was. Even then one had to keep it firmly in mind that the cable was five kilometers in diameter and not the slim spindle into which perspective and the eye's timid bias transformed it.

Rhea was different. For one thing, Chris was closer to the central Rhea vertical cable than he had ever been to Hyperion's great column. A black shadow that leaped from the sea, it dwindled rapidly and kept rising and rising until it vanished completely. To each side of it were the north and south verticals, improperly named because they both angled toward the center, though not nearly so much as the ones behind him, to the west. The cables vanished because of the darkness, but more important, because Rhea did not have a window arching over it. Rhea lived in the shadow of the vast trumpet-shaped mouth known as the Rhea Spoke.

Had he not known its size and shape from pictures, Chris would never have discovered its true geometry. What he could see was a dark, wide oval high overhead. In reality, it was more than 300 kilometers above the sea. Around the edge of that mouth was a valve that could close like the iris of an eye, isolating the space above it from the rim. It was now wide open, and he could see up into a dark, oblate cylinder the upper end of which, he knew, was another 300 kilometers away, where another valve led to the hub. He could not see that far, through that much dark air. But what he could see resembled the barrel of a gun that might have used planetoids for projectiles. It was aimed right at him, but the threat was so overblown he could not take it seriously.

He knew that between the lower valve and the radius of the Hyperion Window—a vertical distance of about a hundred kilometers—the spoke flared like the bell of a horn until it became one with the relatively thin arch of roof that stretched over the daylight areas on each side of Rhea. Try as he might, he could not see that flaring, though it had been discernible from Hyperion. Another trick of perspective, he concluded.

There were lights somewhere up there in the spoke. He supposed they were the windows he had read about. From here they dwindled like runway lights seen from a landing plane.

He gradually became aware of a more immediate light, to his left and over his head as he reclined on the deck. He sat up and turned around and saw that the surface of Nox was being lit from below with a pearly blue luminescence. At first he thought it was a hive of the sea insects Cirocco had told him about.

"It's a sub," said a voice to his right. He was startled; Cirocco had joined him silently. "I sent messengers a few hours ago, hoping to attract one. But it looks like she'll be too busy to give us a tow." She pointed at the sky to the west, and Chris found a big patch of deeper darkness against the night. He didn't need anyone to tell him it was a blimp, and a big one.

"Not many people have seen this," Cirocco said quietly.

"There aren't any subs in Hyperion because there's no seas. Blimps go anywhere, but subs stay where they're born. Ophion won't hold them."

There was a piercing series of whistles from the blimp, followed by a sizzling and hissing from the rear of *Constance*. Chris understood that the blimp had asked for the fire to be put out, and the Titanides had complied.

He felt Cirocco's hand on his shoulder. She pointed over the water. "Right there," she said. He looked, still conscious of her hand, and saw tentacles writhing upward, thrashing slowly against the water. A slender stalk rose from the mass of them.

"That's her periscope eye. This is about as much of a sub as you'll ever see. Notice the long swelling there on the water? That's her body. She never comes out any more than that."

"But what's she doing?"

"Mating. Be quiet, don't disturb them. I'll fill you in."

The story was straightforward, though not obvious. The blimps and subs were male and female of the same species. Both descended from the sexless children of their union, which were snakelike and nearly brainless until competition had reduced their swarms to a small number of twenty-meter survivors. At that point they grew a brain and tapped some racial source of knowledge that neither Gaea nor the blimp-subs had ever explained to Cirocco. It had nothing to do with nurturing, for from the time they were spawned neither the mothers nor the fathers had anything further to do with them.

But they grew wise in some mysterious way, and eventually made a conscious decision to become male or female, blimp or sub. Each entailed a hazard. The water contained many predators which ate young subs. There was no such risk in the air, but a young blimp could not manufacture his own hydrogen. His fate after metamorphosis would be to sit on the water, an empty bladder, and hope a mature blimp would, so to speak, blow him up. No adult could support more than six or seven in his squadron. If there were no openings, it was just too bad. The decision to differentiate was irrevocable.

The blimps and subs had little to do with each other. They might never come together at all at the watery interface between their worlds but for two facts. There was a species of seaweed that grew only in deep water; without it, the blimps could not survive. And the Titan trees—massive spurs of the body of

Gaea herself, growing more than six kilometers tall and only in the highlands—sprouted leaves near their tops which were vital to the diets of subs.

Amicable mating was in the interest of both sexes.

Something fell from the tendrils which dangled below the midships bulge on the great curve of the blimp's belly. It splashed into the water. The sub's tentacles gathered it in and made it vanish. There was a deep sigh as the blimp vented hydrogen and sank toward the outstretched arms of his lover. Beyond that there was not much to see. The tendrils entwined and the massive bodies touched at the surface of the sea, and they just stayed that way. It was only when waves began to roll the raft that Chris realized how much activity might be concealed by distance.

"There is a lot happening," Cirocco confirmed. "There *is* a way to get closer to the action, by the way. I was once a passenger in a blimp when he got smitten by love. Let me tell you . . . never mind. It's a rough ride."

Cirocco went away as quietly as she had come. Chris continued to watch. Before long he heard hooves on the deck, and Valiha came around the cabin to join him. He was sitting on the edge of the raft, his feet dangling over the side to just reach the water. Valiha sat the same way, and for a moment a trick of the shadows made the equine part of her body vanish. She became a very big woman with shrunken, spindly legs, dangling her devil's feet in the water. The image upset him, and he looked away from her.

"Beautiful, isn't it?" she asked, in English so singsong that for a moment he thought she had sung it in Titanide.

"It's interesting." In truth, he was beginning to tire of it. He was just about to get up when she took his hand, raised it to her mouth, and kissed it.

"Oh."

"Hmmmm?" She looked at him, but he could not think of anything to say. It apparently didn't matter. She kissed him on the cheek, the neck, and the lips. He took a deep breath when he was able.

"Wait. Valiha, wait." She did, looking at him with her great, guileless eyes. "I don't think I'm ready for this. I mean . . . I don't know what to tell you. I just don't think I can handle it. Not now." She continued to search his eyes. He wondered if she was looking for madness, decided that was his own fear speaking. At last she briefly pressed his hand between both of hers, nodded, and let him go. She stood up.

"Let me know when you are. Okay?" She hurried away.

He felt bad about it. Though he tried to analyze his reasons for rejecting her, nothing satisfied. Partly Valiha was a reminder of something he had done while possessed. He was a lot braver at those times, unless he was a lot more timid. It looked as if that had been a brave time because try as he might, he could not come up with a comfortable answer to one question: what did a Titanide and a human *do?* And another: how much life insurance would he need before attempting it?

Valiha was *big.* She scared him to death.

It might have been fifteen minutes later that Gaby came around the side of the cabin and joined him in the bow. He only wanted to be alone with his thoughts, but his hideaway was turning into a parade ground.

She leaned on the rail, whistling, then nudged him.

"Feeling the blues, buddy?"

He shrugged. "It's been a weird eight hours or so. You think something's in the air?"

"Like what?"

"I don't know. Everybody's in love. Out there the sky's in love with the sea. Back onshore I found myself acting foolish over Robin."

Gaby whistled. "Poor boy."

"Yeah. Just a few minutes ago Valiha wanted to pick up where my mad alter ego left off, shooting marbles, as they say." He sighed. "It must be something in the air."

"Well, you know what they say. It makes the world go around. Love, that is. And Gaea spins a hell of a lot faster than the Earth."

He looked at her suspiciously. "You didn't have anything. . . ."

She held her hands up and shook her head. "Not me, friend, I won't bother you. With me, it's once in a blue moon, and usually with girls. I don't go in for the short-term stuff either. I want all my relationships to last. All seventeen of them." She made a face.

"I guess you have a different perspective on it," Chris ventured. "Being as old as you are."

"You'd think so, wouldn't you? Not true. It always hurts.

I want it to last forever, and it never does. And it's my fault. I always end up measuring them by Cirocco, and they never measure up." She coughed nervously. "Well, listen to me. I didn't mean to get into that. I came to stick my nose into your business. You don't have to be afraid of Valiha. Not emotionally, if that's what's bothering you. She would not be jealous, or possessive, or expect it to last long. Titanides have no concept of exclusiveness."

"Did she ask you to tell me that?"

"She'd be furious if she knew. Titanides handle their own affairs and don't want interference. This is Gaby the know-it-all butting in. I'll say one more thing, then butt out. If your reservations are moral—bestiality, maybe?—wise up, friend. Didn't you hear? Even the Catholic Church says it's okay. All the Popes agree, Titanides have souls even if they are heathens."

"What if my objection is physical?"

Gaby laughed merrily and patted his cheek. "Oh, boy, do *you* have some pleasant surprises in store."

22.

The Idol's Eye

The sub was unwilling to interrupt her postcoital bliss to tow the raft to Minerva. Cirocco stood in the bow and tried to woo it in a language combining the less pleasant sounds of asthma and whooping cough, but the big bathyzoote's light grew even fainter as she reached for the abyss. The blimp, who might have helped for a short time, turned out to have business in the west. Blimps were always ready to give a free ride, but only if one wanted to go where the blimp was bound.

It didn't matter. In a few hours a breeze came up from the west. Soon they were at the base of the central Rhea vertical cable.

Robin studied it as they drew nearer. Cirocco had not been exaggerating. Minerva was not really an island; it was more of a shelf. It had been formed over the aeons by barnacleoids, pseudolimpets, near corals, and other Gaean equivalents of sessile mollusks and crustaceans. The problem was that the water level was low—it had, in fact, been dropping gradually for a million years as the cables stretched and Gaea expanded slowly as she aged. This was in addition to the seasonal lows, which included a seventeen-day short cycle and a thirty-year long one. They had arrived near the trough of the long fluctuation, with the result that the main body of the "island" shelved away from the cable 50 meters above the water. The thickness of the shelf varied. At some places it jutted out more than a hundred meters; elsewhere the mass of shells and sand had broken away from wave action or its own weight, and the cable rose vertically. But it was encrusted as far as Robin could see. Two kilometers above her were the corpses of organisms that had lived during Earth's Pliocene Epoch.

She wondered how they intended to land *Constance* when the nearest place to stand was fifty meters up. The answer became apparent as the raft was steered to the south side of the cable. There one of the hundreds of strands had broken near the waterline. The upper end curled away from the cable far above. Reef builders had transformed the lower end into a cove that enclosed a flat circle of land only five meters high.

Constance was soon moored, and Robin followed Gaby and Psaltery through a jagged cleft, stepping on meter-wide shells that still housed living creatures. They emerged onto the flat, severed end of the cable strand, 200 meters in diameter.

It was a strange seashore, backed as it was by the limitless vertical wall of the cable. There were skeletal trees growing from sandy deposits and a clear, still pool near the center. The area was littered with bone-white driftwood.

"We'll be here a day or two," Hautbois said as she passed Robin, carrying a huge burden of tent canvas. "Feeling better?"

"I'm fine, thanks." She smiled at the Titanide, but in truth, she was still shaky from her last bout of palsy. Hautbois had taken good care of her. Without her restraint, Robin would surely have injured herself.

She snagged Gaby's arm as she passed by and fell in step beside her.

"What are we stopping here for?"

"It's the garden spot of Rhea," Gaby said, sweeping her arm wide. But the joke seemed forced. "Actually, Rocky has some business here. Better count on two days. Maybe three. Getting tired of us?"

"No. Just curious. Should I be?"

"It might be better if you weren't. She has something to do, and I can't tell you what it is. That's for your own good, believe it or not." Gaby hurried away, back to the raft.

Robin sat on a log and watched the Titanides and Chris pitching camp. A month ago she would have forced herself to get up and help. Honor would have mandated it because to sit here was an acknowledgment that she was weak. Well, damn it, she *was* weak.

She had Hautbois to thank for being able to say that to herself. The Titanide had sung to her all through her recent seizure, in both English and Titanide. She had not let Robin turn away from her helplessness, had forced her to begin looking at ways to cope with it beyond sheer gutsiness. When Robin began to regain control, she found she did not resent what the Titanide had said. She learned Hautbois was a healer. That included doctor and psychiatrist and counselor and comforter,

and possibly other things. Robin had the impression Hautbois
would willingly have made love to her in the private, frontal
mode, if it could have helped anything. Whatever Hautbois
had done had given Robin more peace of mind than she had
felt since . . . she could not recall. She thought she must have
breached her mother's womb ready to fight the whole world.

Nasu was agitating to get out. Robin opened her sack and
let her writhe onto the sand, confident she would not go far.
She dug in her pocket and came up with a piece of hard candy
wrapped in a leaf, peeled it, and sucked on it. The sand was
too cold for Nasu's liking, so she coiled around Robin's ankle.

Cirocco was standing alone near the wall, motionless, looking at a tall crack in it. Robin followed it with her eyes and
realized it was a space between two cable strands. Three of
them abutted the island, which had once been an outer strand
itself, making the little bay semicircular. There was a similar
crack between the center strand and the one on the left. Below
the sea, the strands would splay out widely. She remembered
a picture of the conical mountain and its strand forest in Hyperion. Here the gaps between strands were no more than ten
meters wide and partially clogged with barnacles.

She saw Gaby return from the raft bearing an oil lamp.
Gaby hurried over to Cirocco and handed it to her. They were
talking, but the constant noise of the sea obliterated the words
before they reached Robin. Cirocco was not saying much; it
fell to Gaby to do most of the talking, and she was animated
about it. She did not look happy. Cirocco kept shaking her
head.

At last Gaby gave up. She stood facing Cirocco for a moment. Then the two women embraced, Gaby standing on her
toes to kiss her old friend. Cirocco hugged her once more, then
entered the crack between the cables. The light of her lantern
was visible for a short time, then gone.

Gaby walked to the edge of the circular cove, as far from
everyone else as she could get. She sat and put her head in her
hands. She did not move for two hours.

Cirocco's absence passed in relaxation and games. The
Titanides did not mind it, nor did Chris. Gaby was nervous
much of the time. Robin grew more bored by the hour.

She took up whittling, taught by the Titanides, but did not
have the patience for it. She wanted to ask Chris to teach her

to swim but felt she should not be naked in front of him again. Gaby solved the problem by suggesting she wear a bathing suit. One was quickly improvised. The idea of a bathing suit was as unexpected to Robin as wearing shoes in the shower, but it did the job. She took three lessons in the central body of water she had misnamed a tidepool. (There were no tides in Gaea.) In return, she tutored Chris in fighting, something he knew little about. The lessons had to be called off temporarily when she herself learned something, which was that testicles are amazingly easy to injure and can cause their owner a great deal of pain. She exhausted her store of apologies and was genuinely sorry, but how could she have known?

Only two incidents livened an otherwise comatose two days. The first was soon after Cirocco had left, when Gaby seemed to want to move around. She took them along a narrow trail leading from the campsite to the high ledge girdling the cable. All seven of them spent the next hour walking carefully on irregular ground that sloped toward a fifty-meter drop into the sea. They went almost halfway around the cable to a point where the ledge had broken away. Just short of that was a recess between two cable strands. Standing in it was a squat stone pilaster, and sitting on that was a golden statue of an alien creature.

It reminded Robin of the Frog Queen from a childhood tale. It was obviously aquatic; though it had six legs, they ended in broad flippers. It squatted, looking out to sea, hunchbacked and broad. Nothing grew on it, though it was draped with dried seaweed. Its single eye was a hollow socket.

"That's been here at least ten thousand years," Gaby said. "There used to be an eye in the socket. It was a diamond about as big as my head. I saw it once, and it seemed to glow." She kicked at the sand, and Robin was startled to see a creature the size of a large dog emerge and slink away on six flippered feet. It was yellow and rather ugly. There was very little flesh on its bones. The thing did not look much like the statue, yet there was a family resemblance. It turned once, opened a mouth with several thousand long yellow teeth, hissed, and continued to shuffle away.

"Those things used to be so mean a wolverine would have a heart attack just to look at them. They were so quick your guts would be on the ground before you saw them. They'd hide in the sand like that one was doing. As soon as the first

one jumped out, they'd be coming from all over. I saw one
take seven mortal hits from a rifle and still live to kill the man
who shot it."

"What happened to them?" Chris asked.

Gaby picked up a big shell and threw it to shatter against
the image. A dozen heads immediately appeared above the
sand, open-mouthed. Robin reached for her weapon, but it
wasn't necessary. The creatures looked around in confusion,
then wriggled back into concealment.

"They were put here to guard the idol's eye," Gaby said.
"The race that made it is long gone. Only Gaea knows anything
about them. You can be sure it wasn't really an idol because
nobody in here ever worshiped anything but Gaea. Some kind
of monument, I guess. Anyway, it's been at least a thousand
years since anyone cared about it or visited it.

"Until about fifty years ago. That's when the pilgrims
started coming, and Gaea created these creatures as perversions
of the original ones. She gave them one drive in life, and that
was to protect the eye at all costs. They did a damn good job.
The eye wasn't taken until about fifteen years ago. I personally
know of five people who died right here where we're standing,
and there were surely many more than that.

"But after it was gone, there was nothing left for the guard-
ians to do. Gaea didn't program them to die, so they eat a little
and get a little older. But waiting to die is what they're doing."

"So it was all just for a challenge?" Robin asked. "It wasn't
even here before she started daring people to . . . to go out and
prove themselves. . . ." She was unable to finish the thought.
It brought back her anger in full force.

"That's it. Something she didn't tell you, though, is that
Gaea is rotten with places like this. I'm sure she fed you the
whole spiel about a hundred and one dragons and jewels as
big as blimp turds. The thing is, this place has been scoured
by pilgrims for fifty years, all of them looking for some stupid
thing to do. A lot of them have died trying it, but the thing
about humans is if enough of them keep coming, they'll eventually do just about anything. The dragons have had the worst
of it. There's not many left, and there's plenty of humans.
Gaea can whomp up another dragon anytime she feels like it,
but she's way behind. She's getting old and can't keep up
anymore. Things break down and don't get repaired for a long

time, if ever. I doubt there's a dozen dragons left, or two dozen unplundered monuments."

"There's a quest shortage," Valiha said, and couldn't understand why Robin laughed so hard.

Chris was subdued on the way back. Robin knew he had visions of doing something worthy of tales, even if he was not aware of it. He was, after all, a man and trapped in peckish toy-soldier games. Robin could not have cared less if there were no more dragons.

The second incident was more interesting, however. It happened after their second sleep period. Gaby, who had not slept the first time, awoke and came out of her tent to find huge tracks in the sand. She howled for the Titanides, who came from the raft at a gallop. By the time they arrived Chris and Robin were awake, too.

"Where the hell were *you*?" Gaby wanted to know, pointing at a meter-long footprint.

"We've been down working on *Constance*," Hornpipe said. "Hautbois discovered the waves had damaged one end and—"

"But what about this? You were supposed to be—"

"Now wait a minute," Hornpipe said hotly. "You told me yourself there was nothing to worry about here. Nothing from the land and nothing—"

"Okay, okay, I'm sorry. Let's don't argue." Robin was not surprised Gaby had backed down so quickly. Titanides got angry so seldom that there was something sobering about it when one did. "Let's take a closer look at this."

They proceeded to do that, examining one track in detail and following the whole series to see where the creature had come from and where it had gone. The results were frightening. The tracks appeared at one edge of the cove, went straight to the camp, made a circle around Gaby's tent, then vanished again at the edge of the water.

"What do you think it was?" Valiha asked Gaby, who was down on one knee, studying a track by the light of her lantern.

"I sure as hell wish I knew. It looks like the claw of a bird. There are birds that big in Phoebe, but they can't fly or swim, so what would they be doing here? Maybe Gaea's whipped up something new again. Damn if it doesn't look like a giant chicken."

"I don't think I'd like to meet it," Robin said.

"Me either." Gaby straightened, still frowning. "Don't anybody disturb this one. Rocky should see it when she gets back. Maybe she'll know what it is."

Cirocco returned eight revs later. She looked tired and hungry, yet more confident than when she had gone in. Robin noticed that she smiled more easily. Whatever had happened in there, it had gone better than expected.

Robin wanted to say something, but all she could think of were questions like "How did it go?" or "What did you do?" Gaby had warned her away from that. For the time being she would let it go.

"Maybe you were right, Gaby," Cirocco said as they headed toward camp. "I sure as hell didn't want to—"

"Later, Rocky. We've got something you ought to look at."

She was taken to the site of the mysterious track. It was not as distinct as it had been, but still legible. She knelt in the lantern light, and one by one, deep lines etched themselves in her forehead. She seemed offended by the whole idea of this creature.

"You've got me," she said at last. "It's nothing I've ever seen, and I've been around and around this goddamn wheel." She sang something in Titanide. Robin looked at Hautbois, who frowned.

"Freely translated, she said, 'Gaea likes her jokes as well as the next deity.' This is well known, of course."

"Giant chicken?" Cirocco said incredulously.

Robin could not stand it anymore.

"Excuse me, I'm not feeling good," she said, and hurried into the darkness. When she reached the water's edge, she climbed down into a ravine like the one near the raft mooring. Once safely out of view she began to laugh. She made as little noise as possible, but she laughed until her sides hurt, until the tears rolled down her cheeks. She did not think she could laugh any harder; then she heard Gaby yell.

"Hey, Rocky, come here! We found a feather!"

Robin laughed harder.

When she finally had herself under control, she reached into a crack between round growths of coral and pulled out two contraptions made of sticks, bits of driftwood, and shells. They had ropes to tie around her legs and places to rest her feet.

"Gaby and Cirocco," she said. "The great Gaean wildlife

experts." She kissed one of the devices, then tossed it far out over the water.

"You'd better hurry. Gaby will be coming to see how you are." She looked up and saw Hautbois. She waved the remaining stilt at her and sent it after the first.

"Thanks for the diversion."

"You're welcome," Hautbois said. "I think Valiha is suspicious, but she won't say anything." He grinned broadly. "I think I'm going to enjoy this trip. But no more fooling with the salt, okay?"

23.

Tempest and Tranquil

A stiff breeze from the west propelled *Constance* on her wallowing way from the isle of Minerva. That was good news to Gaby. Looking up, she could see that the lower valve had closed. She knew from bitter experience that meant the spoke above was going through its regular winter. The trees and everything else would be coated in a layer of ice. After the thaw began, all that water and a respectable tonnage of broken branches would pool at the valve. When it opened, Rhea would not be a healthy environment. In fifty revs Nox would rise two meters or more.

No one asked where Cirocco had been. Gaby suspected they would have been surprised to learn the answer, and that included the Titanides.

Cirocco had been to an audience with Rhea, the satellite brain who dominated the land for a hundred kilometers in every direction. She was subject to no higher authority but Gaea herself. She was also quite mad.

The only way to visit the regional brains was through the central vertical cables. All of them lived down there, at the bottom of five-kilometer spiral stairways. Not even the Titanides were aware of this. Their knowledge of the twelve demi-Gods was limited; Gaea, when she made Titanides—complete with a culture and racial wisdom—had seen no reason why they should bother their heads about the regionals. They were Gaea's appendages and no more, the quasi-intelligent servo-mechanisms that kept things running smoothly in their own limited domains. For the Titanides to think of them as even so much as subordinate Gods would detract from their capacity to appreciate Gaea. Obediently the Titanides thought no more about the big clumps of neural matter than did the most ignorant tourist. Hyperion was a place, not a person, to them.

The reality was quite different, and had been since long before the birth of the Titanides. Perhaps the brains had actually been totally subservient to Gaea in her youth. She claimed it was so. But today all twelve increasingly went their own way. To accomplish her will, Gaea had to cajole or threaten.

All it took with a regional like Hyperion was a simple request. Hyperion was Gaea's closest ally on the rim. Yet the fact that she had to ask showed how far things had come. Gaea retained little in the way of direct control on the rim.

Gaby had met several of the regionals; she had been down to see Hyperion dozens of times. She found him dull, an automaton. She suspected that, as usual, the villains were far more interesting than the nice guys. Hyperion managed to use the word "Gaea" twice in every sentence. Gaby and Cirocco had seen him just before Carnival. The Hyperion central cable always made Gaby feel strange. She had visited it with Cirocco and others from the *Ringmaster* crew during her first weeks in Gaea. Unknowing, they had come within a few hundred meters of the entrance. Finding it would have saved them a terrible trip.

Rhea was another story. Gaby had never been able to visit any of Gaea's enemies. Cirocco had met them all except Oceanus. She was able to do that because she was the Wizard and under Gaea's safe-conduct. There was no way to guarantee that protection to Gaby. Killing Cirocco would bring the full wrath of Gaea down on the murderer's lands. Killing Gaby would probably annoy Gaea, but little more.

It was misleading, however, to call Rhea an enemy of Gaea. Though she had allied with Oceanus in the Oceanic Rebellion, she was far too unpredictable for either side to rely on. Cirocco had been down to her once before and barely escaped with her life. Rhea was a hell of a place to start, Gaby knew, but there had been no advantage to be gained by skipping her and coming back. Because their purpose was to visit eleven of the twelve regional brains. It was their fond hope that Gaea did not yet know this.

It was risky, to be sure, but Gaby felt it could be done without arousing suspicion. She did not expect complete security; that would have been foolish. Though Gaea's eyes and ears were not what some people imagined them, she had enough contacts on the rim so that she eventually heard of most things that happened.

They hoped simply to brazen it out. Some of it would be easy. It would have been bad form for the Wizard to pass through Crius, for instance, without dropping in for a visit. If Gaea wanted to know why the Wizard had visited an enemy like Iapetus, Cirocco could say she was simply keeping up with the state of affairs on the rim: part of her job. Asked why she had not told Gaea of this junket, she could protest quite truthfully that Gaea had never demanded she report every little thing.

But visiting Rhea would be hard to explain. Poor, confused, erratic Rhea could be the most dangerous regional in Gaea if confronted face to face. Traveling her lands was not hazardous. She spent so much time internalizing that she seldom noticed what was going on above her. For that reason, Rhea the land was slowly going to hell. But there was no predicting what she might do if one went down to speak to her. Gaby had tried to convince Cirocco to skip Rhea entirely, and the danger was not the only reason. It would be hard to explain why the Wizard had risked the trip.

The mysterious creature that had visited them had given Gaby some bad moments. She thought at first it might have been one of Gaea's tools, like the obscene little creature that greeted new pilgrims in the hub. Now she doubted that. More likely it was one of Gaea's sports. She spent more and more of her time dreaming up biological jokes to unleash on the rim. Such as the buzz bombs. *There* was a nasty bit of business.

When she questioned Cirocco as to how the audience had gone, the Wizard seemed reasonably confident all was well.

"I built up her ego as carefully as I could. I wanted to leave her with the thought that she was far above Gaea so she won't even deign to talk next time Gaea calls. If she doesn't talk, she can't tell her I was there."

"You didn't *tell* her not to tell, I hope."

"Give me some credit, will you? I think I understand her as well as anyone can. No, I kept it all open and as routine as possible, considering I had second-degree burns over half my body the last time I left her. Incidentally, you can put a big black *X* by her name, if you haven't already."

"Are you kidding? I didn't even put her on the list."

Cirocco closed her eyes for a moment. She rubbed her

forehead. "Next is Crius, and another *X*. I don't think this is going to go anywhere, Gaby."

"I never said it would. But we at least have to try."

The wind blew them past the long line of small islands dotting central Nox, then died away. For nearly a day they waited for it to return. When it did not, Gaby ordered everyone, including Cirocco, to the oars.

The valve began to open after they had been working at it for twenty revs. Contrary to what might have been expected, no torrent of water spilled out the rapidly widening hole above them. The valve was like a sponge. It soaked up the big thaw, and when it dilated, the water was squeezed out gradually. It emerged in a billion streams and broke into droplets. From there the process was complex, with cold water and chilled air hitting warm air masses below, moving inexorably downward. Since they were east of the valve—though only slightly—the worst of the resulting storms and torrential rain tended away from them at first, moving as Robin had moved when she took the Big Drop: westward, toward Hyperion. It was impossible to know when the winds would become dangerous.

The fate of the debris littering the valve's upper surface could be determined by simple physical equations. When it hit, it would make quite a splash. Some of the "debris" would be entire trees bigger than redwoods. Gaby knew it would not be a problem since it was relatively unaffected by atmospheric friction and would tend to fall to the west.

They put their backs into it, even when the expected breeze developed, and watched the storm descending. It fell for hours, met the sea, and began to ooze out like an inverted mushroom cloud.

They began to encounter waves and stray gusts that whipped the tough fabric of the sail. Gaby could see the rain approaching, hear the steady hissing get louder. When it hit, it was like a wall of water. What her father had called a "frog-strangler" a long time ago.

The wind was not as bad as she had feared, but she knew it could get much worse. They were still a kilometer from land. Those who were not rowing began using the poles to feel for the bottom. When they found it, the Titanides left the oars to the humans and began poling the raft toward shore. Beaching it was going to be tricky since there were waves two meters high by now, but there were no rocks or reefs to worry about. Soon Hornpipe jumped into the water with a rope, swam to shore, and began hauling.

Gaby was beginning to think it was going to be routine after all when a wave crested the stern and swept Robin into the water. Chris was nearest; he jumped into the water and quickly reached her. Gaby went to help him get back aboard, but he decided it would be easier at that point to take Robin straight to the beach. He rode the waves into shallow water, helped her stand up, and they both were knocked down by a big breaker. For a moment Gaby could not find them; then Chris came up with Robin in his arms and carried her up beyond the reach of the surf. He set her on her feet, and she promptly went to her knees, coughing, but waving him away.

The Titanides got *Constance* onto the beach and spent five minutes dancing through the increasingly angry waves to get everything off. The sail was whipped away when they tried to take it down. Otherwise, everything was salvaged.

"Well, we came through that with some luck," Cirocco said when they had found a campsite on high ground with plenty of trees to break the wind. "Anything lost, aside from the sail?"

"One side of my pack came open," Valiha said. "There was water damage, and Chris's tent rests with the fishes now." She looked so mournful that Chris couldn't help laughing.

"He can double up with me," Robin said. Gaby had not expected that. She eyed Robin, who did not look up from the cup of hot coffee in her hands. She sat close to the small fire the Titanides had built, a blanket over her shoulders, looking like a drowned rat.

"I imagine you critters will want to stay in the tents this time," Cirocco suggested, looking from one Titanide to the other.

"If you critters will have us," Psaltery said. "Though I suspect you're going to be very boring company."

Gaby yawned. "I suspect you're right. What do you say, little ones? Shall we crawl into bed and be boring?"

Gaby had become the leader of the expedition through Cirocco's refusal to have anything to do with it. Since resigning her captaincy, Cirocco had never been eager to accept that sort of responsibility, though she still did well when such a position was forced on her. Now she would not even discuss it; Gaby was in charge, and that was that. Gaby accepted it, did not even become annoyed when the Titanides involuntarily looked toward Cirocco when Gaby told them what to do. They couldn't help it. She was the Wizard, but they would do what Gaby said so long as it was clear Cirocco had no objection.

And Cirocco was improving. The mornings were still the worst. Since she spent more time sleeping than anyone else, she had more mornings to contend with. She looked like death when she woke up. Her hands shook, and her eyes darted around, searching for help and not finding it. Her sleep was not much better. Gaby had heard her crying out in the night.

But it was something she had to handle herself. What concerned Gaby at the moment was a simple matter of routes. They had landed at the northern bend of Long Bay. When Gaby sailed Nox, she always put into Snake Bay, the narrowing finger that led to the Ophion outflow. A rocky neck of land separated the two. Overland it was only five kilometers to the river. Following the beach would be at least twenty-five. She did not know this region well, could not remember if the beach extended all the way around. While she thought there was a pass between the rocky crags to the north, she was not sure of that either. Then there was the storm. The wind would be very bad if they followed the beach. Overland there would be mud and slippery trails to contend with, and the deeper darkness of the forest.

She waited a few hours to see if the storm would abate, consulted with Cirocco—who knew no more about it than Gaby—then ordered the camp broken and told Psaltery to strike out overland.

She never found out if it had been the best choice, but it was not a bad one. They had to pick their route carefully in several places. Yet the land was not as rugged as it had looked. They emerged on the southern beach of Snake Bay. It was not much of a beach—the bay was as sheer-sided as a Norwegian fjord—but she knew her way from there. The Circum-Gaea rejoined Ophion at that point after having made its way through North Rhea and down through the tortuous passes of the western Nemesis Mountains.

For some reason, Gaby's creation had fared better in this 30-kilometer stretch than anywhere else in Gaea. Much of the asphalt was cracked and buckled, some of it washed away, but for 50 and 100 meters at a time they could walk on road surface little changed from when Gaby's work crews had rolled it. The roadbed was particularly hard and stable in this area. Gaby had done a great deal of blasting just to make a path. Yet she would have thought the regular rains would have obliterated it long ago.

Nevertheless, there it was, winding its way up beside the seven massive river pumps lining the gorge. Gaby called the pumps Doc, Happy, Sneezy, Grumpy, Sleepy, Dopey, and Bashful, and no longer apologized for it. She couldn't help it; she had run out of Greek names. Of them all, Sneezy and Grumpy were the most appropriate. The pumps made an awful racket. There was also a lot to be said for Dopey as a generic name.

The storm began to slacken as they approached the top of the system. It was the highest point on Ophion. From the level of Nox—highest of Gaea's ten major seas—the Seven dwarfs raised the water another 4,000 meters. The place was called the Rhea Pass. From it one could look west to the alpine wall of the Nemesis Range: jagged teeth backlighted by the fertile greens and blues of Crius, its northern lakes and southern plains curving up behind the mountains. A steady rain was still falling in the pass, but the weather was clear to the east. Gaby decided that canoes should be built and that the party would take to the river and try to reach dry country before making camp.

Once again Gaby was amused by Chris. He was all eyes as he watched the Titanides select the proper canoe trees and, with a few well-aimed cuts, reap a harvest of perfect curved ribs and floorboards. He shook his head in wonder at the way they dovetailed into frameworks needing only a skin covering—which had been retained from the original fleet in Hyperion. In a little more than a rev they were ready to go.

She found herself watching Chris as the canoes were loaded. She was surprised at herself, but the fact was she found him irresistible in many ways. His almost childlike curiosity and willingness to listen while she and Cirocco pointed out the wonders of Gaea made her wistful and envious. She had once been like that. It was in contrast with Robin, who usually listened only long enough to be sure what was being said had no relevance to her. She supposed Robin's hard life had made her that way, but Chris had not had an easy life either. It showed in his quiet, moody spells. He was rather shy, but not to the point of fading into the background. When he was sure someone was actually listening, he could be a good talker.

And—she might as well admit—she felt a physical attraction. It was remarkable; her last affair with a man had been more than twenty years ago. But when he smiled, she felt good. When she was the reason for the smile, she felt terrific. His face had a lopsided beauty; he had good shoulders and arms and a marvelous ass. The small roll of fat around his waist was already melting away; a few weeks of exertion would turn him lean and narrow-hipped, the way she liked her men. She already had the urge to run her fingers through his hair and reach into his pants to see what that was like.

But not on this trip. Not with Valiha already mooning over him, Cirocco held at bay only by the effects of her megahangover, and—Gaby was beginning to suspect—even Robin showing signs of willingness to experiment in cross-cultural exploration.

He had enough problems without Gaby Plauget's trying to fit him into the disaster she had made of her love life. And she knew the biggest potential problem was the one he was least aware of. Her name was Cirocco. Chris was not ready for her, and Gaby intended to do what she could to protect him from her.

The segment of Ophion they now entered was a far cry from the stretch they had sailed in Hyperion. It necessitated changes. For the worst rapids Gaby insisted on an experienced canoeist front and rear. The Titanides all qualified, as did Gaby and Cirocco. Chris was a little rough, but he would do. Robin was an absolute novice, as well as a nonswimmer. Gaby put her between two Titanides, with the other two in the second boat, and Chris, Cirocco, and herself in the third, towing the fourth. In quiet places she let Robin take the lead and joined her, showing her how to handle the craft. As in everything she did, Robin worked at it single-mindedly and soon showed improvement.

It was an exhilarating trip. Chris was enthusiastic, but Robin bubbled with excitement when they reached the end of a stretch of rapids. Once she even suggested they go back and do it again, looking about three years old as she said it. She was aching to sit alone in the front. Gaby understood it well; there were few things Gaby liked more than a challenging white-water ride. When traveling with Psaltery, she defied the river, taking chances. Now, though she enjoyed herself, she was learning something Cirocco had found out a long time ago. It's not quite the same when you're the leader. Being responsible for others makes one conservative and a bit of a grouch. She had to be firm with Robin about wearing her inflatable life vest.

They reached the twilight zone west of Crius before making camp. Everyone was pleasantly exhausted. They had a light dinner and a big breakfast and set out again toward gradually brightening lands. If anything could enhance the joys of being on the river, it was coming out of the Rhean rain into the Crian sunshine. The Titanides led the singing, which started with the traditional Gaean traveling song: "The Wonderful Wizard of Oz." Gaby was not surprised or abashed to feel tears fill her eyes as they came to the end of it.

Ophion dashed into full daylight at a point slightly north of the western slanted cable, the counterpart of Cirocco's Stairs but leaning in the other direction. The river then turned south and continued in that direction for more than a hundred kilometers. The rapids became less frequent, though the river was still lively. They took it easy, barely paddling in the quiet waters, resting and letting the river's current move them.

Gaby called a halt early when they came to a place she had camped before. She thought it the prettiest site in the Nemesis Range and told everyone they would stay for eight revs, sleep, and then continue on. It seemed agreeable, especially to the Titanides, who planned a decent meal for the first time in several days.

When Chris suggested they try to catch something for the Titanides to cook, Gaby showed him what reeds to cut for fishing poles. Robin showed an interest, so Gaby taught her how to bait a hook and string a line, how to operate the simple wooden reels the Titanides had brought. They moved out into shallow water, smooth stones under their bare feet, and began casting.

"What do you catch around here?" Chris asked.

"What would you take out of a stream like this back home?"

"Trout, probably."

"Then trout it is. I figure we could use about a dozen."

"Are you serious? There are really trout?"

"Not just a Gaean imitation either. A long time ago Gaea thought she wanted to attract tourists. Now she's largely indifferent to them. But she had a lot of streams stocked, and they did well. They get pretty big. Like this one." Her pole was bent into a semicircle. In a few minutes she netted a fish that was larger than any Chris had ever seen, let alone caught.

Robin broke her line with her first bite, then brought in one about the same size. In half an hour they had their quota, but Chris was battling something that felt more like a whale than a trout. Yet when it flashed into the air, it had the familiar lines and colors, the fighting spirit. He played it for twenty minutes and at last could reach down and come up with a fish larger than even Gaby had seen. He looked at it with undisguised delight, then held it up, looking toward the sky.

"How about it, Gaea?" he shouted. "Is this big enough?"

24.

The Grotto

For once Chris had actually been able to see the thing. It was just a tiny speck far to the north and high in the air, but it had to be the source of the sustained roar he had heard twice already. He watched it vanish over a mountain, but he could hear it for nearly a minute after that.

"Valiha," he said, "I'm bearing to the left."

"I'm coming right behind you."

Chris steered close to Gaby and Psaltery. He held the side of the other canoe as he stowed his oar, then jumped easily from one to the other. Gaby frowned at him.

"Don't you think it's about time you told us what that is? You did say you'd teach us things we'd need to know."

"I did, didn't I?" She scowled even more but gave in. "I wasn't trying to keep anything from you, really. It's just that I don't even like to talk about them. I—" She looked up a time to see Robin join them.

"Fine. We call 'em buzz bombs. They're new. Very new. I first saw one no more than six or seven years ago. Gaea must have worked on them for a long time because they're so damn unlikely they shouldn't even be alive. They are the *nastiest* things I ever saw.

"What they are is living airplanes powered by ramjets. Or pulse-jets, possibly. The one I examined was pretty busted up and burned to a crisp. I ordered an old heat-seeking missile from Earth a few years after the first one appeared and shot one down. It was about thirty meters long and definitely organic, though it had a lot of metal in its body. I don't know how; its chemistry must be fantastic, especially when it's being gestated.

"Anyway, I did wonder how it flew. It had wings, and I knew it didn't fly by flapping them. It works like an airplane that uses warpable wings instead of elevons. It had two legs

186

that folded up in flight. I doubt it could walk very far on them.
And it had two fuel bladders that held something that's probably
kerosene. Possibly ethanol or a mixture.

"Right away I wondered how it could eat enough to make
that kind of fuel in the amounts it would need to be useful for
flight. I mean, it was obviously awkward as hell on the ground.
On top of that, if it is a ramjet that makes the damn abomination
go, it wouldn't dare land anywhere but the top of a cliff or a
very tall tree. That engine won't work until it's in motion. So
they'd need a thrust assist or a long fall to reach the speed
where they could flame on. I didn't know any of this; I had
to look it up.

"What I decided was that they didn't make their own fuel.
The food they ate went to a more or less normal animal me-
tabolism, and they must get their fuel from some outside
source. Or several sources. Most likely it's another new creature, and it's probably in the highlands. I haven't found out
where yet."

"Are they dangerous?" Robin asked.

"Very much so. The best thing about them is there aren't
many of them. I thought at first they'd have a hard time sneak-
ing up on anybody, but that turns out to be untrue. They cruise
at about five hundred kilometers per hour. Even with the engine
running they're on you practically before you know it. But
they can also flame out at that speed and skim along the surface,
then fire up after they've made a kill and before they drop
below critical speed. If you see one, try to get in a ditch. They
don't come around for a second pass unless the land is as flat
as stale beer. You're safe behind a rock, and your chances are
improved if you're just stretched out on the ground. They have
barbed noses and what they do is impale you and fly off to eat
the carcass somewhere else."

"How delightful."

"Ain't it?"

"What do they eat?" Chris asked.

"Anything they can lift."

"Yes, but what is that? Running into something as big as
a human might slow them down below their critical speed."

"It turns out they handle humans quite well, thank you. It's
a good point, though, and they do favor prey in the forty-to-
sixty-kilogram range."

"Hey, thanks," Robin snorted. "That's *me*."

"Me, too, little one. But just think how good the big fella here must feel." She smiled at Chris, who was not feeling that good about it. "Actually, they will attack a full-grown human buck if given the chance and so far have always pulled it off. Seven humans have been killed by them. They will also take on a Titanide, but that's closer to the wishful-thinking category. I know of a dozen cases where Titanides have been carried off, but I've heard of two where the buzz bomb crashed and burned while trying to do it.

"I wouldn't worry about them too much. I cringe when I hear one going over because I hate the things intensely. I did even before one of them took a friend of mine. If I ever find the fuel station, there's going to be one hell of a jolly fire. They are obscene, terrible beasts. They don't attack blimps, but they seem to get a kick out of flying around and around them until the poor things are almost insane with fear, and they've got good reason to be. One blimp was accidentally ignited by the exhaust, and the others are still whistling about that.

"But statistically there's a lot of things that are more dangerous. They're as unpredictable as sharks. If they get you, you're gone, but the chances are against it."

Chris liked Crius. Coming out of the Rhean night might have had something to do with it, but in some respects it was nicer than Hyperion. Crius had the Nemesis Mountains in the west to provide a backdrop, and the forbidding frozen sea of Oceanus could no longer be seen.

After Ophion resumed its eastward course far in the south of Crius, it flowed briskly through the grandfather of all jungles. Gaby told him it actually was not as dense as parts of the western Hyperion forest, but it was good enough for him. Earthlike species of trees jostled with alien spikes, feathers, crystals, strings of pearls, films, spheres, and lace veils. They leaned over the water in their intense competition for light and space. Though the river was wide, at some points they met in the middle.

They made one camp in the jungle, and everyone stayed alert. There were creatures in it that could and would attack humans and Titanides. Robin was startled into shooting a creature the size of a bull when it came nosing around her tent, then learned it was harmless. They ate part of it for breakfast.

Five minutes after they threw the carcass into the river it was swarming with eels that tore at the dead flesh. Scavengers, Cirocco said, maintaining that the waters here were not dangerous. Chris still skipped his bath.

It had been Robin's first use of her weapon. Cirocco asked to see it, professing surprise that such a small woman could handle a .45-caliber automatic. Robin explained she was using rocket bullets instead of explosive. Most of the thrust was developed outside the barrel. It was especially helpful in Gaea's low gravity, where the kick of a Colt .45 could topple even a heavy person. She had two types of ammunition loaded into the standard seven-round clips: lead slugs and impact-fused explosives.

It was 120 kilometers from the last ramparts of the Nemesis Range to the end of the jungle. The river no longer gave them much help, but by rowing hard, they came out onto the plains in one more shift and camped a few kilometers beyond the forest verge.

While Chris slept, they were visited by a delegation of Crian Titanides, who were overjoyed to hear that the Wizard was among the travelers and began to plead for a Carnival. Chris later learned they had a good case for one; while the larger Hyperion chords got a Carnival every myriarev, the chords in other regions had to wait for the Wizard's erratic journeys to bring her to them. Crius was overdue.

When Chris awoke, the Crians were accepting the hospitality of the Hyperionite breakfast table. Chris joined them, and the difference between the Titanides of Crius and of Hyperion was immediately obvious. While Valiha was based on the frame of a Percheron, the Crians were more like Shetland ponies. He could actually see eye to eye with the tallest of them. They presented the same riot of color as their Hyperion cousins, however. One had a pelt that was a passable tartan.

None spoke English—it being a skill infrequently useful in Crius—but Valiha introduced him around and translated a few polite greetings. He took an immediate liking to one white-skinned female, and from her shy smiles he felt the interest was mutual. Her name was Siilihi (Locrihypolydian Duet) Hymn. Had she possessed two fewer legs, he would have been extremely attracted.

Gaby went into Cirocco's tent to tell her of the request. There was a loud moan, and Siilihi looked away from Chris, embarrassed. The other Crian Titanides stirred restlessly. Chris was suddenly furious at the Wizard. What a demeaning thing it was for such beautiful people to have to come begging to that miserable drunk!

He wished he could perform the Wizard's function. If anyone ever deserved to have a lovely baby, it was Siilihi. He wondered if, when he saw Gaea again, she would consider making him a Wizard so he could help these people. He was sure he could handle the responsibility better than Cirocco had done.

It sounded like such a fine idea, in fact, that he wanted to get started on it right away. The first step was frontal fertilization, so he reached for Siilihi and saw her eyes go wide.

He returned to consciousness stretched out on Valiha's back. His jaw hurt. When he tried to sit up, he found it impossible. He was strapped down, and his hands were tied in front of him.

"I'm better," he announced to the sky. Valiha turned around and looked down at him.

"He says he's better," she called. He heard changes in the cadence of hooves. Soon Robin and Gaby were flanking him, looking down.

"I wish I could think of a cheap way to test that," Gaby said. "The last time we cut you loose, you attacked Robin. You've been a real pain in the ass."

"I remember it," Chris said tonelessly.

"Will you shut your stupid mouth?" Robin growled at Gaby. Gaby looked surprised, then nodded.

"If you think you can handle it, yeah, I will."

"Then get out of here. I'll take the responsibility." Gaby rode off, and Robin told Valiha to stop while she cut the ropes that bound Chris. He sat up, rubbing his wrists and working his jaw. It had been a short attack and not a very deep one. Still, he had had time to insult the Crian delegation, take a swing at Cirocco in front of the Titanides, and make amorous advances to Robin after he had convinced them he was better. For his troubles he had picked up a black eye from Cirocco and a kick in the balls and a sore lip from Robin. Apparently his miraculous luck didn't work against Wizards and witches. He shifted on Valiha's back, and it hurt.

"Listen," he said. "All I can say is I'm sorry, inadequate as it is. And thanks for not killing me."

"There's no need, and I wish I could have been...done less. But you are getting better; you rushed me. And now I know what rape must be like."

He winced. And he had thought he could be friends with this woman. He felt the black depression beginning to descend.

"Did I say something wrong?" He looked at her, wondering if she could possibly be kidding, but there was only concern on her face.

"I...maybe I see," she said. "You must believe me when I say I had not thought being accused of rape would shame a man. I can see that you are, but you needn't be. I don't hold you responsible. What I meant was that I now see how it can be so traditionally feared by my sisters. It was frightening to come even that close. Even knowing that you would not do me great injury. If I'm making things worse, just tell me to shut up."

"No, you're not," he said. "I tricked you the last time. How did you know I'm not tricking you now?"

"You tricked Gaby," Robin said. "I would have kept you bound. And I don't know how I know. But I do."

"How did you know that I wouldn't hurt you, beyond the—" he found it hard to go on, but forced himself—"beyond the normal hurts of a rape, that is. How did you know I wouldn't beat you or mutilate or kill you?"

"Was I wrong?"

"No. No, I do terrible things, but I've never been murderous. I'll pick a fight, but only to remove someone who's annoying me. After I knock them down I forget about them completely. I've assaulted women. I even raped one once. But that's just—or so I've been told—just normal sex urge with all the social conscience short-circuited. At my worst, I have never gone into homicidal rages or derived pleasure from the act of hurting someone, even at my worst. But that's not to say that in the course of getting my way I won't hurt someone, hurt them badly."

"I thought it was something like that."

There was more he had to say, the most difficult of all.

"It has occurred to me," he said, "that if we both were stricken at the same time...you know, in a rather unlikely circumstance, I suppose, with no one around to protect you or restrain me . . . that I might . . . without meaning to, but unable to stop myself. . . ." He could not finish, try as he might.

"I thought of that," she said casually. "As soon as it was clear to me what your problem was, the possibility arose. I decided to risk it, or I wouldn't be here. As you say, the chance is remote." She reached across and briefly pressed his hand. "What I want you to understand is that *I don't hold you responsible*. Not *you*. I can make that distinction."

Chris looked at her for a long time and gradually felt some of the weight lifting. He ventured a smile, and she smiled back.

Their destination now was once again the central vertical cable. In Crius it was thirty-five kilometers north of Ophion.

To everyone's surprise, upon arrival Cirocco invited them to accompany her. Sooner or later they would notice that the expedition always stopped in the middle of a region, and there was no need to conceal the visit with Crius from anyone.

The Titanides would not go. The whole idea made them visibly uneasy. They remained in the sunlight while Cirocco led the three humans into the forest of titanic columns where the unwinding cable strands emerged from the ground. At what must have been the center was the entrance to a stairway. It was a transparent building, vaguely like a cathedral but nothing so imposing as the monuments at the hub.

The stairs went down in a spiral defined by the unseen central strand of the central cable. The corridor was wide enough to accommodate twenty people abreast, and fifty meters high. They did not need lanterns since the ceiling was festooned with flying creatures that glowed with a ruddy orange light.

Chris thought Cirocco must have been joking when she said the stairs went down for five kilometers. It turned out to be literally true. Even in one-quarter gravity one doesn't climb that many steps without resting on the way. But it did come to an end. He was in better shape than he had thought. Aside from some soreness in his calves Chris felt fine.

They emerged in a cavern that was less than he had expected. This was Crius, after all, and though he was only a subordinate God, Chris still remembered the bizarre grandeur of Gaea's quarters.

Crius was an underworld God, a troglodyte who had never seen the light of day and never would. His domain smelled of sour chemicals and the wastes of a billion creatures, thrummed with the beating of subterranean hearts. He was a working God, an engineer to Gaea's executive, a God who worked in the grease that kept things moving.

They stood on a flat surface rimming an hourglass-shaped crystalline structure reaching floor to ceiling. The cavern was 200 meters in diameter, with passages opening east and west.

The thing in the center was obviously the main attraction. It put Chris in mind of the devices of heavy industry, though he could not say why. He could imagine metals being smelted in a shape like that, or electricity transformed. He wondered if Crius lived inside it. Could the actual brain be that small? Or perhaps it was only the top projection of a larger structure; it sat in a circular moat twenty meters wide and unguessably deep.

"Don't go for a swim," Gaby warned. "That's hydrochloric acid in pretty good concentration. Things are programmed not to come in here—look how well it worked with the Titanides— but the acid is a last-ditch protection, as it were."

"Then that is Crius, right there?"

"In person. We won't introduce you. You and Robin stay back by the wall and don't make any quick motions. Crius knows the Wizard, and he'll talk to me because he needs me. Be quiet, listen, and learn." She watched them sit down and joined Cirocco at the edge of the moat.

"We will speak English," Cirocco began.

"Very well, Wizard. I sent for you nine thousand three hundred and forty-six revs ago. This lack of efficiency is beginning to impair the proper operation of systems. I thought of filing a complaint with the God of Gods but have delayed it."

Cirocco reached into the folds of her red blanket and threw something at the shape in the acid lake. There was a bright flash of light when it struck Crius, and red dots chased each other frantically over its surface.

"I retract the statement," Crius said.

"Did you have any other complaints?"

"None. I made no complaint."

"See that you don't."

"It will be as you say."

Chris was impressed in spite of himself. The exchange had been rapid, emotionless on the part of Crius. Cirocco had not raised her voice. Yet the impression was of a child being chastised by a strict parent.

"You spoke of a 'God of Gods,'" Cirocco said. "Who is this?"

"I spoke as a humble servant of Gaea, the one and only God. The phrase was used in ... in a metaphorical sense," Crius finished, rather lamely, Chris thought.

"Yet you used the word 'God' in the plural. This is a source of surprise to me, who had thought such a construction could not enter your mind."

"One hears heresy."

"Would you be speaking of imported heresy or the local brand? Have you been speaking with Oceanus?"

"As you know, Oceanus speaks to me. It is not in my power to stop listening. I have, however, been completely successful in ignoring him. As to imported, human notions, I am aware of and unimpressed by their many varieties of myth."

Once again Cirocco reached into her blanket. This time she paused, and as she did, more red spots appeared on Crius's surface, dancing anxiously. The Wizard did not take notice. She looked thoughtfully at the floor for a time: then let her empty hand appear in the open once more.

The conversation turned to matters that meant nothing to Chris, concerning the day-to-day affairs of Crius. Throughout it, Crius maintained an attitude that was not precisely subservient, yet left no doubt he knew well who was in charge. His voice was not loud. It had a buzzing quality and was not in the least intimidating. Cirocco dispensed orders casually, as though her role in the exchange were by natural law something like a queen dealing with a respected commoner, but a commoner nonetheless. She listened to the things he said, then would interrupt in the middle of a sentence with her decision. Crius never attempted to argue with her or to explain further.

They spoke for more than an hour on matters of policy; then the talk turned to more prosaic items, and Gaby was invited to join in. Much of it was again meaningless, but at one point they discussed a malfunction in a particle accelerator that was part of Crius, deep beneath his surface. What Crius would do with a particle accelerator was a mystery to Chris.

A preliminary contract was made, Gaby agreeing to look into the matter in less than a myriarev, provided Gaea offered acceptable payment. She mentioned contacting a race in Phoebe that was good at subterranean work.

Chris could tell Robin was bored after the first ten minutes. He held out a little longer than that but soon was yawning himself. It was not that he felt the trip was wasted—it was interesting to see what the regional brains looked like and educational to see Cirocco do something more than drink—but it had been a very long stairway. He dreaded the climb to the top.

The audience was ended without ceremony. Cirocco simply turned, gestured to Robin and Chris, and the four of them entered the stairs again. It was five minutes before the gentle curve of the corridor put them out of sight of the grotto.

Cirocco glanced behind her, then let her shoulders sag. She sat and put her head in her hands, then threw it back with a deep sigh. Gaby sat behind her and began massaging the Wizard's shoulders.

"You did real well, Rocky," she said.

"Thanks. Gaby, I could use a drink." She said it without emphasis. Gaby hesitated, then reached into her pack and took out a small flask. She poured a capful and handed it to Cirocco, who quickly drained it. She gave it back without requesting another, though Chris could see Gaby was ready to give her one.

Gaby gave Chris and Robin an annoyed look.

"You might say something nice," she suggested.

"I would if I knew what you're talking about," Robin said.

"I was impressed," Chris said. "But I thought it was routine."

Gaby sighed.

"Sorry. I guess it was, now that you mention it. I just never get used to it. Even with a relatively sane one like Crius you never know what it's going to be like from one visit to the next. He could squash us like flies, you know. He's not in the least happy about having to take orders from an alien. The only thing that keeps him in line is his fear of Gaea. Or love of her. Frankly, with a relationship like that there's not much distinction."

Chris frowned. "Are you saying we were in danger?"

"What's danger?" Gaby looked at him and laughed. "Ten

minutes before we got there that chamber was flooded with acid. By now it's probably full again. It wouldn't have been hard to arrange an accident. He might even have convinced Gaea it was an accident."

"He'd never do that," Cirocco said firmly. "I know him."

"Maybe not. But Oceanus *has* been talking to him. You know that. I had a bad moment there when he started off with his 'complaint.' Coming from Crius, that's like a billionaire starting to quote Karl Marx."

"I took care of it," Cirocco said contentedly. "Rub a little lower, will you? There, there, that's it."

Chris suddenly felt like sitting down. He wondered what he was doing here. It was obvious he knew little of what had really gone on, what was still going on. These women dealt in things that often seemed less than real to him, but that crystalline brain had been as solidly real as a pair of pliers. Somewhere far away there existed another brain much like it, but malevolent, bent on death and warfare. And above all of them was a diety who collected cathedrals like the poker chips in a game played by megalomaniacs.

It was a forbidding idea. He could not help observing that when mortals stepped into the affairs of Gods, the smart money would pick the Gods to get the better of it.

25.

Inglesina

"What do you think, Rocky?"

Cirocco had been sunk in the mindless rhythms of the near-infinite climb. She looked up in surprise.

"About Crius? Forget it. There might be some way to involve him in an *ad hoc* grouping. You know, afterward. But for now, forget it."

"You didn't think it was a hopeful sign?" Gaby persisted. "The fact that he was talking about complaining to Gaea about you? What did you make of that?"

Cirocco snorted. "Damn little."

"Don't you think you could fan that spark?"

"Don't get so eager, Gaby. I don't know how the ice could be any thinner, but the way you keep heating things up. . . ."

"I'm sorry. You know how I feel about this."

"I sure do. But I'd appreciate it if you'd be a little less forthcoming with those two children. I'm talking about 'need to know.' The less they know, the better for them if things go wrong. You aren't doing them any favors by talking about Crius and his loyalty or lack of it. If that got to the wrong ears, if one of them made an innocent remark, it could start certain thoughts that I'd just as soon were not thought. I wish I hadn't brought them down here."

"You're right, I guess," Gaby said. "I'll be more careful."

Cirocco sighed and touched Gaby's shoulder.

"Just keep on doing what you've been doing. Be a tour guide. Point out the marvels. Tell them funny stories, and keep them entertained, and remember they're along to learn things that will keep them out of trouble, not to get them into anything we're doing."

"Do you think you might be able to open up a little more? There are a lot of things you could teach them."

Cirocco looked thoughtful. "I could tell them a thing or two about drinking."

"Don't be so hard on yourself."

"I don't know, Gaby. I thought I was doing better. But now there's Inglesina."

Gaby winced. She took Cirocco's hand and squeezed.

Just beyond the line of vertical cables Ophion began a series of wide loops. The land was flat and so nearly level that the river slowed to a crawl.

Robin used the time to improve her skills with the oar. She rowed all day, with Hautbois instructing her in the finer points of boat handling. She would set Robin the task of turning the craft by herself, guiding it through tight circles or figure eights in the shortest possible time. Then the two of them would put their backs into it to catch up with the others. Her shoulders grew strong, and she developed blisters and then calluses on the palms of her hands. At the end of the day she was exhausted, but a little less so each morning.

They were in no hurry. Groups of Titanides appeared on the shore, singing for the Wizard. Gaby or Cirocco would shout one word at them, and they would gallop away in high excitement. The word was "Inglesina." Robin learned it was the name of a large island in Ophion. Like Grandioso, it was named for one of the Titanides' beloved marches and was the site of the Crian Purple Carnival.

The Carnival was to be held 120 revs from the time of the first meeting with the Crians. It had to be so to give the local Titanides time to gather. They camped early and arose late. Robin began to feel more comfortable in the sleeping bag, to listen less to the thousand sounds of Gaea. She even came to enjoy the murmuring river as she relaxed and waited for sleep to come. It was not so very different from the purring of the air system she had heard all her life.

There were no further mishaps with the food, nor did they have any visits from unknown creatures. But at one camp, when Robin was feeling particularly bored, she took Chris on a snipe hunt. She judged, correctly, that he would not question her assertion that the Titanides wanted a brace of snipe for the evening meal, nor would he think the approved method of catching them in the least odd. After all, what in Gaea was not odd?

So she took him a good distance from the camp and showed

him how to hold the sack, cautioned him to tie it tightly when the little creatures had run inside, and went off over a low hill to drive them from the underbrush and into his waiting arms. Then she went back to camp and waited for him.

She felt a little guilty about it. He had been so easy to fool that a lot of the enjoyment had gone out of it. And she wondered, not for the first time, if it was ethical to prank her comrades on what everyone kept saying was a dangerous journey. The trouble was that it had not looked very dangerous so far, and—she might as well admit it—she was unable to resist.

He stayed away for nearly two hours. She was about ready to go bring him back when he appeared on his own, looking forlorn. Everyone was sitting around the fire, finishing another superb meal. Gaby and Cirocco looked up in surprise as he sat down and reached for the pot.

"I thought you were in your tent," Cirocco said.

"So did I," Gaby said, then looked thoughtfully at Robin. "Now that I think of it, though, Robin didn't actually say that. She just led me to believe you were."

"I'm sorry," Robin said, directing it to Chris.

He shrugged, then managed to grin. "You sure did get me. I just happened to remember something you said. About the witches appreciating tellers of lies." She was happy to see he was not bitter. There was the inevitable chagrin, but apparently Earth humans as well as witches felt an obligation not to be angry at a friendly con. Or at least Chris did.

The story came out gradually since Robin could not honorably boast of it, nor was Chris eager to admit his gullibility. As it unfolded, Hautbois caught Robin's eye and made a warning sign. The Titanide was watching Cirocco intently. Suddenly, she signaled, and Robin leaped over the rock she had been sitting on and began to run.

"Giant chicken!" Cirocco roared. "Giant chicken? I'll give you a giant chicken. You won't sit down for a month!"

Cirocco had the longer stride; Robin, the quicker moves. It was never established if the Wizard could catch her, however, as the whole party joined in the chase and Robin was soon cornered, laughing hysterically. She struggled hard, but they had no trouble throwing her in the river.

The next day they picked up a hitchhiker. He was the first human they had seen since leaving Hyperion. A small naked man with a flowing black beard, he stood on the riverbank and hailed them, then swam out to climb into Cirocco's canoe when she granted permission. Chris maneuvered his boat close to get a look at him. From the looseness of his pale, weathered skin, he must have been in his sixties. He spoke a clipped, slangy version of English, with a Titanide singsong flavor. He invited them to eat at the settlement where he lived, and Cirocco accepted for the group.

The place was called Brazelton and consisted of several domes set in an area of plowed fields. As they docked, Chris caught sight of a naked man following a plow drawn by a team of Titanides.

There were about twenty Brazeltonians. They were nudists by religion. Everyone had a beard, men and women alike. On Earth, female facial hair was a fad which had come and gone several times in the twenty-first century. Now it was rare, but seeing the bearded women reminded Chris of his own childhood, when his mother had worn a neat goatee. He rather liked it.

Gaby did not know a great deal about the settlement but told him that the group practiced incest. The man they had picked up was known as Gramps, and it was not a nickname. Others were called things like Mother2 and Son3. There was a Great Gra'mama, but no male of her generation. As children were born, everyone moved up into a different name.

Robin thought the arrangement very strange, and Chris heard her say so to Gaby.

"I agree," Gaby said. "But they're no loonier than a lot of other little groups of exiles scattered through Gaea. And you'd do well to remember that your own Coven probably looked pretty odd when it got started. Hell, it still would, if anybody on Earth was asked about it. Your mothers went to Sargasso Point; these days the fringe groups come here if they're small enough to get Gaea's permission."

The customs were not the only strange thing about the group. There were some odd individuals. Chris saw his first human-Titanide hybrids. One woman, otherwise unremarkable, had the long ears of a Titanide and a naked tail that reached to her knees. There were two Titanides with human legs and feet. By the time he saw them Chris was sufficiently accustomed to Titanide legs that it was the hybrids who seemed misshapen.

He spoke to Cirocco about it, but his knowledge of genetics was not sufficient to understand what she was saying. He suspected she might not know as much about it as she claimed.

The fact was that Gaea had allowed no human studies of Titanide genes, nor had any hybrid ever left Gaea. It remained mysterious how two such dissimilar animals could be cross-fertile.

Inglesina was a low island eight kilometers long and three wide in the eastern reaches of Crius, near Phoebe, the Twilight Sea. Near its center was a perfect ring of trees, carefully tended, two kilometers in diameter. Everything outside that circle was covered with the tents of the celebrants.

The island was reached by six wide wooden bridges, now decked in ribbons and banners. To the north and south were marinas where broad-beamed Titanide barges docked. Near them were beaches for the landing of smaller craft. The river was alive with them. Crian Titanides spent more time on the water than their cousins in Hyperion. Fully as many arrived on the river as poured over the causeways after overland treks.

They would stay the traditional two hectorevs—nine Earth days. Valiha pitched a tent for Chris behind the airy white confection set aside for the Wizard, and the tents of Robin and Gaby went up beside his. He went out to sample the festivities.

The Crians were fully as hospitable as the Hyperionites had been, but Chris found it difficult to enjoy himself. He kept fearing he would run into Siilihi. There was the persistent feeling that the story of his attempted assault on her had made the rounds, that everyone knew about him and held something in reserve, fearing he would repeat the incident. No one did or said anything to make him think that; no one was less than completely friendly. It was certainly his own fear and no one else's, but knowing that did not help. He was reserved and unable to change it.

Robin was still spending many nights with him, though his lost tent had now been replaced. He was not sure why she did so. He welcomed the companionship, but sometimes it was difficult. She was careful not to undress in front of him after her discovery on the beach of Nox. This annoyed him because the efforts required to remain modest while they shared a tent pointed up her unavailability. Several times he thought of asking her to leave. Yet he thought she might be demonstrating her lack of fear and thus her acceptance of him as a friend. It was a gesture he did not wish to discourage, so he tossed and turned while she slept like a child.

On the fifth night it was worse than ever. He could not get

to sleep, try as he might. He put his hands behind his head and stared at the pale light coming through the tent ceiling and thought black thoughts. Tomorrow he would kick her out, one way or the other. There were limits.

"Is something the matter?"

He looked at her, surprised to see that she was awake.

"Can't get to sleep."

"What's the problem?"

He threw his hands up, searched for words, then thought, why be delicate?

"I'm horny. You go too long without making love, you're surrounded by attractive women all day long . . . it builds up, that's all."

"I've got the same kind of problem," she said.

He opened his mouth to suggest a solution, thought about it, and closed his mouth again. What a waste of such a symmetrical solution, he thought. You scratch my back. . . .

"You did say we were much the same," she said. "I thought that's what had been bothering you." When he only grunted, she opened her sleeping bag and sat up. She reached across and touched a finger to his lips. "Would you show me how?"

He looked at her, not daring to believe, but feeling more desire than he had known since he was a teenager.

"Why? Do you find me attractive, or are you just curious?"

"I'm curious," she admitted. "I'm not sure about the other yet. There is something there. Cirocco said that what I have been told is raping can be a lot like making love. She said a woman can get pleasure from it. I'm dubious." She raised one eyebrow. A few weeks ago Chris would not have seen the gesture behind the elaborate facial tattoos, but now he felt more in tune with her. He threw off his sleeping bag and took her in his arms.

She seemed surprised that he did not simply enter her and get to work. When she understood that they could make love in the same way two women would, she showed no hesitation in the matter. In fact, she did things that Trini would certainly have charged extra for. There was nothing shy about her. She told him what she wanted and when she wanted it, talking as though she assumed he had never done this before. In a way, she was right. Though he had been with his share of women, he had never met one as certain of her own needs or as assured in expressing them.

She learned rapidly. At first she was full of questions and observations, wanting to know what he felt when she did this or that, surprised at the tastes and feels of things. None of the surprises seemed unpleasant, and by the time he felt ready to move on she had developed an obvious enthusiasm for the project.

Her skepticism returned when he entered her. She admitted it had not been painful, even that it was a pleasant sensation, but observed pointedly that the arrangement seemed unnatural in that it failed to provide for her needs. He tried to assure her that it would work out all right and then realized with dismay that it was going to because he was already too close and it was too late to stop.

He had time to hope that Robin would be willing to wait until he was ready for a second time before he was seized by the shoulder and pulled roughly away.

"You idiot, get away from her!" It was Cirocco. Chris did not have time to understand anything beyond that because too much was happening at once. He rolled on the ground, curling into a foetal position, and spasming into violent ejaculation. In a feverish confusion he did not know whether to be embarrassed, angry, or hurt. In a moment it was over and Chris came up off the floor, swinging at Cirocco. With a perfect roundhouse he hit her squarely on the chin. For a moment, reeling back, she looked almost as surprised as he felt. But his triumph lasted only a second. As Cirocco folded like a puppet with her strings cut, his hand began to throb, and Gaby appeared from nowhere, flying at him as though she'd dropped from the sky. The next thing he knew she was kneeling on his chest and about to drive her stiff fingers right through his face.

Instead, she hesitated, and the fire went out of her eyes. She hit the ground with her fist, rolled off him, and patted his cheek.

"Never hit the bones with your fist," she counseled. "That's what sticks and stones were made for."

She helped him to his feet where he saw Robin still on her back and looking baffled. Hornpipe had squeezed into the tent and was seeing to Cirocco, who was working her jaw cautiously.

Chris's fury was obviously still mounting, but with Gaby and a couple of Titanides stationed between him and Cirocco he was forced to voice his anger.

"You had no right to do that," he raved. "Damn it, I can't even think why you would. But this is it! You're getting out or I am."

"Shut up," Cirocco said coldly, waving Hornpipe away and sitting up. "There's a small chance I did something terrible. If that's true, I'll stand still while you both beat the daylights out of me. But hear me out first. Robin, what kind of birth control are you using?"

"I don't know what you're talking about."

"Right. What about you, Chris?"

Chris felt a distinct chill but shrugged it off. She couldn't possibly be right.

"I take pills, but it doesn't—"

"I remember you telling me that. When was the—"

"—but she *can't have children!* She told me so, and if you had—"

"Stop. Hear me out." Cirocco held her hand up until she was sure everyone would listen to her.

"I think you misunderstood her. She said 'can't,' and you thought she meant she was unable to. What she really meant was, because her children would have her condition, she will not impregnate herself. What's the use of sterilization when the act of conception is so complicated?" She looked at Robin, who was shaking her head in exasperation.

"But we were only making love," she said.

Cirocco went to her, took her shoulders, and shook her. "How do you think babies get *made,* damn it? Everywhere but in the Coven it's just like it was for—"

"But I *trust* him, can't you see that?" Robin shouted back. "We were just making love, not making a baby. He wouldn't have. . . ." She wound down and for the first time looked uncertainly at Chris. He had to look away.

As Cirocco explained the true situation, the color slowly drained from Robin's face. Chris had never seen her look frightened, but it was clear she was terrified in retrospect, as well she might have been. The whole bizarre misunderstanding had arisen from Robin's failure to realize that the male orgasm involved ejaculation, and that it was not under his control, and from the impression Chris had formed that Robin was sterilized. She was not, and he was fertile, as the production of the egg with Valiha had established. The fact was that his pills had been lost during his episode in quarantine, and he had been unable to replace them.

Robin was reduced almost to tears. She sat with her head in her hands, shaking, saying, "I didn't know, I didn't know, I really didn't know."

Chris did not know what long-term effects there would be between himself and Robin, but there was one thing that was clear.

"I owe you an apology," he said to Cirocco.

She grinned at him. "No, you don't. I'd have done the same thing. It's not a situation where you hang around for explanations." She rubbed her jaw. "Actually, it's my own fault for not getting out of the way quicker. I think I'm slowing down."

"Maybe I'm speeding up."

"That's a possibility."

As though by mutual accord the others turned back to their tents, leaving Robin and Chris alone. The moment hung awkwardly in the air and Chris felt frightened. If Rocky had realized the score why hadn't he? Maybe because he'd been too eager for sex. Robin seemed to have some of the same feeling. He could tell she was thinking of their earlier conversation and perhaps reassessing it. She turned away from him briefly to collect her thoughts and then very carefully said she was sorry. In a few words she professed not to blame him any more than she blamed herself. It had been a simple misunderstanding, fortunately averted in time. She said she was no more afraid of him now than she had ever been.

But she moved back into her own tent that night.

Cirocco came reeling in after the last day of Carnival, singing loudly. Gaby put her to bed and in the morning loaded her into a canoe and once more covered her with a blanket. They shoved off and soon left the diminishing gaiety of Inglesina Island behind them. Ophion was again quiet, undisturbed, as the party, much subdued, paddled steadily toward the Twilight Sea.

26.

Path of Glory

The body of water half in Crius and half in Phoebe was usually designated on maps as Phoebe or the Phoebe Sea, but no one ever called it that. One traveled through Phoebe and sailed on the Twilight Sea.

It was an apt name. The western end of the sea was in Crius, and thus in daylight, but it extended through the twilight zone and into the night of Phoebe. Seen from a distance sufficient for Gaea's curvature to upend it, the waters of Twilight began in shades of deep blue and green, faded through orange and copper, and ended in black. Roughly in the center was a large island known as Unome, always in twilight, that held two lakes known as Tarn Gandria and Tarn Concordia. A race of insectile creatures lived on the island and nowhere else, and they were known to humans and Titanides as the Iron Masters. Robin gathered from what little was said that they were thoroughly unpleasant, starting with their smell and continuing to just about every aspect of their culture and morals. She was just as glad that the Wizard had no business with them on this trip.

In fact, they planned to take the conservative path. The northern shore of the Twilight Sea was close enough to the straight-line route across it that it made sense to stay near a safe haven, particularly since Twilight was known for its sudden, violent storms.

The navigation of Twilight passed without incident, but Robin spent her time withdrawn from the others. The incident with Chris had upset her greatly. She did not blame him but could not help a certain queasy feeling when she caught him, sometimes, looking at her. Her policy was to draw lessons from the bad things in life, and what she learned from her experiment in heterosexual love was that her worst enemy in Gaea was usually her own ignorance. It was not a new reali-

zation. All through her life she had tended to shut out things
that seemed to have no immediate bearing on her survival. By
doing that, she often missed the things noticed by more patient,
less discriminating people who listened to and watched everything, no matter how trivial it appeared.

And it was time to discard an opinion, which was that the
Wizard was an alcohol-soaked zombie, commanding respect
only through a title and tales of her past deeds. It was a small
thing, really, yet Robin had been impressed when she had time
to think about it. Cirocco could not have heard them until Chris
began to moan, meaning he had already been on the edge of
disaster. Cirocco had thought quickly, putting together such
details as the lost contraceptives and Robin's genetic disorder,
deducing their shared ignorance and Robin's probable fertility,
and had immediately acted on her answer without worrying
about the consequences. No matter that what she had done was
socially unthinkable; she had been right, had known it, and
had acted.

She wondered if Chris's blow had actually surprised Cirocco
or if it had been allowed to land. It was obvious that he felt
bad about being the worst fighter in a group of three women
and one man. Being able to hit her at a moment of such in-
dignity had allowed him to salvage some self-respect.

That was something she would never know. What she did
know was that she would not underestimate Cirocco again.

Ophion emerged from Twilight in much the same way it
had from Nox: the sea narrowed gradually and at some point
became a river. But instead of a series of river pumps, the
group confronted five kilometers of the swiftest water they had
yet seen. They paused in the last quiet pool, and the four boats
drew together to discuss the approach. Only Cirocco and Gaby
knew this part of the river. The Titanides listened, paddling
slowly backward to stay out of the current.

They moved into the current one at a time, Cirocco and
Hornpipe in the lead, Gaby and Psaltery bringing up the rear.
When her turn came, Robin exulted in the speed and noise.
She knelt in the bow and paddled vigorously until Hautbois
advised her to save her strength and let the river do most of
the work. She could feel the results of the Titanide's strong,
calculated strokes and did her best to help rather than hinder.
There was a rhythm to find, a way of becoming attuned to the
river. Twice she fended off submerged rocks with the end of

her paddle and once was rewarded with a shout of encouragement from Hautbois. She was still grinning when they swung around a bend and confronted a hundred meters of chaos that seemed to go straight down.

There was no time for second thoughts. Robin recited a prayer almost before she realized what she was doing and held on tight.

The canoe shuddered. Water spilled over the side and sprayed in her face; then she was battling to keep the nose pointed downstream. She thought she heard Hautbois shout, but the roaring of the river was too loud for words. The wood splintered beneath her, and suddenly she was in the river, clinging to the side of the canoe.

When she got her head above the water and opened her eyes, she saw that Hautbois was also in the river, but standing on the bottom submerged to the waist. She had wrestled them to an area of relative quiet at the side of the river and now clambered onto a rocky shelf and lifted the stern of the canoe.

"You all right?" she called, and Robin managed to nod. When she looked up, she saw Gaby and Psaltery.

After an inspection and a shouted conference they decided the canoe would have to complete the trip down the rapids; that was fortunate since the other would have been dangerously overloaded with the two Titanides and two humans. Robin would have to ride with Gaby, while Hautbois managed the task of nursing the disabled craft down the river. Robin did not argue but climbed into Gaby's boat with a sense of failure.

"I can't fix that," Hautbois told them after inspecting the broken ribs of the canoe. "We'll have to salvage the skin and wait until we get into another stand of canoe trees."

"Robin can ride with me and Valiha," Chris offered.

Robin hesitated only a moment, then nodded to him.

They were beached on a wide mud flat at the confluence of Ophion and the river Arges, near the center of Phoebe. The land was dark, with only an occasional spindly tree silver and translucent in the moonlight. Phoebe was actually a tiny bit brighter than Rhea had been. The reason was the Twilight Sea, part of which was in sunlight, was a better reflector than the lands which curved up on each side of Nox. But the slight gain was lost in the dreariness of the land itself. Rhea at least had been rugged; central Phoebe was swamp.

Robin hated it. She stood in mud that covered her ankles and looked out over land that must have been heaven for eels and frogs but for nothing else. It was already hard to remember the exhilaration of the white water. She was drenched and saw no chance of drying out soon. It didn't help to think that had she not been in the front of the canoe, the accident might not have happened. She wondered once again what she was doing here.

She was not the only one who didn't like it. Nasu squirmed restlessly in the bag slung under her arm. The trip had not been easy on the snake. She knew she should have left the demon at the Coven—had planned to do so but at the last moment had not been able to. When she loosened the string, Nasu poked her head out and sampled the air with her tongue. Finding it at least as cool and damp as the inside of the sack and seeing no dry place to curl up, she soon retreated.

Hautbois and Psaltery were busy breaking down the damaged canoe, transferring its contents to the other three. Robin saw the others some distance away, standing on what passed for high ground in Phoebe, which meant their feet were a few centimeters above the water. Cirocco sat on a rock facing the central Phoebe cable, which loomed above them, but the others looked north. Robin could not find anything worth seeing, but she slogged through the mud to join them.

"What's so interesting?" she asked.

"I don't know yet," Chris said. "I'm waiting for Hornpipe to get to it."

Hornpipe stamped the ground restlessly.

"Maybe I shouldn't have brought it up," he said.

"You certainly shouldn't have," Valiha agreed, glowering at him. But Hornpipe went ahead doggedly.

"Well, you are here to find a way to prove your heroism to Gaea. I just thought I should point out opportunities. Take it or leave it."

"I leave it," Robin said. She looked at Chris. "You aren't serious, are you?"

"I don't really know," Chris admitted. "I came because Gaby said it was better than sitting around and waiting for opportunity to come to me, and that made sense. I never did really decide if I was rejecting Gaea's rules. I'm here, so I must not have rejected them completely. But I'll admit I hadn't given much thought to taking off on my own."

"And you shouldn't," Valiha said.

"Still, I ought to hear what's out there."

Robin snorted but had to admit she was interested to know.

"That mountain," Hornpipe said. Robin saw a conical black smudge. "It's nearly at the northern rampart," he went on. "It's a bad area, from all accounts, where little lives. I have never been there myself. But all know it is the home of Kong."

"What's Kong?" Chris asked.

"A giant ape," said Gaby, who now joined them. "What else? Let's get going, folks. The canoes are ready."

"Just a minute," Chris said. "I'd like to hear more."

"What's to hear? He sits up there. . . ." She looked suspicious. "Say, you weren't thinking of . . . right. Come over here, Chris, and I'll tell you about Kong." She took him a few meters away, glancing at Cirocco. Robin followed, but the Titanides did not. When Gaby spoke, she kept her voice low.

"Rocky doesn't like to hear about Kong," she said, and grimaced. "I can hardly blame her. Kong is a one-shot, about a hundred years old and the only one of his species. He's in the same class with the dragons Gaea told you about; each one different, no provision to breed. They pop out of the ground after Gaea creates them, live as long as they're programmed to live, which is usually quite a long time, and die. Kong was based on a movie Gaea saw, like the giant sandworm in Mnemosyne. There're several things like that in here. Of course, they become objects for quests by pilgrims. I hate to think how many people have been slaughtered by Kong. Short of a gun the size of a tree or one hell of a lot of dynamite, he's unkillable. Believe me, a lot of people have tried it."

"It must be possible," Chris said.

Gaby shrugged. "I guess anything is if you try long enough. I don't think *you're* ready to take him, though. I know I wouldn't try it. Come on, Chris. There are simpler ways to commit suicide."

"Why does Cirocco fear him?" Robin asked. "Or perhaps 'fear' is not the right word."

"'Fear' is *precisely* the right word," Gaby said almost in a whisper. "Kong will eat anything that moves. The Wizard is the one exception. Gaea built him with a tropism. He can smell her at a hundred kilometers, and her scent is the only thing that will bring him from his mountain. I don't think you can call it love, but it's a strong compulsion. He'll follow her right to the edge of the twilight zone. Whatever else I might say about Gaea, she usually leaves an escape clause, so she made Kong with an aversion to light, like the sandworm hates the cold on either side of Mnemosyne. He won't follow her into Tethys or Crius.

"But if the wind were from the south, we wouldn't be in Phoebe right now. Rocky crosses at the southern rampart when she can—if she has to visit Phoebe at all—because if Kong smells her, he will come running. If he catches her, he takes her back to his mountain. He did catch her once, about fifty years ago. It was six months before she could get away."

"What did he do?" Robin asked.

"She won't talk about it." Gaby raised her eyebrows and looked at each of them, then turned and walked away.

Robin looked back to the mountain, then saw that Chris was staring at it, too.

"You aren't—"

"What has she been telling you?"

Robin was startled at the nearness of the Wizard and wondered how she had approached so silently.

"Nothing," she said.

"Come on, I heard some of it before she so cleverly moved you away. You didn't believe all that, did you?"

Robin thought back over it and realized, with some chagrin, that she had.

"Well, it wasn't *all* lies," Cirocco conceded. "Kong is there, and he is twenty meters tall, and he did capture me and hold me prisoner, and I don't talk about it much because it was extremely unpleasant. He fouls his nest. By now the compressed shit in his cave must be ninety meters deep. He likes to take his prisoners out and look at them from time to time, but as for the sexual innuendo, forget it. He isn't even equipped; he's neuter.

"He does have a terrific sense of smell, too, but that business about smelling just *me* is bunk. He is attracted to all human females. What he homes in on is menstrual blood."

Robin felt concerned for the first time. Why had they come through Phoebe *now?*

"Don't worry," Cirocco soothed. "His nose is so good there's not really any time when you're safe. Anyhow, your smell is what would protect you, in a way. When he catches a man, he eats him. Titanides confuse him. He doesn't rely on his eyes too much, but when he gets a Titanide, he bites off part and saves the torso because at least it looks right. Then he plays with it until it falls apart." She frowned at the memory, looking away from them.

"But he *is* killable," she went on. "I could think of a couple of ways that should turn the trick. There was one go-getter about thirty years back who even managed to capture him. I think he planned to bring him back alive, though I don't know how because Kong got loose and ate him. The point is the guy had him tied down and could have killed him.

"But nobody goes to his mountain to kill him because there's something that's marginally easier and will get the same result if you're a pilgrim. You can rescue one of his captives. If you're a woman, there isn't even the risk of getting killed yourself because he never kills women. Not that I'd recommend being captured by him; there're more pleasant ways to spend your time. Still, he's usually got somebody up there. I know for sure there's one woman he's had for six months now, and there might even be more."

She turned away from them, reconsidered, and came back.

"One thing Gaby didn't tell you is how I got out. If you think it was a case of turning my knowledge of Gaea to good use or of out-thinking the old bastard, you're wrong. I might still be there if I had been left to my own devices. The fact is that Gaby got me out at great risk to her own freedom, and I don't talk about it because it frankly doesn't fit well with my image of myself. Kong is a pretty scruffy monster, but he's nothing to laugh about, and Gaby fills the role of knight in shining armor as well as anyone could, but I'm afraid I was a miserable damsel in distress. I didn't have much self-respect left by the time she dragged me out of there." She shook her head slowly. "And I couldn't give her the traditional reward." She hurried away from them.

Robin looked once more toward the mountain, then back at Chris, saw a suspicious look in his eye, and remembered what she had been about to say before Cirocco interrupted.

"No," she said firmly, taking his arm and pulling him toward the waiting canoes. "That's what Gaea wants you to do. She wants you to put on a good show for her, and she doesn't care whether you live through it."

Chris sighed but did not resist her.

"You must have a pretty low opinion of my ability to take care of myself."

The remark surprised her, and she searched his face. "Is that what you think? Look, I understand the need to prove yourself. I probably have it stronger than you do, after all. But personal honor cannot be placed at the service of malevolence. It must *mean* something."

"It would mean something to that woman up there. I'll bet she doesn't see it as a game."

"She's not your affair. She's a stranger."

"I'm surprised to hear you say that about a sister."

Robin had been a little surprised to hear it herself and uneasily searched for a motivation. When she found it, she was not delighted but faced it anyway. Part of it was, truly, that she detested the thought of anyone doing anything to impress the slime-Goddess, Gaea. The other part. . . .

"I don't want to see you hurt. You're my friend."

27.

Burst of Flame

"This could be the most dangerous part of the trip," Cirocco told them.

"I disagree," Gaby said. "Iapetus will be the worst."

"I thought Oceanus would be," Chris put in.

Gaby shook her head. "Oceanus is tough, but I've never had too much trouble getting across. He's still lying low, making his plans. I don't expect to live to see the results. These beings think in terms of millennia. Iapetus is the most actively hostile region. You can count on him to notice you when you pass through and to try to do something about it."

The group was gathered around the base of the central Phoebe cable, which, like the one in Hyperion, came to ground in a wide bend of the river. It was actually more accurate to say the cable had created the bend through a process Cirocco called millennial sag. Gaealithic evidence beneath the cable proved that in earlier times Ophion had flowed among the cable strands. As its rim stretched, the land beneath the juncture had been pulled up and the river had found a new path.

"You're right about Iapetus and Oceanus," Cirocco said. "Though I'm not sure Oceanus will stay quiet much longer. The thing is that this is the only place where two strong regionals opposed to Gaea's rule are border to border. Rhea's too insane to be called an enemy. Beyond Tethys is Thea, who is still loyal to Gaea, and past her is Metis, who's an enemy but cowardly. Dione is dead, and beyond her—"

"One of the regional brains is dead?" Robin asked. "What effect does that have on things?"

"Not as much as you'd suspect," Cirocco said. "Dione's bad luck was to be squeezed between Metis and Iapetus when the war came. She was too loyal to cooperate or even to stay in the background, so they attacked her and she was mortally wounded. She's been dead for three or four centuries, but the land itself is doing okay. Iapetus has tried to take it over, but he hasn't had much luck. I believe Gaea is able to handle most things that need doing."

"I've had a fair amount of work there," Gaby pointed out. "Things break down more rapidly in Dione. But it's pretty peaceful."

"The point is," Cirocco continued, "that only here with Phoebe and Tethys do we have a situation with two strong enemies of Gaea side by side. I blimp over it when I can, and I thought you two ought to know you have that option if you want to leave us now. We're going to cross Phoebe and Tethys just as quickly as we can, but it has to be on land because while I can get a blimp to come in here and pick us up, none of them would take us from central Phoebe to central Tethys, which is what I have to do." She looked at Chris, then at Robin.

"I'll stick it out," Robin said. "But I would like to get out of here. I worry that Kong has . . . you know. I've got two more days to go."

"As long as the wind holds, we're okay," Gaby said. "If it shifts, we'll get moving very fast, I promise you. What about you, Chris?"

Chris was still thinking about Kong, too, but not in the way Robin seemed to assume. He was not anxious to become a hero, dead or alive, but was bothered to know that this was the first real opportunity he had seen.

"I'll stick around," he said.

The Titanides did not like Phoebe. They tended to jump at unexpected sounds. Valiha almost stepped on Robin's foot at one point. They stayed near the fire a short distance from the outlying cable strands and sang their songs, which sounded to Chris like whistling in the dark.

He didn't blame them. He felt it, too.

Cirocco had said she did not expect to be long. There had been no question of anyone, even Gaby, going with her when she called on Phoebe. The Wizard knew Phoebe would not go as far as to drain her acid pool, so she would have to stand on the stairs and communicate as best she could. There seemed little reason why the encounter should last more than a few minutes. Cirocco would ask Phoebe to return to Gaea's arms and reap the benefits of her love—which meant avoid the consequences of her wrath since there was little Gaea could do to improve anything but a lot she could do to hurt Phoebe. Phoebe would refuse and send Cirocco on her way, possibly with a demonstration of power meant to frighten but not to seriously injure her. Phoebe was no fool. She was aware of the spoke pointed at her like a cosmic siege gun, and she knew about the Big Squeeze.

Cirocco had told Chris about the Squeeze, which had been Gaea's final weapon in the Oceanic Rebellion. The interior of each of the six spokes was lined with a thick coat of green which, when examined closely, turned out to be the trees of the vertical forest. It was vertical because of the ground; the trees grew horizontally from the spoke walls and dwarfed any redwood.

To apply the Big Squeeze, Gaea first deprived the forest of moisture for several weeks. It became the tallest pile of firewood ever conceived. It was not necessary for Gaea to squeeze too hard to dislodge the trees in their millions to shower over the night below. She had done this to Oceanus, setting it afire as it fell, then closing the lower spoke valve. The fire storm had scorched Oceanus down to the bedrock. He had apparently been impressed because it was ten thousand years before he dared defy Gaea again.

The hours dragged by, and Cirocco did not arrive. She had been up and down the staircases to the regional brains enough times to know within a few minutes how long the journey should take her. It had seemed unlikely that she would spend more than an hour with Phoebe, but that time came and passed, marked by the slow movements of the gyroscopic clock, and still no Cirocco. When Gaea had completed another sixty-one-minute rev, Chris joined the conference to determine whether the tents should be pitched. There was not much sentiment for the idea, though Robin and Chris had been awake a long time. Gaby hardly bothered to talk about it; unstated but known to all was the certainty that before much longer she would go after her old friend, with or without help.

Chris moved away from the group and reclined on the dry ground. He oriented his body north and south and placed the Gaean clock on his belly, its axis in the east-west plane of rotation. He could no more see it move than he could watch water freeze, but when he looked away and then looked back, the motion was apparent. They had a mechanical clock which was much more useful because it worked all the time, regardless of orientation, but this one was more fun. It seemed to him that he could feel Gaea spinning beneath him. He recalled a similar feeling on a clear night back on Earth, and suddenly he wanted to be home, with or without his cure. It was not the same to be overwhelmed by the vastness of a starry night as it was to look up the dark, towering spoke to an unseen but tangible heaven.

"Strap on those bags, you quartet of quadrupedal quacks!"

"How about I ride *you* this time, Captain?" Hornpipe shouted.

"Hey, Rocky, how do you stay balanced so long?"

Her return brought Chris back from the edge of sleep. The group was transformed into a swirl of energy that Cirocco shaped toward the task of breaking the rough camp and getting back to the canoes. But finally, Gaby asked the question they all wanted answered.

"How did it go, Rocky?"

"Not bad, not bad, I guess. She was more . . . talkative than I've seen her. I almost got the impression that it was *she* who. . . ." She looked up and into Chris's eyes, then pursed her lips. "Tell you later. But I'm nervous. Not anything I can put my finger on, but I had the feeling she was up to something. The sooner we're out of here, the better I'll feel."

"Me, too," Gaby said. "Let's get moving."

Chris had worries of his own as he swung astride Valiha. The palms of his hands were wet, and there was a fluttering in his stomach, heat flashes washing over his body. Combining these symptoms with the sense of foreboding that now crept over him, he was as sure as he had ever been that another attack was imminent.

And so what? Tough it out; let it happen; these folks can take care of themselves. If anyone got hurt, it would probably be he, not they. It was not the first time he had thought of telling someone an attack was coming on. As before, he now decided against it, changed his mind, again elected to say nothing. Part of him knew this process of vacillation was the perfect defense because there was little chance he would act until it was too late.

No! Not this time. He turned to Gaby, who rode a meter to his right. As he did, he saw from the corner of one eye that Valiha had turned her head to look at him, and from the other he detected a flicker of motion.

He saw it a fraction of a second before Valiha did. Just a
gaping mouth bristling with spikes, silently expanding, a circle
cut by a thin horizontal line. It was far away and it was upon
them, just like that. So little time.

He leaped, hit Gaby hard enough to carry her from Psaltery's
back.

"Down! Get down!" he shouted, while Valiha shrieked an
alarm in Titanide.

The sound hit like a fist, solid as an avalanche, as the buzz
bomb ignited its torch and accelerated no more than a meter
off the ground. The air pulsed with the rhythm of its engine;
then Chris was blinded by what seemed like a flashbulb exploding in his eyes, and the sound dopplered far down the
scale. He put his hand to the back of his head and felt hair
singed into little knots.

Gaby struggled out from under him, fighting for breath.
Robin was prone, ten meters away. Her hands were held together in front of her. A thin blue-white line grew from her
fists, followed rapidly by another. The tiny warheads popped
like firecrackers, far short of their goal.

"It came from the cable," Cirocco called out. "Everyone
stay down."

Chris did as she said, then squirmed until he faced the dark
prominence silhouetted against the upturned sands of Tethys.
He realized that was what had saved them; he had seen the
buzz bomb's motion before it was on the deck, during the last
part of its fall from a perch on the cable.

"There's another!" Cirocco warned. Chris tried to make his
spine meet his belly. The second attacker roared by to his right,
followed in echelon by two more, seconds apart.

"I don't like this," Gaby yelled, very close to Chris's left
ear. "The Titanides are too big, and the ground is too flat."
Chris turned and saw her face, a few centimeters from his own
and smeared with dirt. He felt his hand squeezed tightly.
"Thanks," she whispered.

"I don't like it either," Cirocco shouted back. "But we can't
get up yet."

"Crawl to the lowest place you can find then," Gaby suggested. "Come on," she said quietly. "Psaltery's in the lowest
spot around here."

The brown-skinned Titanide was two meters behind them,
in the center of a depression that even wishful thinking could

not make more than forty centimeters deep. Gaby slapped Psaltery's flank as Chris edged in beside them.

"Don't get up and look around, old friend," Gaby said.

"I won't. You keep your head down, Boss." Psaltery coughed, a strange and oddly melodious sound.

"Are you all right?" Gaby asked.

"I hit the ground pretty hard," was all he would say.

"We'll get Hautbois to take a look when we get out of here. Damn!" She wiped her hand on her pants. "Wouldn't you know we'd land in the only patch of wet ground on this stinking hill?"

"Northwest," Valiha called from a position Chris could not see. He did not try to find the approaching buzz bomb but did succeed in making himself smaller and flatter than he would have thought possible. The monster roared by, again followed by two more. He wondered why the first had not come in formation.

When he risked a look, he was actually able to see one dropping away from the cable. It was just a speck, and it must have been three kilometers up. It had clung there, nose down, waiting for the right opportunity. It might have come at them when they approached the cable but had sense enough to know that when the group left, their backs would be turned.

This one also seemed to know it was now useless to try for a kill. It passed fifty meters above them, snorting an insolent challenge. Another ignited shortly after dropping from the cable and could not resist making a pass at about the same altitude. That was a bad mistake since it gave Robin a good wide target at a realistic range, plenty of time to follow it, and three tries to get it right. Both the second and third shots connected. Chris got his best view yet as the swift shape was captured in the twin flashes of the exploding bullets. It was a tapered cylinder with swept-back rigid wings and a double tail. There was an eye tucked under the wing. The buzz bomb was a great black shark of the skies, all mouth and appetite, with sound effects added.

For a moment it looked as if the creature had not been harmed by Robin's shots. Then the creature began to bleed fire that spilled across the sky, and the landscape was washed in a dull orange light. Chris looked up in time to see the explosion and could barely hear it for the shrill, warbling victory cry of Robin the Nine-fingered.

"Send me more buzz bombs!" she shouted.

They all watched as the creature arced high and began its death roll. There was a supersonic keening just before it hit ground on the far side of Ophion.

When ten minutes had passed with no more sign of the creatures, Cirocco crawled to Gaby and suggested they make a run for the boats. Chris was all for it; he worried about being out on the river, but anything was better than hugging this little patch of ground.

"Sounds good," Gaby agreed. "Here's the plan, folks. Don't waste any time. When I give the signal, humans will mount and Titanides will head for the boats at top speed. Ride facing backwards, and keep your eyes open. We've got to cover all points of the compass and be ready to hit ground instantly because we may not have more than two or three seconds. Any questions?"

"I think you must find another mount," Psaltery said quietly.

"What? Is it that bad? What is it, your leg?"

"Worse, I think."

"Hand me that lamp, will you, Rocky? Thanks, now. . . ." She froze, cried out in horror, and dropped the lamp. In its soft light Chris had seen her hands and arms smeared with dark red blood.

"What has she done to you?" Gaby moaned. She fell on the prone body and began trying to turn him over. Cirocco shouted for Hautbois to come quickly, then ordered Robin and Valiha to stand watch. It was not until she turned back to the injured Titanide that Chris realized the sticky mud on his own face and chest was mixed from the spilled blood of Psaltery. He moved away, appalled, and still he was sitting in mud. The Titanide had bled rivers of it, was lying in a pool of his own making.

"Don't, don't," he protested as Gaby and Hautbois tried to turn him. Hautbois did stop, but Gaby ordered her to start again. Instead, the Titanide healer put her head close to Psaltery's and listened for a moment.

"It's no use," she said. "His death is arrived."

"He can't be dead."

"He still lives. Come, sing good-bye to him while he hears."

Chris moved away, went to kneel beside Robin. She said nothing, looked at him for only a moment, then resumed her watch on the night sky. He recalled, shakily, that minutes before he had been sure an attack was coming. In fact, one had, but not the kind he expected.

There was no sound but the singing of Hautbois and Gaby. Hautbois's voice was sweetly melodic, not sorrowful. Chris wished he could understand it. Gaby would never be a skilled singer, but it did not matter. She choked but kept at it. At last there was just the sound of her sobbing.

Cirocco insisted they turn the body over. They had to examine the death wound, she said, to understand how it had happened and learn more about the buzz bombs. Gaby did not argue but stood by herself some distance away.

When they lifted his legs and began to turn him, a bushel of shapeless wetness spilled in the mud. Chris hurried away and fell to his hands and knees. His stomach continued to heave long after it was completely empty.

Later he learned that the wound had run the length of Psaltery's body, had come quite close to severing his trunk from his lower body. They decided that the long right wing of the creature had swept along his side seconds after Chris threw Gaby to the ground. It had cut so neatly that it had to be razor-edged in front.

They brought Psaltery to the bank of the river, to a place protected from attack by a few trees. Chris stayed back with Robin, watched as Gaby knelt and cut off the bright orange hair, then stood and tied it securely. Without ceremony, the three gathered. Titanides rolled the body into the water and pushed it out into the current with long poles. Psaltery was a dark shape bobbing in the gentle ripples. Chris watched him out of sight.

They stayed there for ten revs, not wanting to catch up with his body. No one felt like doing much, and there was very little talk. The Titanides spent the time weaving and singing quietly. When Chris asked Cirocco to translate the songs for him, she said they were all about Psaltery.

"They're not particularly sad songs," she said. "None of these three was really close to Psaltery. But even his best friends won't mourn the way we do. Remember, to them he's gone. He doesn't exist anymore. But he *did* exist, and if he is to live in any sense, it must be in song. So they sing of what

he was to them. They sing of the things he did that made him
a good person. It's not much different from what we do, except
for the lack of an afterlife. It's doubly important to them because of that, I think."

"I'm an atheist, myself," Chris said.

"So am I. But it's different. We both had to reject the
concept of life after death, even if we weren't brought up to
believe in it, because all human cultures are steeped in the
idea. You get it everywhere you turn. So I think in the back
of your mind and my mind—no matter how we deny it—there's
some part that hopes we're wrong or maybe even is *sure* the
reasoning mind is wrong. Even atheists experience out-of-body
transformations when they die and are brought back. It's deep
in your soul, and it just does not exist in theirs. What amazes
me is that they're such a cheerful race in the face of that. I
wonder if Gaea built that into them, too, or if it's their own
invention. I won't ask her because I don't really want to know;
I'd prefer to think it's their particular genius to rise above the
futility of it all, to love life so much and demand nothing more
of her."

Chris had never thought about the advantages of a "decent
burial." He could not help, in his human way, thinking of the
body as the person. That connection was what caused humans
to seal their dead in caskets to keep the worms away or to burn
them and remove all possibility of further depredation.

The river burial had a certain rustic poetry, but Ophion
cared not at all about preserving the decency of the dead. The
river deposited Psaltery on a mud flat three kilometers downstream. When they passed her ruined body, the Titanides did
not even glance at it. Chris could not look away. The corpse
crawling with scavengers haunted his sleep for a long time.

28.

Triana

Maps of Gaea often used the device of shading the six night regions to emphasize that the sun never shines on them. This made the days all the more vivid. Tethys was usually printed in yellow or light brown to indicate that it was a desert region. It sometimes led travelers to believe that the desert began in the Phoebe-Tethys twilight zone. This was not the case. The hard bare rock and drifting sand enfolded the central swamp of Phoebe, extending arid arms north and south of it and as far west as the central cables.

Ophion flowed due east through the middle of eastern Phoebe, apparently gouging out a hundred-kilometer watercourse known as Confusion Canyon. But as the name suggested, few geological concepts applied inside Gaea. The canyon was there because Gaea wanted it; her three million years was not nearly enough time for water to have cut so deeply. Nevertheless, it was a passable imitation, though bearing a closer kinship to the subsidence formations of the Martian Tithonius Lacus than to the hydrologically formed Grand Canyon of Arizona. Why Gaea chose to imitate such planetary geology no one could say.

After flowing down the river for some time, Robin was able to stand at the *top* of the canyon and look down at where she had been. As in Rhea, river pumps were responsible. They had made two difficult portages, during which Robin had bettered her mountaineering skills. The buzz bombs had made the highway too dangerous since the road was through the tableland to the north, too open to attack. They were thankful for the sheer protecting cliffs even as they struggled up them.

In all, it took three hectorevs to get out of the canyon. It was their slowest progress to date. The fresh fruits that had formed the more appetizing portion of their meals were no longer to be found. They subsisted on dried provisions from their packs. There was still game to be taken. At one point, when they found a plateau rich in small scaly ten-legged creatures, the Titanides killed more than a hundred of them and spent three days preserving them with smoke and curatives obtained from leaves and roots.

Robin had never felt stronger. She had found to her surprise that the rugged life agreed with her. She woke up quickly, ate a lot, and slept well at the end of the day. Had it not been for Psaltery's death, she thought she might actually have been happy. She had not been able to say that for a long time.

It was oddly disorienting to see Ophion stop at the edge of day, but that is just what it did. At its eastern end it emptied into a small brown lake known as Triana, and it did not come out the other side. The river had been the constant factor in their journey so far; they had left it only to skirt the pumps. Even Nox and Twilight were just wide places in the river. It felt like a bad omen to Robin.

That omen was as nothing to the sight that confronted them as they paddled their reduced fleet to the Trianan shore. It was a boneyard. The skeletal remains of a billion creatures littered the white sand beach, made great still waves and dunes, heaped into rickety golgothas. When they gained the shore, they stood in the shadow of a single bone plate eight meters high, while beneath their feet they crunched the ribs of creatures smaller than mice.

It looked like the end of all things. Robin, who did not think of herself as superstitious, could not shake a feeling of foreboding. She seldom noticed the pale texture of Gaean daylight. Everyone spoke of the "perpetual afternoon" that prevailed in the wheel; Robin had as often been able to imagine it as morning. But not here. The shores of Triana were frozen at an instant just before the end of Time. The heaped bones were the necropolitan skyline of death, set in the vast brown desert of Tethys.

She recalled something Gaby had said, likening Ophion to a toilet. It certainly looked that way from Triana. All the death of the great wheel had come to rest on the shores of the lake. She almost said something to Gaby, stopped herself just in time. Psaltery would probably end up here.

"Feeling bad, Robin?"

She looked up and saw the Wizard facing her. She shook

herself to get rid of the sense of melancholy that had stolen over her. It did not help much. Cirocco put a hand on her shoulder and led her down the beach. A few weeks ago Robin would have rejected the gesture, but now she welcomed it. The sand was as fine as powdered sugar, pleasantly hot between her toes.

"Don't let it get you down," Cirocco said. "This isn't what it looks like."

"I'm not sure what it looks like."

"It's not Gaea's waste bin. It *is* a graveyard. But it's not the end of Ophion. The river flows underground and comes up on the other side of Tethys. The bones are brought here by scavengers. They're about half a meter long, and one form lives in the sand and another in the lake. It's a complex story, but it boils down to, neither type can get along without the other. They meet here at the shore to exchange gifts, mate, and spawn. It's a common pattern in Gaea."

"It's just depressing," Robin said.

"The Titanides love it. Not many of them get here, but those that do take lots of pictures to show the folks back home. It is kind of pretty, if you can get used to it."

"I don't think I could." Robin wiped her forehead, then removed her shirt and went to the water's edge. She soaked it, wrung it out, and put it back on. "Why is it so hot here? The sun isn't enough to heat your skin, but the sand's blazing."

"It comes from below. All the regions are heated and cooled by fluids running underground. It's pumped out to the big fins in space to be heated on the sunside or cooled on the darkside."

Robin looked at Cirocco's browned face, at the tanned skin on her bare arms and legs. She recalled that the body under the red blanket that was apparently the only article of clothing she owned was just as brown. But damn it, it looked like a tan, and it had been bothering her for weeks now. Her own skin was as milky white as the day she arrived.

"Are you and Gaby naturally dark-skinned? You don't look it, but I can't believe you got that tan in here."

"I'm a little darker than Gaby, but she's as light as you are. And you're right, the sun didn't do this. Maybe I'll tell you about that someday." She stopped walking and looked to the east. There was a break in the high bone cairns, and it was possible to see a range of low hills several kilometers away. She turned and called to the group, which Robin was surprised to discover was more than 200 meters down the beach.

"When you get the boats broken down," Cirocco shouted, "join us over here."

In a few minutes they were gathered around Cirocco, who squatted on the sand and used her finger to draw a long map.

"Phoebe, Tethys, Thea," she said. "Triana." She stabbed a small circle, then drew a series of peaks just east of it. "The Euphonic Range. To the north of them, here, the Northwind Range. Out here by itself, La Oreja de Oro." She glanced up at Chris. "That means 'Ear of Gold,' and there's the possibility of a quest there, if you're interested. Otherwise, we won't be going near it."

"Not interested," Chris said with an amused smile.

"Okay. To the east—"

"Don't we get to hear the story?" Robin asked against her better judgment.

"No need for it," Cirocco said. "The Ear of Gold can't possibly concern us unless we go there. It's not a mobile threat, like Kong." While Robin wondered if she was being toyed with, Cirocco was drawing a long line of peaks, from the north to the south, cutting across the width of Tethys.

"The Royal Blue Line. Somebody was in a poetic frame of mind, I guess. They do take on a blue tint when the air is right, but they're pretty dull mountains for the most part. Some rocky cliffs, but if you go up the southern slopes down here, you can walk from one peak to the next without much trouble.

"The road goes northeast from the lake, through the big space between the Northwinds and the Euphonics, which is called Tethys Gap." She looked up, deadpan. "Or, as it's sometimes called, Orthodontist Pass."

"Except we agreed not to use that joke anymore," Gaby said.

Cirocco grinned. "My apologies. Anyhow, through the gap the road goes due east over a lot of very gradual up-and-downs, passes the central cable, through the Royal Blue Line, and so on to this lake with the slanted cable in the middle, known as Valencia. As, yes, it is sort of orange-colored."

"With a very long stem," Gaby put in.

"Right. Well, that wasn't one of my names." She straightened, slapping sand from her hands.

"Frankly," she said, "I don't know what's the best thing to do from here. We originally planned to follow the road and not worry too much about the sand wraiths, but now that we've—"

"Sand wraiths?" Chris asked.

"More about them later. As I was saying, I'm more worried about the buzz bombs right now. We've never heard of a concerted attack like what happened at Phoebe. Before this, they've always traveled alone. It could be that we disturbed a nesting place, but there's also the possibility they're exhibiting new behavior. That can happen in Gaea."

Gaby had her arms folded in front of her. She was looking straight at Cirocco, who would not meet her eyes.

"It's also possible the attack was deliberate," Gaby said.

Robin looked from one to the other. "What do you mean by that?"

"Never mind," Cirocco said quickly. "I don't think so, and if it was, they weren't after either of you."

Robin assumed that meant Gaby and Cirocco were wondering if it had something to do with Cirocco's visit to Phoebe. Possibly Phoebe had some influence with the buzz bombs, had persuaded them to try to kill the Wizard. Once again she was struck with the odd lives these two women led.

"The other possibility is to go through the mountains," Cirocco resumed. "They would give us some protection from the buzz bombs, though we'd still have to stay alert. What I'm suggesting is that we go down the Euphonics here." She knelt once more and traced the route as she spoke. "It's a short dash, no more than twenty kilometers, from here to the hills. It's about thirty from the end of the Euphonics to the southern reaches of the Royal Blues. How long would that take, Hornpipe?"

The Titanide considered it. "With Gaby doubling up, one of us will be slower. We could have her trade mounts twice in the course of the journey. I should say we could make it in one rev, pacing ourselves. More like two or two and a half for the second crossing because we will be tired."

"Okay. No matter how we look at it, this route would slow us down."

"Maybe I missed something," Robin said. "Do we have an appointment?"

Cirocco smiled. "You've got a point. Better safe than swift. I'm not sure, myself. I figure we could make our way to the central cable, dash across to it, and if we haven't seen any buzz bombs to that point, we could make a decision again about whether to stick to the highway. But I'd like to hear what you think." She looked from face to face around the group.

Robin had not realized until that point that Cirocco had taken over the group. It was an odd way to do it—asking the other six to advise her on a decision—but the fact remained that a week earlier it would have been Gaby doing the asking. She looked at Gaby and could detect no resentment. In fact, she seemed happier than she had been since Psaltery's death.

The consensus was to follow the mountain route, since that seemed to be the one Cirocco preferred. They mounted, Gaby sitting behind Cirocco for the first third of the trip, and set off under skies that were growing cloudy in the west.

29.

Across the Sands

The clouds arrived overhead as the Titanides were resting after their long run across the dunes between Triana and the foothills of the Euphonics. Cirocco glanced at Hornpipe, who consulted his clock.

"The second decirev of the eighty-seventh," he told her.

"Right on time."

Chris didn't understand it for a moment.

"You mean you...."

Cirocco shrugged. "I didn't make the clouds. But I did ask for them. I called while we were still in the canyon. Gaea said she could give me an overcast but wouldn't go so far as to make it rain. You can't have everything."

"I don't understand what you wanted clouds for." Or how one could just ask for them, he added to himself.

"That's because I haven't told you about the sand wraiths yet. Hornpipe, are you folks ready to go yet?" When the Titanide nodded, Cirocco stood and wiped the sand from her legs. "Let's mount up, and I'll tell you as we go."

"Sand wraiths are silicon-based creatures. We call them that because they live beneath the sand and they're translucent. They'd be hell to fight if they lived in a night region, but you can see them well enough in Tethys.

"The scientific name for them is something like *Hydrophobicus gaeani*. I may have gotten the endings wrong. It describes them pretty well. They are intelligent and have the sweet disposition of a rabid dog. I've spoken with them twice, under carefully controlled conditions. They are so xenophobic

229

that the word 'bigotry' is pitifully inadequate; racists to the tenth power. To them there is only the race of wraiths and Gaea. Everything else is food or enemies. They will pause in the act of killing you only if they aren't sure which you are, but more likely they'll kill first and decide later."

"They are very bad people," Valiha confirmed solemnly.

The Titanides were riding three abreast now so Cirocco could tell Chris and Robin about the wraiths. Chris was not sure this was good strategy, and he kept scanning the sky nervously. The Euphonic Mountains were more rugged than the dunes they had just crossed, but not enough for his tastes. It would have felt better to be in canyons so narrow that they had to proceed single file. The hills ahead did go higher, sometimes reaching up in mesalike formations. Of course, the more rugged the country, the slower they would go, and thus, the longer they would stay in the country of the sand wraiths.

On balance, he feared buzz bombs more. Perhaps when he saw the wraiths, he would change his mind.

"They live under the sand," Cirocco was saying. "They can run or swim or something, under the sand, and do it about as fast as I can run on the ground.

"Their existence is fairly precarious since water is poisonous to them. I mean, if it touches their bodies, it kills them, and it doesn't take much to do it. They'd die on a sunny day if the humidity were much over forty percent. The sands of Tethys are bone dry in most places because the heat from below blasts the water right out of the ground. The exception is where Ophion goes under the sand. It flows in a deep bedrock channel, but it still pollutes the sand for ten kilometers in every direction as far as the wraiths are concerned. So all of Tethys is divided into two totally separate tribes of wraiths. If they could ever meet each other, they'd probably fight to the death because they're always fighting even in the smaller divisions that are marked off wherever water flows in times of flash flood."

"Then it does rain here?" Robin asked.

"Not a lot. Say once a year, and just a trickle. It would have killed the wraiths long ago, but they can grow a shell and hibernate for a few days when they smell it coming. That's how I talked to one; I came in here during a storm and dug one up and put him in a cage."

"Always the peacemaker," Gaby said with teasing affection.

"Well, it was worth a try. The thing about this route is that the mountains are pretty dry right now. The highway, as it happens, closely parallels the path of Ophion under the desert."

"That was no accident, believe me," Gaby said. "I thought it made as much sense as keeping to the high ground when going through a swamp."

"Yes, that's true. The point is, we might meet some wraiths up here. I'm hoping the cloud cover will keep them down, but I don't know how long it will last. The good news is that they seldom band together in groups larger than about a dozen, and I think we have enough hands to fight off an attack."

"I should have traded my gun in on a water pistol," Robin said.

"Were you making a joke?" Hautbois asked, digging into her left saddlebag. She came up with two items: a large slingshot and a short tube with a handle and trigger and a pinhole in one end. Robin took it, squeezed the trigger, and a fine stream of water squirted from the end and sailed ten meters before hitting the sand. She seemed delighted.

"Think of it as a flamethrower," Cirocco suggested. "You don't have to be accurate. Shoot in the general vicinity and fan it around. Even a miss will hurt them, and enough shots will put water vapor in the air and drive them back underground. And don't shoot it anymore now," she said, hastily, as Robin squeezed off another shot. "The bad news is that there are no springs in Tethys, and what water we use in battle will be water we won't have to drink later."

"Sorry. What's the slingshot for?" Robin was looking at it eagerly, and Chris could see she wanted to hold it and give it a try.

"Long-range stuff. Water balloons. You put one of these into the cup, pull back, and let fly." Cirocco was holding something the size of a Titanide egg. She tossed it to Chris. When he squeezed it gently, a trickle of water ran into his hand.

Valiha was looking through her saddlebags, too. She removed a slingshot and a short club, which she stowed in her pouch, and another water pistol, which she handed to Chris. He looked at it curiously, trying to get the feel of it, wishing he could shoot a few practice shots.

"The sling takes skill, which I have," Valiha explained. "Do as the Wizard says, do not be too selective in your targets. Just shoot."

He looked up and saw Cirocco grinning at him.

"Feeling like a hero?" she said.

"Like a little boy playing at being one."

"You'll change your mind if you ever see a wraith."

30.

Rolling Thunder

"I never said it worked all the time." Cirocco put her hands on her hips and scanned the sky again, with no better result. Gaby watched her, feeling for the first time in years that irrational desire for the Wizard to make something happen. It did no good to know that Cirocco's powers did not work that way. She wanted her to make it *rain*.

"She said she'd provide cloud cover," Gaby pointed out.

"She said she'd try," Cirocco corrected. "You know Gaea can't control every detail of the weather. It's too complex."

"So she keeps saying." Seeing the look on Cirocco's face, Gaby kept the rest of her remarks to herself.

"We haven't seen any wraiths yet," Robin said. "Maybe the clouds were enough to scare them off before they broke up."

"They're probably down deep in the sand," Hautbois agreed.

Gaby said nothing. Instead, she reached into Hornpipe's saddlebag and took out a bladderfruit the size of a baseball.

The group was at the end of the foothills leading to the eastern slopes of the Royal Blue Line. Not far to the east was the central Tethys cable, and barely visible beyond it was the fine line of the Circum-Gaea Highway. A last outpost of naked rock formed a wide bowl filled with sand just in front of them, its rim submerged in several places.

Standing on Hornpipe's back, steadying herself with a hand on Cirocco's shoulder, Gaby lobbed the bladderfruit in a high arc that brought it down in the center of the bowl.

The results were dramatic. Nine lines quickly diverged from the point of impact. There were humps at the heads of the lines and shallow depressions behind them that quickly filled in with sand. The humps moved as swiftly as cartoon gophers under a suburban lawn. In a few seconds there was no sign they had been there.

Cirocco had risen to her knees when the missile hit the sand. Now she slumped back to a sitting position.

"What do you want to do?" she asked. "Head on west to Thea?"

"No. I'm sure you recall who wanted to do this and who wanted to stay home."

"And drink," Cirocco added.

Gaby ignored it. "I'd look silly advising you to skip Tethys after all the time I spent convincing you to come here at all. Let's see what we can do."

Cirocco sighed. "Whatever you say. But look out, everybody. I want the humans watching the air. Titanides, keep an eye on the ground. You can usually see a spurt of sand before the wraiths come out onto the surface."

When Robin was nine, she read a book which had made a lasting impression on her. It was about an old fisherwoman who, alone in a small boat, hooked a huge fish and battled it for days, through storms and high seas. It was not so much the struggle with the fish that had frightened her. It was the evocation of the sea: deep, cold, dark, and unforgiving.

She thought it odd that she had not recalled the book while crossing Nox or Twilight. It seemed even stranger that she would think of it now, in broad daylight, crossing the arid desert. Yet the sand was a sea. It undulated in broad waves. In the distance, some atmospheric effect made it shimmer like glass. And beneath its surface were monsters more terrible than the old woman's fish.

"I just thought of something," Cirocco said. She was riding alone on Hornpipe, followed by Robin on Hautbois and Chris and Gaby on Valiha. "We should have gone north to the road, then back west to the cable. It would have been a shorter distance over dry sand."

Robin recalled the map Cirocco had drawn. "But we would have spent more time covering flat ground," she said.

"That's true. But somehow I'm more worried about wraiths than buzz bombs."

Robin did not say it, but she was, too. Though she was supposed to be scanning the sky, her eyes were constantly drawn to Hautbois's hooves as they kicked up the loose grains of sand. She could not understand how the Titanide could bear it. Her own toes curled in her boots in sympathetic horror. Any moment now some hideous mouth would appear and engulf the Titanide's forelegs. Except Cirocco had said the wraiths had no mouths, eating by directly ingesting through their crystalline carapaces. They did not even have faces. . . .

"Do you want to go back and do that?" Gaby called out.

"I don't think so. We're about halfway there."

"Yeah, but we know there aren't any wraiths back—"

As soon as Gaby stopped shouting, Robin's heightened awareness told her that something was wrong. She had a pretty good idea of what Gaby must have seen, and it took only a few seconds of scanning the near side of the five-meter dune behind them to find the telltale grooves in the sand, deep in front, trailing away like the tail of a comet. She saw a dozen of them, then realized that was only one of five or six groups.

There was no need to raise an alarm. Robin saw Cirocco standing on Hornpipe, facing backward. Valiha increased her pace until she was beside Hautbois and Robin. Gaby was passing bladderfruit to Chris and Valiha.

"Hand me one of those," Hautbois said, and Robin did, feeling the Titanide increase her pace. For the first time on a Titanide she felt some of the bouncing associated with horseback riding.

"Hold your fire for now," Gaby said. "That's as fast as they can move, and we're staying ahead of them easily."

"That's easy for you to say," Valiha said. Her mottled yellow skin glistened with foamy sweat.

"It's time to switch," Hautbois said. "Valiha, give me Gaby for a while. Robin, you move to the front." Robin did as she was told, noting that she would be sandwiched between Hautbois and Gaby and, though it was painful to admit it, not objecting at all. The unseen wraiths frightened her more than anything she had encountered in Gaea.

"Just a second," Gaby said. Ignoring her own order, she turned around and lobbed a bladderfruit into the path of one approaching group of wraiths. They sensed it while still fifty meters away. Some swung wide to avoid the poisonous area, while others vanished entirely.

"That's got them," Gaby said with satisfaction as she landed on Hautbois's back. She settled in behind Robin. "The ones that disappeared went deeper in the sand, but that slows them down a lot. They can only move at top speed near the surface, where the sand is looser." Robin looked back again and saw that the ones which had swung wide were only now resuming the chase, far behind the vanguard.

"How about it, friends?" Cirocco said, addressing the Titanides. "Can you keep up this pace until we reach the cable?"

"It shouldn't be any problem," Hornpipe assured her.

"Then we're all right," Gaby said. "Rocky, you'd better throw a small bomb ahead of us every few minutes. That ought to scatter any ambushes."

"Will do. Robin, Chris, stop looking at the ground!"

Robin forced herself to look at the sky, still painfully clear and fortunately empty of buzz bombs. It was one of the hardest things she had ever done. It could not have been harder if her own feet were touching the hated sea of sand; like a backseat driver reaching for an imaginary brake, she found herself lifting her feet in an effort to make Hautbois step more carefully.

The group had crested a dune and was starting down the other side when Cirocco called out a warning.

"Hard right, people. Hang on!"

Robin put her arms around Hautbois's trunk as the Titanide dug her hooves into the sand, heeling over almost forty-five degrees as she turned. The ride was definitely getting bumpier as Hautbois began to tire. Robin caught a glimpse of a commotion at the foot of the dune, saw several of the telltale trails as wraiths fled from the bladderfruit that had suddenly exploded in their midst. A stream of water came from behind her, angled left, sizzled when it hit. There was a fountain of sand. For a moment a supple insubstantial tentacle writhed in the air. Where the water touched it, the thing hissed and shed glass scales that turned slowly in the low gravity. Robin freed one hand and took the butt of her water pistol in the other, peering around Hautbois's broad shoulder. She squeezed the trigger and sprayed what turned out to be a harmless patch of desert.

"Save it," Gaby cautioned. Robin nodded quickly, mortified that the gun was shaking in her hand. She hoped Gaby couldn't see it. Gaby's voice was calm and controlled and made Robin feel ten years old.

The Titanides had made a wide circle around the nest of wraiths Cirocco had exposed; now they were back on course for the Tethys cable. Robin remembered to look up at the sky, saw nothing, looked back at the sand, once more forced herself to look up. She did that for an hour while the cable base grew no closer. Finally she asked Gaby how long they had been running.

"About ten minutes," she said, and looked behind them again. When she turned back, she was frowning. On the crest of a dune five or six hundred meters to the rear Robin thought she saw a wraith track. It paralleled the imprints of the Titanide's hooves.

"They're still back there, Rocky."

The Wizard looked, frowned, then shrugged.

"So? They can't catch us if we keep going."

"I know. They must know that, too. So why do they keep coming?"

Cirocco frowned again, and Robin didn't like that. Eventually Gaby reported she could no longer see the pursuers. Though the Titanides were tired, they agreed not to slacken their pace until the cable was reached.

Hautbois topped the final giant dune before the cable. Ahead Robin could see the land rising unbroken. She estimated the distance to the welcoming darkness between the strands at about a kilometer.

"Buzz bomb to the right," Chris called out. "Don't go down yet! It's still a long way off." Robin found it, banking around the eastern side of the cable, perhaps a thousand meters high.

"Back over the dune," Cirocco ordered. "I don't think it's seen us yet."

Hautbois wheeled, and in a few seconds the seven of them were prone together on the far side.

All of them but Robin.

"Get down, you silly idiot! What's the matter with you?"

She was on her knees, leaning forward, her hands almost touching the sand.

She could not make them move. The sand seemed to writhe before her eyes. She could not make herself reach out and touch its loathsome heat, could not press her belly to it and await the arrival of the wraiths.

A great weight fell on her, and she cried out. She screamed when she felt the sand press against her, then began to vomit.

"That's good," Hautbois said, easing up enough to allow Robin to turn her head. "I wish I'd thought of that. All that moisture will keep them away."

Moisture, moisture . . . Robin heard only that word on a conscious level and quickly blocked everything but that thought. The sand was wet. Wet would keep the monsters away. Sweat, weep, spit, vomit . . . any of those things were suddenly the smart thing to do. She hugged the sand and thought about how wonderfully wet it was.

"What's the matter? Is she having a seizure?" Cirocco called out.

"I think so," Hautbois said. "I'll take care of her."

"Just keep her down. It still may not see us."

Robin heard the sound of a buzz bomb high and far away. She turned her head enough to see it come into sight over the edge of the dune, still at altitude. It turned sharply, showing a swept-wing profile, and began to come toward them.

"That's that," Cirocco said. "Everyone stay low. It's not at a good angle to hurt us."

They watched the buzz bomb in growing doubt until it became clear that the creature was not going to make a low pass. It cruised over them at five or six hundred meters, going much more slowly than Robin remembered from the last time.

"That thing looks odd," Gaby said, daring to sit up a little.

"Never mind that," Cirocco said, standing to scan the air. "It's going to come back around. Gaby, keep a watch for more, and the rest of you start digging. I'd like a wide hole two meters deep, but I'd settle for one. It's going to be tough in this sand. Throw some water around before you dig. Oh, and if anyone has even the slightest urge to pee, do it now, don't be shy. It's useless in your bladder." Cirocco stopped talking when she saw the look on Robin's face and realized the condition of the younger woman's pants was not intentional.

Robin had disgraced herself. She thanked the Great Mother that none of her sisters was here to see it, but it was small consolation. These six were her sisters now, for the duration of the trip and probably beyond.

But things are never so bad they cannot get worse. Robin appreciated the truth of that principle when she tried to move and found she could not. Hautbois's statement—certainly meant as a facesaving out for Robin—had come true; she was paralyzed.

For a moment she thought she would surely lose her mind. She was sprawled bonelessly, face down, on the hateful sands of Tethys, a surface she feared so much that she had possibly betrayed the whole group by her inability to touch it. But instead of insanity, she achieved a fatalistic detachment. Mind-less, serene, she heard the sounds of frenzied activity and understood little of it. It was no longer important if a wraith emerged beneath her and tore her apart. There were grains of sand and the taste of vomit in her mouth. She felt a trickle of sweat run down her nose. She could see a few meters of sand and her own arm extended across it. She listened.

Cirocco: "Since they can't get too close to us, they have to use some kind of medium-range weapon. They used to chunk rocks, but in the last ten years they've used some kind of spear thrower or bow and arrow."

Chris: "That sounds bad. We're not going to get much cover in this sand."

Cirocco: "It's good and bad. They were pretty mean shots with those rocks. They're built . . . well, you haven't seen them, and they're hard to describe, but they were very good at throw-ing rocks. But they're basically cowardly, and they had to get in pretty close to throw them. With the arrows they can stand farther back."

Hautbois: "Now tell us the *bad* news, Rocky."

Cirocco: "That's it. The good news is that they're lousy shots with arrows. They can't aim them. But they'd rather stay back and take potshots."

Gaby: "They make up for it by shooting a *lot* of arrows."

Hautbois: "I knew there'd be something."

There was the familiar staccato roar of a buzz bomb some distance away.

Gaby: "I still say there's something weird about that crea-ture. I can't make it out, but it looks like a swelling on its back."

Hornpipe: "I see it, too."

Cirocco: "Your eyes are better than mine."

For a time there were just the sounds of breathing and occasionally the rustle of someone crawling over sand. Once Robin felt someone brush against her leg. Then Hornpipe shouted a warning. Something fell to the sand in Robin's range of vision. She had been staring at her thumbnail; now she shifted her eyes and looked at the intruder. It was a thin shaft of glass, half a meter long. One end was notched, the other buried in the sand.

"Anybody hit?" It was Cirocco's voice. There were a few negative replies. "They just shot those in the air. They must be behind that dune. In a while they'll get up the nerve to look over it, and they'll get a little more accurate. Get your slingshots ready."

Shortly after that Robin heard the twang of the Titanides' weapons.

Chris: "I think you hit that one, Valiha. Oops! Those were closer."

Cirocco: "Damn it, look at Robin. Can't we do anything about that? It must be hellish."

Robin had heard the last flight of arrows hitting the sand, felt a few grains rain on her legs. It was not a matter of importance. She heard more slitherings, and a hand grasped the arrow she had been looking at, pulled it out, and tossed it away. Gaby's face appeared, a few centimeters from her own.

"How are you making it, kid?" She took Robin's hand and squeezed it, then stroked her cheek. "Would it be easier if you could see things better? I can't think of any way to protect you, or I'd use it for all of us."

"No," Robin answered, from a great distance.

"I wish . . . shit." Gaby hit the ground with her fist. "I feel helpless. I can imagine how you must feel." When Robin made no answer, she leaned close again.

"Listen, do you mind if I take your gun for a while?"

"I don't mind."

"Do you have any of those rocket slugs left? With the explosive tips?"

"Three clips."

"I'll need them, too. I'm going to try to pot a buzz bomb if it ever gets down low enough. You just hang on and try not to think of it. We're going to make a dash for the cable pretty soon."

"I'm all right," Robin said, but Gaby was gone.

"And I'll take you," Hautbois said, from behind her. She felt the Titanide's hand come around her and briefly touch her cheek, which was wet. "Do not begrudge the tears, little one. Not only is it good for the soul, but every drop protects us all."

31.

Heat Lightning

"Just how smart do you think those things are?" Chris asked, watching the lone buzz bomb bank to the left for another high circling pass.

Gaby looked at it and scowled.

"It never pays to underestimate the intelligence of anything you meet in Gaea. A good rule of thumb is to assume it's at least as smart as you and twice as mean."

"Then what's it doing up there?"

Gaby patted the barrel of her borrowed weapon. "Maybe it heard about the one Robin shot down." She looked at the sky once more and shook her head. "But I don't think that's the whole reason. I don't like it. I don't like it at all." She looked at Cirocco.

"Well, you've convinced me. I don't like it either."

Chris looked from one to the other, but neither had anything more to say.

Above, the buzz bomb continued to circle. It seemed to be waiting for something, but for what? Periodically the arrows of the wraiths rained down in flights of three or four dozen. Fired almost straight into the air, the arrows had lost their lethal speed by the time they reached the ground. One had hit Hornpipe in the hind leg. It penetrated five or six centimeters into the muscle: painful, but easily plucked out since the point was not barbed. The barrages seemed designed to keep them pinned down more than anything else. Chris had read somewhere that in a war, millions of rounds were expended for just that purpose.

But if the wraiths wanted them to stay put, there must be a reason for it. They were preparing some surprise, or a larger force was on the way. In either case Chris thought the logical move was to make a dash for the cable. They surely would have done so if not for the presence of the buzz bomb.

"Do you think the wraiths and the bombs are working together?" he asked.

Gaby looked at him and did not answer immediately.

"I certainly doubt it," she said finally. "So far as I know, the wraiths have never worked with anybody but other wraiths, and not very well then." But when she looked back at the sky, she seemed thoughtful. She caressed the butt of Robin's gun and trained it on the distant target, keeping it in her sights, coaxing it down with soft, cajoling whispers.

"The arrows have stopped," Valiha said.

Chris had been aware of it for several minutes but had not mentioned it in the illogical fear that the barrage would begin again out of pure spite. But it was true; for the half hour since they had dug their community foxhole the arrows had come in at one- or two-minute intervals, and now they were not.

"Maybe I'm a pessimist," Gaby said, "but I don't think I like that either."

"They could be gone," Hornpipe ventured.

"And I could be a half-assed Titanide."

Chris could contain himself no longer. There was no point anymore in reminding himself that Gaby and Cirocco were much older, wiser, and more experienced in this sort of thing than he was.

"I think we should make a run for it," he said. "Hornpipe is already hurt. If we wait for them to start shooting again, it could get much worse." He waited, but though everyone was looking at him, no one said anything. He plunged ahead. "This is just a feeling, but I'm worried that the buzz bomb is waiting for something. Possibly reinforcements."

He might have expected the Wizard to call him on that one. He had nothing to base it on except the fact that the buzz bombs had acted in concert once, in the attack that had killed Psaltery.

To his surprise, Cirocco and Gaby were looking at each other, and they both looked troubled. He realized that beyond a certain base of knowledge, it was impossible for even the Wizard to know just what Gaea might throw at them next. So many things were possible, and even the things you thought you knew could change overnight as Gaea created new creatures, changed the rules that governed the old ones.

"That's a very lucky man saying that, Rocky," Gaby said.

"I know, I know. I'm not discounting his feelings at this

point. I don't have much more to go on, myself. But it could
be that's just what that bastard up there is waiting for. No
matter how fast we go, he'll have time for at least one shot
at us, and the ground out there is flat as a pancake."

"I don't think I'll be slowed down," Hornpipe said.

"I can take care of Robin," Hautbois said.

"Damn it, it's you Titanides who have the most to lose out
there," Cirocco shouted. "I think I could dig into that sand in
a few seconds, but when you people lie down flat, your butts
stick up a meter and a half."

"I'd still rather make a run for it," Hornpipe said. "I don't
fancy lying here and becoming a pincushion."

Chris was beginning to think no decision would be reached.
Cirocco, faced with two unreasonable choices, had suddenly
lost the assurance she had gained during the trip. He did not
really think that leadership, in any sense but that of fostering
morale, was her strong point. Gaby needed time to gear herself
up to assume a role that was basically distasteful to her. Robin
was paralyzed, and the Titanides had never shown a tendency
to dispute the commands of first Gaby, then Cirocco.

As for Chris, he had never been the captain of his childhood
sports teams or the one who decided where he and his friends
would go or what they would do when they got there. In his
troubled adulthood no one had ever asked him to be the leader
of anything. But an urge to take control was growing in him.
He began to think that if something were not resolved very
quickly, this might be his hour at last.

And then, in an instant, everything was changed. There was
a deafening explosion, as if lightning had struck no more than
ten meters away, followed by the hollow, receding rumble of
a buzz bomb.

Everyone flattened reflexively. When Chris dared look up,
he saw the silent approach of three more, skimming the tops
of the dunes, shimmering and unreal in the heat-distorted air.
He pressed his cheek to the sand but kept his eyes on them as
they blossomed from points bisected by lines into voracious
mouths with enormous wingspans. The wings had a slight
camber, so that viewed head-on, they looked like frozen black
bats.

They passed overhead at an altitude of fifty meters. Chris
saw something fall from one of them. It was a cylindrical
object that wobbled through the air to land behind a dune to

his left. When the fountain of flame appeared, Chris could feel
its heat on his skin.

"We're being bombed!" Cirocco cried out. She had half
risen. Gaby tried to pull her down, but she was pointing to a
third flight of buzz bombs coming from the northeast. They
were far too high for the ramming tactic, and just before they
were directly overhead, they lifted slightly, exposing ebony
underbellies with landing legs drawn up tight. More of the
deadly eggs were released. Hornpipe combined with Gaby to
pull Cirocco down just as the bombs exploded, sending a
shower of sand over the prone bodies.

"You were right!" Gaby shouted over her shoulder as she
leaped to her feet. Chris took little comfort from it. He got up,
turned to find Valiha, and was lifted bodily before he quite
knew what was happening.

"To the cable!" Valiha called. Chris almost dropped his
water gun as she sprang forward. He looked over his shoulder
and saw a river of flame running down from the dune behind
them, and out of it emerged all the denizens of hell.

There were hundreds of them, and most were on fire. The
wraiths were disorganized clusters of tentacles, tangled snarls
that bore no resemblance to anything Chris had seen. They
were the size of large dogs. They scuttled like crabs, and just
as rapidly, all at once with no wind-up. They were translucent,
and so were the flames, so that, burning, they became writhing
areas of violent light that cast no shadows. Chris's ears were
tortured with an almost supersonic screeching and metallic
pings like red-hot metal cooling.

"That was great bomb placement," Gaby shouted, suddenly
appearing to his right, mounted on Hautbois. The Titanide had
Robin cradled in her arms. "It's hard to think the buzz bombs
are working with the wraiths."

"I wouldn't count on them being on our side, though," Chris
said.

"Neither would I. You got any ideas on what to do next?"
She pointed to the sky, where Chris saw two flights of three
buzz bombs wheeling around for another pass.

"I'd say keep running," Valiha said before Chris could get
anything out. "It looks to me like they're not used to dropping
bombs. They had two chances while we were helpless and they
missed both times."

Hornpipe and the Wizard had matched the pace of the other

two Titanides and now galloped along beside them.

"Okay. But they could change tactics. If it looks like they're coming in low, hit the dirt. And if we're going to run, don't do it in a straight line. And spread out a little. More targets might confuse them."

The Titanides put the orders into effect. Valiha began a zigzag progression toward the cable, totally different from her usual effortless glide. Chris had to hold tight to stay on her back. When the buzz bombs were positioned for another run, she redoubled her efforts, sending up great sprays of sand as she leaned into her turns, hooves churning.

"They're keeping high," Chris told her.

"Good. I'll keep—"

"Turn toward them!" he shouted. Valiha obeyed instantly, and Chris ducked as three bombs sailed over his head, seeming close enough to touch. Yet they hit fifty meters away. Chris saw that he had been right. The momentum of a bomb that fell short could still spray them with the liquid fire. His ears rang, but the main force of the devices was expended in incendiary effects rather than concussion.

"That's napalm," Cirocco shouted as for a moment Hornpipe and Valiha drew close in their erratic paths. "Don't let it get on you. It sticks and burns."

Chris wanted no part of it, sticky or not. He was about to say so when Valiha shrieked and stumbled.

He was thrown forward against her back, hitting his chin and snapping his teeth together. He sat up, spit blood, and looked over her shoulder. Glassy tentacles had wrapped around her left foreleg. They seemed too ephemeral to exert the force that was tearing her flesh and pulling her down into the sand. Yet they were doing it. Her knees were already buried.

His hand had no feeling in it as he aimed the gun and squeezed a stream of water over the wraith. It released Valiha, backed off half a meter, and began to shake. Chris thought it was dying.

"The water's not hurting it!" Valiha shouted. She was using her club to flail at the thing. Two tentacles broke off and slithered independently before slipping into the sand. "It's shaking it off."

Chris could see it. Injured, the creature nevertheless began to close on Valiha again. It was a nest of glass snakes. Somewhere near the center, not held to a defined spot, was a large pink crystal that might have been an eye. It more nearly resembled one of the invertebrate chimeras of the sea than any land creature, yet it had the supple strength of a whip.

Valiha reared on her hind legs while Chris held on only by winding his fingers in her hair. She didn't seem to notice. She came down on the creature with her front hooves, reared and did it again, then jumped over the twitching remnant and hit it so hard with her hind legs that pieces were still rising when she leaped forward again.

Chris looked up, and the sky was filled with buzz bombs.

Actually there were no more than twenty or thirty of them, but one was too many. Their pulsing exhaust rattle shook the world.

The next thing he knew, Valiha was kneeling in front of him, shaking his shoulders. His ears were ringing. He noticed that Valiha's hair was singed on one side and that her left arm and the left side of her face were bleeding. Her yellow skin was nearly invisible behind a coat of sand which adhered to the sweat.

"You're not bleeding too badly," she said, causing him to look down and see tears in his clothing and redness beneath. A patch on his pants was smoldering, and he quickly slapped it out. "Can you understand me? Can you hear me?"

He nodded, though he was very shaky. She lifted him again, and he fumbled with his feet, trying to straddle her back. When he was in place, she took off again.

They were only a hundred meters from the first of the cable strands. Just before they arrived, Chris heard a subtle alteration in the sound of Valiha's hooves. Instead of the muffled thumps of deep sand, it was turning into a satisfying clop-clop as they emerged onto hard rock. Soon they were close enough to touch the massive strand. Valiha wheeled around, and they looked out over an empty expanse of desert. Nowhere could they see Cirocco and Hornpipe, Gaby, Hautbois, or Robin. Though they could hear the distant thunder of pulsejets, the sky was clear of buzz bombs.

"Over there," Valiha said. "To the east."

There was a commotion on the sand. Many wraiths created a shifting cloud over something lying motionless.

"It's Hautbois," Valiha said quietly.

"No. It can't be."

"But it is. And over there, to the right of the remains. I fear that is our companion Robin."

The small figure had come into view from around the curve of the cable strand. She was three or four hundred meters from the two of them. Chris saw her stop short of the carnage. She crouched. She put her hands to her mouth, then straightened, and Chris was sure he knew what she was about to do.

"Robin! Robin, don't!" he shouted. He saw her stop and look around.

"It's too late," Valiha called out. "She no longer lives. Come to us." She turned to Chris. "I'm going to get her."

He held her wrist tightly.

"No. Wait for her here." It felt like a damnably unheroic thing to say, but he couldn't help it. He kept seeing the tentacles of the wraith pulling Valiha down into the sand. He looked at her legs and gasped.

"That thing. . . ."

"It's not as bad as it looks," Valiha said. "The cuts are not deep. Most of them."

It looked awful. Her left leg was covered in drying blood, and at least one of the gashes had torn loose a flap of her skin. He looked away, helplessly, back to where Robin was running toward them. She was unsteady, her legs and arms flying without much control. Chris ran out a short way to meet her and hurried back, supporting her under one arm. She collapsed on the rock, gasping, unable to speak but clutching the hard surface to her like an old friend. Chris turned her over and took her hand. It was the one without a little finger.

"We were here," she finally managed to say. "Here under the . . . cable. Then Gaby saw the buzz bomb, and . . . and it was coming in low. The first one. And she shot it down! And something came out of it in a parachute . . . and she ran off after it. The water didn't kill them! They came up right in front of us, and . . . and—"

"I know," Chris soothed. "We saw it, too."

". . . and then Hautbois ran off looking for Gaby and . . . didn't take me. I couldn't move! But I did move, and I got up and went . . . after her. She was out there, and then you called me . . . and Gaby's out there somewhere. We've got to find her, we—"

"Cirocco and Hornpipe are missing, too," Chris said. "But they might be under the cable. You must have come in farther to the west than we did. Cirocco might be in the other direction. We . . . Valiha, how long was I out?"

The Titanide frowned. "We were under the cable, too," she

said. "We made it to safety, then saw Gaby running alone, and we went to help her, and that is when we were nearly hit. I was out myself for a short time, I think."

"I don't remember any of that."

"It has been possibly four or five decirevs . . . possibly thirty minutes, since the bombing began."

"So Cirocco has had plenty of time to make it to the cable. We should search the outer cable strands first." He did not add that he felt sure anyone still out there on the sands was dead.

They all felt a sense of urgency, yet found it difficult to move from their hard-won refuge. They managed to use up some time in the examination and treatment of wounds. Robin was the least injured, and Chris had nothing wrong that a few bandages would not cure. Valiha's treatment took more time. When the torn leg was bound up, she did not seem eager to put much weight on it.

"What do you think?" Chris asked them. "Any of them could be just on the other side of this strand, looking out over the sand, trying to locate us."

"We could split up," Robin suggested. "They'd be around the edge. We could search in both directions."

Chris chewed his lip. "I don't know. Every movie I ever saw, splitting up happened just before the big disaster."

"You're basing your tactics on movies?"

"What else do I have? Do you know more about it?"

"I guess not," Robin admitted. "We have drills for different sorts of invasions, but I don't know how much of that would apply here."

"Don't split up," Valiha said firmly. "Division is vulnerability."

But they did not have time to make the decision. Robin, looking out at the desert, saw Gaby appear over the top of a dune. She was bounding in the long, easy low-gravity lope which no longer looked odd to Chris. He knew it well enough by now to be able to tell she was tired. She was bent slightly, as if favoring a stitch in her side.

She gradually closed the distance. When still half a kilometer from them, she waved one hand and shouted, but no one could hear what she said.

And she could not hear them when all three began to shout frantically, trying to warn her of what she could not see because it was approaching her from behind.

Valiha was the first to start running. Chris followed quickly, but the Titanide quickly outdistanced him. She was still 300 meters from Gaby when the buzz bomb tilted its nose up and released its deadly cargo. Chris watched it tumble slowly through the air, his feet pounding the sand, oblivious to what might be under it. It came down just in front of her, and she threw up her hands as a wall of flame appeared in her path.

She came out of it running fast. She almost seemed to fly.

She was on fire.

He saw her hands slapping at the flames, heard her scream. She no longer knew where she was going. Valiha tried to grab her but missed. Chris did not pause. He smelled burning hair and flesh as he hit her with his shoulder and knocked her sprawling; then Valiha was holding her down as she thrashed and cried out, and Chris used both hands to throw sand on her. They rolled her, held her down, ignoring the pain as their own hands were burned.

"We'll suffocate her!" Chris protested when Valiha pressed Gaby down with her entire body.

"We must smother the fire," the Titanide said.

When she stopped struggling, Valiha scooped her up and grabbed Chris, almost pulling his arm from its socket. He swung onto her back, and she flew toward the cable, holding Gaby, unconscious or dead, in her arms. They caught up with Robin, who had already turned back, just short of the cable strand where they had watched most of the drama. Chris caught her hand and pulled her up behind him. Valiha did not slacken her pace until they were on hard rock again.

She was about to set Gaby down when she looked back and saw yet another buzz bomb on its approach. Incredibly, it was aiming at the cable at high speed, on a course that would deposit its bombs just where Valiha stood. As it nosed up to release them, its engine bellowing at full thrust as it reached for the power to climb fast enough to survive, Valiha headed deeper into the darkening maze of monolithic cable strands.

There were explosions behind them. It was impossible to know if one signaled the death of the buzz bomb. Valiha did not slow down. She raced deeper into the strand forest and paused only when the darkness had deepened to gloom.

"They're still coming," Chris said. He had never felt so hopeless. Behind them, silhouetted against a thin wedge of sky visible between strands, were the convex slivers of shadow

that marked buzz bombs seen head-on. He counted five, knew
there were more. One banked right, then left, threading its way
through the strands with suicidal speed. There was an explosion
far behind them, then one nearer, and the creature roared
overhead. In the darkness its blue exhaust flame was once more
visible.

There was a monstrous explosion ahead of them, and the
cable interior suddenly flared orange. The shadows of the
strands danced in time to the unseen flames; then, for a brief
instant, Chris saw the broken body of the buzz bomb dropping.
Valiha ran on.

A second creature came up behind them, and they heard the
crash as a third hit a cable strand to their left. Burning napalm
dripped down the strand to splash a hundred meters away from
them, like wax from a candle. More bombs exploded ahead
of them.

The concussion began to shake large stones and other massive debris from the narrowing spaces between the unwinding
strands far above. A boulder as big as Valiha crashed in a
shower of sparks twenty meters ahead of them. Valiha went
around it as they heard another buzz bomb impact, followed
rapidly by two more, punctuated with the lesser sounds of
released bombs.

Valiha did not stop until she saw the stone building that
marked the entrance to the regional brain of Tethys. She halted,
unwilling to enter. Only the driving force of the buzz bombs
had brought her this far, into a place traditionally avoided by
her kind.

"We've got to go in," Chris urged her. "This place is falling
apart. One of those things is going to get us if a falling rock
doesn't kill us first."

"Yes, but—"

"Valiha, do as I say. This is Long-Odds Major talking to
you. Do you think I'd make you do something that wasn't a
sure bet?"

Valiha hesitated one second more, then trotted under the
arched doorway and across a stone floor until she reached the
beginning of the five-kilometer stairs.

She started down.

32.

The Vanished Army

The chemical fires had long guttered to their death when Cirocco, on foot, rounded the curve of the great cable with Hornpipe following behind. The Titanide used a three-legged gait, his right hind leg held up by a sling tied around his middle. The lower joint of the leg was splinted.

Cirocco, too, bore signs of the battle. There was a bandage wrapped around her head, covering one eye. Her face was streaked with dried blood. Her right arm was in a sling, and two fingers of her right hand were swollen and askew.

They walked on the hard rock that surrounded the base of the cable, not venturing onto the sand. Though the last wraiths they had encountered had been free of whatever bewitchment had enabled some of them to ignore water and actually to grapple with the humans and Titanides, Cirocco was taking no chances. One she had killed had sloughed off a clear, supple skin at the moment of death. It had felt like vinyl.

She saw something out on the sand, stopped, and held out her hand. Hornpipe handed her a pair of binoculars, which she awkwardly put to her good eye. It was Hautbois. She could be sure only because there were a few patches of green-and-brown skin undamaged. Cirocco looked away.

"I fear she will never see Ophion," Hornpipe sang.

"She was good," Cirocco sang, not knowing what else to say. "I hardly knew her. We will sing of her later."

Aside from the one body, there were few signs that a terrible battle had been fought here. A few patches of sand were blackened, but even now the relentless dunes were marching over them, the rising wind heaping grain after grain over the body of the Titanide.

Cirocco had expected much worse. They might be dead but she would not accept it until she saw the bodies.

They had been forced toward the east as their flight degenerated into chaos. Hornpipe had tried again and again to bear toward the other two Titanides but every time came upon another concealed cadre of the waterproof wraiths. There was little he could do but flee. The attacks had been so intense that Cirocco had decided the wraiths were after her alone. Thinking she could draw them off and thus relieve the pressure on her friends, she had told Hornpipe to run as fast as he could around the cable to the east. They were pursued by a lone buzz bomb, which nearly killed them when it dropped a bomb so close they were lifted into the air and slammed against one of the cable strands.

By then it was clear she had been wrong. The wraiths had not been after her; they had not followed her, nor had the buzz bombs, except for the one that had wounded them. Miserably, they sought shelter beneath the cable strands and listened to the sounds of battle far away, helpless to do anything about it. They had to bind their own wounds first.

Cirocco had been about to go on, but Hornpipe called her back. He was looking at the hard surface of the rock.

"One of our people came this way," he sang, pointing to parallel scratches that could have been made only by the hard, clear keratin of a Titanide's hoof. A few steps further he found a patch of drifted sand that bore two hoof marks and the imprint of a human foot.

"So Valiha made it here," Cirocco said, in English. "And at least one other." She put her free hand beside her mouth and shouted into the darkness. When the echoes had died away, they could hear no sound. "Come on. Let's go in and find them."

As they journeyed deeper into darkness, they began to encounter looming, irregular shapes that blocked their path. Hornpipe lit a lantern. By its light they could see a great deal of debris had fallen from the narrowing spaces overhead. The strands rose at least ten kilometers before entwining to form a single entity: the Tethys cable. Cirocco knew the maze harbored its own complex ecology—plants that rooted in the cable strands and animals that scuttled up and down them.

Cirocco led the way through the debris, conscious that under any of the larger piles could be all four of her friends. Yet from time to time Hornpipe called out to tell her he had seen another hoof mark. The two of them moved deeper until they came upon a massive pile of stone. Cirocco knew that she was dead center under the cable. She had been here before, and in the spot had been the usual gremlin-constructed entrance building. Now there was just rubble and, in the center of a huge scorch, the twisted corpses of three buzz bombs. There was not much left of them but the metal that had formed the combustion chamber linings and blackened steel teeth.

"Did they go in there?" Cirocco asked.

Hornpipe bent to study the ground in the light of his lantern.

"It is hard to say. There is a chance they got into the building before it was brought down."

Cirocco was breathing deeply. She took the lantern from Hornpipe and walked a short distance around the pile of rubble. Then she gingerly climbed a few steps until she had to give it up, handicapped by her broken arm and a feeling of dizziness. She came down. She sat with her forehead in her hand for a moment, sighed, got up, and began picking up small rocks and throwing them into the darkness.

"What are you doing?" Hornpipe asked after she had kept it up for several minutes.

"Digging."

Hornpipe watched her. There were rocks from fist-sized up to several hundred kilograms that the two of them would probably be able to move. But the great bulk of the pile, the rocks that gave the small mountain its massive shape, would have made good building blocks for an Egyptian pyramid. At last he came up behind her and touched her arm. She flinched away from him.

"Rocky, it's no use. You can't do it."

"I have to. I *will*."

"It's too—"

"Damn it, don't you understand? *Gaby's down there*."

She trembled and fell to her knees. Hornpipe eased himself down beside her, and she came into his arms to sob on his shoulder.

When she once more had control of herself, she drew back from his embrace, stood, and put both hands on his shoulders. Her eyes were burning with a determination Hornpipe had not seen in the Wizard for a long time.

"Hornpipe, my old friend," she sang, "by the blood tie that binds us, I must ask you to do a great thing for me. By the love we both know for your grandhindmother, I would not ask this thing if there were any other way."

"Command me, Wizard," Hornpipe sang, in formal mode.

"You must return to your homeland. There you must implore all who will to come to the great desert, to come to Tethys for their Wizard's sake, in her hour of need. Summon the great leviathans of the sky. Call Dreadnaught, Pathfinder, The Aristocrat, Ironbound, Whistlestop, Bombasto, His Honor, and Old Scout, himself. Tell them that the Wizard will make war on the skyrockets, that she will wipe their kind forever from the great wheel of the world. Say to them that in return for this sworn pledge, the Wizard asks them to take all who will come and bring them to Tethys. Will you do this thing for me, Hornpipe?"

"I will, Wizard. Yet I fear not many of my people will come. Tethys is far from home, the way is full of danger, and my people fear these places. We believe Gaea did not intend for us to come here."

"Then tell them this. Say to them that to each who will come, a baby is granted next Carnival time. Tell them that if they help me in this, I will give them a Carnival the people will sing of for the next thousand megarevs." She switched to English. "Do you think that will get them here?"

Hornpipe shrugged and replied in the same language. "Only as many as the blimps can lift."

Cirocco clapped the Titanide on the shoulder, stood, and tried to help him to his feet. He was slow to rise. She stood looking at him, then stretched up to kiss him.

"I will be waiting here," she sang. "Do you know the whistle of great distress, to call down the sky leviathans?"

"I know it."

"One will pick you up soon. Until then be extremely cautious. Get there safely, and return to me with many workers. Tell them to bring ropes, block and tackle, their best winches, picks, and hammers."

"I will." He looked down. "Rocky," he said, "do you think they are alive?"

"I think there's a chance. If they're trapped down there, Gaby will know what to do. She'll know nothing will stop me from getting her out, and she'll have the others stay at the top of the stairs. It's too dangerous to go down to Tethys without me to hold her in check."

"If you say so, Rocky."

"I say so. Now go with love, my son."

33.

Firebrand

"It was Gene," Gaby said in a hoarse whisper. "I could hardly believe it, but it was Gene who jumped out of the buzz bomb before it hit."

"Gaby, you have to take it easy," Chris said.

"I will. I'll sleep in a minute. But I wanted to tell you this first."

There was no way for Robin to tell how long the four of them had been on the stairway. She thought it might have been a full day. She had slept once, only to wake to the sound of Gaby's screams.

Robin could hardly look at her. They had stripped away what was left of her clothing and put her on top of one of their two sleeping bags. Valiha's first-aid kit contained tubes of a salve for the treatment of burns, but they had run out of it long before they had covered all the seared skin. They had not even been able to spare enough water to wash the sand from her adequately, for when the waterskins were empty, there would be no more.

It was merciful that the one lantern, turned low to conserve fuel, cast so little light. Gaby was a mass of second- and third-degree burns, painful to behold. Her entire right side and most of her back were charred black. The skin cracked when she moved and oozed clear liquid. She said she could feel nothing there; Robin knew that meant the nerves had been destroyed. But the reddened areas that surrounded the destruction hurt her terribly. She would doze fitfully for a few minutes, then come to tortured awareness with croaking screams tearing at her throat. She would beg for water, and they would give her a few sips.

But now she seemed calmer, in less pain, more aware of the people around her. She was on her side, legs drawn up, head cradled in Valiha's lap, and she spoke of the minutes before her immolation.

"That was his doing. He contacted the buzz bombs—they're damn intelligent, by the way. He contacted the wraiths, too; only they don't work with outsiders. I knew that, and he knew it, and he tried not to tell me how he got them to cooperate. I persuaded him." She smiled, a terrible sight with half her face ruined.

"I've got to give him credit for one thing. That stunt with the wraiths surprised me completely. He dipped the bastards in plastic. He had them all go through a sprayer that coated them with some gunk, and he marched them out to do battle.

"But then he assumed we were smarter than we actually were, and that's what fouled him up. Remember, halfway to the cable, Rocky pointed out if we'd gone north to the road, doubled back on it, and *then* struck out for the cable, we'd have had less distance to travel over deep sand? If we had, we'd have run right into his ambush. He had his waterproof army deployed between the road and the cable, and a flotilla of buzz bombs hiding in the north mountains to bomb us to hell after we were pinned down. Where we came through, he had only a small force, not waterproofed. He said the plastic couldn't last long, it got worn away in the sand, and he had only the one machine to put it on. He had to station that with his main force."

She coughed, and Robin offered her more water. She shook her head.

"We'll have to make that stuff last," she said. She seemed weakened from talking so long, and Chris again suggested she rest.

"Got to tell this first," she said. "Where was I? Oh. You were right, Chris. We allowed ourselves to get stopped by the small force of wraiths; then we hid when that buzz bomb appeared. That was Gene, looking for us. When he saw us, he radioed his main force to join up with him. If we'd gone then, we'd have been under the cable before the infantry or the air force could have reached us. I don't think Gene would have risked his neck trying to get us from the air, but I could be wrong. He had a pretty powerful motive.

"He was after *me*," she said, and began to cough again. When she had it under control, she resumed her story. "The whole thing and just about all our troubles on this trip, was

Gene trying to kill me. The wraiths and the buzz bombs had orders to go for me first, get the rest later if they could. Cirocco was not to be harmed, but I think Gene had other ideas."

"What do you mean?" Robin asked. "Was he under orders himself?"

"Yes," Gaby said. "Goddamn right. He *really* didn't want to tell me about that. I told him if he didn't, I'd see to it he lived at least a day and I'd take him apart piece by piece. I had to take off a few pieces to make sure he believed me."

Robin swallowed nervously. She had thought herself no stranger to violence, but the scale of recent events had shaken her. She knew about bloodied noses and broken bones and even death, but war had been just a tale of the forsaken Earth. She did not know if she could have done the things Gaby now described. She could have slit his throat or stabbed him in the heart. Torture was foreign to her, yet she felt the deep current of hatred that flowed in Gaby, with this man Gene as its source. Once again she knew the tremendous gap between her nineteen years in the Coven and Gaby's seventy-five in the great wheel.

"So who was it?" Chris was asking. "Oceanus? Tethys?"

"I wanted it to be Oceanus," Gaby said. "But I didn't expect it to be. Gene was getting his orders from who I suspected all along. It was Gaea who told him I must be killed and Cirocco spared. That's why when Psaltery died, I couldn't help crying out that she had done it to him. I think she heard me and told Gene to step up his efforts. She gave him a source of napalm and explosives."

"Gene was behind that attack, too?"

"You remember what happened? Chris saw the buzz bomb and pushed me off Psaltery. If he hadn't, we both would have been dead. After that Gene had to make it look like an attack on us all because it was necessary that Rocky not know she were after just me." She coughed again, then grabbed Chris by the collar, lifting herself with hysterical strength.

"And that's what you have to tell Rocky when she gets here. She has to know it was Gaea that did it. If I'm asleep when she gets here, tell her the very first thing. Promise me you'll do that. If I'm delirious or too weak to talk, you have to tell her."

"I'll tell her, I promise," Chris said. He glanced at Robin. He thought she was delirious already, and Robin agreed. Cirocco was probably dead, and even if she wasn't, there was

little prospect she could move the mountain of stone clogging
the stairway above them.

"You don't understand," Gaby said, sagging back. "All
right, I'll tell you what we were really doing while we pretended to be taking you two on a little walk in the park.

"We were plotting the overthrow of Gaea."

What Gaby and Cirocco had been doing was more an exploration of ways and means than an actual plot. Neither of
them was at all sure it was physically possible to overthrow
Gaea or if Gaea the being could be disposed of without wreck-
ing Gaea the body, upon which all of them depended for survival.

As with so many things in Gaea, the situation had its roots
in events long past. Gaby had felt an itch to change things at
least thirty years before. Robin sat beside her in the flickering
darkness and heard her speak of things she had been able to
confide to no one but Cirocco.

"Rocky didn't even want to hear about it for a long time,"
she told them. "I don't blame her. She had a lot of reasons to
be satisfied with things the way they were. So did I, for that
matter. I didn't find life in Gaea a terrible thing. Every once
in a while I found something I didn't like, but hell, it was
worse on Earth. The universe isn't fair, and it isn't pretty,
whether or not it's governed by a living God. I honestly believe
that if the Christian God existed, I'd hate him more than I do
Gaea. She isn't even in his league.

"And yet, just because you *could* talk to this god, just
because she was actually *there* and I had spoken to her and
knew that she was responsible, that every injustice and every
pointless death was the result of a conscious decision . . . it
made it much harder to take. Cancer is acceptable to me only
if I feel it just grew, that no one thought it out and decided to
inflict it on people. On Earth, that's the way it was. If an
earthquake happened, you suffered and patched your wounds
and picked up the pieces and moved on to whatever the universe
threw at you next. You didn't rail against God, or at least not
many of the people I knew did.

"But if the government passed a law you didn't like, you
raised hell. You either tried to throw the bastards out at the
next election or organized to take power away from them by
other means. Because those injustices came from people, and

not an indifferent universe, you felt you could do something about it.

"It took me a long time to realize that it's the same way here, but I finally did. The obstacle was in thinking of her as a God, and believe it or not, for a long time I guess I did. There are so many resemblances. But she doesn't operate by magic. Everything she does is theoretically within the reach of beings like ourselves. So I gradually moved away from the God proposition and began viewing Gaea as City Hall. And damn it, I guess I can't resist fighting City Hall." She had to stop talking because she was seized by a coughing fit. Robin held the waterskin to her lips, and she drank, then looked down at herself with tears in her eyes. "You can see where it got me."

Valiha gently stroked Gaby's forehead. "You should rest now, Gaby," she said. "You must save your strength."

"I will," Gaby said. "I just have to get this out first." She breathed heavily for a short time, and Robin saw her eyes widen. She tried to raise herself, but Valiha kept her down, carefully not touching her burned skin. Robin could see a realization growing in the other woman as she looked wildly from one to the other. When she spoke, her voice was childlike.

"I'm gonna die now, aren't I?"

"No, you should just—"

"Yes," said Valiha, with a Titanide's directness about death. "There can be very little hope now."

Gaby inhaled with a racking sob.

"I don't want to die," she moaned. Once again she tried to sit up. She fought them, gaining strength with hysteria. "I'm not ready yet. Please don't let me die, I don't want to die, I . . . I don't want . . . *don't let me die!*" She suddenly stopped resisting them and collapsed. She wept bitterly for a long time, so long that when she tried to speak again, her words were broken almost beyond understanding. Robin bent to put her ear close to Gaby's mouth.

"I don't want . . . to die," Gaby said. And a long time later, when Robin had hoped she was alseep, she said, "I didn't know it could hurt so much."

Finally she slept.

It might have been eight hours before she spoke again. It might have been sixteen; Robin could not know. None of them had expected her to awake at all.

Over the next several hours she told them the rest of the story. Her strength had failed alarmingly; she was barely able to lift her head to take the sips of water that she needed with increasing frequency if she was to speak at all. She had inhaled flames. Her lungs were filling up, and her breath bubbled. She drifted in and out of dreams, talking to her mother and other people who must have been long dead, calling often for Cirocco. But always she returned to the story of her private heresy, her quixotic and ultimately fatal mission to topple the arbitrary power that held sway over her life and those of everyone dear to her.

She told of grievances great and small, and often it was the little things, the injustices on a personal level, that meant more than the great wrongs. She spoke of the institution of the quests and how she grew more disgusted with each passing year as unfortunate people were compelled to fight and die to provide amusement for a God who was weary of the smaller passions. She detailed the cruel joke of the Wizard and the Titanides, ran down the roster of Gaea's macabre toys: a long and infamous list that had its culmination in the buzz bombs.

At one point she had dared to wonder if it must be this way. Having thought it, she was led inexorably to wonder what the alternative might be. At first she could tell no one, not even Cirocco. Later, when Cirocco had suddenly found cause to resent Gaea's machinations, she had approached the subject cautiously, been rebuffed, and let it lie for five years. But gradually Cirocco became interested. At first it was only a theoretical problem: could someone or something take Gaea's place? If so, what? They discussed and rejected Earth computers; none was large or complex enough. Various other solutions were also found wanting. At last they had narrowed the possible candidates for a heavenly succession to eleven—the living regional brains of Gaea.

For a long time Cirocco was content to leave it at that. It seemed possible that one of them, or a team, might conceivably take over Gaea's functions if she were to die. There were myriad problems with any of the possibilities, but they were at least thinkable. And that was as far as Cirocco cared to go. Gaby did not think it was cowardice, though this was during the worst of Cirocco's alcoholism. It was merely that the second part of the problem looked insignificant compared to the first. All their discussion presupposed the absence of Gaea. But who will bell the cat? Gaby could dismiss that, knowing from experience that the world is full of stupid heroes and knowing herself to be one of them. Cirocco was, too, if suitably goaded to it. She and Cirocco would dispose of Gaea.

But then they reached the question that had so far been unanswerable.

How does one dispose of Gaea?

"That one had me completely beat," Gaby confessed. "The whole thing was left at that point for a good seven or eight years. Rocky was pleased to forget it, but I never could. All that time my conscience was working on me, telling me I ought to be doing something. There was only one thing I could think of . . . let me admit this, this seems like the right time for confessions. I never thought that by myself, I'd come up with the final answer. I knew Rocky could if she set her mind to it. So my job was to find a way to get her interested in doing something. I had to make it seem possible. I began to badger her about making a survey. I worried at her for several years, until she would hardly speak to me because I was getting to be such a pest. But I worked at *her* conscience—because she didn't like the things I've told you any more than I did; it's just a little harder to get her moving than it is me. She finally gave in.

"We used you people. I said I was confessing, didn't I? I will say we didn't think we were putting you in any more danger than you would have had anyway if you stayed here. But we were wrong. You would have been safer if you'd gone on your own. Because Gaea got wind of something, or she just decided she'd had enough of my being my own boss. Maybe she couldn't stand the thought of someone she didn't have anything on. Her only hold on me was the need for renewals of my youth—and you can believe this or not, as you wish—I countered that by being ready to reject it if the terms were too dear. I *think* I could have grown old and died gracefully. I'll never know, but I wasn't afraid of it like I'm afraid of this.

"So what Rocky's been doing is speaking to the regional brains, not even coming close to talking revolution. If you think Rocky planned to go up and offer any of them the Godhead on a silver platter, you're out of your mind. She was feeling them out, trying to find hidden resentments. We'd pretty much eliminated half of them before we started but thought it best to see them all. That way we could tell Gaea we were making another kind of survey, sort of scouting the mood of the land." She tried to laugh but succeeded only in coughing. "Gaea's the only place where that can be done literally.

"What the next stage would have been I don't know. We hadn't had any luck so far. Rhea's a spook, and Crius is a toady—he *did* make a few unexpected remarks . . . ah, what's the use? The project is over, and we struck out. Why the *hell* didn't I let her skip Tethys?"

She licked her lips but rejected water when it was offered.

"You people are going to need that. Do you see why it's vital you tell Rocky all this? That Gene was behind it and that he was under Gaea's orders? If she knows what we were doing, Rocky is in bad trouble. She needs to know, so she can figure out what to do. Will you promise to tell her?"

"We promise, Gaby," Valiha said.

Gaby nodded wearily and closed her eyes. She opened them again and looked troubled. Her voice was nearly inaudible.

"You know," she said, "the only thing I really regret is that Rocky couldn't be here with me. Chris, would . . . no." She looked away from him and found Robin's eyes. Robin took her hand. "Robin, when you see her, give her a kiss for me."

"I will."

Gaby nodded again and quickly went to sleep. After a short time her breathing became ragged and then stopped. When Valiha listened for a heartbeat, she could find none.

34.

Revelation

It was strange.

Gaby had read of the commonality of near-death experiences. Those who had gone to the edge of death so often saw the same things that she had some idea of what to expect. People spoke of serenity, an absence of pain, of achieving a peace so sweet and alluring they could calmly take stock and decide whether to live or die. Whether real or hallucinatory, many had also reported standing outside themselves and looking at their bodies.

She knew what they were talking about now, and words could not describe it. It was wonderful, and it was strange.

They thought she was dead, but she knew she wasn't, not yet. She soon would be because she had stopped breathing. Her heart stopped, and she waited for the final experience with what might have been amused curiosity: I know what it's like to *be*; what will it be like to *not* be? Does one come apart, gradually shut down, or just fade away? Will there be trumpets and harps, fire and brimstone, rebirth, or the steady-state hum of cold intergalactic hydrogen? Will it be *nothing*? If so, what *is* nothing?

Her body no longer held her. It was good to be free, to drift in space and time, to look back on the scene frozen behind her. It made a striking tableau.

And there was Cirocco, sitting patiently on the pile of stone. Her arm was in a sling. It was good to have had a friend. For the early part of her life Gaby had been in dire danger of dying without one, and that would have been worse than any hell. Thank you, Rocky, for being my friend. . . .

It was taking more time than she expected. Now there was open sky and the vast desert below, and she continued to drift upward. Higher and higher she went, up through the roof and into space, up and up. . . .

To where?

For the first time she began to have doubts.

Wouldn't that be the cosmic joke to end them all? What a surprise to theologians if it turned out the Answer really was. . . .

What if she were *not* City Hall?

Presently it could no longer be ignored. Whatever Gaby had become, her destination was clear. She was going to the hub.

She wished she knew how to scream.

35.

Runaway

Chris and Robin talked it out, explored it from all angles, and it added up to a hopeless situation. But the human animal is seldom hopeless, really hopeless in the real world. Had they been sealed off above and below, they could have waited to die. It might almost have been easier to do so. But while the stairs still beckoned, they both knew they had to descend them.

"It's in the best tradition of heroes," Chris pointed out. "To die trying."

"Will you stop that hero business? We're talking about survival. We don't have a chance here, so if there's even a million-to-one shot at the bottom of the stairs, we have to take it."

But it was not easy to get Valiha moving.

The Titanide was a bundle of nerves. Logical argument had little effect on her. She could agree that they must look for a way out and that the only possible route was downward, but at that point her mind stopped, and something else took over. It was wrong for a Titanide to be in this place. To go deeper was almost unthinkable.

Chris was beginning to feel desperate. For one thing, there was Gaby. It was not pleasant to remain near her body. Before long . . . but that did not bear thinking about. To be unable to bury her was terrible enough.

They never found out how long it took to descend the stairs. The clocks had been in Hornpipe's pack, and there was just no other way to measure the passage of time. It became an endless nightmare, relieved only by meager meals taken when hunger became intolerable and by the dream-ridden sleep of exhaustion. They might make twenty or thirty steps down before Valiha would sit and begin to shake. It was impossible to budge her until she had screwed up her own courage. She was too big to move, and no words they could say did any good.

Robin's temper—none too even at the best of times—became volcanic. At first Chris tried to restrain her language. Later he began to add comments of his own. He thought it unwise when Robin began to pummel the Titanide, to get behind her and push in her desperate urge to get moving, but he said nothing. And he could not just leave her. Robin agreed.

"I'd love to strangle her," she said, "but I couldn't abandon her."

"It wouldn't have to be abandonment," Chris said. "We could go ahead and try to get help."

Robin scowled at him. "Don't kid yourself. What's at the bottom? Probably a pool of acid. Even if there's not, and if Tethys doesn't kill us and we make it to one of those tunnels—if there even *are* tunnels down here like the other place—it's gonna take weeks to get out and weeks to get back. If we leave her, she's dead."

Chris had to admit the truth of it, and Robin went back to physically trying to force Valiha to move. He still thought that might be a mistake, and Valiha proved him right. It happened suddenly and began with Robin slapping her.

"That hurt," Valiha said.

Robin slapped her again.

Valiha put her huge hand around Robin's neck, lifted her off the ground, and held her at arm's length. Robin kicked a few times, then held completely still, gurgling.

"The next time I pick you up," Valiha said, with no particular menace in her voice, "I will squeeze until your head comes off." She set Robin down, held her shoulder while she coughed, did not let go until she was sure Robin could stand on her own. Robin backed away, and Chris thought it was fortunate her gun had been safely stowed in Valiha's pack. But Valiha did not seem to bear her any malice, and the incident was never mentioned again, nor did Robin ever again so much as raise her voice to the Titanide.

He thought they must be past the halfway point. It was the fifth time they had slept. But this time, when he awoke, Valiha wasn't there.

They started to climb.

One thousand two hundred twenty-nine steps later they

found her. She was sitting with her legs folded under her, glassy-eyed, rocking back and forth gently. She looked no more intelligent than a cow.

Robin sat and Chris collapsed next to her. He knew that if the tears started now, he might never stop weeping, so he fought them back.

"What now?" Robin asked.

Chris sighed and stood up. He put his hands to Valiha's cheeks and rubbed them gently until her eyes focused on him.

"It's time to go again, Valiha," he said.

"It is?"

"I'm afraid so."

She stood and let him lead her. They made twenty steps, then thirty, then forty. On the forty-sixth step she sat down again and began to rock. After more coaxing Chris got her to her feet and they made sixty steps. When he got her up the third time, he was optimistic, hoping to make one hundred steps, but what he got was seventeen.

Two sleeps later he awoke to the sound of Robin crying. He looked up, saw that Valiha was gone again. He put his arm around her, and she made no objection. When she was through, they got up and once more began to climb.

It seemed that no one had done any talking in years. There had been arguing and once he and Robin had come to blows. But even that could not be sustained long; neither had the energy for it. He limped for a while after the fight, and Robin sported a black eye.

But it was amazing what a little adrenalin could do.

"It looks like the floor is dry," Robin whispered.

"I can hardly believe it."

They were concealed behind the gradual curve of the spiraling wall, looking out and down at what had to be, incredibly, the end of the line. All along they had expected to find an acid lake, with Tethys safely submerged in it. Instead, they saw what appeared to be a high-water—or high-acid—mark only ten steps from where they stood, then a section of bare floor. Tethys herself was invisible around the curve.

"It's got to be a trap," Robin said.

"Right. Let's turn around and go back."

Robin's lips drew back, and her eyes blazed for a moment; then she relaxed and even managed a faint smile.

"Hey, I don't know how to say this . . . it feels like we've been at each other's throats forever . . . but if this comes out badly . . . what I mean is—"

"It's been fun?" Chris suggested.

"I wouldn't put it that way. Hell." She put out her hand. "It's been good knowing you."

He held her hand in both of his briefly.

"Me, too. But don't say any more. Every word is going to sound awkward as hell later if we *do* survive."

She laughed. "I don't care. I didn't like you when we started out, but don't feel bad. I don't think I liked *any*body. I like you now, and I wanted you to know that. It's important to me."

"I like you, too," he said, and coughed nervously. His eyes left hers, and when he forced them back, she had already looked away. He released her hand, aware of things he would like to say and unable to say them.

He turned to Valiha and began talking to her quietly. He had become better at that, speaking of nothing in particular, letting the melody of his voice soothe in a language they held in common. Gradually he began working meanings into what he said, repeating them, telling her what she must do without stressing it enough to activate her ever-present fears. He spoke to her of getting out in the sunshine again.

A strange fatalism had overcome Valiha during the last kilometer. She stopped less frequently but moved more slowly. She seemed drugged. Once Chris would have sworn she was asleep. She had a hard time keeping her eyes open. He supposed it was Titanide fear, or whatever they used in place of fear. Now that he thought of it, he had never seen any of the Titanides displaying what he thought of as fear, not in the face of the wraiths and not even down here in the dim stairway. She apparently did not fear Tethys in any way Chris could understand. Instead, there had been first a repulsion, like a physical force acting to keep her away from Tethys. She had been unable to give an explanation of many of her acts; when he and Robin were not impelling her downward, she simply went up, with the inevitability of heated air rising. That force had faded, to be replaced by a physical and mental numbness. Her mind worked sluggishly, her senses were dulled, and her body almost seemed to be shutting down.

"In a moment we . . . Valiha, listen to me." He had to slap

her to get her attention. He had the impression she barely felt it. "Valiha, we have to do this part of the trip quickly. It's only a few hundred steps. I don't think we'll have time to sit down and rest like we've been doing."

"No rest?"

"I'm afraid not. What we'll do is hurry down the last steps, stay close to the wall—stay close to *me*, and *I'll* be near the wall—and into the tunnel. Once we're there, we'll be on our way up and out. Do you see, Valiha? To start going up, we have to go just a little bit down, just a little bit, that's all, and we'll be okay. Do you understand?"

She nodded, but Chris was far from sure she did. He thought of saying more but realized there was little use. It would work, or it wouldn't. If he were betting, he would have to put his money against them.

They started the final descent hand in hand. It did not take long to come around the curve of the corridor and into the presence of Tethys, who sat unmoving in her acid bath, just as Crius had done. In fact, there was no way Chris could tell the two apart. He hoped the things he could not yet see were also the same. He would not know until they actually emerged on the floor of the chamber.

"What took you so long, Wizard?"

The voice hit Chris like a physical blow. He had to pause and take a deep breath. Until that moment he had not realized how keyed up he had been. His heart was pounding, and his breathing was shaky. Luckily Valiha was still moving. The three of them continued to approach, with only ten steps in front of them.

"I knew you were up there, of course," Tethys said. "I understand you ran into some trouble. Now I hope you aren't blaming me for that because it was none of my doing, and you can tell that to Gaea."

Tethys's voice was identical to the voice of Crius. It was the same flat drone, without humanity: indistinct, without source. And yet there was a contemptuous, hectoring quality that chilled his blood.

"So you brought Gaby with you. I was beginning to wonder if we'd ever meet. She's not too good to do business with Crius, is she? Are you, Ms. Plauget? And yet we've never seen her down here. I wonder why?"

Robin leaned in front of Valiha, and her eyes were wide.

"Chris," she whispered, "the damn thing's *nearsighted!*"

Chris frantically signaled with his hands, afraid to talk and break the spell. Tethys would not mistake the voices.

"What was that?" Tethys asked, confirming his fears. "Why don't you speak up? Is it polite to keep me waiting for so long and then whisper secrets when you get here? I hate secrets."

They were on the floor now, and Chris saw the two tunnels he had noted in the chamber of Crius, one leading west and the other east. All they had to do now was traverse the sixty or seventy meters to the eastern tunnel. Chris nervously fingered the unusual weapon he had removed from Valiha's saddlebag. It felt reassuringly cold and hard and unyielding as he ran his thumb over the two sharp points. Perhaps he would not have to use it.

"I confess I didn't see until just now why you brought *that* creature along," Tethys said. "It should have been obvious. Am I right?"

Chris said nothing. They were ten meters from the tunnel entrance and still moving.

"I'm getting impatient," Tethys said. "You may be the Wizard, but there are limits. I'm talking about the Titanide. How thoughtful of you to bring dinner. Come here, Valiha."

Valiha stopped and her head turned slowly. She looked at Tethys for the first time. Chris did not wait to see what she would do. He took a firm grip on the large fork which had been part of Valiha's carving set, dropped back a step, and thrust it solidly into the fleshy part of Valiha's rump. For one awful moment there was no reaction; then Valiha moved so fast she seemed to blur. He caught a glimpse of her tail as it vanished into the tunnel, heard her shriek and the clatter of her hooves; then all other sounds were drowned by a piercing whistle. They were into the tunnel, followed by a blast of heat and a rising wind. They were surrounded by choking fumes. Tethys was filling her lake as quickly as she could. The floor they were running on seemed level; when the acid brimmed over the edge of the moat, it would follow them.

As they ran, they were joined by fluttering, batlike creatures. Chris knew by their orange glow that they were the same animals which had lighted their long descent and which he hoped would also populate the tunnels. Whatever they were, they did not like acid fumes any more than he did.

One part of his mind noted that he had found one more thing he could do better than Robin. He was a faster runner. She had fallen behind, and he slackened his pace to allow her to catch up. They both were coughing, and his eyes were watering, but the fumes were not as thick as they had been.

He heard her gasp and fall. It was not until he had stopped himself and turned back that he heard the sound of a trickling liquid he suspected was not water. For one wild moment he was ready to run away, but instead, he hurried back to her, toward the sound of the approaching wave of acid. It was almost completely dark now since the luminescent creatures, less altruistic than he, had not halted in their flight.

He collided with her. Why had he assumed she would need help getting up?

"Run, idiot!" she yelled, and he did run, behind her this time, the only light coming from the distant fliers, the pale glow of which made a halo around the animated shadow she had become.

"How long do you think we need to keep running?" she called back to him.

"Until I can't hear the acid splashing behind me."

"Good plan. Do you think we can outrun it? Is it getting closer?"

"I can't tell. I can't hear it unless I stop."

"Then we might keep running until we drop," she pointed out.

"Good plan," he said.

It didn't seem likely that the glowbirds were flying faster. Yet they were farther ahead than they had been, so he and Robin must be slowing down. His own breath was coming in ragged gasps, and his side was hurting badly. But he had detected no rising of the floor. For all he knew, their present location might actually be lower than the floor in the grotto of Tethys. It was possible that Tethys could flood the entire length of what Chris devoutly hoped was a 300-kilometer tunnel linking Tethys with her sister, Thea. But of course, it was possible the tunnel did not lead to Thea at all. It might end at any moment. It might begin to slope down, and they would find they had been seeking their salvation in what was actually a drain for excess acid. But there was nothing to do but run. If there were an end to the tunnel, Valiha would find it first, and they had not yet caught up with her.

"I think . . . it's gone . . . up. Don't . . . you?"

"Maybe. But how . . . far?" Privately Chris did not think they had gained any ground at all, but if thinking they were rising made it easier for Robin to put one foot in front of the other, that was fine with him.

"I can't . . . do this much . . . longer."

Neither can I, he thought. The darkness was nearly complete now. The floor was not as level as it had been, so the danger of falling was increased. Getting up again would be quite a project.

"A little longer," he wheezed.

They bumped into each other, moved away, and hit again. When Chris moved to his right, he hit his shoulder against the invisible tunnel wall. He had his hands out in front of him, no longer able to tell if the glow he was following—seemingly many kilometers ahead—was real or just an afterimage on his retinas. He was afraid the tunnel would make a turn and he would crash into the wall. Then he realized he was moving so slowly by now that he could not be badly hurt in a collision.

"Stop now," he said, and fell to his knees. Robin was somewhere in front of him, gasping and coughing.

For an undetermined time it did not really matter that acid might be creeping along the tunnel behind him. He pressed his cheek to the cool stone floor and let himself go limp. Only his lungs continued to labor, at a steadily decreasing tempo. His throat was burning, and his saliva was thin but so plentiful he had to keep spitting out sticky ropes of it. At last he raised his head, put his palms to the floor, got to his knees, and, by force of will, held his breath for a few seconds, listening. It was no good. His ears thrummed with blood, and Robin, close enough to touch, still gasped and panted loudly. He thought he might hear the approach of the acid if it came in a roaring wave, but it would not. If it were still coming, it would be rising silently. He reached over and touched Robin's shoulder.

"Come on. We'd better get moving again."

She moaned but got up with him. She fumbled for his hand, and they began to walk. His shoulder rubbed the right wall; they continued that way, Chris touching cool solidity with one hand, warm flesh with the other.

"We have to be going up," Robin said finally. "If it was down, the stuff would have washed over us a long time ago."

"I think so, too," Chris said. "But I don't want to bet my

life on it. We have to keep going until we can get some light."

They walked on, Chris counting the steps, not really knowing why he was doing it. He supposed it was easier than thinking about what might lie ahead.

After several hundred paces Robin laughed.

"What's funny?"

"I don't know, I...I guess it just occurred to me... *we made it!*" She squeezed his hand.

Chris was astonished by her reaction. He was about to point out that they were far from safe, that the road ahead was certainly filled with dangers they could not even guess, when he was suddenly filled with an emotion as powerful as any he had ever experienced. He realized he was grinning.

"Damn. We did, didn't we?" Now they both were laughing. They embraced, slapping each other on the back, shouting incoherent congratulations. He squeezed her hard, unable to stop himself, but she made no objection. And just as suddenly he found himself crying with a smile still on his face. Neither of them could control the swift passage of emotions brought about by the release of unbearable tension. Nothing they said made sense. And in time they were spent, still clinging to each other, still standing, rocking gently and wiping away stray tears.

When Chris finally chuckled again, Robin nudged him.

"What's funny now?"

"Oh... nothing."

"Come on."

For a while he wouldn't say anything, but she kept at him.

"All right. Damn it, I *don't* know how I can laugh. It isn't funny. A lot of our friends are dead. But back there... back when we were pinned down...."

"Yeah?"

"Well, you couldn't see this because you were out of it. You know." He hurried on, wishing he'd never started now that he remembered how much she probably wanted to forget that time. "Anyway, Cirocco told us all to pee. Well, hell, I had to. I pulled my pants open and... you know, got it out... and let go. Spreading it around, you understand, so it'd do the most good... and suddenly I thought, Take that, you lousy sand wraiths!"

Robin laughed herself to the ragged edge of hysteria. Chris laughed with her but eventually began to worry. It hadn't been *that* funny, had it?

* * *

They had walked a thousand steps before they saw the first
glowbird clinging to the ceiling. It was their first realization
that the tunnel had widened around them. The creature was at
least twenty meters above, possibly more, and its orange light
touched walls that were thirty meters apart. Chris turned and
looked for reflections of moisture behind them but found nothing.

In a little while they passed beneath another glowbird, then
five in a group. They blazed like torches after so many hours
of darkness.

"I wonder what they find to eat down here?" Chris said.

"There must be something. I would think it would take a
lot of energy to glow constantly like that."

"Gaby said it was a catalytic reaction," Chris recalled. "But
still, they must eat. Maybe we could eat what they eat."

"We're going to need something sooner or later."

Chris was thinking of the supplies still in Valiha's saddlebag. That thought led to Valiha herself. He was beginning to
worry about her. By now the glowbirds were plentiful, illu-
minating a tunnel that stretched far ahead of them. He could
see 500 meters ahead, and there was no sign of the Titanide.

"I just thought of something," Robin said.

"What's that?"

"Are you *sure* this tunnel goes east?"

"What are you—" He stopped walking. "You know as well
as I do that. . . ." That what? The stairs had corkscrewed downward for five kilometers. Early in the descent Robin had pointed
out that orientation would be critical when they arrived at the
bottom. Accordingly, they had performed laborious calculations to discover the rate of curvature of the spiral stairs. When
they knew how many steps it took to complete one revolution,
once again to be headed in the same direction, orientation
became a matter of counting steps. They had determined that
they were at the south side of the chamber when they emerged
in Tethys, so west would be to the left and east to the right.

Yet their figures had always contained uncertainty. The fact
that their calculations might be off by a few steps was not
relevant, but not knowing their precise starting point was. They
had entered the surface building from the west. But the confusion surrounding their flight and the destruction of the grem-
lin-built structure made it impossible to know how many steps
Valiha had covered before coming to rest. And when things

had quieted down, the top part of the stairs had been clogged in rubble.

"You don't think she ran through half a revolution, do you?" he said at last.

"I don't think so. But she *might* have. If she did, this tunnel leads to Phoebe, not Thea."

Chris wished he could put it out of his mind. Their situation was so precarious; it depended on so many factors beyond his control. It was possible that even if they reached Thea—who Cirocco had said was a friendly region—she would not be kindly disposed to three invaders of her realm.

"We'll face that problem when we come to it," he said.

Robin laughed. "Don't give me that. If Phoebe is at the other end of this tunnel, what we'll do is sit down and starve to death."

"Don't be such a pessimist. We'd die of thirst *long* before that."

The tunnel began gradually to widen, to look less like an artificial passageway and more like a natural cave. Though there were more of the glowbirds, their light was correspondingly less effective in the larger space. Chris saw branch tunnels to the north and south, but they both felt it made better sense to continue in the direction they hoped was east.

"Valiha must have still been panicked when she came through here," Robin said. "I presume she would have kept going straight. If she'd started to think again, I'd expect her to come back for us, or wait, before she started exploring the side tunnels."

"I agree. But I didn't expect her to come this far. And I keep remembering she's got all our food and water. I could sure use a drink."

The cave floor had become irregular. They found themselves going up and down gentle slopes that reminded Chris of the sand dunes they had traversed on the surface of Tethys. The roof was by then so distant that the glowbirds clinging to it looked like stars turned orange by atmospheric haze. Little detail could be discerned above, and only the general shapes of things on the ground. When they heard running water, they approached it cautiously until the stream betrayed itself by coppery reflections. Chris dipped a finger in it, ready to wipe it dry if it proved to be acid. When he was not burned, he raised some to his lips. It had a faintly carbonated taste.

They removed their shoes and waded, found that it was only ten meters across and never more than half a meter deep.

Beyond the stream the ground changed character again. They could see jagged spires rising around them. Once Chris fell over a two-meter drop. For an eternal second he did not know if the fall might be his last moments of life, until he hit on his hands and knees, cursing loudly more from relief than anger. He had a few bruises to add to his cuts and scrapes but was otherwise uninjured.

His increased caution after the scare paid off quickly. Reacting more from instinct than any sure knowledge, he found himself reaching out to stop Robin. When they moved forward more carefully, they saw she had been no more than a meter from a precipice that tumbled down thirty or forty meters.

"Thanks," Robin said quietly. He nodded, distracted by a glow to his left. He was having no luck making it out when he heard the sound. Someone was singing.

They moved toward the light. As they did, detail emerged from the endless shades of gray and black. Shapeless blurs became rocks, dark traceries like the webs of spiders turned into emaciated vines and shrubs. And the light could be seen to flicker like a candle. It was not a candle, but the lamp Valiha had been carrying in her saddlebag when she took flight. In one last clearing of perceptions he could see one of the shapes near the light was Valiha herself. She was on her side, lying on the far slope of the small canyon twenty meters from the bottom. He called out to her.

"Chris? Robin?" she shouted back. "It is you! I've found you!"

He thought it an odd thing to say but did not dispute her. He and Robin picked their way down the slope on their side, then climbed to her position. It seemed a strange place to rest. Another twenty meters, and she would have been on level ground. He had suspected something was wrong, and now he was sure of it. There was something about her that reminded him, with a flash of fear, of Psaltery lying in his blood-soaked dying ground.

When they reached her, the light of the lamp showed her face smeared with dried blood. She sniffed loudly and drew her hand across her upper lip.

"I'm afraid I've broken my nose," she said.

Chris had to look away. Her nose was broken, and so were both her front legs.

36.

Carry On

Robin sat quietly twenty meters from Chris and Valiha and listened to him shouting at the Titanide. Valiha had suggested, shortly after he determined just how bad her injuries were, that they might as well put her out of her misery. Chris had exploded.

Her body grew heavier each minute. Soon she would be one with the rocks and the darkness. It would be a relief. It would mean an end to frustration. She now realized her momentary elation after their escape from Tethys had been a mistake. She would not make it again.

But she could see that Chris wasn't going to make it easy. He still thought there were things they could do. He was coming toward her now, and she felt sure he wanted to make plans.

"Do you know any first aid?" he asked.

"I can put on a Band-Aid."

He grimaced. "That about sums it up for me, too. We're going to have to do more than that, though. I found this." He opened the leather case he carried. Its sides folded out in all directions, lined with pouches and compartments. Metal glinted in the light of his lamp: scalpels, clamps, syringes, needles, all neatly laid out for the amateur surgeon. "One of them must have known how to use this stuff, or they wouldn't have brought it along. Valiha says Hautbois had a lot more. It looks to me like there's enough equipment here to perform minor surgery."

"If you know what you're doing. Does Valiha need surgery?"

Chris looked tortured.

"She needs some kind of sewing up. Both breaks are in the . . . what do you call it in a horse? Between the knee and the ankle. I think just one of the bones is broken in her right leg; she can't walk on it anyway. But the left leg is bad. She must have taken most of her weight on that one. Both bones snapped, and one of the edges broke through the skin." He had picked up a slim booklet. "It says here that's a compound fracture, and the problem with it is usually fighting infection. We'll have to set the bones, clean out the wound, and sew it up."

"I don't really want to hear about it. You figure it out, and when you understand it, call me and tell me what you want me to do. I'll do it."

He did not respond for a while. When she looked up, she found him studying her face intently.

"Is there something wrong?" he asked.

She could not even laugh. She thought of mentioning that they were lost five kilometers underground in the dark with little food and less light and a demented demi-God to the east and west and an injured companion too big to carry to safety even if they could find their way out in the first place, but why spoil his day? Besides, that wasn't what he meant and she knew it and she was certain that he knew it, too, but she wasn't going to talk about it. Not ever.

So she shrugged tiredly and looked away from him.

He continued to look at her for a long time—it was as if she could feel his gaze on her, and how could he not know?—then reached over and put his hand on her knee briefly.

"We'll get through this all right," he said. "We just have to stick together and take care of each other."

"I'm not so sure," she said, but she was thinking that perhaps he didn't know. While she had feared him when she thought he knew, his apparent ignorance prompted a feeling of contempt. Could it be that her vigilance had been in vain? Could no one see through her? She felt her lip curl on the side of her face that was in shadow and quickly put her hand up to cover it. A hot flash of anxiety swept over her, leaving her filmed in sweat. What was happening to her? It did not even hurt. It was easy to sneer, easy to keep her mouth shut. Could the careful structure of honor built over a lifetime be swept away this easily? He was on his feet now, moving away, going back to tend Valiha, and when he was gone, her secret would be safe.

There was a low roaring in her ears. Something trickled down her chin. She forced her jaw to loosen and felt a sharp pain as air touched the fresh bite in her lower lip.

"It isn't true!" She had been unable to stop the words, but when he turned and was waiting for her to go on, she had to think of something to say that would make it all as if it had never happened, as if she had never said it wasn't true.

"What isn't true?" he said.

"It isn't . . . it . . . I never said . . . you didn't—" Suddenly her stomach felt really awful. She found herself staring stupidly at a clump of hair held in her fist. It was the same color as her own. She was kneeling, and Chris was beside her with his arm around her shoulder.

"Feeling better now?"

"Much better. Up there when there was fire and the things in the sand bite you and you can never see them because they live in the sea came after me and I couldn't get away but I thought of a way nobody will ever know because it happens all the time to me and I can't do anything about it anymore and I *don't* want to do anything I just want to go *away* because they bite and you can't see them and that's not fair and I *hate* them because they live deep deep in the sea."

She allowed him to lead her away. He took her to a level spot and unrolled the sleeping bag and helped her stretch out on it. She stared up at the blank nothing.

He did not know what to do beyond that, so he left her there and returned to Valiha.

Robin heard him approach some time later.

She had not been asleep or even unaware of what had been happening around her. She flexed her fingers and found they moved easily, so she was not having a seizure. Yet she was not existing in any way she was used to. She had heard Valiha groaning, and it had no effect on her. A few times the Titanide had shouted in pain, but Robin was not sure how many times, and the shouts had not been separated by rational amounts of time. She could no longer recall if she had cried or if the weeping was still in the future. She could not explain it and did not try to.

"Do you want to talk some more?" he asked.

"I don't know."

"I'm not sure what you said awhile ago, but it seemed important to you. Do you want to try again?"

"That wasn't a seizure."

"Do you mean just—"

"You know what I mean."

"While we were pinned down. Back in the desert."

"Yes."

"You really could move? You were faking it? That's what you're saying?"

"That's exactly what I'm saying."

She waited, but he said nothing. When she looked at him, he was just sitting there, watching. She wished he wouldn't do that. She was determined not to say any more.

"No, that's not what I'm saying," she said at last.

"You could talk," he observed.

"Then you *did* know! You were just . . . why didn't you—" She was sitting up, but his hands were on her, gently pushing her back onto the sleeping bag. She resisted for a moment, then gave in.

"I noticed you could talk," he said reasonably. "I thought it was odd. Okay?"

"Okay," she said, closing her eyes.

"You couldn't, before," he said when she remained silent. "The other times, I mean. You mumbled."

"That's because a seizure affects all my voluntary muscles. That's why I knew when I couldn't move up there, it wasn't one. It was something else." She waited for him to name it since it seemed he had the right to make the accusation, but it looked as if he weren't going to.

"It was fear," she said.

"*No!*" he said. "You can't mean it!"

She glared at him. "This isn't funny to me."

"Sorry. I get tickled at all the wrong times. Okay, what do you want? I'm astonished, I'm ashamed of you, I never suspected you would turn out to be such a coward, and I'm humiliated that I thought I'd met the perfect, fearless human and now it turns out you're not."

"Will you get the fuck out of here and leave me alone?"

"Not until you've heard the diagnosis of the surgeon-trainee and apprentice psychologist."

"If it's gonna be as funny as your last couple of lines, why don't you save it?"

"Aha! A sign of life."

"Will you go away?"

"Not until you make me. See, a few days ago you would have ripped my guts out for saying any of the things I just said.

It disturbs me to see you just lying there and taking it. Somebody has to restore your self-esteem, and I guess it's got to be me."

."Is that your diagnosis?"

"Part of it, I guess. Malignant lack of self-worth and fear of fear. You're phobophobic, Robin."

She was about to laugh or cry and did not want to do either.

"Will you finish what you have to say and leave me alone, please?"

"You're nineteen years old."

"I never denied it."

"What I'm suggesting is that no matter how tough you think you are, thought you were, you haven't been around long enough to be tested in many, many ways. You went into Tethys thinking nothing could terrify you, and you were wrong. You pissed in your pants and threw up and cried like a baby."

"I'll always appreciate you sparing my feelings like this."

"It's about time someone rubbed your nose in it. You've lived with your seizures most of your life and still haven't really faced them."

"I haven't *surrendered* to them."

"Of course not. But you won't reach an accommodation. You barely admit they exist. You stood watches over important machinery in the Coven, and by doing it, you put your whole world and all your sisters in danger."

"How did you—" She put her hand to her mouth and bit down on her finger until some of the heat of shame had passed.

"You talk in your sleep," he explained. "Robin, they don't allow epileptics to pilot airplanes. It's not fair to the people the airplane might fall on."

She sighed and nodded jerkily.

"I won't argue with you. But what does that have to do with what happened in the desert?"

"Everything, as I see it. You found out something unpleasant about yourself. You got scared, and you froze. And you're dealing with it the same way you've dealt with your seizures, which is not to deal with it at all. I take that back. You cut off your finger. What are you going to cut off now? If you were a man, I'd have a gruesome suggestion, but I don't know what the heroic gland is supposed to be in a woman. Do you have any ideas? I'm learning surgery. Some practice might do me good."

She hated listening to him, wanted nothing more than for

him to stop talking and go away. Far, far away. There was tremendous anger in her somewhere, the pressure was building inexorably, and she felt sure that if he did not leave soon, it would explode and she would kill him. Yet she could not even look at him.

"What would you have me do, then?"

"I already said that. Face it. Recognize that it happened and that you're not proud of it and that it might even happen again. It looks like what you're doing now is trying to pretend it didn't happen, and you can't bring that off, so you just lie there and can't do anything. Tell yourself you were a coward— once, in a very bad situation—and go on from there. Then maybe you can start thinking of how to prevent it happening the next time."

"Or have to face the fact I might do the same thing next time."

"There's always that chance."

She had finally managed to look at him. To her surprise, she was no longer angry when she saw his face. There was no mockery in it. She knew that if she asked him to, he would never say another word about it and never tell anyone else. It somehow didn't seem as important as it had.

"You're a great believer in facing things," she said. "I'd rather fight them. It's . . . more satisfying." She shrugged. "It's easier."

"In some ways."

"It would be easier to cut off another finger than do what you say."

"I guess I can believe that, too."

"I'll think about it. Will you leave me alone now?"

"I don't think so. I'm going to be ready to set Valiha's legs soon. While I'm reading everything again and getting the equipment ready, you can make us something to eat. There's still a fair amount of food in Valiha's pack. There's water on the other side of that ridge. Take the lantern with you; I've improvised a torch I can use to read by."

She stared at him. "Is that all?"

"No. While you're going for water, you can look for something we can use for splints. Most of the plants I've seen are pretty small and twisted, but there might be something. Say, five to six straight poles about a meter long."

She rubbed her face. She wanted to sleep for a few years and did not really want to wake up.

"Poles, water, dinner. Anything else?"

"Yes. If you know any songs, go sing them to Valiha. She's in a lot of pain, and there's not much to take her mind off it. I'm saving most of the drugs to use when I set the legs and sew up the wounds." He started to leave, then turned back. "And you could pray to whoever it is you pray to. I've never done anything like this before, and I'm sure I'm going to do it badly. I'm terrified."

How easily he says it, she thought.

"I'll help you."

37.

West End

Nasu ran away sometime during the early part of their stay in the cavern. Chris was never able to say precisely when it happened; time had become an irrational quantity.

Robin went through hell trying to find the snake. She blamed herself. Chris was unable to ease her sorrow because he knew she was right. Gaea was no place for an anaconda. Nasu had probably suffered more than anyone, coiled in Robin's shoulder bag, allowed out only briefly. It had been with many misgivings that Robin finally let her out to explore the camp. The rocks were warm, and Robin had expressed the opinion that her demon would not wander far from the light of the small camp-fire. Chris had his doubts. He felt Robin was unconsciously attributing to the snake almost arcane powers of intelligence and loyalty merely because she was her demon, whatever that meant. He thought it was too much to expect of a snake, and Nasu proved him right. One morning they woke up and Nasu was gone.

For many days they searched the vicinity. Robin scoured every corner, calling Nasu's name. She left out fresh meat in an attempt to lure her back. Nothing worked. It gradually came to a stop as she realized she would never see the animal again. Then she compulsively questioned Chris and Valiha, asking them if they thought the snake would survive. They always said Nasu would have no problem, but Chris was not sure that was the truth.

Gradually both the searches and the questions tapered off, Robin accepted her loss, and the incident melted through the event horizon of their timeless existence.

The problem was that Hornpipe had carried both the clocks. He still had them, assuming he was still alive.

Chris had a hard time convincing himself that it was a problem, even as the evidence mounted. He had experienced a sense of dislocation even on the surface, where the degree of light varied only with distance travelled and, to a lesser extent, with the weather. But then they had had the clock to tell them how much time had gone by, and Gaby had kept them all punctual. Now he realized he had no clear idea how long it had been since they set out from Hyperion. Going back over it, he arrived at figures from thirty-five to forty-five days.

Down in the cavern the timelessness was intensified. Chris and Robin slept when they were tired and called each period a day, while aware that one might be ten hours and another fifty-five. But as the days began to accumulate, Chris found that he had increasing trouble recalling the sequence of things. Further confusion resulted from their late realization that keeping a tally calendar of sleep periods could be of some help. Thus, from fifteen to twenty sleeps went by before they began to make notches in a stick, and all their calculations were plus or minus an unknown number of days. Even the calendar was useful only if they assumed their days averaged twenty-four hours, and Chris was far from sure it was safe to assume that.

And it mattered. For though they had no timepiece, there was a process going on that was measuring time as surely as atomic decay: Valiha was making a baby Titanide.

She estimated she had been injured on the twelve hundredth rev of her pregnancy but admitted she could be off because she had no recollection of the climb down the Tethys stairway. She recalled little from Gaby's death to her own return to consciousness after her failed attempt to leap the crevasse which had cost her two broken legs. Chris translated 1,200 revs into about fifty days, turned that into one and two-thirds months, and felt a little better. He then asked her if she knew how long her legs should take to heal.

"I could probably walk on crutches in a kilorev," she said, adding helpfully, "That's forty-two days."

"You wouldn't get too far on crutches in here."

"Probably not, if there's climbing to be done."

"There's climbing to be done," said Robin, who had been exploring the area as far as two or three kilometers from the camp.

"Then the time for complete healing would be as much as five kilorevs. Possibly four. I doubt I'd be much good in as little as three."

"As much as seven months. Possibly five or six." Chris

added it up and relaxed slightly. "It will be close, but I think we can get you out of here before your time."

Valiha looked puzzled; then her face cleared.

"I see your mistake," she said placidly. "You thought I would take nine of your months to get the job done. We do things more quickly than that."

Chris rubbed his palm over his eyes.

"How long?"

"I have often wondered why it takes human females so much longer to produce something not so large and still so far from completion—no offense meant. Our own young are born able to—"

"How long?" Chris repeated.

"Five kilorevs," Valiha said. "Seven months. It's certain I'll birth him before I can hope to walk out of here."

The timelessness began to frighten Chris. One day he found himself trying to establish the sequence of events following their discovery of Valiha and found he could not. Some things he knew because they had followed each other during a particular waking period. He was sure he had set Valiha's legs soon after his talk with Robin because he recalled leaving her to prepare for the task. He knew when they had captured their first glowbird because that had happened after their first sleep.

The little luminescent animals were unafraid of them but avoided areas of activity. While they moved around in their camp, the glowbirds would not come near, but when they settled down to sleep, the creatures flew in and perched within meters of them.

Robin had been able to approach one that first "morning," even go so far as to reach out and touch it. They had been thankful for the light cast by the dozen or so glowbirds until a few minutes later they began to drift away. Robin caught the last one and tied it to a stake, where it fluttered all day, and the next morning another dozen had returned. She caught them all this time because they did not make any strong attempts to escape.

They were globular creatures puffed up with air. They had beady eyes with no heads to speak of, wings thin as soap bubbles, and a single two-toed foot. Try as he might, Chris could find nothing resembling a mouth, and all his efforts to feed them came to nothing. They died if kept captive more than two sleeps, so he and Robin used them only during one waking period, catching a fresh group every morning. A dead one had no more presence than a punctured balloon. If touched in the wrong place, they could give a nasty electrical shock. Chris had a theory that they contained neon—the orange light looked very much like it—but it was so wildly unlikely he kept it to himself.

He and Robin had moved Valiha one day fairly early in their stay. They all had grown tired of perching on a twenty-degree slope with a ten-meter drop below them. Chris had worried a long time about the best way to move her. To his surprise, it worked. They fashioned a stretcher and shifted her a few meters at a time until they had reached the plateau above. In the one-quarter gee the two of them could just lift the Titanide, though they could not carry her far.

It was on the plateau that they established their camp and settled in for the long wait. At the time of the move they were still far from optimistic about their chances for survival, for even with the most severe rationing they had food for no more than five or six hundred revs. But they went about making a home as though they expected to stay the six or seven months it would take Valiha to heal. They erected the tent and spent a lot of time in it, though there was no weather and the temperature was an even twenty-eight degrees. It simply felt good to get in from the echoing cavern.

Valiha began to carve things for them. She did so much of it that Robin was kept busy hunting for the scarce, stunted trees which had the only wood worth carving. The Titanide seemed the least affected by boredom; to her, this was simply an extended rest period. Chris thought it must be what a six-month sleep would be to a human.

They were in the west end of an irregular cavern that averaged one kilometer in width and stretched an unguessable distance to the east. The floor was a hopeless jumble of fallen rocks, crags, spires, pits, and slopes. They could deduce from the dimensionless points of light the glowbirds became when festooning the ceiling that it was at least a kilometer high, possibly more. To the north and south was a bewildering variety of openings. They were tunnel mouths that led to corridors much like the one they had fled through. Many of these looked as if they had been bored through the rocks; some actually had timber shorings. Some went up, and others down. Some stayed level, but all of them branched within a hundred meters into two or three other tunnels, and if they were followed for any distance, the branch tunnels divided again. In addition, there were fissures in the rock walls of the sort found in natural caves. The environment beyond these cracks was so chaotic it seemed pointless to explore them. A promising path would dwindle to a passage so narrow even Robin could barely squeeze through, then open into a chamber the size of which she could only guess at.

At first Chris went with Robin on her explorations, but when he returned, he always found Valiha in such a state of despair that he soon stopped. After that Robin went alone, as often as she could talk Chris into agreeing.

Chris was impressed with the change in Robin. It was not a revolutionary one, but to anyone who knew her it was dramatic. She listened to him and would usually do as he said, even if it went contrary to what she wished to do. He was astonished at first; he had never expected that she would take orders from a man. On more careful reflection he decided that his being male was not the crux of the issue. Robin had functioned reasonably well as part of a group with first Gaby and then Cirocco as the leader, but Chris suspected that if either of them had told her to do something she strongly did not wish to do, she would have left them on the spot. She would never have done anything to harm the group—unless leaving it could be called harm—but she always had the option in her own mind of striking out on her own; she was not a team player.

Nor had she magically transformed herself into a follower under Chris's leadership. Yet there was a difference. She was more willing to listen to his arguments, to admit it when he was right. There had been no struggle. In a sense, there was little need for a leader when their group had been reduced to three, but Robin seldom initiated anything, and Valiha never did, so the role, such as it was, devolved on Chris. Robin was too self-centered to be a leader. At times it had made her insufferable to those around her. Now she had added something, which Chris thought was a little humility and a little responsibility. It was humility which allowed her to admit she might be wrong, to listen to his arguments before making up her mind. And it was responsibility to something larger than herself that made her stick with Chris and Valiha day after weary day instead of striking off on her own to bring back help, which was all she really wanted to do.

They compromised on many things. The most trouble was caused by Robin's exploration of the cavern. They had the same argument countless times, in almost the same words, and neither of them really minded it. Boredom had become intense, they had talked out every subject they held in common, and even disagreement became a welcome diversion.

"I don't like it when you go out there alone," Chris said for what might have been the twentieth time. "I've read a little about caving, and it's just not something you do, like swimming in deep water by yourself."

"But you can't come with me. Valiha needs you to stay here."

"I'm sorry," Valiha said.

Robin touched the Titanide's hand, assuring her she didn't blame her and apologizing for bringing up the touchy subject. When Valiha had been soothed, she went on.

"Somebody has to go out. We'll all starve if I don't."

What she said was true, and Chris knew it. There were animals other than glowbirds living in the cavern, and they, too, lacked both fear and aggression. They were easy to approach and easy to kill, but not so easy to find. Robin had discovered three species so far, each about the mass of a large cat, slow as turtles, all without hair or teeth. What they did with their lives was anyone's guess, but Robin always found them lying immobile near conical gray masses of a warm, rubbery substance that might have been a sessile animal or a plant but that was firmly rooted and almost certainly alive. She called the rubbery masses teats because they bore a resemblance to the udders of a cow, and the three sorts of animals cucumbers, lettuce, and shrimp. It was not for the tastes—they all tasted more or less like beef—but after the three Terran organisms they mimicked. She had walked by the cucumbers for weeks before she accidentally kicked one and it opened big, mooning eyes at her.

"We're doing all right," Chris said. "I don't see why you think you have to go out more often than you already are." But he knew it was not true even as he said it. They had some meat, it was true, but hardly enough for Valiha's huge appetite.

"We can always use more," Robin argued, indicating with her eyes that they would not talk about what they both were thinking while Valiha was present. They had discussed her pregnancy and mentioned some of their fears to her, to find out she shared them and was worried she was not getting enough food, or enough of the right diet, for proper development of her child. "Those things are hard to find," Robin went on. "I'd almost like it better if they ran from me. As it is, I can walk within a meter of one and never see it."

The discussion went on and on, and nothing was changed when it was over. Robin went out every other day, half as much as she wanted to and a thousand times more often than Chris liked. Every moment she was gone he saw her lying broken at the bottom of a pit, unconscious, unable to shout for help, or too far away to be heard. Every moment she was in camp she squirmed, paced, shouted at them, apologized, shouted some more. She accused him of acting like her mother, treating her like a child, and he retorted that she *was* acting like a child, and a wild, willful one at that, and each knew both allegations were true, and neither could do anything about it. Robin ached to strike out for help but could not so long as they needed her to hunt, and Chris wanted to go nearly as badly but could not say so for Valiha's sake, so they both seethed and fought, and there seemed to be no solution to the problem until the day Robin angrily plunged her knife into one of the gray teats and was rewarded with a faceful of sticky white liquid.

"It is the milk of Gaea," Valiha said happily and immediately drained the waterskin Robin had filled. "I had not expected to find it so deep. In my homeland it flows two to ten meters below the ground."

"What do you mean, 'the milk of Gaea'?" Chris asked.

"I don't know how to explain further. It is simply that: Gaea's milk. And it means my worries are over. My son will grow strong on this. Gaea's milk contains everything needed for survival."

"What about us?" Robin asked. "Can pe . . . can humans drink it, too?"

"Humans thrive on it. It is the universal nutrient."

"What's it taste like, Robin?" Chris asked.

"*I* don't know. You didn't think I'd just drink it, did you?"

"The humans I know who have tried it say it has a bitter

flavor," Valiha said. "I myself find some of that but believe its quality varies from one rev to the next. When Gaea is pleased, it becomes sweeter. In times of Gaea's anger, the milk thickens and cloys but is still nourishing."

"How would you say she's feeling now?" Robin asked.

Valiha upended the skin again, letting the last drops fall into her mouth. She tilted her head thoughtfully.

"Worried, I would say."

Robin laughed. "What would Gaea have to worry about?"

"Cirocco."

"What do you mean?"

"What I said. If the Wizard still lives, and if we live to tell her of Gaby's last moments and her last words, Gaea will tremble."

Robin looked dubious, and Chris privately agreed with her. He did not see how Cirocco could ever present a threat to Gaea.

But the significance of her discovery had not been lost on Robin.

"Now I can go get help," she said, beginning an argument that would last for three days and that Chris knew from the start he was certain to lose.

"The rope. Are you sure you have enough rope?"

"How can I know how much is enough?"

"What about matches? Did you get the matches?"

"I have them right here." Robin patted the pocket of her coat, tied to the top of the pack they had improvised from one of Valiha's saddlebags. "Chris, stop it. We've been over the supplies a dozen times."

Chris knew she was right, knew that his last-minute fussing was simply to delay her departure. It had been four days since his final capitulation.

They had located the nearest of Gaea's teats and laboriously moved Valiha. Though it was only 300 meters from the old camp in a straight line, that line had crossed two steep ravines. They had taken her half a kilometer north to find passable land, then a kilometer south, then back again.

"You have the waterskin?"

"Right here." She slung it over her shoulder and reached for her pack. "I have everything, Chris."

He helped her get it settled on her back. She looked so small when it was in place. She was weighted down with gear and reminded him with an irresistible protective tug of a toddler dressed to go out and play in the snow. He loved her at that moment and wanted to take care of her. That was exactly what he could not do, what she did not want him to do, so he turned away before she could see the look on his face. He did not want to get the argument started again.

But he could not keep his mouth shut.

"You'll remember to mark the trail."

Wordlessly she held up the small pick, then slipped it back into a belt loop. It was a wonderful belt, fashioned from cured cucumber hide by Valiha's skilled hands. The plan was that when Valiha got well enough to move with crutches, she and Chris would follow the trail Robin had blazed. Chris did not like to think about it, for if Robin had not made it out and returned with help long before that, it would be because calamity had befallen her.

"If you stop finding the teats, you can go three sleeps beyond the point when your waterskin is empty, then turn back if you don't find another."

"Four. Four sleeps."

"Three."

"We agreed on four." She looked at him and sighed. "All right. Three, if it'll make you happy." They stood looking at each other for a moment; then Robin went to him and put one arm around his waist.

"Take care of yourself," she said.

"I was about to say the same thing." They laughed nervously; then Chris embraced her. There was an awkward moment when he did not know if she wished to be kissed; then he decided he didn't care and kissed her anyway. She hugged him, then backed away with her eyes averted. Then she did look at him, smiled, and started moving away.

"'Bye, Valiha," she said.

"Good-bye, little one," Valiha called back. "I'd say, 'May Gaea be with you,' but I think you prefer to go alone."

"That's exactly right." Robin laughed. "Let her stay in the hub and worry about the Wizard. I'll see you people in about a kilorev."

Chris watched her out of sight. He thought he saw her stop and wave but could not be sure of it. Soon there was nothing but the bobbing light of the three glowbirds she carried in a cage woven of reeds, and then even that was gone.

Gaea's milk was indeed bitter, made all the more so by Robin's departure. Its taste did change slightly from day to day, but not nearly enough to provide the variety Chris craved. In less than a hectorev he gagged at the thought of it, began to wonder if starvation might be better than subsisting on the filthy, revolting stuff.

He went foraging as often as he could, careful never to leave Valiha alone for too long. On these trips he gathered wood and from time to time brought back one of the indigenous animals. That was always a signal for rejoicing, as Valiha would bring out her hoarded spices and prepare each one in a different way. It soon became clear to him that she was eating only sparingly of the things she cooked. Chris was sure it was not because she preferred the milk. He thought many times of insisting she take her share but never had the determination actually to say it. He ate his portions like a miser, making the meal last for hours, and always took more when it was offered. He did not like himself for doing it but was unable to stop.

Time blurred. All the sharp edges of time's passage had been worn away since the day he arrived in Gaea. Since before that, actually; the trip in the spaceship had begun his detachment from Earthly time. Then there had been the freezing of duration into one eternal afternoon in Hyperion, the slow crawl into night and once again into day. Now the process was complete.

He started going crazy again, after a long hiatus that had lasted from before the Carnival in Crius until his arrival in the cavern. He thought of it that way now—as going crazy rather than having an "episode," as his doctors had so mincingly called it—because it was simply what happened. He no longer believed Gaea could cure him even if she wanted to, and he could think of no reason why she should want to. He was certainly doomed to go through life as a collection of maniacal strangers, and he would have to cope with them as best he could.

That was actually easier to do in the cavern than it had ever been. He often literally did not notice it. He would become aware of himself in a place he did not recall coming to and could not tell if he had gone crazy or had simply been woolgathering. Each time it happened he would anxiously turn to Valiha to see if he had done her any harm. He never did. In fact, often she would look happier than she had been in days. That was another thing that made the craziness easier: Valiha did not care if he went crazy and actually seemed to like him better that way.

He wondered giddily if this was the cure Gaea had in mind. Down here craziness did not matter. All on his own he had found his way into a situation where he was normal and as well as anyone.

With no discussion between them, Valiha took over the chore of notching the calendar after each of his sleeps. As much as anything else he took that as a sign that he was indeed suffering lapses into manic states. He did not know what he did during those times. He did not ask Valiha, and she never spoke of it.

They spoke of everything else. The chores around camp took up no more than an "hour" each "day," and that left anywhere from nine to forty-nine hours with little to do but talk. At first they spoke of themselves, with the result that Valiha soon ran out of things to say. He had forgotten how impossibly young she was. Though she was a mature adult, her experience was woefully small. But it did not take much longer for Chris to exhaust his life as well, and they turned to other things. They spoke of hopes and fears, of philosophy— Titanide and human. They invented games and made up stories. Valiha turned out to be only mediocre at games but great at stories. She had an imagination and a perspective just enough askew from the human to enable her to astonish him time and again with her reckless, disturbing insights into things she should not understand. He began to see as he never had before what it was to be so nearly human, yet not human. He found himself pitying all those billions of humans who had lived before contact with Gaea, who could never have communed with this improbable engaging creature.

Valiha's patience amazed him. He was going crazy, yet his freedom of movement was much greater than hers. He began to understand why it was the common practice to kill horses with injured legs: the frame was not designed for reclining. A Titanide's legs were much more flexible than those of an Earthly horse, yet she had a terrible time. For half a kilorev she could do little but lie on her side. When the bones began to knit, she started sitting up but could not maintain the position long because her stiff, splintered forelegs had to be straight out in front of her.

His first hint that she was finding it difficult to bear was when she mentioned in passing that Titanides being treated in a hospital would be suspended in a sling with the injured legs hanging down. He was astonished.

"Why didn't you tell me that before?" he asked.

"I didn't see what good it would do, since—"

"Horseshit," he said, and waited for her to smile. It had become his favorite expletive, something he used to tease her gently by pretending to bitch about his daily chore of cleaning up. But this time she did not smile.

"I think I could rig something like that," he said. "You'd stand on your hind legs, right? So some kind of sling that went behind and between your front legs . . . I think I could do that." He waited, and she said nothing. She would not even look at him. "What's the matter, Valiha?"

"I don't want to be any trouble," she said almost inaudibly, and began to weep.

He had never seen her cry before. What an idiot he had been, to assume that because she had not cried, everything was fine. He went to her and found her eager for his touch. It was awkward at first, comforting someone so huge, and the position enforced on her by her injury did not simplify things. Yet he soon relaxed and could soothe her with no thought to anything but the moment. She had really been asking so little all this time, he realized, and he had not given her even that.

"Don't worry about it," he whispered in the long, terete shell of her ear.

"I've been so stupid," she moaned. "It was stupid to break my legs."

"You can't blame yourself for an accident."

"But I remember it. I don't remember much, but I remember that. I was so frightened. I don't know what happened back there . . . back there on the stairs. I remember a terrible pain, and all I could think of was running. I ran and ran, and when I came to the ravine, I jumped, even though I knew I'd never make it to the other side."

"We all do crazy things when we're frightened," he reasoned.

"Yes, but now you're stuck here because of me."

"We're both stuck here," he admitted. "I won't pretend that this is where I want to be; that would be silly. Neither of us

wants to be here. But so long as you're hurt, I'll stick by you
wherever you are. And I don't blame you for anything that
happened because the simple truth is none of it was your fault."

She said nothing for a long time as her shoulders shook
quietly. When she had stopped crying, she sniffed loudly and
looked into his eyes.

"This is where I want to be," she said.

"What do you mean?" He drew back slightly, but she held
him.

"I mean I love you very much."

"I don't think you really love *me*."

She shook her head. "I know what you mean, and it's not
true. I love you always, when you're quiet and when you rage.
There are so many parts to you. I think perhaps I am the only
one who has ever known them all. And I love them all."

"A few doctors claimed to know them all," Chris said un-
happily. When Valiha did not respond, he went to the question
he had been afraid to ask for a long time. "Do I make love to
you when I'm crazy?"

"We make love in glorious tumult. You are my virile stal-
lion, and I your erotomanic androgyne. We have anterior romps
and frontal communion, and then we diddle around in the
middle. Your penis—"

"Stop, stop! I didn't ask for the dirty details."

"I said nothing rhyparographic," Valiha said virtuously.

"I don't . . . what did you do, eat a dictionary?" he asked.

"I must know all English words for the experiment," she
said.

"What . . . never mind, tell me about that later. I knew I
made love to you once. I just wanted to know if I still do."

"Only twenty or thirty revs ago."

"And it doesn't bother you that I do it only when I'm crazy?"

She considered it. "I really have had a hard time understanding what you mean by crazy. Sometimes you lose some
inhibitions—another word I have trouble with. This gets you
into trouble with human women who don't wish to copulate
with you and with any human who thwarts your desires. I have
no trouble because if you ever become obstreperous, I simply
pick you up by your hair and hold you at arm's length. When
you calm down, I reason with you. You respond to this very
well."

Chris laughed, and it sounded hollow even to him.

"You amaze me," he said. "I've been studied by the best

doctors on Earth. They couldn't do a thing with me but give me some pills that are damn near useless. They'll be fascinated to hear your cure. Pick him up by the hair, hold him at arm's length, and reason with him. Ah, sweet reason."

"It works," she said defensively. "I suppose it would be efficacious only in a society where everyone was larger than you."

"My behavior at those times doesn't put you off?" he asked. "Titanides never assault one another, do they? I would expect you to see me as . . . well, repulsive when I'm acting like that. It's so un-Titanide."

"I find most human behavior un-Titanide," Valiha said. "Yours when you are 'crazy' becomes perhaps a trifle more aggressive than is normal, but all your passions are magnified, love as well as aggression."

"I'm not in love with you, Valiha."

"Yes, you are. Even this part of you, the sane part, loves me with a Titanide's love: unchanging, but too large to give all of it to one person. You have told me so when you were crazy. You told me your sane self would not admit his love."

"He lied to you."

"You would not lie to me."

"But I'm here to be cured of all that!" he said, in mounting frustration.

"I know," she moaned, once more on the verge of tears. "I'm so afraid Gaea will cure you and you'll never know your love for me!"

Chris thought this conversation was as crazy as any he had ever heard. Maybe he *was* crazy: permanently. It was within the realm of possibility. But he did not want to see her cry, he *did* like her, and suddenly it did not make sense to resist her any longer. He kissed her. She responded instantly, alarming him with her strength and passion, then paused and put her mouth close to his ear.

"Don't worry," she said. "I'll be gentle."

He smiled.

It was not easy, but eventually he made the sling she needed to rest comfortably while her legs healed. Finding three poles long and strong enough among the stunted shrubs that passed for trees in the cavern took quite a while, but when he had them, he soon fashioned a tall tripod. There was just enough rope to make the sling and pad it with material from clothes they didn't need in the warm cave. When it was finished,

Valiha carefully pulled herself up with her hands, and Chris
positioned her legs through the loops. She settled down in it
and heaved a sigh of contentment. Thereafter she spent most
of her time with her front hooves dangling a few centimeters
from the ground.

But not all her time. In the sling, it was impossible for them
to make frontal love, and that activity quickly became an important part of their lives. Chris was soon wondering how he
had survived so long without it, then realized that, of course,
he hadn't, he had been making love with Valiha all along.
Now he felt he would most probably have succumbed to despair
and simply wasted away, starving in the midst of plenty. Even
Gaea's milk tasted a little better, and he wondered if it was
his mood and not Her Majesty's that made the difference.

Valiha was not like a human woman. It would have been
pointless even to try to say if she was better or not as good;
she was different. Her frontal vagina fitted him within lubri-
cious tolerances too close to be the result of cosmic happen-
stance. He could almost hear Gaea chuckling. What a joke she
had played on humanity, to arrange it so the first intelligent
nonhumans the race encountered could play the same games
humans played, and with the same equipment. Valiha was a
vast, fleshy playground, from the tip of her broad nose across
acres of mottled yellow skin to the softness just above the
hooves of her hind legs. She was completely human—on a
large scale—in the caress of her hands, the mass of her breasts,
the taste of her skin and her mouth and her clitoris. And she
was at the same time wildly alien in her bulging knees, in the
smooth, hard muscles of her back, hips, and thighs, and in the
imposing slither of her penis as it emerged moist from its
sheath. When he kissed her in the hollow behind her expressive
donkey ears, she smelled human.

He was at first reluctant to admit the presence of most of
her body. He tried to pretend she existed from the head to the
forecrotch and ignored the sexual superabundance she contained. Valiha led him gently to experience the surprising possibilities of her other two-thirds. Part of his hesitation was a
lingering misconception he had fought when he found it in
others and had not realized he shared: part of her body was
equine, meaning she was part horse, and one does not become
intimate with animals. He had to discard all that. He found it
surprisingly easy. In many ways there was less equine about
her than there was simian in him. Another hurdle had been

stated early by Valiha herself: she was an androgyne—though gynandroid was the closer of two words never meant to cover Titanides. Chris had never been homosexual. Valiha made him see that it meant nothing when making love with her. She was all things, and it made no difference that her anterior organs were so huge. He had always known that coitus was only a small part of making love.

Titanide crutches were long, stout poles with padded crescents to fit the armpits, little different from the sort used by humans for thousands of years. Chris had no trouble making a pair.

At first Valiha walked only fifty meters before resting, then a similar distance back to the tent. Soon she felt she was able to handle more. Chris struck the tent and packed everything on his back. It was a large burden, especially the poles of her tripod sling. He would never have attempted it but for the low gravity. Even with that advantage it was hard.

Valiha walked by rolling her shoulders, lifting first one crutch, then the other, following with her hind legs. It put an unaccustomed strain on her shoulders, her human back, and the right-angle bend of her spine. Chris had no idea what her skeleton looked like in there; he was sure only that her vertebral structure must be very different from his to enable her to turn her head around and do some of the other improbable contortions he had seen. But she was enough like him to get backaches. The end of each day's journey found her grimacing in pain. The muscles in the bend of her back were like stiff cables. Massage was not enough, though Chris tried. In the end he had to pound her with his fists to give her any relief, as though he were tenderizing meat.

They toughened up, though both knew it would never get easy. For a while each trek was a little longer than the previous day until they reached a maximum Chris judged at about a kilometer and a half. Each day they passed many of the marks made by Robin in her earlier traverse. There was no way to tell how old they were and no use discussing what they both were thinking. By any accounting she should have been back with help long ago.

They struggled on, and each day the question grew larger in their minds.

Where was Robin?

38.

Bravura

It was no longer a matter of admitting Chris had been right. Robin knew that, had known it for quite a long time. She had had no business going off on her own in a place like this.

She tried once again to move her arm. This time she got some results: one finger twitched slightly, and she felt a rough texture beneath it. She swallowed carefully. One of her seemingly endless fears now was drowning in her own saliva. It could happen. Even worse things could happen. She might find, when she got her body back, that it was broken. In that case she would lie here in the dark forever, and while the bulk of that time would pass in peaceful nirvana, the first few weeks promised to be ugly.

How odd to realize that less than a year ago she had been nineteen, and fearless. It did not seem like such a great age, yet it was ancient for someone who could stumble tomorrow and fall a thousand meters to her death.

There was no reason death had to wait until tomorrow. While she lay helpless, the Night Bird could creep up on her and . . . do whatever it did to helpless witches.

Her breath caught in her throat, and she once more strained to turn her head just the few centimeters that would enable her to see if, as she suspected, the Night Bird was actually crouching on the ledge a few meters above her head. Once again she failed to see it, but a drop of sweat ran from her brow to sting her eye.

You were supposed to whistle, she remembered. Then: that's ridiculous. You're nineteen years old, maybe twenty already. You haven't been afraid of the Night Bird since you were six. Nevertheless, if she could have puckered, she would have warbled like a canary.

She was half convinced that the faraway sounds she had been hearing since shortly after she left Chris and Valiha were echoes of her own footsteps, the faint whispers of glowbirds shifting on their perches, the distant sounds of falling water. But being half convinced leaves a lot of room for the imagination, and the picture of the Night Bird had leaped from her childhood memories to shriek and gibber just out of her sight.

She did not believe it *was* the Night Bird; even in her present state she knew no such animal had ever existed, either here or on Earth. It was a story little girls told each other and nothing more. But the thing about the Night Bird was that no one ever saw it. It swooped down on wings of shadow and always attacked from behind; it could change its size and shape to conform to whatever dark place was available, hiding with equal ease in a gloomy cubicle, under a bunk, or even in a dusty corner. Whatever was trailing her—if there was anything—seemed to belong to that dreamworld. She saw nothing. From time to time she thought she heard the sound of claws snapping together, the rattle of a ghastly beak.

Robin knew there were more living things in the cavern than the glowbirds, the cucumbers, shrimp, and lettuce, and the various plant species. There were tiny glass lizards with from two to several hundred legs. They liked heat and had grown more abundant as she moved west, so that her first morning chore was to rid her sleeping bag of the ones that had crept in. There were things like starfish and snails with shells as varied as snowflakes. Once she had seen a glowbird in flight snatched away by some unseen flier, and another time she had found something that might have been part of the ubiquitous body of Gaea denuded of her rocky covering, or could as well have been a creature beside which a blue whale would have seemed no more than a minnow. All she knew for sure was that it was warm and fleshy and, luckily, somnolent.

If all these things lived in a cavern that was, at first glance, endless kilometers of rocky sterility, why not the Night Bird?

Once more she tried to look over her shoulder, this time succeeding in lifting her chin a little. Soon she was able to twitch her feet. But long after she could move her legs and arms, she remained perfectly still, her feet almost a meter lower than her head, to be sure she was completely in control before she dared to try to move from the slope where she had fallen.

When she did move, it was with infinite caution. She edged backward on her heels and elbows until she felt the ground leveling out, then turned to hug the warm rock. Gravity was a wonderful thing when it was pressing you down against a stable surface, not so nice when it tried to pluck you from an uncertain perch. She had seldom thought about gravity before, as either friend or foe.

When her trembling stopped, she crept to the edge of the ravine where she had lain helpless for so many hours. One of her glowbirds had been crushed beneath her when she fell. The other was flickering, near death, but it cast enough light for her to look down and see the bottom, no more than a meter and a half from where her feet had been.

When she came to Gaea, she would have laughed at such a distance. She did not laugh now. After all, it did not take a hundred meters to kill; it did not even take ten. One or two would do, if she hit right.

She took stock of first her body, then her equipment. There was a sharp pain in her side, but after careful probing she decided no ribs were broken. There was blood dried under her nose; she had smacked it when her legs gave way, just before starting her terrifying, feet-first slide into the unknown. Aside from that and some scrapes and a torn fingernail, she was all right. An inventory of the equipment she had kept after several episodes of weeding revealed nothing missing. Her glowbird cage was crushed, but she no longer had any animals to keep in it, and she could make a new one from reeds and vines at her next camp.

She had lost track of how many times she had brushed disaster, was to some degree unsure of just what counted as a brush. Even if she eliminated all the times she had felt her hands slipping on the rope, the momentary losses of footing, the falling rocks that hit only a few meters away, the quicksand that turned out to be only waist-deep, the flash flood that came from nowhere and thundered through a gully she had been about to cross . . . even if she counted only the times she had actually felt the grasp of death as a cold, malefic presence, as though its clammy hand had brushed her and left its spoor of fear on her soul, it was too many times. She was lucky to be alive, and she knew it. There had been a time when danger exhilarated her. That time was no more.

Each day brought its new fear. There were so many by now that she was no longer even ashamed of them; she was too beaten down, too crushed by the collapse of the person she had thought herself to be. If anyone ever emerged from this cavern, she knew it would not be Robin the Nine-fingered but some subdued stranger.

It had not been easy to be Robin, but she was a person to respect. No one had ever pushed her around. Once again she wondered why she kept on. It would be more honorable, she felt, to live her life here where no one could see her. To emerge into the light would be to expose her shame.

But sometime later, urged on by a force she did not understand and would have resisted if she had known how, she got up and resumed her long walk east.

It had seemed so simple when she explained it to Chris and Valiha. She would make her way through the cavern, heading always toward the east, until she reached Thea. Of course, that was assuming the direction they were calling east really *was* east, but if it wasn't, there was little she could do about it.

But it soon became apparent she would have to make more leaps of faith than that first, basic one. She had to assume that the cavern, which was one or two kilometers across at the west end and reached into the unguessable east, would keep going in that direction. And there was no reason to assume that. By the pinpoint lights of the glowbirds she was able to tell the general trend of the passage for two or three kilometers in each direction. It *seemed* to average out as a straight line, but there were so many twists and curves she could not be sure.

There was another possibility. It was impossible to tell if the cavern was rising or descending. They had started at a level she knew to be five kilometers beneath the surface because Cirocco had said so. She also knew Gaea's outer skin was thirty kilometers thick. There was room to miss Thea's chamber by quite a margin.

Two simple instruments could have banished her disorientation. To go up in Gaea was to become lighter, while descending would have made her weigh fractionally more. A sensitive spring scale could have measured those differences. Her own senses were inadequate. The gyroscopic Gaean clock could have been used as a compass because when its axis was oriented north and south, it no longer turned. By aligning the clock until it stopped and then turning it ninety degrees, she could learn east and west by whether the clock ran backward or forward. But neither Gaby nor Cirocco had ever needed a spring scale in her travels, so they had not packed one. And the clock had stayed with Hornpipe.

She wasted a great deal of time trying to fix her position and direction using simple equipment, and ended up being completely baffled. In particular, it should have been possible to determine east and west by the behavior of falling objects. She tried setting up long plumb lines and dropping things, with inconclusive results.

So in the end she blundered on, lost in the dark. She had been doing it for at least three kilorevs, possibly more. She followed the north wall. It had seemed a good idea until she came to the end of a passage, no more than twenty sleeps into her trip. She had followed the south wall back until it began to bend and kept bending through 180 degrees, and she realized she had entered a side passage without knowing it. There was nothing to do but go back across the passage until she reached the marks she had made to guide Chris and Valiha, cross out one and chisel in a new one, directing them to the other passage. Until it, too, ended abruptly three sleeps later.

From that time it had been a nightmare of long treks and heart-breaking backtracks, of gaining slowly as she eliminated false trails one after the other by fighting her way to the ends of them. It was grueling, dangerous work. Her overriding fear was that there was, in fact, no way out, that after all the tears and frustration and the growing realization that she had no real idea *where* she was going, she would one day see Chris and Valiha's camp in the distance and know it had all been for nothing.

The possibility began to grow that Chris and Valiha would one day catch up with her. She would not have minded that at all. In face, she often wondered why she did not sit down and wait for them to arrive. It would be nice to have some company. She longed to see the two of them . . . or it could very well be three by now. She wondered what the baby Titanide would be like.

The more she thought about it, the more sense it made. Three of them working together would do better than Robin working alone. It would be safer, there was no getting around that. Chris would bear some of the danger of leading the way, so her risk would automatically be halved.

And every time she thought that, she pressed ahead with

more determination than ever. If she could no longer be fearless, she could at least be dogged. If she must face the fact that she was fearful, she would also face the fear and overcome it.

She entered an arched corridor much like the one she and Chris had fled through. There was nothing unusual about that fact; she had explored a hundred just like it. But she had come to expect so little of her journey that it was more than a surprise when she saw what lay at the end of it. For a moment she was too stunned to move. There was an unpleasant smell in the air. Robin looked vaguely to the left and right, then down, where a thin sheet of clear liquid lapped at her toes. The tips of her boots were smoking.

She jumped back and hastily kicked them off. She might have waded right into it. She could have fallen on her face. It might have gotten into her lungs. . . .

"Stop it!" she said, aloud, shocked to hear the sound of her own voice. It would never do to stand here and worry about the things that might have happened. She had to deal with what still *could* happen.

"Thea!" she called. But what if it was Tethys she faced, or Phoebe? She doubted she could tell the difference even up close, and from where she stood, several hundred meters down a dark corridor with the conical regional brain only a speck of light, there was no hope at all. It might be best to go back, to think it out better, maybe approach the problem later. . . .

"Thea, I need to speak to you!"

She listened intently, keeping her eyes on the level of acid covering the floor a few meters from her. If it began to rise even the tiniest little bit, she would teach the glowbirds a thing or two about flying.

But the voice of Crius had been faint—hardly a sound to reach down acid-filled tunnels—and though Tethys had sounded louder, it was probably because she had been so frightened, hanging on every word. There was no reason to think Thea could speak any louder than the others.

Robin shouted again, listened, heard nothing. She had not counted on this. She had expected trouble in a million variations but had never thought she might be unable to make Thea aware of her presence.

"Thea, I am Robin of the Coven, a friend of Cirocco Jones,

the Wizard of Gaea, Empress of the Titanides, and. . . ." She tried to recall the titles Gaby had rattled off in a bitter moment back at the Melody Shop, but had no luck.

"I'm a friend of the Wizard," she finished, hoping the assertion would be enough. "If you can hear me, you should know I come on the Wizard's business. I need to speak to you."

She listened again, with no better result.

"If you're talking to me, I can't hear you," she shouted. "It is very important to the Wizard that I be able to speak to you. If you could lower the level of the acid so I could get closer, it would be much easier for us to talk." She was about to add that she could not harm Thea, but something in Cirocco's attitude when addressing Crius made her change her mind. She had no idea if it was a dangerous thing for her to assume any of the airs Cirocco had put on. It might be the worst thing she could do. Yet it was equally possible that Thea understood nothing but strength and would slaughter her the moment she showed weakness.

That thought almost made her laugh, frightened as she was. What did she have but weakness? It was possible she would lose control of herself while in Thea's presence and lie helpless while the huge being decided what to do with her.

Never mind all that, she thought. She would get nowhere but back to the far end of the corridor, back to the darkness of bitter defeat, if she kept thinking like that. She must do what she had to do and ignore the trembling in her hands.

"It is necessary that I speak to you," she went on firmly. "For that to happen, you must lower the level of acid. I tell you that the Wizard will be displeased, and through her, Gaea, if you do not do as I say. As you love and respect Gaea, let me approach. As you *fear* Gaea, let me approach!"

It sounded so hollow, it rang so falsely in her ears. Surely Thea would hear it as plainly as she did, the fear lurking behind her words, ready to betray her.

Yet the level of acid was receding. She approached it cautiously and saw that where there had been a few centimeters of liquid there was now just a slippery, fuming film.

She sat down quickly and opened her pack. Into her boots she stuffed rags from a shirt ruined many hectorevs ago. Her toes were cramped when she put them back on. She tied the rest of the shirt and a corner of her blanket around the outsides of her boots. Then she stepped forward onto the wet floor. She examined the blanket after taking a few steps. It looked as if the acid was not strong enough in that concentration to eat away the material quickly. She would have to chance it.

Thea was being cautious, too. The acid withdrew with painful slowness while Robin danced with impatience. The corridor sloped downward. Soon the walls were dripping acid. Drops began to fall from the ceiling. She drew her blanket over her head and walked on.

At last she came to stand on a ledge identical to the ones she had seen in the lairs of Crius and Tethys.

"Speak," came the voice, and she had never been closer to turning and running than at that moment because the voice was the same, the same as Tethys's. She had to remind herself that Crius had sounded like that, too: flat, emotionless, without human inflection, like a voice constructed on an oscilloscope screen.

"Do not move," the voice continued, "on peril of your life. I can act much faster than you suspect, so do not rely on past experience. I am within my rights to slay you because this is my holy chamber, given to me by Gaea herself, inviolate to all but the Wizard. It is only my long friendship with the Wizard and my love for Gaea that have brought you this far alive. Speak, and tell me why you should continue to live."

She's not one to mince words, Robin thought. As to the words themselves . . . if they had come from a human she would have thought the speaker insane. And perhaps Thea was insane, but it hardly mattered. "Insanity" was a word the connotations of which were not broad enough to cover an alien intelligence.

"If you mean to turn and run," Thea went on, apparently getting suspicious, "you should know that I am aware of what occurred when you visited Tethys. You should know that she was unprepared, whereas I have known of your approach for many kilorevs. I do not need to flood my chamber; beneath the surface of the moat is an organ capable of propelling a jet of acid powerful enough to cut you in half. So speak, or die."

It occurred to Robin that Thea's threats were a hopeful sign, in the same way that her willingness to speak at all was unexpectedly meek for a second-string God.

"I *have* spoken," she said, as firmly as she was able. "If you were listening, you know the importance of my mission. Since you apparently were not, I will repeat it. I come on an errand of great importance to Cirocco Jones, the Wizard of Gaea. I bear information she must hear. If I do not reach her to give it to her, she will be greatly displeased."

As soon as she said it, she wished she could bite her tongue out. This was Thea, an ally of Gaea, and the information she was bringing to Cirocco was that Gaea had murdered Gaby. That would not have mattered but for the possibility that Tethys, who must have been involved, had bragged to Thea. Since Thea seemed to know a lot of what had happened in Tethys's chamber, it was clear there was some communication.

"What is the information?"

"That is between me and the Wizard. If Gaea wishes you to know it, she will tell you."

There was a silence that could not have been more than a few seconds. It was enough time for Robin to age twenty years. But when the jet of acid did not come, she could have shouted for joy. She _had_ her! If she could say a thing like that to Thea and still live, it had to be because Thea's respect for Cirocco was a pretty powerful thing.

Now if she could only keep it up for a few more minutes.

She began to move slowly, not wishing to startle Thea. She had gone three steps toward the stairs she could see on the south side of the chamber when Thea spoke again.

"I said you should not move. We have things still to speak of."

"I don't know what they could be. Will you impede one who carries a message to the Wizard?"

"The question may not be relevant. If I destroyed you—as is my right; indeed, my obligation under the laws of Gaea— there would be nobody to tell tales. The Wizard need never know you passed this way."

"It is not your obligation," Robin said, once more muttering prayers under her breath. "I myself have visited Crius. I have been to his inner chambers and lived to talk about it. It requires only the Wizard's permission. This I know, and you must know it, too."

"My chambers have always been inviolate," Thea said. "This is how it must be. No creature but the Wizard has ever been where you stand."

"And I say to you that I have seen Crius. There is no one more loyal to Gaea than Crius."

"I bow to none in my loyalty to Gaea," Thea said virtuously.

"Then you can do no less than Crius did and let me leave unharmed."

Possibly this was a difficult moral dilemma for Thea; for whatever reason, there was another long pause. Robin was bathed in sweat, and her nose burned from the acid fumes.

"If you are so loyal to Gaea," Robin prompted, "why have you been speaking to Tethys?" Once again she wondered if she had said the right thing. But she was possessed by a maniacal urge to play the charade out to its end, come what may. It would not do now to grovel or plead. She sensed that what chance she had lay in putting on a strong front.

Thea was no fool. She realized she had committed an indiscretion in revealing what she knew of Robin's experience in Tethys. She did not attempt to deny it but instead replied in much the same vein Crius had when confronted by Cirocco.

"One cannot help listening. It is how I am built. Tethys is a traitor. He persists in whispering heresy. All is promptly reported to Gaea, of course. From time to time it is of some use."

Robin concluded that Tethys either did not know what Gaby had told them or had not told Thea. With all the talk of Gaea's eyes and ears, Robin had not been sure just how far Tethys's own senses might reach. She suspected that the threshold to his chambers, five kilometers above him, was too far for direct spying on his part. But Thea did not know, for it was certain that if she did, she would have passed it on to Gaea, who would not be eager for Cirocco to learn the circumstances of Gaby's death. And in that case Robin would already be dead.

"You still have not answered my question," Thea said. "What is to prevent me from killing you now and destroying your body?"

"I'm surprised to hear you speak so disloyally," Robin said.

"I said nothing disloyal."

"Yet the Wizard is an agent of Gaea, and you propose deceiving her. We can leave that question for a moment and consider only the practical side. The Wizard, if she lives, knows—" She coughed, trying to make it look like the effects of the fumes. Robin, she said to herself, you have a very large mouth.

"You do not even know if she lives?" Thea asked, and Robin thought she detected a menacingly sweet overtone to the question.

"I did not," she said hastily. "But of course now it is obvious that she does. We would not be talking if she did not, would we?"

"I concede the point. She lives." Red sparks chased themselves over Thea's conical surface. Robin would have been alarmed if she had not seen a similar display when Crius was chastised. Thea was having a painful memory.

"As I was saying, then, the Wizard knows I went down the stairs with my friends. They are still alive and quite likely to remain so. Sooner or later the Wizard will come and find them and...." There were more sparks, and Robin wondered what she had said. She thought she might be treading on dangerous ground, then realized it was odd that Cirocco had *not* been down to look for them. Of course, she could be lying drunk on the front porch of the Melody Shop, but the implications of that in Robin's current situation did not bear thinking about. And apparently Thea was still sufficiently cowed by the threat of a search by Cirocco to keep on listening.

"The Wizard will come looking," she resumed. "When she finds them, they will tell her I came this way. You will object that I might have become lost in the maze to the west, but do you think the Wizard will be satisfied until she finds my body? And not only that, but a body dead by natural causes, not burned with acid?"

Thea was silent again, and Robin knew she had said all she could. Having posed that last question, she was no longer sure it was such a good one. *Would* Cirocco come looking for her? Why had she not done so already? Surely she would not abandon Gaby. She wasn't that far gone, was she?

Thea did not think so.

"Go then," she said. "Leave quickly, before I change my mind. Carry your message to the Wizard, and may you never have a day's luck with it for the impudent desecration of my chambers. Go. Go swiftly."

Robin thought of mentioning that she would never have come here if there was any other way out, but enough was enough. The acid was rising already, and she began to fear Thea might still engineer a plausible accident. She hurried to the stairs and took them five at a time.

She did not slow down when she was out of sight. She did not intend to slow down at all, ever, but eventually exhaustion overtook her and she stumbled, fell to her knees, and lay gasping, sprawled across three steps.

She had escaped, but there was no elation this time. Instead, there was the impulse she by now knew all too well: the overpowering urge to cry.

But this time the tears did not come. She shouldered her pack and began to climb.

The entrance to the Thean staircase was clogged with snow. At first Robin did not know what it was and approached it cautiously. Books had told her snow was soft and fluffy, but this was not. It was hard-packed and drifted.

She stopped to put on her sweater. It was nearly pitch-black now that the wild glowbirds were gone. Her last glowbird in the rebuilt cage was nearly dead. There had been no chance to catch another in her hurried ascent of the stairs.

The first order of business was to get out in the open. If it was not overcast, she ought to be able to see the Twilight Sea and thus establish which way was west. Beyond that she was unsure. She tried to recall the map she had studied so long ago. Did the central Thea cable touch ground to the north or south of Ophion? She could not be sure, and it was important. Gaby had said the best way to cross Thea was on the frozen river. Once oriented, she would strike out to the south, and if she seemed to be rising, she would turn around because she did know the cable was very close to the river.

Before she was even out of the strand forest, she had to stop and put on all her clothes. She had never imagined such cold. She wondered uneasily if it had been a mistake to discard the bulky parka Chris had insisted she take. It had made sense at the time; the thing had taken up nearly half the space in her backpack, had made her unbalanced and awkward, and she had been sure the two sweaters, the light jacket, and the rest of her clothes would be enough for anything. But he had told her to keep the parka. He had been quite emphatic about it.

At least she had her boots. They had been handy in the roughest stretches of climbing, though she had torn out the fur padding that had made her feet sweat. Like everything she owned, they had seen a lot of wear but were well-made and still intact. She rubbed snow over the acid-marked toes, hoping the corrosion would go no further once the stuff was diluted with water.

She was about to start again when she remembered one piece of equipment carried uselessly for so long that would finally come in handy. She dug in her pack and came up with a little mercury thermometer, held it close to the guttering glowbird, and squinted. She could not believe what she saw. But after she had shaken it, the thing still read negative twenty degrees. She breathed on it and saw the slender silver column rise, then slowly fall again. Now she had something else to fear. She could freeze to death if she didn't keep moving.

So get off your butt, she told herself, and eventually obeyed. It would have been nice to be more rested, she thought, but sleeping on the Thean stairs had been out of the question. Now she considered it, standing knee-deep in snow. She could go down a short way until it warmed up, sleep, and start out fresh.

In the end she did not and thought she was being cautious. There was no telling if she was safe from Thea on the stairs.

She looked again at the dying glowbird and knew she had better hurry. If she didn't get out from under the cable soon, the darkness would be complete.

She made it out, learning a few things about snow and ice on the way. Ice was a lot more treacherous than rock, even when it looked solid. As for snow . . . she found enough of the properly fluffy variety to last a lifetime. In places it drifted higher than her head. Several times she had to find her way around huge piles of it.

But she saw gray light about the time the glowbird was becoming useless. She tossed the cage away and headed for it.

It was a strange sensation to see so far again. The weather was clear in Thea. The air was crisp and biting with an intermittent wind gusting up to five or ten kilometers per hour. It sucked the heat from her skin where it touched. She could see Twilight to her left, so that was west, meaning she had to circle the cable before she could go south.

Unless she was remembering wrong. It would be wise to consider it again before starting around the cable on a trip she would have to retrace if Ophion were north of the cable. She had had enough backtracking, and this time she had to consider her toes, which were already getting cold.

She remembered that Thea was dominated by a rugged mountain range that reached from the north to the south highlands. Ophion, which kept to a nearly central course through the region, divided into a north and south fork somewhere near the middle of Thea. The central cable attached near the point where the streams reunited. For most of its length the south branch flowed beneath one of the two glacial sheets that covered most of Thea and would be nearly impossible to find. But the north branch was free of permanent ice. At times, during some part of Gaea's thirty-years climatic cycle, it thawed, and a narrow valley in central Thea experienced a brief, bleak springtime. Now was not one of those times. Still, even frozen, it should not be too hard to find. It would be relatively level and would be at the bottom of a wide valley.

The more she thought about it, the more she felt her first recollection had been wrong. The ground before her sloped gently down. It was too dark to tell if the river was ahead, but she now thought it was. And what the hell? The chances were even, and this way she would not have to begin by circling the cable. She started off to the north.

The wind picked up before she had gone half a kilometer. Soon snow was whipping from the tops of high drifts, stinging her cheeks. Once more she stopped to rearrange her clothing, this time wrapping her blanket around herself and fashioning a hood which she could hold tight at her neck and thus protect everything but her eyes from the wind.

While she sat, something approached her. She never did get a clear look at it through the blowing snow, but it was white, about the size of a polar bear, and had massive arms and a mouthful of teeth. It sat watching her, and she watched it until it decided to move in for a closer look. Possibly it wanted to say hello, but she didn't wait to find out. It absorbed her first bullet with no change of expression but paused to look down at a spreading red stain on its fur. When it kept coming, she emptied the magazine, and it folded up like clean white linen and did not move again. She fought the shaking in her hands as she reloaded the gun with her last clip, cursing under her breath and blowing on her fingers to make them bend. The creature had still not moved when she was through, but she did not try to approach it. She made a wide detour and resumed her downhill slog.

In a way it was good that she had not thought of what to do once she reached the river. If she had, she might still be huddled under the cable. Better to set one's goal a few steps at a time, she thought, as she stood on the wide, flat, windy plain that must be the frozen Ophion. She looked east, then west. Each direction looked equally impossible. She was in the dead center of Thea, with more than 200 kilometers to go in either direction before she reached daylight.

To the east was Metis, which looked warm and inviting but was not, according to Cirocco. Metis was an enemy of Gaea, though not so dangerous as Tethys. West, of course, was Tethys, and the desert. Somehow it did not look so bad from here. She thought of the baking heat of the sands, then of the wraiths beneath those sands, and turned east. There had really been no choice, but pretending there was had given her a few minutes to stand still and not think about her feet.

The terrible thing was that she was burning up as she froze to death. She could not feel her toes while sweat ran down her back and arms. The exertion was keeping her warm—in fact, overheated—but the wind was killing her. There was nothing to do for either condition; she kept walking.

When she stumbled several hours later and then jerked her head up with the realization she had almost fallen asleep, she forced herself to take stock. She had enough experience by now with the drugged, careless rapture so common among people who tried to live in Gaea without a clock that she knew she was far gone under its spell. She had no idea how long she had been awake, but it was probably something like two or three days. She had already been tired when she reached the corridor that led to Thea, and she had been exerting herself continually since that time. It was possible to fall asleep standing up, she knew, because she had done it several times in her traverse of the cavern. She had to find a place to sleep, and fast.

Nothing looked promising. Trying to get her brain to work, she suddenly recalled something about burrowing in the snow. It didn't make sense, but then sleeping out in the wind sounded even crazier.

At the edge of the frozen river was a place where snow had drifted eight meters high. She went to the downwind side and began to hack at the snowbank. It was hard and crusty on the surface, but the digging quickly became easier. She scooped out the snow with both arms, working feverishly to hollow out something big enough to take her body. When she had it, she crawled in, fitfully tried to pack snow around the entrance, then curled up as tightly as she could and was instantly asleep.

She had thought "chattering teeth" was a figure of speech, and not a very good one, like knees knocking when one is afraid. Then she realized her knees were knocking too. Her whole body was quivering, and she could not stop it. She began to cough, and a lot of wet matter came up before she was through. She was soaking wet and burning with fever. She knew she was going to die.

That thought was enough to bring her scrambling out of her cubby to stand unsteadily on the riverbank. She coughed again, could not stop until she threw up the bitter contents of a nearly empty stomach. She was surprised to find herself on her knees.

She was even more surprised to find herself walking over the ice. Looking back, she could not find the spot where she had stopped. She must have been moving for some time, and she had no recollection of it.

Things began to fade in and out as she walked. Her vision would narrow as if she were looking through a long pipe; then the edges would redden, and she would have to pick herself up from where she had fallen. Her outline looked comical as she stood there swaying, regarding the human cookie-cutter shape she had made. Snow angels, they were called, and she had no idea how she knew that.

Sometimes people walked beside her. She had a long conversation with Gaby and did not remember she was dead until long after. She fired a shot at what could have been another snow monster or just a gust of snow-laden wind. The gun was deliciously warm for a few minutes after that, and she thought of firing it again until she realized it was pointed at her stomach. When she tried to put it back in her pocket, some of her skin came away, stuck to the metal handle. Part of the tail of one of her snake tattoos went with it. Even worse, the lashes of one eye froze together, and she wasn't seeing all that well out of the open one.

The flashing light, when she saw it, was a bother at first. It irritated her because she could not explain it. She wanted no part of paranormal phenomena like the ghost of Gaby or hallucinations of Chris and Valiha, and she was sure this light was something like that. If she went there, she'd probably find Hautbois all saddled up and ready to gallop away with her.

On second thought, why not? If she were going to die, she might as well do it with a friend. So what if the Titanide was dead? She was not prejudiced. They would have a good laugh, and Hautbois would have to admit that there really *was* a life after death, that she and her whole race had been wrong about that. She laughed at the thought and struck out over the low rise where the light had been.

She was considerably sobered when she reached it, aware of how dangerously close to complete delirium she was getting. She had to keep her wits about her. The light was real, and though she had no idea what it might be, if it wasn't her salvation, then she *had* none.

Her vision was getting worse. If she had not run into the metal leg, she might well have blundered past it and into oblivion. But the thing rang when her head hit it, and she staggered up one more time, dazed, and peered up into the darkness. A red light was flashing up there, once every ten or fifteen seconds. She could dimly make out a building set on four stilts tied together with metal girders like a fire lookout tower. The tower was about ten meters high. There was a ladder with wooden rungs that went all the way to the top.

Something caught her eye beside the ladder. It was a small sign set just below eye level. She brushed snow away and read it:

PLAUGET CONSTRUCTION COMPANY
REFUGE NUMBER ELEVEN
"WELCOME, TRAVELERS!"
—Gaby Plauget, Prop.

Robin blinked at it, read it through several times to see if it would fade away as Gaby's ghost had. It didn't. She licked her lips and fumbled around, trying to get a grip on the wooden rungs. Her hands would not work. Still, it was thoughtful of Gaby to have made the ladder from wood, she thought, recalling the terrible cold of the metal gun butt.

So she hooked her arms over the rungs and dragged herself up that way. She had to look down to see if her feet were on the steps; she could not feel them. Three steps and rest, then five and rest again, then three, then two. Then not even one. She could not raise herself any higher. She looked down and saw that she was almost halfway up, so she must have blacked out and lost count. She looked up and it might as well have been Mount Everest.

So close.

The door opened above her. A face peered down over a narrow ledge. She hoped it was Cirocco because she could believe that; the Wizard had business in Thea—good, sound, logical business. If it were anyone else, she would know it was a mirage, a phantom.

"Robin? Is that you?"

She smelled coffee and something cooking on the stove. That was too good to be true, and no, it was not Cirocco. It was so ridiculous there was no point in even bothering to look back because the face she finally recognized belonged to Trini, her lover a million years ago back in Titantown. At that instant she knew it was all a dream, probably the tower as well as Trini.

She let go and landed on her back in a deep snowdrift.

39.

The Outpost

Cirocco's money had been piling up on Earth for more than seventy-five years. There were the royalties from her scholarly works and travelogs of Gaea and from her autobiography, *I Chose Adventure* (publisher's title, not her own), which had been a best seller and the subject of two movies and a television series. In addition, she owned a piece of the cocaine trade which was quite lucrative. There was even the NASA salary accrued during the voyage of *Ringmaster*, until her resignation.

She had hired a Swiss investment counselor and a Brazilian lawyer and given them two instructions: to keep her ahead of inflation and to avoid confiscation of assets by communist governments. She had hinted that she would like her money to go into firms dealing in space travel and that she would not like it to be used in ways contrary to the interests of the United States. Her lawyer had suggested the last requirement was old-fashioned and almost impossible to define anymore, and she wrote back saying that Earth was full of lawyers. He got the point, and his descendants were still working for her.

After that she forgot about it. Twice a year she got a report, which she would open to glance at the bottom line, then throw away. Her fortune weathered two depressions when countless short-lived investors were wiped out. Her agents knew she could look to the long term and knew she would not get excited by temporary losses. There had been bad years, but the overall trend had been relentless growth.

It all had been a meaningless abstraction. Why should she care to know that she owned X kilograms of gold, Y percent of corporation Y Prime, and Z deutsche marks in rare postage stamps and works of art? If the report arrived on a dull day, she might spend a few minutes chuckling over the lists of assets, from airliners to Airedales, from Renoirs to rental housing. Only once did she send a letter, when she discovered by accident that she owned the Empire State Building and that it was scheduled for demolition. She told them to restore it again, instead, and lost millions during the next two years. After that she made it all back, and her agents undoubtedly thought she was a financial genius, but she had spared the building because her mother had taken her to the top when she was seven years old, and it was one of her fondest memories of her mother.

She had thought from time to time of willing her fortune to someone or something, but she was so removed from Earthly concerns she had no idea where it would do any good. She and Gaby used to laugh at thoughts of picking a name from the phone bank and dumping it all on one person or of endowing homes for unwed goldfish.

But now it was coming in handy after all.

Trini saw the plane when it was still quite a distance away by the glare of its landing lights. She heard the high whine of its tiny jet engine much later. She was not sure she approved. Cirocco's equipment had not yet arrived when Trini took up her vigil at Refuge Eleven; she had blimped in as a decent person should. One of the reasons she had come to Gaea was to escape the pressures of mechanical civilization. Like most humans in Gaea, she viewed any but the simplest technology with deep suspicion. But she understood the Wizard's reasons. Cirocco was waging all-out war on the buzz bombs, and Trini did not doubt they would soon be wiped from the skies.

The plane crawled through the last meters before touchdown, its exhaust raising clouds of snow. Ophion did not look like a promising landing field, hummocked as it was with drifted snow, yet the little plane made it easily in less than thirty meters of runway. The low gravity and Gaea's thick atmosphere provided a lot of lift, making the plane spry as a butterfly. It had transparent wings of plastic film. When the snow settled, Trini could see dark shapes embedded in them and assumed they were lasers or machine guns. It was a six-seat puddle jumper modified for aerial combat.

Cirocco got out from the pilot's seat, and someone else, about her size, from the other side.

Trini went back to her tiny stove and turned up the gas burner under the coffeepot. She had volunteered for the duty—though she and all the other humans in Gaea owed no allegiance to the Wizard—when she heard Cirocco was looking for human help for a rescue mission involving Robin of the Coven. Trini had not been able to stop thinking of Robin since the day she left, and thought waiting in the refuge was more in keeping with her talents than going down the stairs to see Thea. She had been brought in with crates of food, blankets, medical supplies, and bottled gas to prepare the long-abandoned way station for occupancy should any of the missing people show up. Cirocco had helped her get the beacon working again, but aside from that, there had not been much to do. The structure was still sound, and it kept out the wind. She had spent her time at the window, reading, but had been away from it when she felt the tower vibrate slightly with the sound of someone climbing the ladder.

Now it was vibrating again, more noticeably, as Cirocco and the other person hurried up outside. She opened the door for them. Cirocco went immediately to Robin, who was sleeping beneath a big stack of blankets. She knelt beside her and touched her face, looked back with concern.

"She's awfully hot."

"She drank some broth," Trini said, wishing she could say more.

Cirocco's passenger was a familiar figure to Trini and anyone else who had spent time in Titantown. He was Larry O'Hara, the only human doctor in Gaea. Nobody cared that he was there because he was barred from practicing on Earth, and nobody asked why. He probably wasn't much at open-heart surgery, but could set a bone or dress a burn, and he charged nothing. He carried a genuine black bag without a gram of electronic equipment in it. This he now set down while removing his fur coat. Beneath it he was a big man with a black beard and rosy cheeks, more of a lumberjack than a surgeon. Cirocco stood back while he made his examination. He took his time about it.

"She may lose those toes," he announced at one point.

"Nonsense," Cirocco said, which struck Trini as a funny thing to say.

She really looked at the Wizard for the first time and was surprised to see she was wearing what she had always worn for as long as Trini had known of her: the faded brick red Mexican blanket with a hole cut in the center. It draped carelessly around her body, reached to the knees, and was modest enough when she stood still but not when she moved. She was barefoot. Snow still clung to the sides of her feet but was melting rapidly.

What was she? Trini wondered. She had known for a long time that Cirocco was different but had assumed she was still human. Now she was not so sure. Perhaps she was something more, but the differences were subtle. The only visible one was something she shared with Gaby Plauget. All the dark-skinned humans in Gaea had been born that way. Yet Gaby and Cirocco always looked freshly tanned.

At last Larry turned away from her and took the mug of coffee Trini offered him. He smiled his thanks and sat with the white mug warming his hands.

"Well?" Cirocco asked.

"I'd like to get her out of here," he said. "But I don't believe we should move her. I don't suppose I could do much more for her back at Titantown, at that. She's got some frostbite, and she's got pneumonia. But she's young and strong, and that Titanide drug I gave her is hell on pneumonia, and she should make it all right, with the proper care."

"You'll stay here to see that she gets it," Cirocco announced. Larry shook his head.

"Impossible. I have a practice in Titantown to take care of. You can care for her, or Trini can."

"I said—" Cirocco stopped herself with an effort that was visible on her face. She turned away for a moment. Larry looked interested; no more. Trini knew he was impossible to talk into anything. Once he had decided what his duty was, he would do it and not even bother to argue with you. Whatever had happened to him on Earth, he took his medical oath very seriously in Gaea.

"I'm sorry I snapped at you," Cirocco said. "How long can you stay?"

"As much as twenty revs, if need be," Larry assured her. "But really, I can tell you what to do for her in ten or fifteen minutes. The treatment's as old as the hills."

"She was talking awhile ago," Trini offered. Cirocco turned to her at once, and for a moment Trini thought she would grab her shoulders and shake her. But she restrained herself, while her eyes bored into Trini.

"Did she mention any of the others? Gaby? Chris? Valiha?"

"She wasn't really awake," Trini said. "I think she was talking to Thea. She was afraid, but she couldn't let Thea know that. It was jumbled."

"Thea," Cirocco whispered. "My God, how did she get past Thea?"

"I thought you expected them to," Trini said. "Or why else did you have me stay here?"

"To cover all the bases," Cirocco said, distracted. "You were a backup to take care of a low probability. I don't see how she found her way *through* all that, much less got past. . . ." She frowned, and her eyes focused on Trini.

"I didn't mean that the way it sounded, I hope you—"

"That's all right. I'm glad I was here."

Cirocco's face softened, and she smiled at last. "So am I. I know you've been here a long time, and I appreciate it. I'll see that you get—"

"I don't want anything," Trini said quickly. Again those eyes bored into her.

"All right. But I won't forget it. Doctor, can we wake her up?"

"Call me Larry. You'd better let her rest for now. She'll wake up in her own time, but I don't promise she'll make any sense. She's got a high fever."

"It's very important that I talk to her. The others could be in trouble."

"I realize that. Give her a few more hours, and I'll see what I can do."

Cirocco did not wait very well. Not that she paced or chattered; in fact, she said nothing and never got up from her chair. But her impatience filled the room and made it impossible for Trini to relax. Larry had had a lot of practice at waiting. He spent his time reading one of the books Trini had finished during her long vigil.

Trini had always liked to cook, and the refuge was filled with food she had no chance to use. Robin had been able to take no more than a few sips of broth. For something to do she cooked eggs, bacon, and pancakes. Larry appreciated them, but Cirocco waved it away.

"Thea!" she said at one point, prompting the others to look up. "What am I talking about, Thea! How the hell did they ever get past *Tethys?*"

They waited for her to say more, but that was it. Larry returned to his book, and Trini began to straighten things for the seventeenth time. On the cot, Robin slept quietly.

When Robin groaned, Cirocco was instantly at her side, and Larry was not far behind. Trini hovered behind them and had to retreat quickly when Cirocco moved to let Larry in to take Robin's pulse.

Robin opened her eyes when Larry touched her arm, tried to pull away, and blinked slowly. Something in Larry's voice calmed her. She looked at him, then at Cirocco. She did not see Trini in the shadows.

"I dreamed I . . ." she began, then shook her head.

"How do you feel, Robin?" Cirocco asked. Robin's eyes moved slowly.

"Where were *you?*" she said petulantly.

"That's a good question. Can you listen to the answer? That way you won't have to talk for a while."

Robin nodded.

"Okay. First, I sent Hornpipe back to Titantown to get a crew to clear out the entrance to the stairs. If you remember, it was completely cut off."

Robin nodded again.

"It took awhile to get everyone there and longer than I'd thought to clear it all away. The Titanides were willing to work, but they behaved strangely under the cable. They'd wander away, and when you found them, they didn't remember leaving. So I had to hire some human help, too, and wasted even more time.

"But we got it clear and took a team of seven humans down to Tethys. The chamber was flooded higher than I've ever seen it. She wouldn't speak to me, and there was nothing I could do about it since even Gaea carries no weight with Tethys.

"So I came here. I was sure you all were dead, but I wouldn't believe it until I found your bodies, no matter how long it took. If Tethys had killed you, I . . . I don't know what I would have done, but I would have done something to her she'd never forget. Anyway, there was that outside chance you had made it by her and into the catacombs."

"We did. And Valiha—"

"Don't talk yet. Save your strength. Now, as far as I know, me and Gaby are the only humans who have ever been down there, and I knew little about the catacombs except that they go on forever and are impossible to find your way through. I went to see Thea anyway and told her that if any of you showed up, she was to let you through without hindrance. Then I tried to explore the east end of the catacombs, and I had to give it up after a few weeks. I wasn't getting anywhere. I decided I'd risk leaving and organizing a group to come down there properly equipped and explore every meter of the place, and for that I had to order a lot of things from Earth. I didn't really think any of you had made it, you see, and I—"

"I understand," Robin said with a sniff. "But Thea . . . oh, damn it. I thought I had . . . I thought I made it past her on my own. But she was just playing with me." She looked as if she were going to cry, but in the end she was too weak to do it.

Cirocco took Robin's hand.

"Pardon me," she said. "You misunderstood. I was a long way from satisfied Thea would take an order from me if I wasn't there to enforce it. She's obsessive about her privacy. I was afraid that if any of you *did* show up, she'd kill you and destroy the bodies and let Tethys take the blame since she knew I already thought that's what happened and there wasn't a damn thing I could do about it unless I wanted to camp out on her doorstep for a few months. Maybe I should have done that anyway because—"

"That's all right," Robin said. She smiled weakly. "I handled it."

"You sure did, and someday I'd like to know how. Anyway, I did what I could—though I sure as hell wish I'd done more now—and I was going to start down to Thea in three or four more days when I got a call from Trini that you'd come knocking at her door. I got here as fast as I could."

Robin closed her eyes and nodded.

"Anyway," Cirocco went on after a pause, "there are a lot of things I've wanted to ask you, and if you feel up to it, maybe I can ask them now. The biggest thing that's been on my mind is why Gaby let you go down to Tethys in the first place. I know her, and she knows me, even if we don't always get along, and she should have known I'd find a way to clear those rocks and come in to get you all. Then, when she didn't show up with you, I wondered why she didn't, and now I'm wondering if she was hurt and couldn't. . . ." Her voice trailed off. Robin had opened her eyes, and the look of horror there was so plain to Trini that she knew instantly what had happened. She turned away.

"I thought when you cleared away the rocks . . ." Robin wailed.

Trini turned back, and it was as if Cirocco had turned to stone. Finally her lips moved, but her voice was dead.

"We found nothing," she said.

"I don't know what to say. We left her there. We wanted to bury her, but there was just no...." She trailed off into tears, and Cirocco stood. Her eyes looked at nothing as she turned, and Trini knew she would never forget those dead eyes that swept over her as if she were not there as the Wizard of Gaea fumbled for the door latch and stepped outside onto the narrow porch. They heard her going down the ladder; then there was no sound at all but Robin's weeping.

They worried about her, but when they looked out, she was standing with her back to them, a hundred meters away, knee-deep in snow. She did not move for more than an hour. Trini was going to go out and get her, but Larry said give her more time. Then Robin said she had to talk to her, and he went down the ladder. Trini could see him speaking to her. Cirocco did not turn her head but did follow him when he put his hand on her shoulder.

When she was back inside, her face was still dead to all emotion as she knelt beside Robin's cot and waited.

"Gaby told us something," Robin began. "I'm sorry, but I think she wanted just you to hear it, and this room is too small for privacy."

"Larry, Trini," Cirocco said, "would you wait in the plane? I'll flash the lights in here when you can return."

Neither Cirocco nor Robin moved as the two of them put on their coats and boots and left, pulling the door closed quietly behind them. They spent an uncomfortable hour in the plane, protected from the wind but cold all the same. Neither of them complained. When the lights flashed, they returned, and Trini did not immediately see the difference in Cirocco's face, but it was there. It was still painful to look at, and it was still dead, in a sense. But it was not dead like the face of a corpse; it was more like a face carved in granite.

And the eyes burned.

40.

Proud Heritage

There had to be easier things than shepherding a pregnant, disabled Titanide through a dark terrain that would have daunted a mountain goat. On the other hand, Chris could think of some things that were probably harder, and many things less pleasant. The company was some compensation, and the fact that the path was marked for them.

Everything balanced, and it came to seem as if that were the way it should be. Valiha's arms grew stronger, but their pace did not improve because she was gaining weight. They had to be more careful than ever lest her growing awkwardness provoke a slip that might hurt her still-fragile forelegs. As she neared her term, the new delights of anterior sex play tapered off and stopped. But the frontal sex got even better as her legs improved. He gradually lost the exciting, exotic sense of alienness he had once felt when he was around her, to the point he sometimes wondered how she had ever looked odd. Yet with familiarity grew an easy acceptance that drew them closer.

Valiha swelled like a ripening pumpkin. She grew more radiantly beautiful and, curiously, more mottled with brownish freckles.

There would be few surprises. Chris began completely ignorant of Titanide birthing, but by the time Serpent was ready to be born he knew as much as Valiha. He had been making many assumptions that led to needless apprehension.

He knew, for instance, that Valiha was not using a general pronoun when she called her child he. That had been planned with the other two parents. He knew—but still could not quite believe—that Valiha was in communication with the fetus in a way she never satisfactorily described. She claimed they had decided on his name together, though she had influenced him because of a circumstance beyond her control. That concerned the Titanide custom of naming a child after the first instrument

326

he or she owned. The custom was no longer universal, but Valiha was traditional and had been working for some time on the first instrument for her son: the serpent, a sinuous tube of wood played like a brass horn. In the cavern, her choice of building materials had been limited.

He knew the birth would not be painful, would not take long, and Serpent would be born able to walk and talk. But when she told him she hoped the child would be able to speak *English*, Chris's first thought was that she was a fool. He did not say that but expressed his doubt.

"I know," Valiha said. "The Wizard is dubious, too. This is not the first time an attempt has been made to birth a child with two milk tongues. Yet even the Wizard will not say it cannot be done. Our genetics is not yours. Many things happen differently inside us."

"Like what?"

"I know nothing of the scientific side of it. But you must admit we are different. The Wizard has successfully crossed Titanide eggs with the genetic matter of frogs, fish, dogs, and apes in the laboratory."

"That goes against everything *I* ever read about genetics," Chris admitted. "Not that I know much either. But what does that have to do with Serpent speaking English? Even if he had human parents—which you say he doesn't—all we can do when we're born is yell."

"The Wizard calls it the Lysenko effect," Valiha said. "She has demonstrated to her own satisfaction that Titanides can inherit acquired characteristics. We—those of us who postulate that English might be passed on—speculate that if sufficiently reinforced, it could be done. You once asked me if I had swallowed a dictionary. That is almost true. For the experiment it is necessary that all the parents know all English words. This is a goal one can never attain, but we have good memories."

"I can vouch for that." Something about it disturbed Chris, and it took him a long time to put his finger on it. Even when he had it, he was not sure just why it upset him, but it did.

"What I want to know is why," Chris said much later. "Why English when your own language is so beautiful? Not that I understand it, though I wish I could. From what I gather, aside from Cirocco and Gaby, who got it implanted in them, no human has ever gone beyond the pidgin stage in singing Titanide."

"It's true. We know the language instinctively, and humans, despite their often great intellectual attainments, have had no luck with it. Our songs will not parse and are seldom the same, even when the same thought is expressed. The Wizard has speculated there is a telepathic component."

"Whatever. My point is—or maybe I should say it's my question—why are you working so hard at this? What's wrong with Titanide? I think it's a miracle you're born knowing *any* language. Why try for English?"

"Perhaps you misunderstood," Valiha said. "Serpent will know how to sing. This is assured. I would not dream of trying to take that ability away from him. I would as soon wish he be born with only two legs as . . . oh, dear. Please—"

Chris laughed and said it was okay.

"I was alluding to a saying used when one is experiencing great difficulties. Then we say, 'Going at it on two legs, both of them on the left.'"

"Sure you were."

"I promise you that . . . you're teasing me again. I suppose I'll get used to it one day."

"Not if I can help it. You still haven't told me why you're doing this."

"I would think it would be obvious."

"Not to me."

She sighed. "Very well. As to why English, the first humans in Gaea spoke it, and it just caught on. As to why any human language . . . since first contact there have been more humans living here all the time. You don't come in great numbers, but you keep coming. It seems a good idea to know as much about you as we can."

"The unpleasant neighbors who've moved in to stay, huh?"

Valiha considered it. "I don't wish to sound disparaging about humans. As individuals, some of them are as nice as anyone could wish—"

"But as a race we're a pain in the ass."

"I shouldn't make judgments."

"Why not? You're as entitled to them as anyone else. And I agree with you. We're pretty ugly when we put our heads together and start thinking up atomic bombs and such. And as for most of the individuals . . . hell." He was experiencing a twinge of chauvinism he did not like but could not avoid. It made him think, try to find some defense to throw back at her. He could not. "You know," he said finally, "I'm just realizing that I've never met a Titanide I didn't like."

"I've met many," Valiha said. "And I know a lot more than you do. But I have never met a Titanide I could not get along with. I've never heard of one Titanide killing another. And I've never met a Titanide I hated."

"That's the key, isn't it? Your people get along a lot better than we do."

"I would have to say yes."

"Tell me. Tell me the truth. Just for a minute forget I'm human and—"

"I forget it all the time."

She was trying to lighten it, but Chris was not having it.

"Just tell me what you think of having humans in Gaea. What you think, and what Titanides in general think. Or are they divided?"

"Of course, there is division, but I agree with most that we would like to have more control. We are not the only intelligent race in Gaea and do not speak for anyone but ourselves, but in the lands where we live, in Hyperion and Crius and Metis, we would like to have a say in who is allowed to enter. I believe we would turn back ninety percent."

"That many?"

"Perhaps less. You asked me to be frank, and I will be. Humans brought alcoholism to Gaea. We have always enjoyed wine, but the beverage you call tequila and we call"—she sang a brief melody—"which translates as Death-with-a-pinch-of-salt-and-a-twist-of-lime, has addictive properties for us. Humans brought venereal disease: the only malady of Terran origin that affects us. Humans brought sadism, rape, and murder."

"This all reminds me of Indians in America," he said.

"There is a resemblance, but I believe it to be fallacious. Many times on Earth a powerful technology met a weaker one and overwhelmed it. In Gaea, humans bring in only what they can carry, so that is not such a factor. In addition, we are not a primitive society. But we are powerless to do anything because humans have good connections."

"What do you mean?"

"Gaea likes humans. In the sense that she is interested in

them and likes to observe them. Until she tires of them, we must accept whoever comes." She saw his face and suddenly looked as troubled as he did.

"I know what you're thinking," she said.

"What's that?"

"That if standards were set, you would not have passed them."

Chris had to admit she was right.

"You're wrong. I wish I could explain it to you better. You are upset about your episodes of violence." She sighed. "I see I must tell more. It is easy to deliver a righteous diatribe against the things about humans one doesn't like. There are *many* humans my people would bar unconditionally: the prejudiced, the small-minded, the faithless, the misguided. Those badly reared, who, when blameless children, were not taught how to be proper persons. We believe the root of human troubles lies in the fact that you must be taught, that you are born with nothing but savagery and appetite and more often than not have those urges reinforced into a way of life.

"Yet we have a love-hate relationship with your species. We admire and sometimes envy the fire of your emotions. Each of you has a streak of violence, and we accept that. It's easier since we are so much larger; without a gun, there is little chance any of you could harm any of us. One of the things we would like to do is ban those equalizing weapons. Lacking the spur of aggression, we cannot afford to let you be our physical equals.

"And there are among you individuals with life burning so brightly within them that we are dazzled by your brilliance. The best of you are better than the best of us. We know that and accept it. None of you is so nice as we are, but we have realized that niceness isn't everything. We have much to offer the human species. So far it has shown only the mildest interest, but we remain hopeful. But we would learn from you, too. We have tried long to absorb your fire by getting to know you. And since, in Gaea, Lysenko was right, we are now trying to breed you into us. *That's* why we learn English."

Chris had never heard her speak so long on anything, or so forcefully. He had thought he knew everything about her, and now he wondered why, since he was not normally such a fool as to think he could know everything about anyone. He knew, and had even mentioned to Valiha, that her manner of speech had gradually improved from the time he first met her. Now her vocabulary often left him far behind. When she needed to, she could express herself in his native language ten times better than Chris. This did not bother him; he knew she had revealed more of herself as she came to trust him more, and that was as it should be. But something else disturbed him.

"I don't want to sound harsh, but I have to ask this. Is that what that business with the egg was all about? Lysenkoism?"

"I don't want to sound harsh either, but I will not lie to you. Yes, that entered into it. But I would never have done it with you without something much stronger. I speak of love, which so far as I know is the only emotion identical in humans and Titanides."

"Cirocco didn't think so."

"She is wrong. I realize that, commonly, love is bonded with jealousy and covetousness and territoriality in humans, and it never is in Titanides. That does not make the emotion different. It is simply that few humans experience love uncolored by these other things. You must take my word for that; it is one of the things I mentioned that we do better than humans. Humans have written and sung for thousands of years on the nature of love and never succeeded in defining it to anyone's satisfaction. Love is no mystery to us. We understand it thoroughly. It is in song—and its close friend poetry—that humans have come closest to it. That is one of the things we could teach humans."

Chris wanted to believe that but was still disturbed by something he could not quite bring into the open. She had explained how she could tolerate his spells of violence. Maybe it was just that, deep down, he could not believe it.

"Chris, would you come touch me?" she asked. "I feel I have upset you, and I don't like that feeling."

She must have seen his hesitation because tears started in her eyes. They sat only a meter apart, yet he felt a gulf had opened between them. It frightened him because only a short time ago he had felt very close to her.

"I'm terribly afraid," Valiha said. "I'm afraid that in the end, we will be too alien to each other. You will never understand me, and I will never understand you. And you *must!* *I* must!" She stopped and made herself slow down. "Let me try again. I will never give up.

"I said the best of you are better than us.

"I tell you that any of us can see it. Serpent will see it immediately, newborn, when he looks at you. I can see it, and I could not describe it if I had read a thousand dictionaries. When one of those better humans appears, we can tell it. But if I brought a group of them together, you would be at a loss to say what they had in common. It is no one quality, and it is not even always the same qualities. Many of them are brave, and others are cowards. Some are shy, and others brash. Many are intelligent, but others are far from geniuses. Many are outwardly exuberant; they taste life better; they burn with a brighter fire than we have ever seen. Others, to human senses, are quite subdued, as you are at times, but to our eyes the light shines through. We don't know precisely what it is, but we want some of it if we can have it without the urge to self-destruction that is the bane of your species. Perhaps even then, because its warmth is so glorious.

"We have a song for it. It is—" She sang it, then rushed on in English, as if she felt time were against her and she would once again fail to reach him. "In translation, that is, roughly, 'Those-who-might-one-day-sing,' or, more literally, 'Those-who-can-understand-Titanides.' If they want to. The word grows unwieldy, I fear.

"Cirocco is such a human. You have not felt one-hundredth of her heat. Gaby was one. Robin is. A handful of people back in Titantown. The settlement we passed in Crius. And you. If you were not, I could no more love you than a stone, and I love you fabulously."

That was a funny way to put it, Chris thought. And: what a coincidence that all four of us possessed this elusive quality. And again: it's such a shame, because she's a great person, but how do I tell her . . . ?

But that was all swept away by a feeling Chris was later to describe as like a drowning man's having his life pass before him all in an instant, or possibly the flash of genius that is so often spoken of—with a corollary that read "How have I been an idiot for so long?"—and, in the end, might best be expressed as the sudden realization that he loved her fabulously, too.

She saw the flash of his emotion—if he had wanted proof of her propositions, that would have been it, but he didn't need it—and while he was trying to think of something more intelligent to say than "I love you, too," she kissed him.

"I told you you loved me," she said, and he nodded, wondering if he would ever stop grinning.

Knowing the processes of Titanide birth was not the same thing as understanding the linked minds of the mother and child. Nor did Chris comprehend the nature of that link. He pestered her with questions about it, and determined that, yes, she could ask Serpent a question and he could answer it, and no, Serpent could not tell her if he knew how to speak English.

"He thinks in pictures and song," she explained. "The song is not translatable except emotionally; in a sense Titanide song never is, and that's why no human has been able to compile a dictionary of Titanide. I hear and see what he thinks."

"Then how did you ask him what he wanted to be named?"

"I pictured the instruments it was feasible to make down here and played them in my mind. When his awareness indicated delight, I knew he was Serpent."

"Does he knew about me?"

"He knows you very well. He doesn't know your name. He will ask that quite soon after birth. He is aware that I love you."

"He knows that I'm human?"

"He knows it very well."

"What does he think about that? Will it be a problem?"

Valiha smiled at him. "He will be born without prejudice. From that point, it is up to you."

She was lying on her side in a comfortable spot Chris had prepared. The birth was close, and Valiha was serene, delighted, in no pain. Chris knew he was acting as badly as any first-time father outside the delivery room and could not help it.

"I guess I still don't understand a lot of things," he admitted. "Will he come out, sit up, and start offering his opinions on the price of coffee in Crius, or will there be a goo-goo and ga-ga stage?"

Valiha laughed, paused for a moment while the muscles of her belly worked like a hand squeezing a water balloon, and took a sip of water.

"He will be weak and confused," she said. "He will see much and say nothing. He is not truly intelligent at this point. It is as if his thinking pathways have been packed in grease for shipment, needing to be cleansed upon arrival before use. But then. . . ." She paused, listening to something Chris could not hear, then smiled.

"You'll have to let that wait," she said. "He is almost here, and there is a ritual I must perform, passed down through my chord for generations."

"Sure, go ahead," he said hastily.

"Please indulge me," she said. "I could do it with beauty in my own song, but since he will speak English, I've decided to break with tradition and sing it in that language . . . also because you are here. But I'm not sure of my ability to make it beautiful in English, so my prose might sound awkward in—"

"Don't apologize to me, for God's sake," he said, waving his hands. "Get on with it. There may not be time."

"Very well. The first part is set, and I merely quote. I add my own words at the end." She licked her lips and looked into space. "'Yellow as the Sky Are the Madrigals.'" She began to sing.

"'In the beginning was God, and God was the wheel, and the wheel was Gaea. And Gaea took from her body a lump of flesh and made of it the first Titanides and gave them to know that Gaea was God. The Titanides did not dispute her. They spoke to Gaea, saying, "What would you have us do?" And Gaea replied, "Have no other Gods but me. Be fruitful and multiply, but be aware that space if limited. Do unto others as you would have them do unto you. Know that when you die, you return to dust. And do not come to me with your problems. I will not help you." And thus the Titanides received the burden of free will.

"'Among the first was one called Sarangi of the Yellow Skin. He went with many others to the great tree and saw that it was good. In time he was to found the Madrigal Chord. He looked out upon the world and knew that life tasted sweet, yet one day he would die. This thought was a sad one, but he remembered what Gaea had said and wondered if he could live on. He loved Dambak, Violone, and Waldhorn. The four of them sang the Sharped Mixolydian Quartet, and Sarangi became the hindmother of Piccolo. Dambak was the forefather, Violone the foremother, and Waldhorn the hindfather.'"

The song went on in that vein for some time. Chris listened more to the music than the words because the lists of names had little meaning for him. Descent was traced exclusively through the hindmother, though the other parents were always mentioned.

Chris could not have traced his parentage back through ten generations as Valiha proceeded to do, yet he knew his fore-bears went back through thousands or millions of generations to apes or Adam and Eve. With Valiha, ten generations was the entire story. Serpent would be the eleventh. It brought home more forcefully than anything he had heard just what it was to be a Titanide, a member of a race that knew it was created. While he did not know how accurate the opening words of her song were, they could be literally true. The Titanides had been created around the year 1935. Even an oral tradition could cope with that time span, and the Titanides were meticulous record keepers.

But the song was more than just a list of her hindmothers and the ensembles they had used to produce the next generation. She sang songs of each, sometimes lapsing into the purity of Titanide, more often staying in English. She listed the brave and good things they had done but did not omit failings. He heard tales of suffering from the years of the Titanide-Angel War. Then the Wizard arrived, and the songs, more often than not, mentioned the stratagems employed to attract her attention to proposals at Carnival.

"'. . . and Tabla was favored of the Wizard. Singing the Aeolian Solo, she gave birth to Valiha, of whom little has thus far been sung and who will leave the singing of her song to future generations. Valiha loved Hichiriki, born by the Phrygian Quartet in another branch of the Madrigal Chord, and Cymbal, a Lydian Trio from the Prelude Chord. They quickened the life of Serpent (Double-flatted Mixolydian Trio) Madrigal, who will sing his own song.'"

She stopped, cleared her throat, and looked down at her hands.

"I told you it would be rough. Perhaps Serpent will do better, when his time comes. Though the song flows like a river in Titanide, in English—"

"You did him proud," Chris said. "This isn't the best beginning, though, is it?" He waved his hand at the darkness and the barren rocks. "You should have had Hichiriki and Cymbal and all your friends gathered around."

"Yes." She thought about it. "I should have asked you to sing."

"You'd have soon regretted it."

She laughed. "Hum, then. Chris, he's here."

He certainly was. A glistening shape was moving slowly but inexorably. Chris felt the powerful urge to *do something*: boil water, call a doctor, comfort her, ease his passage . . . anything. But if his entrance into the world had been any quicker, he would have squirted across the ground like a pinched watermelon seed. Valiha had her head pillowed on her arm and was chuckling softly. If a doctor was needed, it was for Chris, not Valiha.

"Are you sure there isn't anything I should do?"

"Trust me." She laughed. "Now. You can pick him up—being careful not to step on the umbilicus, which he will need a little longer. Carry him to me. Lift him with both arms beneath his belly. His trunk will fall forward, so don't let him hit his head, but do not be alarmed by it."

She had already told him all that, but it was well she repeated it. He did not feel competent to pick his nose at the moment, much less handle a newborn Titanide. But he went, knelt, and looked at him.

"He's not breathing!"

"Don't be alarmed by that either. He will breathe when he's ready. Bring him to me."

Serpent was a shapeless puddle of sticks and moist skin. For a moment Chris literally could not make head or tail of him; then it all sprang into focus, and he saw a sweet-faced little girl-child with matted pink hair pasted to her sleeping face. No, not a child . . . she had fully formed breasts. And not a girl either. That was merely the trick all Titanides played on all humans, which was to seem female no matter what their actual sex. The forepenis was there between his front legs, complete with pink pubic hair.

He was going to be gentle, do it gingerly. After a few tries, he gave that up and put his back into it. Serpent massed nearly as much as Chris. He was a slippery bundle, but there was not a drop of blood on him. He looked like a starving urchin, with matchstick legs longer than Chris's own. He was narrow-hipped and had a short body and long trunk, which promptly fell forward loosely when Chris lifted him. As Chris carefully played out the loops of umbilical cord while bringing him around to his mother, Serpent stirred, and one of his hind legs kicked Chris in the shin. It was not too painful, but then he began a fitful struggle. Valiha sang something, and he calmed instantly.

Chris handed him to Valiha, who arranged him in front of her and held his upper body against her own. His head lolled. Chris noticed that it was as Valiha had said it would be: the umbilical did not attach under his belly but vanished into his anterior vagina, just as the other end still trailed from Valiha.

He had not known what to expect. He had seen young Titanides but none as young as this. Would he be able to love it? So far, he thought Serpent looked . . . he would not go so far as to say ugly. Funny-looking was the best he could come up with. But then he had always thought newborn humans were funny-looking, at best, and they were bloody into the bargain. He hated the squeamishness he felt—it did not mesh well with Valiha's description of him as a lusty, life-loving human, and that had been the nicest thing anyone had said about him in a long time—but he still felt it. Serpent most closely resembled an undernourished fourteen-year-old girl who had just been fished out of the bottom of a lake. Mouth-to-mouth resuscitation seemed called for.

Serpent wheezed loudly, coughed once, and began to breathe. He did it noisily for a few breaths, then found the rhythm. Shortly afterward he opened his eyes and was looking right at Chris. Either the sight was too much for him, or he was not seeing anything too well; he blinked and burrowed his face between his mother's breasts.

"He'll probably be cranky for a while," Valiha said.

"I would be, too."

"What do you think of him?"

Here we go, Chris thought. "He's beautiful, Valiha."

She frowned and looked at Serpent again, as if wondering if she had missed something.

"You can't be serious. Your use of English is better than that."

Feeling as if he were jumping off the deep end, Chris cleared his throat and said, "He's funny-looking."

"*That's* the word. He'll get a lot better rather quickly, though. He has a lot of promise. Did you see his *eyes?*"

They busied themselves cleaning up. Valiha combed his hair and Chris washed and dried him. And Valiha had been right: he did improve. His skin was warm and soft when dry, quickly banishing the picture of a drowned ragamuffin. The umbilical cord soon withered, and he was on his own. It would be a long time before he stopped looking skinny, but there was no longer the suggestion of starvation. Rather, as his muscles toned, he looked supple and glowing with health. It was not long before he held his torso erect unaided. He watched them with glittering brown eyes as they fussed over his young body, but he did not say a word. Valiha was watching him, too. She was as excited as Chris had ever seen her.

"I wish I could explain this to you, Chris," she said. "This is the most wonderful . . . I remember it so well. Suddenly to be aware, to feel yourself awakening from a state of simple desires and to feel a larger world taking shape around you, full of other creatures. And the growing urge to talk, almost like the building of an orgasm. The first formation of the idea that it is possible to communicate with others. He has the words, you see, but without experience to give them substance they are still mysteries. He will be full of questions, but he will seldom ask you what something is. He will see a rock and think, So *that* is a rock! He will pick it up and think, So *this* is picking up a rock! He will be asking many questions of himself, providing his own answers, and the sensation of discovery is so glorious that a Titanide's most common fantasy is of rebirth, the desire to live it over. But there will be plenty of questions for us. Sadly, a lot of them will be the unanswerable ones, but that is the burden of life. We must do our best with them and try at all times to be kind. I hope you will be patient and let him develop his own armor of fatalism at his own pace with no prompting from us because it can be a—"

"I will, Valiha, I promise. I'm sure I'll be watching you for quite a while to get hints on what you want, and I'll stay in the background as much as possible. But the big question on my mind is still the crazy experiment of yours, whether or not he will be able to—"

"You are a human," Serpent said quite distinctly.

Chris stared into the wide-set eyes looking guilelessly back at him, realized his mouth was still open, and shut it. Serpent's mouth carried the hint of a smile as elusive as the Mona Lisa's. The conversational ball was in his court, and all he had wanted to do was stay in the background.

"I'm a very surprised human. I—" He stopped when Valiha shook her head almost imperceptibly.

Chris examined his words. All right, wit was not called for. He had to hit a middle ground between goo-goo and the Gettysburg Address, and he wished he knew where it was to be found.

"What is your name?" Serpent asked.

"I'm Chris."

"My name is Serpent."

"I'm happy to meet you."

The smile emerged in full, and Chris felt warmed by it.

"I'm pleased to meet you, too." He turned to his mother. "Valiha, where is my serpent?"

She reached behind her and handed him the lovingly carved serpentine horn clad in soft leather. He took it, and his eyes sparkled as he held it and turned it in his hands. He put the mouthpiece to his lips and blew, and a dark bass tone drifted into the air.

"I'm hungry," he announced. Valiha offered him a nipple. His curiosity was such that he could not give it his whole attention. His eyes roamed, and his head twisted, and he just managed to keep the nipple in his mouth. He looked at Chris, then at his instrument, still held tightly in his hand, and Chris saw an expression of awed wonder come into the Titanide's eyes. Chris knew, at that moment, that he and Serpent were thinking the same thought, though each with a different meaning.

So this *is a Serpent.*

The child lived up to everything Valiha had said about him. The word "coltish" might have been coined for him alone. He was lanky, awkward, eager, and frisky. When it came time to walk, he tottered for all of ten minutes and then lost interest in every gait but the breakneck gallop. Ninety percent of him was legs, and most of that was knees. His angularity precluded the elegant bearing of his elders, yet the seeds of it were there. When he smiled, there was no need of glowbirds.

He had great need for affection, and they did not spare it. He was never far from a physical touch. A kiss from Chris was accepted as eagerly as one from his mother, and as eagerly returned. He loved to be stroked and petted. Valiha tried to nurse him lying down, but he would have none of it. She stood supported on her crutches while he embraced her. Often he would fall asleep while nursing, standing up. Valiha could then move away and leave him there, his chin on his chest. He would sleep irregularly for three kilorevs, then give it up forever.

For many days Chris regarded him as a disaster looking for a place to happen. It had been trouble enough easing Valiha through the rough places. All he had needed was an adventurous youngster to age him prematurely, and Serpent filled the role well. But nothing happened, as Valiha had predicted. Eventually Chris stopped worrying about it. Serpent knew his limits, and while he was constantly seeking to expand them, he did not go beyond them. Titanide children had a built-in governor; while they could not be made accident-proof, they suffered mishaps at about the same rate adult Titanides did. Chris wondered about this—toyed with the idea that the difference between humans and Titanides might be the absence of foolhardiness—but he was in no mood to complain.

Serpent succeeded so well in brightening things that for quite a long time Chris seldom thought of something that had caused him much worry for the first part of the trip. But the worry came back strongly when they found Robin's heavy winter coat and a pile of equipment beside one of her trail marks.

"I *told* her to keep this at *all costs*," he fretted, holding it up for Valiha to see. "Damn it, she doesn't understand cold at all, does she?"

"What does cold taste like?" Serpent wanted to know.

"I can't answer that, child," Valiha said. "You'll have to wait and taste it yourself. She had other clothing, Chris. If she wore all of it. . . ."

"Who is Robin, Chris?"

"A good friend and companion," he said, "who I'm afraid will be in very bad trouble if we don't catch up to her."

"May I wear that?"

"You can try it on, but you'll get too hot. Then you can carry it and these other things. Will you?"

"Sure, Chris. If you can catch me."

"We'll have none of that, my man. And stop giggling at me. I can't help it if I'm slow. But can you do this?" He stood on one pointed toe—easy in the low gravity—and did a ballet dancer's pirouette, one finger touching the top of his head, and finished with a bow. Valiha applauded, and Serpent looked suspicious.

"What, on one foot? I can't—"

"Ha! Gotcha. Now come and. . . ."

He stopped and turned. Behind him was a light brighter than any he had seen in . . . he had no idea how long. There was a low rumble that he realized had been on the edge of his hearing for quite a while. There was the sound of a distant explosion.

"What's that? Is it—"

"Hush. No questions yet. I . . . Valiha, get him down behind that rock. Stay as low as you can until—"

Suddenly a voice was speaking through an amplifier. The echoes distorted it almost beyond recognition, but Chris heard his own name and Valiha's. More flares burst and floated gradually down on little parachutes, and the roaring became the familiar sound of helicopters. The voice was Cirocco's.

She had come for them at last.

41.

Entry of the Gladiators

The dancing man met them again as they stepped from the elevator. He was just as elegant and just as enigmatic as he had been the last time, his face in shadow, a dazzling shine on his shoes, with white leather spats, cane, top hat and tails. Robin stood silently with Chris and watched, not daring to interrupt. The dancing man executed a series of pullbacks with easy aplomb, went into a twirling motion whereby his head seemed locked in place until a flicker of motion brought it completely around.

"Well, I don't understand the cathedrals either," Chris sighed when he was gone.

Robin said nothing. She recalled from her last visit the kind of song and dance Gaea would do as she manipulated people for her amusement. Everything would have significance, and she did not expect to understand it all. The dance had left her cold; she was going now to listen to the song.

"I keep having this dream," she said. "We sit down with Gaea, and the first thing she says is, 'Now for the *second* part of your test. . . .'"

He looked askance at her. "At least you've kept your sense of humor. Did you bring your novelty palm buzzer?"

"Already packed in my luggage."

"Too bad. How are the feet? You need any help?"

"I can manage, thanks." She had already noted that she did not need the crutches here in the hub. Her feet were still bandaged, but walking on them in the low gravity caused no pain. She and Chris made their way through the jumble of stone buildings, this time without a guide.

Heaven was just as she remembered it. There was the same monstrous rug, the scattering of couches and elephantine pillows, and low tables heaped with food. There was the same air of gaiety rubbing elbows with blank despair. God sat in the middle of it, holding perpetual court for her retinue of idiopathic angels.

"So the soldiers return from the wars," she said by way of greeting. "A bit subdued, a little the worse for wear, but, by and large, intact."

"Not quite," Chris said. "Robin is missing some toes."

"Ah, yes. Well, she will find that has been taken care of if she wishes to remove her bandages."

Robin had been getting strange feelings from her feet all during the walk but had thought it was the phantom awareness she already knew well. Now she lifted her feet and felt through the bandages. They were back, all ten of them.

"No, no, don't thank me. I can hardly expect your thanks when you would never have lost them without my interference in your life. I took the liberty of correcting what I took to be a slip of the tattooist's needle when restoring the bit of snake that formerly adorned one missing digit. I hope you don't mind."

Robin minded a hell of a lot, but she said nothing. She would find the change, she swore, and have it lasered out and put back the way it had been. Gaea was right to say she was subdued—during her first visit she would have shot Gaea for such a suggestion—but she still had enough pride to resent tampering.

"Have seats," Gaea suggested. "Help yourselves to food and drink. Sit down, and tell me all about it."

"We prefer to stand," Chris said.

"We were hoping this would not take long," Robin added.

Gaea looked from one to the other and made a sour face. She lifted a drink from the table beside her and tossed it down. A sycophant hurried up and put a new one in the wet ring left by the first.

"So it's like that. I should expect it by now, but I'm always a little surprised. I'm not denying you took risks you would rather not have taken. I suppose I can to some degree understand your resentment for having to prove yourselves before receiving my gifts. But consider my position. If I gave the things I have the power to give for free, I would soon be swamped with every mendicant, solicitator, fakir, conjuror, sponger, and just plain bum from Mercury to Pluto."

"I don't see the problem," Robin could not resist saying.

"There are plenty of chairs, and you've made a good start already. You could form a choir."

"So you still have a sharp tongue. Ah, would that I were human so its delicious lash would sting properly. Alas, I am indifferent to your contempt, so why waste it? Save it for those who are weak, who desert their comrades in time of need, who weep and soil themselves in the depths of their fear. In short, for those who have not proved themselves as you have done."

Robin felt the blood drain from her face.

"Did anyone ever tell you," Chris put in quickly, "that you talk just like the villain in a cheap murder mystery?"

"If you are telling me so now, you are the twelfth this year." She shrugged. "So I like old movies. But I tire of this. The second feature of the night begins in a few minutes, so—"

"What was the dancer about?" Robin blurted. She was surprised as soon as she asked it, but for some reason she felt it was important.

Gaea sighed.

"Do you people cherish no mystery? Must everything be made plain? What's wrong with a few minor enigmas to invest your lives with a little spice?"

"I hate mysteries," Chris said.

"Very well. The dancer is a cross between Fred Astaire and Isadora Duncan, with a few pinches of Nijinsky, Baryshnikov, Drummond, and Gray. Not the actual people, mind you— though I'd love to rob a few graves and sift bones for genes suitable for cloning—but homologues made from the records they left in life, written up in nucleic acids by yours truly, and given the breath of life. The dancing man is a very adept tool of my mind, as this meat is also a tool,"—Gaea paused to thump her chest—"but he is a tool nonetheless. In a sense, both he and this speaker dance in my brain; this one for talking to ephemeral creatures, he for a purpose I will get to in a moment. But first, I would expect that despite your distaste, you are curious to know the answer to a certain question, namely: did you or did you not grab the golden ring? Will I send you home as you are or cured?" She lifted an eyebrow and looked at each of them in turn.

Robin, though it pained her to admit it, was all ears. Part of her said that it was all right, that she had not set out to play Gaea's game, and if she had done something along the way to earn the prize, it would be monumental stupidity to refuse it. But something deeper whispered treason. You did not fight very hard when invited on this geste, it said. You *always* wanted the prize. But she would not let Gaea see her eagerness.

"I always like to get your own opinions first before announcing my decisions," Gaea said. She leaned back in her chair and laced her stubby fingers together over her belly. "Robin, you go first."

"No opinion," Robin said promptly. "I don't know how much you know of the things I did or failed to do. I might as well assume you know it all, down to the blackest secrets of my heart. This is an interesting reversal, I guess. Before, it was me who scorned your rules and Chris who was fascinated by them—or at least I thought he was. Now I don't know. I've thought a lot about the things that happened. I'm ashamed of many of them, including my inability when I got here to admit any human weaknesses. Whatever you do or don't do to me, I've gained something. I wish I knew exactly what it was, and I wish it didn't hurt so much to have it, but I wouldn't go back to what I was."

"You sound a little wistful about that."

"I am."

"Things are usually easier when you don't have to look at yourself. But that attitude would not have worn well."

"I suppose not."

"There will be greater satisfactions ahead."

"I wouldn't know about that."

Gaea shrugged. "I could well be wrong. I never assume the cloak of infallibility when predicting the behavior of creatures with free will. I do have considerable experience, however, and I feel that as you said, win or lose, you are stronger for what you have gone through."

"Perhaps."

"My decision, then, is that you have earned a cure."

Robin looked up. She would not say thank you, and it saddened her a little to see that Gaea did not expect her to.

"In fact, you have already been cured and are free to go any time you choose. I'll wish you good luck, though I wonder—"

"Just a minute. How could I already be cured?"

"While you watched the dancing man. When you and Chris entered the elevator down at the rim, I quickly put you to sleep, just as I did the first time. Then it was necessary to determine the nature of your affliction and the means to cure it, if indeed it could be cured. Some things elude even me. Without that examination I could not have offered the pact I did. This time was more to my advantage than yours. I needed to know what you had done since I last saw you. I examined your experiences, tasted them thoroughly, and made my decision. You were aware of no transition. You didn't notice waking up because I fabricated your ride in the elevator and eased you back into consciousness, blending the man who dances in my mind with the real fellow who wears real spats. You probably noticed a sense of unease, but I am quite adept at this by now, and while I can't explain my methods, I can assure you they are sound and scientific. If you object, you should—"

"Just a minute," Chris said. "If you—"

"Don't interrupt me," Gaea said, wagging a finger. "Your turn will come . . . you should, as I was saying, bear in mind the old warning about accepting rides from strangers. Especially in here."

"I remember a very long ride," Robin said, suddenly angry. "It was a long way down. Now I find the ride back up was a trick, too."

"I don't apologize for it. I don't need to, and I don't want to. Everyone takes that long ride down. It usually impresses them with their own mortality; Chris, I believe you are the only person so far who has not remembered that Big Drop to his dying day."

"I want to say something that—"

"Not yet. Robin, you were about to speak."

She looked hard at Gaea.

"All right. How do I know I'm cured? You can't expect me to trust you after what you did the last time I was here."

Gaea laughed. "No, I suppose not. There is no consumer protection in here. And I admit a fondness for tricks. But my reputation in this is flawless. I swear to you now that—barring future injuries to your head, which has been known to prompt epileptic seizures—you have thrown your last fit. Chris, it is now your turn. What do you think of—"

"I want to say something. I don't know if you've cured me or not, but if you did, you shouldn't have. You had no right."

This time both of Gaea's eyebrows lifted.

"You don't say. I was just going to ask if you thought you

deserved a cure, but you've grown so cocky that the answer must surely be yes."

"My answer is no answer. But I do have an opinion. You sent me out to be a hero, and I returned alive. That alone should count for something. But I don't believe in heroes anymore. I just believe in people coping with their lives as best they can. You do what you have to do, and in some ways you have no more choice about it than a rock has about falling from a high place. I spent the first part of my trip examining everything I did, from shooting the rapids to brushing my teeth, wondering if it was a heroic thing to do. Then I did a few things I was pretty sure passed the test, and I realized the test was a fake. You take your standards from comic books and then watch people dance. I despise you."

"Do you? You presume too much. Since you won't answer my question, I will tell you that you, too, are cured. Now, how do you know if I based my decision on your exploit in saving Gaby's life in Phoebe or your decision to endure boredom to stay at Valiha's side?"

"You—" Robin could see the anger boiling in Chris and see it contained. She was sure he had checked himself because of the same realization that had suddenly frightened her at the mention of Gaby's name: how much did Gaea know?

"I don't want to be cured," Chris was saying. "I'm not going back to Earth, and my problems don't matter so much here. And I don't want to accept a cure from you."

"Because you despise me," Gaea said, looking away with a bored expression. "You said that. Granted, you can't hurt the Titanides, but what about the humans who live here? Who will look out for them?"

"I'm not going to be around them. Besides, I've improved on my own. Since I got back to Titantown, my episodes have been more uniform and not nearly so violent. Listen, I...I'll admit it. I'm not too proud to accept something from you. I shouldn't have said I was. I had it in my mind that if you did offer to cure me, I would propose that you do something else instead. I mean, you said I had earned the cure, whether I think I did or not. I thought you might consider the idea that you owed me something."

Gaea was smiling now, and Robin's face burned with sympathy for what she knew must be humiliating for Chris.

"We had a verbal contract," Gaea said. "Quite specific. I admit I had all the better of it, I dictated all the terms, and they were non-negotiable, but I do run this place, don't forget. But I'm dying to hear what you thought I might agree to." She adopted an exaggerated listening posture and blinked several times at him.

"You did it for Cirocco and for Gaby," he said quietly, not looking at her. "If you're waiting for me to beg, I'm not going to."

"Not at all," Gaea said. "I knew you wouldn't—I have some idea what this is costing you after all the high-flown prose— and I'd have been appalled if you did. I've never been *that* far wrong about even a human. I'm merely waiting for you to spell it out. Be specific. What do you want?"

"The ability to sing."

Gaea's laugh rang in the empty darkness of the hub. It went on and on. Soon all the regulars at her heavenly film festival were laughing, too, on the well-known principle that what's funny to the boss is *funny*. Robin watched Chris, thinking he would surely attack the obscene little potato-faced pustule, but he somehow managed to hold it in. Gradually the laughter died away, Gaea's first, then everyone else's.

She cocked her head and appeared to be thinking about it.

"No. No to both requests. I will not uncure you, and I will not teach you to sing. You should have read the fine print and known your own desires before you came here. I am enforcing the letter of the contract. This may seem harsh, but you will find that things are not so bad as you think. When I cured you, there was some blending of your various personalities. You'll find yourself a little more in touch with the violent tendencies that so turned on your Titanide bitch. That, combined with a little more skilled use of your penis, ought to keep the animal quite tame and loyal for at least—"

Chris was on her by then. Robin moved in to help but had to deal with the swarms of Gaea's guests, who—while not the strongest collection of backbones Robin had ever seen—were unanimously eager to shine in Gaea's eyes if all it cost them was a broken nose. Robin handed out several. Not many of them would be getting up soon, but before long they over-whelmed her and pinned her to the ground. She saw that Chris was down, too, and Gaea was being shown back to her chair.

"Let them up," she said, sitting. There was blood dripping

from her mouth, and she grinned in spite of it. Perhaps because of it; Robin could not know. Robin got up and stood beside Chris. She had cut her hand and raised it to her mouth to suck on it.

"See what I mean?" Gaea said, as if nothing had happened. "The man who came here so long ago would not have done that. And I like it, though you really went too far, you know. But I will make a deal with you. I don't think you will stay with me very long. I know more of these matters than you do, I know something of Titanide love and how it differs from the human variety. Your friend will soon begin to open her fine legs for others—please, there's no need to go through that again." She waited until he seemed calmer. "Your reaction tends to prove my point. I won't deny she loves you, but she will love others. You will not handle it well. You will leave in great bitterness."

"Will you bet on that?"

"That's the deal. Come back in . . . oh, say, five myriarevs. No, I'll be generous. Make it four. That's about four and a half years. If you still want to be uncured and if you still want to sing, I'll do both things for you. Do we have a deal?"

"We do. I'll be back."

Robin was never sure if he said more. It had finally penetrated to her conscious mind what part of her hand she was sucking on. She looked at it, stared in growing horror, screamed, and leaped. Once again Gaea went tumbling from her chair, and Robin's memory of what happened next blurred until she found herself sitting on the floor with pain in her little finger, the one that should not have been there. She was biting it, and Chris was trying to pull it from her mouth. He needn't have bothered. She released it and looked dumbly at the toothmarks.

"I can't do it," she said.

"You never could," Gaea reminded her. "You cut it off with a knife, remember? The story about biting was public relations. You were good at that back then; to enhance your image, you could have disemboweled yourself. I'm afraid you were a pain in the ass that only a mother could love." She was wheezing slightly. "As you are now. Really, children, this must stop. Twice in one day? Must I endure assault and battery? What God would put up with it, I ask you?"

Robin no longer cared what Gaea said. The sad fact, the

one she must now face as she had faced so many others, was that Gaea was at least partly right. She was no longer Robin the Nine-fingered.

"Don't bother to say good-bye. Just leave," Gaea said.

Chris helped Robin up, and all the way back to the elevator which she knew might drop her through the Rhea Spoke Robin wondered if the tattoo on her belly was intact, and knew she would not look for as long as possible.

42.

Battle of the Winds

Cirocco sat on a flat rocky outcropping above the Place of Winds, the last western march of the mesalike formation that made the cable known as Cirocco's Stairs look so much like a hand gripping the soil of East Hyperion. Below her the strand fingers splayed over the ground, knotted knuckles blasted smooth by millions of years of ceaseless wind. Between the strands, where the webs between fingers would be, elliptical chasms yawned to gulp air, feeding it to interstitial ducts in the cable, lifting it to spill in the distant hub and fall through the spokes in the grand cycle of replenishment that was the essence of Gaea's life. The ground was barren, yet the larger life that lay beneath it and around it and in some ways penetrated it to the uttermost molecule vibrated Cirocco's bones.

Gaea was so God-awful big, and it was so easy to despair.

It was possible that in all of Gaea's history, there had been only one who had dared defy her. Cirocco, the great Wizard, had pretended to, had put on airs as though she really could speak to Gaea as an equal, but only she herself knew just how empty that had been. Only she could count the loathsome list of her own crimes. At first it had been necessary for Gaea to stamp the ground quite close to the Wizard to bring her properly to heel. As time went by, she did not even have to lift her foot; Cirocco would wriggle under like a worm and feel any pressure as only right and good.

That her course had been wise was now obvious. The one who had dared to stand defiant was now dead, her corpse consumed by the angry ground which was the body of Gaea. It was a powerful object lesson. There could be no doubt that Gaby had been a fool. Her rebellion, pitifully small and tentative as it had been, was gone with her life. No sooner had she taken the first steps than all of Gaea's might had come down on her. Gaea had killed Gaby with about as much concern as a sleeping elephant rolling over on a flea.

Cirocco had not moved for many hours, but at the shout from behind her she turned her head, then stood. The angel was a winged speck but quickly grew larger. His multicolored wings twisted skillfully in the tricky winds, brought him to ground two meters from Cirocco. Not far behind him were five more angels.

"They're back in Titantown," the angel said. Cirocco's shoulders relaxed slightly. They had insisted on going. Apparently they were too small for Gaea's wrath. The angel was regarding Cirocco with narrowed eyes.

"Are you sure you want to do this?" he said.

"I'm never sure of anything. Let's get going."

She walked with them to the lip of the precipice. Below her was the intake called the Great Howler, also known as the Forecrotch of Gaea for the way the mammoth vertical slit set between two rocky thighs resembled a vagina. It sang constantly in a mournful bass.

The angels moved up behind her. One on each side took her arms in their wiry hands. The other four were to provide relief for the dangerous flight in total darkness.

Cirocco stepped off the edge, and the wind caught her like a leaf. She entered the cable and sped toward the hub.

43.

The Thin Red Line

Cirocco called it the Mad Tea Party and knew it was not appropriate; it was just that for some time she had felt a little like Alice. The retinue of despair that surrounded Gaea might have fitted better on Beckett's existentialist stage than in Carroll's Wonderland. Yet she would not have been surprised had someone offered her half a cup of tea.

The crowd was exquisitely sensitive to Gaea's mood. Cirocco had never seen them more restive than as she approached the party, or as suddenly wary as when Gaea finally spotted her.

"Well, well," Gaea boomed. "If it isn't Captain Jones. To what do we owe the honor of this spontaneous and unannounced visit? You there, whatever your name is, bring a large glass of something cold for the Wizard. Never mind what it is so long as it contains no water. Take the chair over there, Cirocco. Is there anything else I can get you? No? Well." Gaea seemed at a momentary loss for something to say. She sat in her wide chair and mumbled until Cirocco's drink arrived.

Cirocco looked at it as if she had never seen anything quite like it before.

"Perhaps you'd prefer the bottle," Gaea suggested. Cirocco's eyes came up to meet Gaea's. She looked back at the drink, turned it over, and moved the glass in a slow circle until a sphere of liquid was formed, sinking slowly toward the floor. She tossed the glass into the air, and it was still rising when it left the circle of light. The sphere flattened and began soaking into the rug.

"Is this your way of telling me you're on the wagon?" Gaea asked. "How about a Shirley Temple? I just received the cutest mixer from an admirer on Earth. It's ceramic, shaped just like

353

America's Sweetheart, and I daresay worth a lot of money. You can make martinis in it by mixing gin to the chin and vermouth to the—"

"Shut up."

Gaea cocked her head slightly, considering it, and did as she was told. She folded her hands on her stomach and waited.

"I'm here to give you my resignation."

"I have not asked for it."

"Nevertheless, you have it. I no longer wish to be Wizard."

"You no longer wish." Gaea clucked sorrowfully. "You know it's not that simple. However, it is coincidental. For the last few years I have been contemplating whether I should terminate your employment. The fringe benefits would have to go, too, of course, which would make it tantamount to a death sentence, so I didn't move hastily. But the fact is, if you recall the qualities I mentioned when I first took you on, you have not been living up to the job for some time now."

"I won't even resent that. The fact is that I'm through with the job, effective immediately after the next Hyperion Carnival. Between now and then I will visit all the other Titanide lands to—"

"'Effective immediately after. . . .'" Gaea burst in with feigned surprise. "Will you listen to her? Who would believe a day could be so full of impudence?" She laughed and was quickly accompanied by some of her disciples. Cirocco looked at one of the people and did not take her eyes off him until he had thought it well to slink back out of her sight. By then it was quiet again, and Gaea motioned for her to go on.

"There's little to add. I promised a Carnival to remember, and I will deliver it. But after that I am demanding that you establish another way for the Titanides to reproduce, subject to my approval, and with a ten-year waiting period, during which I will observe the new method and weed out any tricks."

"You are demanding," Gaea said. She pursed her lips. "I'll tell you, Cirocco, you have me going back and forth on this thing. I frankly never thought you'd have the gumption to show up here, knowing what I just learned. That you have speaks well for you. It demonstrates those qualities I first observed in you that caused me to make you Wizard in the first place. If you recall, among them were courage, determination, a sense of adventure, and the capacity for heroism: qualities you have sadly lacked. I was not going to speak of my recent wavering.

But then you follow it with these foolish demands, and I wonder if you have lost your sanity."

"I have regained it."

Gaea frowned. "Let's get it out in the open, shall we? We both know what we're talking about here, and I'll concede I acted hastily. I admit I *over*reacted. But she was foolish, too. It was not wise for her to have used those children as the medium for her message; no doubt in her condition she couldn't think of everything. But the fact remains that Ga—"

"*Don't speak her name.*" Cirocco had raised her voice only slightly, but Gaea was stopped short, and the first rows of her audience unconsciously edged back. "Never speak her name to me again."

Gaea, to all appearances, was genuinely surprised.

"Her name? What does her name have to do with it? Unless you have been taken in by the tales of your own magic, I don't see the sense. A name is just a sound; it has no power over anything."

"I will not hear her name coming from your lips."

For the first time Gaea looked angry.

"I put up with much," she said. "I allow insults from you and from others that no God would ever endure because I see no point in slaughtering day in and day out. But you try my patience. I will go only so far, and you should take that as a warning."

"You put up with it because you love it," Cirocco said evenly. "Life is a game to you, and you control the pieces. The better show they give you, the more you like it. You have all these people to kiss your ass any time you tell them to. And I will insult you as I please."

"They would, too," Gaea said, smiling again. "And of course, you're right. Once again you prove that when you try, you can give me a better show than anyone." She waited, apparently thinking Cirocco would go on. Cirocco said nothing. She leaned her head against the back of her chair and looked up at the distant, geometrically straight, razor-sharp line of red light overhead. It was the first thing she had seen on her first trip to the hub, so very long ago. She had stood side by side with Gaby, and they had wondered what it was, but it was so high above them there seemed little point in speculating. They could never have reached it.

But Cirocco had felt even then that it was important. It was just a feeling, but she trusted her feelings. Some vital part of Gaea lived up there in the most inaccessible spot of a world filled with daunting vistas. It was at least twenty kilometers from where she sat.

"I would think you would be curious as to the answers to your requests," Gaea finally said. Cirocco brought her head forward and looked at Gaea again. There was no emotion on her face, as there had not been from the time she arrived.

"I couldn't be less interested. I told you what I was going to do, and then I told you what you were going to do. There is nothing further to say."

"I doubt that." Gaea looked at her narrowly. "Because this is absolutely impossible. You must know that, and you must have some threat to make, though I can't imagine what it might be."

Cirocco merely looked at her.

"You could not imagine that I would meekly grant your . . . very well, accede to your demands, if you prefer it that way. Demand or request, it matters little if the answer is no. Then you must tell me what you will do."

"The answer is no?"

"It is."

"Then I must kill you."

There was now no sound to be heard in the vastness of the hub. Several hundred humans stood grouped loosely behind Gaea's chair, hanging on to every word. They all were fearful people or they would not have been there, and certainly most of them were wondering only how Gaea would dispose of this woman. But a few, looking at Cirocco, began to wonder if they had put their allegiance in the right place.

"You really have taken leave of your senses. You have no plutonium or uranium and no way to get any. I doubt if you could fashion a weapon if you did. If you could conjure a nuclear device with the magic you seem to believe you possess, you would not use it because to do so would destroy the Titanides you have such affection for." She sighed again and turned one hand over carelessly. "I never pretended immortality. I know how much time I have left. I am not indestructible. Atomic bombs—in large quantities and placed with calculation—could fragment my body or at least render me uninhabitable. Short of that, I know of nothing that can do me serious harm. So how do you propose to kill me?"

"With my bare hands, if necessary."

"Or die in the attempt."

"If it comes to that."

"Exactly." Gaea closed her eyes, and her lips moved soundlessly. At last she looked at Cirocco again.

"I should have expected it. You would find it less painful to throw away your life than to live with what has happened. It *is* my fault, I admit it, but I don't want to see you wasted. You are worth this entire group, and more."

"I am worth nothing unless I do what I must do."

"Cirocco, I apologize for what I did. Wait, wait, hear me out. Give me this chance. I thought I could conceal what I was doing, and I was wrong. You won't deny that she was plotting my overthrow and that you were helping her—"

"I regret nothing but the fact I hesitated too long."

"Surely. That's understandable. I know the depth of your bitterness and of your hatred. It's all so unnecessary because what I did was done more from pride than fear; you can't think I was seriously worried that her puny efforts would—"

"Watch what you say about her. I won't warn you again."

"I'm sorry. The fact remains that nothing she or you could do would cause me any discomfort. I destroyed her for the insolence of thinking it would be done and, by doing so, have cost myself your loyalty. I find that a heavy price to pay. I want you back, fear I cannot, and yet want you to stay if for no other reason than to give the place some class."

"It needs some, but I can't do it, even if I had any."

"You underrate yourself. What you have demanded is impossible. You are not the first Wizard I have nominated in my three million years. There is only one way to leave the job, and that is feet first. No one has survived it, and no one will. But there is something I can do. I can bring her back."

Cirocco put her head in her hands and said nothing for a very long time. At last she moved, putting both arms under her shapeless blanket, hugging herself, and rocking slowly back and forth.

"This is the only thing I was afraid of," she said, to no one.

"I can re-create her *exactly* as she was," Gaea went on. "You are aware that I carry tissue samples of you both. When you were examined initially, and when you report for the immortality treatments, I tap your memories. Hers are quite up to date. I can grow her body and fill it with her essence. She will be *herself*, I swear it; it will be impossible to tell any difference. It is what I will do with you if despite everything, it becomes necessary to kill you. I can give her back to you, with only one change, and that is to remove her compulsion to destroy me. Only that and nothing more."

She waited, and Cirocco said nothing.

"Very well," Gaea said, waving a hand impatiently. "I won't even change that. She will be herself in all respects. I can hardly do better than that."

Cirocco had been looking at a point slightly above Gaea's head. Now she brought her eyes down and shifted on her chair.

"This was the only thing I was afraid of," she repeated. "I thought about not even coming here so I wouldn't have to listen to the offer and be tempted. Because it is tempting. It would be such a nice way to feel better about so many things and to find an excuse to go on living. But then I wondered what Gaby would have thought of it and knew just what a stinking, corrupt, foul deviltry it would be. She would have been horrified to think she would be survived by a little Gaby doll made by you out of your own festering flesh. She would have wanted me to kill it immediately. And thinking a little more, I knew that every time I saw it I would eat out a little more of my guts until there was nothing left."

She sighed, looked up, then down to Gaea.

"Is that your last offer then?" Cirocco said.

"It is. Don't do—"

The explosions could not be separated. Five closely spaced holes appeared in the front of Cirocco's serape, and her heavy chair slid backward two meters before she was through firing. The back of Gaea's head erupted blood. At least three of the bullets entered her body near chest level. She was thrown backward and rolled loosely for thirty meters before coming to rest.

Cirocco stood, ignoring the pandemonium, and walked to her. She brought Robin's Colt .45 automatic from beneath her wrap, aimed it at Gaea's head, and squeezed off the last three shots. Moving rapidly now in a gathering quiet, she took out a metal can and opened it, poured a clear liquid over the corpse. She dropped a match and stood back as flames burst into the air and began to creep along the carpet.

"So much for gestures," she said, then turned to the crowd. She pointed with her gun toward the nearest cathedral.

"Your only chance is to run toward the spoke," she told them. "When you reach the edge, jump. You will be picked up by angels and landed safely in Hyperion." Having said that, she forgot them totally. It was a matter of no consequence if they lived or died.

She was breathing rapidly as she ejected the empty magazine and took a loaded one from her concealed pocket. She snapped it in, pulled the slide back and let it return forward, then walked away from the growing fire.

When she was far enough away to see clearly, she set her feet wide and raised the gun over her head. Aiming nearly straight up, she fired at the thin red line. She spaced the shots, taking her time, and did not stop firing until the clip was empty.

She pulled out another clip and snapped it home.

44.

Thunder and Blazes

It was in the middle of her fourth magazine that the feeling began to trouble her. At first she could not put her finger on it. She shook her head, aimed, and fired another round. She swallowed dryly. It was quite possible the "gesture" was still going on; she could not know. Even if she hit the thing, her bullets were small and probably harmless. Nevertheless, she fired another shot and was about to shoot again when the feeling returned, stronger than before.

Something was telling her to run. That this should strike her as an unusual feeling to have in her present situation might have amused her at another time, but it did not now. She fired twice more, and the slide locked open on the empty chamber. She released the empty clip and let it fall beside her, where it clattered noisily. She swallowed again.

The feeling came back, stronger than ever. Unaccountably tears came to her eyes and ran down her cheeks. Damn it, she was waiting to die, and it was taking longer than she had thought.

But she knew what she was feeling now, and the tiny hairs stood up on her arms and the back of her neck. For whatever reason, she was sure Gaby was telling her to move.

It was some trick of Gaea's. She moved a few uncertain steps, and it felt good. But she stopped moving, and the feeling started again.

Why was she determined to die? It had not been in her plan when she started, except in the sense that she had been prepared to die if it had to be. There were certain things she had to do. She had done them, and it had been her intention to flee afterward. Was this the trick? Was Gaea putting Gaby's voice in her mind to confuse her until vengeance could arrive?

But suddenly she trusted it. She began to walk toward the cathedrals.

The air seemed to split as a bolt of lightning crashed into the spot where she had been standing. She ran, and Gaea's wrath poured from the world all around her. The red line above glowed more brightly than ever.

Jump!

She obeyed, cutting sharply to her left, and another bolt crashed where she had been.

It was possible to build up a frightening speed in the negligible gravity of the hub, but it came slowly. Feet on the ground could not provide enough traction to accelerate quickly. She had to begin with short, choppy steps, gradually lengthening them until her feet touched the ground many meters apart. And the speed, once attained, stayed with her. She streaked along, touching the ground infrequently, as the lightning crashed.

The biggest difficulty was changing direction. When she decided she must veer to the right, it was hard to put the urge into action, but she managed and could not tell this time if it had done any good. No bolt hit where she had been.

The ground was shaking. Some of the cathedrals, hit by repeated bolts and now attacked from beneath, were coming apart. Stone gargoyles crashed around her as she overtook some of the people who had fled. Spires tottered in slow motion, fragmented, and monstrous blocks of stone started to float inexorably down. Though they might weigh only a few kilograms, their mass would crush anything they encountered.

Too late to turn, she found herself heading straight for the replica Notre Dame. She lifted both feet from the ground, continuing to skim along the surface until she had sunk half a meter; then she pushed off with both feet and soared into the air. She cleared the peaked roof, came slowly down, and bounced up again. Below her, the remnants of the Mad Tea Party milled like a disturbed anthill. She could see the sloping edge of the Rhea Spoke mouth just ahead. She would not touch the ground again; her momentum would carry her over nothingness. A few people had reached the edge and stood gazing down at a leap they could never make.

Cirocco reached into her wrap and took out a small bottle of compressed air. Twisting to face the red line, she held one end of the cylinder to her stomach and turned the valve on the other end. It hissed, and a steady pressure threatened to turn her around, but she kept it in balance. Soon she could see she was building up speed.

When the bottle was empty, she threw it as hard as she could, then removed the two remaining clips for the automatic and threw them, following it with everything in her pockets. She was about to throw the gun itself but hesitated. Robin deserved to have it back, if that were possible. Instead, she slipped out of the red blanket, balled it up as tightly as she could, and threw that. Every ounce of reaction mass counted in her haste to get moving.

Damn! She should have *fired* the remaining bullets instead of throwing them away. She might have been able to save her serape. But she could not think of everything, and besides, when she turned around, she saw it did not matter as much as it might have. The entire cylindrical interior of the Rhea Spoke crackled with a million electrical snakes. She had hoped to get quickly out of range, but now she must run this gauntlet.

Below her she spied the slowly circling shapes of her angel escort, waiting where she had instructed them. As she watched, one of them was struck, and seemed to explode in a shower of feathers. She looked away for a moment, sickened. When she brought her eyes back, she saw the remaining five had not scattered as she had feared they would. At first glance it might have appeared they were fleeing, for all she could see of them was their feet and their frantically flapping wings, but she quickly realized they had spotted a problem before she had, with their incomparably better ballistic senses. A few seconds later she streaked past them and had occasion to feel relief that she had not fired the remaining bullets. Her velocity was already high enough to put her in jeopardy of outdistancing them.

She turned and fell with her back to the ground. There was no point in looking for lightning flashes as she could do nothing to avoid them. She spread her arms to kill some of her speed, and the angels chased her falling body through the flickering tunnel.

45.

Fame and Fortune

Valiha had traded in her crutches for the Titanide version of a wheelchair. It had two rubber-rimmed wheels a meter in radius, attached to a wooden framework slightly wider than her body. Stout bars were supported just ahead of and behind the lower part of her human torso, and from them was slung a canvas cup with holes for her forelegs and straps to hold the arrangement secure. Chris thought it peculiar at first but quickly forgot about it when he saw how practical it was. She would be in it for a short time yet; her legs were healed, but Titanide healers were conservative about leg injuries.

She could walk in it faster than Chris could run. Her only problem was cornering, which she had to do slowly. And like wheelchairs everywhere, it coped badly with stairs. She looked at the broad wooden staircase coming down from the green canopy at the edge of the Titantown tree, frowned with one side of her mouth, then said, "I think I can get up that."

"And I can vividly see you tumbling down," Chris said. "I'll just be up for a minute to get Robin. Serpent, where's the picnic basket?"

The child looked surprised, then abashed.

"I guess I forgot it."

"Then run right home and pick it up, and don't stop off anywhere."

"All right. See you." He was gone in a cloud of dust.

Chris started up the staircase. It had a rustic touch in keeping with the arboreal surroundings: a set of letters made of sticks tied together with ropes, like the entry to a Boy Scout camp. The letters spelled out "Titantown Hotel." He climbed to the fourth level and knocked on the door to room three. Robin called out that it was open, and he entered to find her stuffing clothing into a rucksack.

"I never used to accumulate stuff," she said, wiping sweat

363

from her brow with the back of her hand. It was another hot day in Hyperion. "There's another thing that seems to have changed about me. Now I can't seem to throw anything away. Why don't you have a seat? I'll clear a place for you. . . ." She began moving stacks of shirts and pants, mostly of Titanide manufacture.

"I'll confess I'm surprised to see this," he said, sitting. "I thought you were going to stick around at least until we found out if Cirocco made out—"

Robin tossed an ugly hunk of metal onto the bed beside him. It was her family heirloom, the Colt .45.

"That was delivered a few hours ago," she said. "Haven't you heard? I thought the whole town was buzzing with the news. The signs a few days ago were right: there was a great battle in heaven, and the Wizard got away. But Gaea is not satisfied, and her spies are all over. Carnival is permanently canceled; the race is doomed. Or Carnival will still happen, but it will be late. Cirocco is badly injured. She's in a coma. Or she's just fine and she injured Gaea. Those are the rumors I've heard, and I haven't even left the hotel."

Chris was surprised, but not that he had missed the news. He had spent the day indoors with Valiha and Serpent, then come straight to the hotel when lunch was packed. They had talked of the commotion several dekarevs earlier, when the Place of Winds cable had been seen to sway slowly and the sound of continuous thunder had been heard from Rhea.

"What do you know for sure?"

Robin reached out and patted the gun. "That's it. This is here, so Cirocco made it to the rim. I hope she got some good use out of it. What happened to her from there I can't even guess."

"Maybe she doesn't dare show up here," Chris suggested.

"There's a rumor to that effect. I had been hoping . . . oh, that she would come and give me the gun so I'd have a chance to . . . well, when she left, I still hadn't thanked her properly. Now maybe I never will. For sending Trini to wait for me."

"I doubt you'd come up with the right words. I didn't."

"You're probably right."

"And the last time I saw her she kept apologizing to me for getting me into so much trouble."

"Me, too. I think she was expecting to die. But how could I blame her? There was no way for her to know what was... going to...." She put her hand to her stomach and looked uncertain for a moment.

"Careful," Chris cautioned.

"I'm supposed to be able to talk about it with you, aren't I?"

"Were you feeling sick?"

"I don't really know. I think I was frightened that I *would* feel sick. This isn't going to be easy to live with."

Chris knew what she meant but was of the opinion that in a few months they would hardly notice Gaea's parting joke.

It had solved a mystery, but the nature of the solution precluded their divulging it to anyone else. They both had thought it odd, when they had time to think about it at all, that with all the analysis done on Gaea and the experiences of pilgrims going to her for a cure, no book had made mention of the Big Drop. The reason was simple. Gaea would not let anyone talk about it. Nor could they discuss anything about their individual quests or the quests of others; indeed, they could not mention that pilgrims to Gaea would be asked to do anything at all for their cures.

Chris was sure it was the best-kept secret of the century. Like the several thousand others who shared it, he was not surprised no one had spoken. He and Robin had each felt compelled to test the security system they had been told about soon after their return to Titantown.

Neither of them would ever do it again.

Chris was not proud of that fact, but he knew it to be true. Gaea had given him a psychological block. It was flexible in some ways—he could talk freely to Robin or anyone else who already knew. But should he try to speak to others of the Big Drop, his adventures in Gaea, or anyone else's exploits in pursuit of a miracle cure, he would experience pain so disabling he would be unable to utter even one word. It would start in his stomach and rapidly progress through all his muscles like red-hot snakes burrowing through his flesh.

There were no escape clauses, or so he had been informed. Again, he knew he would never test that either. If he tried to write of his experiences, the result would be the same. Asked questions that strayed onto forbidden ground, he could not even say yes or no; "no comment" was a permissible reply, and "mind your own business" was even better. Safest of all was to tell an interrogator nothing.

The system had a certain beauty if one was not its victim. So far as Chris could see, it was infallible. All visitors to Gaea had to ride in her capsular elevator system even to reach the inner rim from the docks on the outside, and while doing so, they were put to sleep, examined, and cleared for release. No one with any forbidden knowledge could leave Gaea without receiving the block.

Chris had found it best to observe absolute circumspection with anyone but Robin, Valiha, or other Titanides. There were other humans in Gaea who knew what he knew, but it was hard to be sure who they were. Unless he was positive, he would get a warning twinge like a toothache by opening his mouth to talk about the trip. It was all he needed. One dose of Gaea's aversive conditioning had been enough.

Robin had filled one bag and was starting on another. Chris saw her pick up a small thermometer, consider it, and toss it in the sack. He could imagine her problem. A lot of the equipment she had taken on the trip had acquired a sentimental value. On top of that, since their return it seemed that every Titanide in town wanted to stop by and make them a gift of some lovely trinket. They had run out of shelf space in Valiha's home to display all his booty.

"I still don't understand all this," Robin said, carefully wrapping tissue paper around an exquisitely carved set of wooden knives, forks, and spoons. "I'm not complaining—except that I don't know how I'm going to pack it all—but why do we rate this stuff? We didn't do anything for them."

"Valiha explained it, in a way," Chris said. "We're sort of famous. Not like Cirocco, but moderately. We were pilgrims, and we came back cured, so Gaea judged us heroes. That means we're worthy of gifts. Also, Titanides will protest all day long that they're not superstitious, but to have survived what we did, they figure we're pretty lucky. They hope some of it will rub off if they're nice to us, come next Carnival time." He looked down at his hands. "With me there's another reason. Call it the welcome wagon or a bridal shower. I'm going to be part of the community. They want to make me feel at home."

Robin looked at him, opened her mouth to say something, then closed it again. She resumed her packing.

"You think I'm making a mistake," Chris said.

"I didn't say that. I never would, I guess, even if I did think

that, but I don't. I know what Valiha means to you. At least
I think I do, though I've never felt that way about anyone,
myself."

"I think *you're* making a mistake," Chris said.

Robin threw up her hands, turned, and shouted at him.
"Listen to you. Suddenly *I'm* the diplomatic one and *you* just
say any old thing that comes into your head. *Damn you!* I was
trying to be nice, but I could have said that I *know* you're not
sure of what you're doing. Not completely sure. You're going
to fear Gaea for the rest of your life, for one thing, and for
another, you don't know yet just how it will make you feel
when Valiha brings home her other lovers. You *think* you can
live with that, but you're not sure."

"Can I apologize?"

"Just a minute, I'm not through shouting yet." But then she
shrugged, sat on the bed beside him, and went on in a quieter
voice.

"I don't know if I'm making a mistake, either. Trini...."
She shook her head furiously. "I've had my eyes opened to a
lot of things in here, not all of them bad. I'm scared that the
ways I've been changed will make it very hard for me back
home. And speaking of home, some days I can hardly remember what it looks like. I feel I've been here a million years.
I've learned that some things my sisters believe are just fairy
tales, and I don't think I'll be able to tell them that."

"Which things?"

She looked sideways at him, and one corner of her mouth
curled.

"You want the final report of the woman from Mars, huh?
Okay. What I know for sure is that the human penis is not as
long as my arm, no matter what men might wish. My mother
was dead wrong about that. She was off base to say that all
men want to rape all women all the time. And to say that all
men are evil.

"But I've been doing a lot of talking to Trini these days.
It's the first chance I've had to spend some time with a woman
who knows Earth society. I find there were some exaggera-
tions. The system of repression and exploitation is not as bad
or as open as I was led to believe, but it's there, still, even
after the century my sisters have held themselves away from
it. I asked myself if I would advise making any changes in the
Coven, and my answer is no. If I had found a completely equal

society, my answer might have been different, but I'm not sure even then. What purpose would it serve? We're doing fine. There is nothing abnormal about us. Very, very few of my sisters could ever trust a man at all, much less love one, so what would we do back on Earth?"

"I can't imagine," Chris said. He thought it sounded too disapproving, so he added, "I don't have any quarrel with the Coven. I didn't mean for you to defend your way of life to me. It needs no defense."

Robin shrugged again. "Maybe some of it does, or I wouldn't have jumped into it so rapidly. It doesn't worry me too much. It will be hard at first to keep my mouth shut about some of the things I've learned, but it will be good practice for the other things I'll have to keep my mouth shut about."

They sat together without saying anything for a while, each wrapped in private thoughts. Chris was thinking about what he felt had almost happened between them—or the door that had almost opened to allow the possibility of something happening. It was too remote for speculation. He had felt a great deal of respect and affection for the fiery young woman she had been. She was slightly subdued now, but far from beaten down, and his affection was unchanged.

He had a thought and decided to take a chance on it.

"I wouldn't worry too much about your standing in the community," he said.

"How do you mean?"

"Your new finger. There must be tremendous labra in growing one back."

She stared at her hand for a moment, then grinned wickedly.

"You know, I think you're right."

He went to the room's single window, looked down at Valiha patiently waiting at the foot of the stairs.

"What time does your ship leave?"

She glanced at her wristwatch, and Chris smiled. He was wearing one, too. They shared a compulsion always to know what time it was.

"I've still got a deka—ten hours."

"Valiha made a picnic lunch. She has a nice cool spot in mind, down by the river. We were going to invite you anyway, but now it can be a farewell party. Will you come?"

She smiled at him. "I'd love to. Let me get this stuff packed."

He helped her, and soon three bulging sacks were lined up on the floor. Robin lifted two and struggled with the third.

"Can I give you a hand?"

"No, I can . . . what am I talking about? I'll take these, and you grab that one. We can leave them at the desk, and they'll send them to the ship."

He followed her out of the room and down the stairs, helped her check the luggage. They joined Valiha and Serpent. The four of them walked at a leisurely pace out from under the Titantown tree to find themselves under the titanic arch of Gaea's Hyperion window. The day was hot with a slight breeze blowing from Oceanus, promising cooler weather. There was a haze in the air, its source a remote spot in the highlands where Cirocco's air force had found a fuel-producing creature, parent and succorer to the buzz bombs. It had been blazing for half a kilorev.

But the air was sweet in spite of it, full of the smell of the Titanides' crops near harvest, and free for now of all threat. They walked a dusty path between rolling hills. The mighty curve of Gaea rose on each side like the enfolding arms of a mother.

They spread their cloth on the banks of Ophion. While they ate, Chris watched the river, wondering how many times the waters had flowed past that point and how many times the river would yet revolve before Gaea's long life came to an end. When the Titanides began to sing, he joined in without reserve. After a time Robin sang with them. They laughed, drank, cried a little, and sang until it was time to go.

EPILOGUE:

Semper Fidelis

The wheel still turned, and Gaea was still alone.

The Terran death ship remained where it had always been, deep in the gravity well of Saturn. Its crews alternated yearly to relieve the boredom of duty there. Each decade its cargo of nuclear weapons was serviced, and those found defective were replaced.

It was not an empty threat, but Gaea ignored it all the same. She would never give them an excuse to attack. As long as Earth needed her, she was utterly safe, and she would see to it that Earth did need her. It would have been politically unthinkable to impugn her in any dictatorship or deliberative body on the globe. The story of the quests, had it reached the ears of Earth's people, might have caused a momentary unease, but little more. Gaea had a thousand gifts to bestow. Her security system was for her own enjoyment; it amused her for pilgrims to arrive in ignorance.

It was a measure of her confidence that she rated the danger from Earth slightly below the new danger of the renegade Wizard, and that danger was so small as to be nearly incalculable. But she was a cautious being. High in the hub her thoughts whirled faster than light through a crystalline matrix of space the very existence of which defied the edicts of human physics. Great holes yawned in the matrix like the sockets of rotten teeth, yet even in decay her mind held a power to beggar the capacity of all human computing machines taken together.

The answer was as she had expected. Cirocco was no threat at all.

The highlands were unique in Gaea. Though every kilometer of them was associated with some regional brain, the control that could be exercised that far from the centers of power was negligible. In a sense, it was neutral territory.

In the twilight zone between Rhea and Hyperion, far above the land in the most inaccessible reaches of the highlands, a lone Titanide stood guard outside a cave. Not far away, a billion coca plants thrived. He heard a sound from within, turned, and entered.

Cirocco Jones, until recently the Wizard of Gaea but now called Demon, had awakened and was writhing in a cold sweat. She was naked, and so thin her ribs showed. Her eyes were deep hollows.

Hornpipe went to her and held her down until the shaking subsided. She had found a supply of liquor soon after landing in Hyperion, though the Melody Shop had been obliterated by the most singular phenomenon ever seen in Gaea: a rain of cathedrals. Hornpipe had found her and brought her to the cave.

He held her head and helped her drink a cup of water. When she coughed, he let her back down.

But soon her eyes opened. She sat up on her own for the first time in many days. Hornpipe looked into those eyes, saw the fire he had seen there so long ago, and rejoiced.

Gaea would be hearing from the Demon.

TITANIDE SEXUAL ENSEMBLES

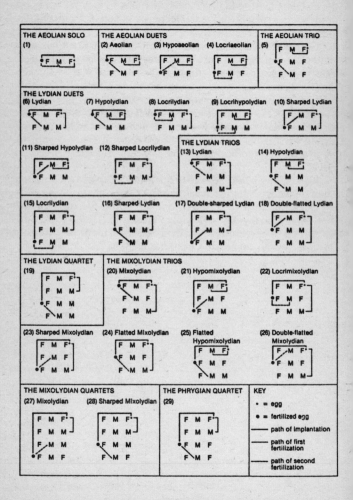